BACK PLEASE

CITY OF SCARS

A DCI JACK LOGAN NOVEL

JD KIRK

CRIME

CITY OF SCARS

ISBN: 978-1-912767-62-5

Published worldwide by Zertex Media Ltd.
This edition published in 2022.

1

www.jdkirk.com
www.zertexmedia.com

BOOKS BY J.D. KIRK

A Litter of Bones

Thicker Than Water

The Killing Code

Blood & Treachery

The Last Bloody Straw

A Whisper of Sorrows

The Big Man Upstairs

A Death Most Monumental

A Snowball's Chance in Hell

Ahead of the Game

An Isolated Incident

Colder Than the Grave

Come Hell or High Water

Northwind: A Robert Hoon Thriller

Southpaw: A Robert Hoon Thriller

CHAPTER ONE

ANGELA SHEEN WAS sick of apologising. She'd said the words half a dozen times on the drive over. She'd offered to make it up to him. She'd even brought them coffee—good stuff, too, made fresh that morning, none of your chain store shite.

Not that any of the chain stores were open at this time of the morning.

The worst thing was, he hadn't asked for an apology. He'd quickly dismissed those she'd offered.

"It's fine," he'd said. "Don't worry about it," he'd said. "I don't mind. Honest."

And, as far as she could tell, he didn't. He genuinely didn't seem bothered. But then, very little seemed to bother Josh Holder.

They'd been working together for nearly six months now. He had been her first hire when her new cleaning business had started to take off. And in that time, despite overflowing toilets, vomit-stained upholstery, and more used condoms than you could shake a stick at, she'd never seen him get upset.

The reason she felt the need to apologise so profusely was not for his benefit, though. It was for hers. If the tables were turned, the roles reversed, she'd have been fucking raging with him.

"No, it was out of line. It was unprofessional," she insisted, jerking the van to a stop at the back of the club, and almost spilling the coffees. She quickly apologised for that, too.

"Calm down. It's fine," Josh said. He smiled at her. It was a goofy sort of smile, all teeth and gums. He was uninhibited like that. He kept nothing back. Everything about him was an open book.

The exact opposite of her.

Angela yanked out the van's key, but the engine coughed and spluttered on for a few more revolutions, before begrudgingly accepting its fate.

"No, it's not fine," she continued, picking up her plastic cup and opening the door. "This one is meant to be a night-time job, not..." She checked her watch and visibly flinched. "...half-five in the sodding morning. I shouldn't have cancelled on you like that. We should've had this done last night. We should both be in bed right now."

Josh raised his eyebrows in mock outrage. "Careful, Ange," he said, joining her around the back of the van. "That's skirting dangerously close to sexual harassment."

She frowned like she had missed the joke, then it clicked and she gave him a dunt with her elbow. "Not together. Perv!" she said, and as they laughed, the worst of her guilt left her.

Usually, she wouldn't joke about such things. Hadn't done for years. But it was different with Josh. He was... unthreatening. He could reference sex without her wanting to scream, or lash out, or curl up into a ball on the floor.

Handing over his coffee cup, Josh opened the back doors of the van and launched into a wrestling match with a big industrial vacuum cleaner, the long hose of which not only appeared to have a life of its own, but seemed to have some sort of vendetta against him.

It was the same routine every time. Josh was... not short, exactly, but below average height for a man, and with a slender build that nature had never intended to do any heavy lifting. Still, some sort of gentlemanly instinct meant he always insisted on carrying any large items, and Angela had long-since given up trying to dissuade him.

Eventually, he managed to tame the Hoover, and let out his usual grunt of effort as he heaved it out of the van. Angela shut the door and followed behind Josh as he waddled towards the rear entrance of the club, leaning left to counteract the weight he was lugging in his right hand.

"You sure you're alright with that?" she asked.

"Oh, just dandy, yeah," Josh replied through gritted teeth. "What did you last suck up with the thing, though? A fucking neutron star?"

"You know it's got wheels, yeah?" she asked, though she knew fine well that he did.

"Please," he said, shooting a look of mock outrage back over his shoulder. "What do you take me for?"

She chuckled, then shut her eyes and surrendered to it when the laugh became a yawn.

By the time she was finished, Josh was standing by the door and nodding emphatically at it.

"Well, get a bloody move on!" he told her. "Arm's about falling off here!"

"Sorry, sorry!" Angela said, adding two more apologies to the morning's long list of them.

She sat the coffee cups down on one of the bins by the nightclub's back door, fished an enormous bundle of keys from her bag, and hurried to let them inside.

———

Refuge had been open for just over a year, but had rapidly risen to become one of the hottest nightclubs in Inverness.

Or so the guy who ran the place kept telling them, anyway. Neither Angela nor Josh were really into that sort of thing. And even if they had been, then the sight—not to mention the smells —that they often encountered during their late-night clean-ups would've put them right off.

The small private car park tucked away on Bank Lane, allowed them access through the back door of the building. The entrance led directly onto the dance floor, which could usually be guaranteed to be strewn with disposable plastic drinkware, and puddles of liquid that were best not identified.

This morning, though, with several hours of drying time behind them, the puddles had mostly become sticky stains that pulled at the bottom of their shoes as they made their way towards the toilets.

They always started there. They had done since their second night in the place. It was best, they'd agreed, to get it out of the way.

With a sigh of relief, Josh sat the vacuum cleaner down on the carpet by the bar and took a moment to realign his spinal column.

He followed Angela to a locked cupboard that was set into the wall directly between the male and female toilets, and watched as she rifled through her bundle of keys, searching for the right one.

She was moving slower today. Something was off.

"What were you up to last night, anyway?" he asked. "How come you had to cancel?"

Angela stopped looking through the keys, but only for a second. Maybe less. "Nothing," she said, not looking at him. "I wasn't up to anything."

"Oh. Right." Josh bit his tongue, but couldn't contain the question. "It's just, when you phoned, you sounded..."

"Sounded what?" Angela asked, her head snapping around, her glare pinning him to the spot.

Josh raised his hands, suddenly defensive. "Nothing. No, nothing," he said. "I just... I thought you sounded a bit, I don't know, stressed. But I could be wrong."

"Yeah, well, you are wrong," Angela replied. "I just... it was nothing. I, eh, I wasn't feeling up to it. That's all."

She turned her attention back to the keys, and Josh decided not to push the matter any further. They got on well—they always had done—but she was still his boss. She had no obligation to tell him anything.

"Right, here we go," she said, finding the correct key and unlocking the cupboard door.

They both chose their weapons—a mop for him, a spray gun and toilet brush for her—then turned back-to-back like they were prepping for a duel.

"Meet back here in a minute?" Josh asked. Normally, he wouldn't bother. It would be taken as given. They'd each go into a different bathroom, assess the damage, then regroup at the cleaning cupboard and decide which one they were tackling first. Today, though, things felt different. Today, he felt the need to check.

Angela's reply was a firm nod, and a barked, "Good luck, soldier!"

Josh snapped off a salute. "I'll see you in hell!" he rasped, then they headed to their respective doors—her to the ladies, him to the gents—and with a final nod of support, they both took a deep breath, nudged open the doors, and stepped inside.

It was almost fifteen seconds before the screaming started.

CHAPTER TWO

THE AREA outside *Refuge* was cordoned off when DCI Jack Logan pulled up in his BMW, and he groaned at the sight of the Scene of Crime Officers' vans parked nose to nose on the cobbled stretch of the pedestrianised thoroughfare.

The SOC team was here, which meant Geoff Palmer would be lingering around somewhere like a fart without the charm or the comedy value. Just what he bloody needed.

Logan searched the dash for the button that switched the engine off, muttered something unkind about those responsible for the vehicle's design, then blew out his cheeks and sighed when he finally found what he was looking for.

"You shouldn't be here."

He looked to the driver's side window, searching for who had spoken, then remembered that he wasn't alone in the car.

Shona Maguire, pathologist, proud Irishwoman, and... what? His *girlfriend*? No. That sounded too juvenile. *Partner* sounded too professional, though. He wasn't really sure if there even was a word that accurately described their relationship status. And, if there was, then—just like the engine stop button had been a moment before—it was evading him.

Whatever you wanted to call her, she was sitting there in the passenger seat, a look of concern furrowing the lines of her face.

"What?" Logan slurred. His eyes flicked down, as if he thought the word had fallen out of his mouth and was looking for it in the cup holders between the seats.

"I said, you shouldn't be here. You're not well."

"It's nothing," Logan insisted. "It's just a..." He gestured at his head and made a vague sort of spinning motion with his hand. "Just a cold, or something."

"Flu. It's the flu," Shona said. "And you should be in bed."

"It's nothing. Anyway, duty calls," Logan insisted, then he opened the door and almost toppled sideways out of the SUV. Only the seat belt across his chest stopped him spilling out onto the cobbles.

"Oh, aye," Shona remarked. "You're right as rain, so you are. You don't need to be here, you know? The others can take care of it."

"I'm fine. Honest," Logan insisted again. He tried to smile reassuringly, but the grimace that twisted across his face had rather the opposite effect.

"Right, well, you can't say I didn't try," Shona sighed. She unclipped her seat belt, watched Logan fumbling around unsuccessfully for the button that would release his, then rolled her eyes and got out of the car.

"Morning, all!"

Shona turned to see Detective Inspector Ben Forde come striding towards her. He had a spring in his step and a broad smile on his face. Both of which could be considered inappropriate, given the circumstances, but it was nice to see him so upbeat.

"Morning, Ben," she replied, and she watched the DI's smile falter as he watched Logan slowly extricating himself from the driver's seat.

"What's up with him?" Ben asked.

"Nothing," Shona said. She raised her eyebrows meaningfully. "So he tells me, anyway."

"Oh. Well, he looks like absolute shite." Ben's eyes widened, and he leaned in closer, dropping his voice to a whisper. "He's not hungover, is he? He's not back on the drink?"

"No, I am bloody not," Logan said, answering on Shona's behalf.

He rounded the front of the car to join them, leaning a hand on the bonnet to help him balance. He looked smaller than usual, his giant stature hidden by the way his head and neck were stooping forwards.

"Are you sure? Because you sound hungover. And you look hungover," Ben said.

"I'm not hungover."

"I've seen you hungover. And it looks a lot like this," Ben continued.

Logan waved a hand in Ben's direction and shot an imploring look at Shona. "Can you shut him up, or make him go away?"

"He's got the flu," Shona explained.

"I don't have the flu," Logan argued. "I've got..." He made the same vague spinning motion as earlier. "Alright?"

Ben nodded sagely. "Right. I see. And that's the official diagnosis, is it?" He copied the DCI's hand gesture. "That's clinically confirmed?"

Logan pinched the bridge of his nose, swayed on the spot for a few seconds, then pointed impatiently at the vans parked outside the front door of the nightclub. "That arsehole here, is he?"

"Aye, he's inside," Ben said. There was no need to ask which particular arsehole the DCI had been referring to. The venom in his voice had been enough of a clue. He turned to Shona. "I think they're waiting on you to go and do your bit."

"Sorry, yeah, running a bit late," Shona said. She opened the back door of the BMW and collected her medical bag. "We would've been here earlier, but I had to help someone—naming no names—put their shoes on."

"I could've put them on myself," Logan retorted.

"What, the laces and everything?" Ben asked, feigning surprise. "I'm impressed."

Logan tutted. "Aye, well, you try finding your feet when the room's spinning in bloody circles, and—"

There was a sound from somewhere inside him, like the croak of a startled bullfrog. Ben and Shona both stepped back as Logan slapped a hand across his mouth, his eyes bulging in shock and horror.

Nobody moved. Nobody dared.

Then, after several tense moments, Logan lowered his hand again. "False alarm," he said.

"You should be home in your bloody bed," Ben told him.

"That's exactly what I said," Shona agreed. "But will he listen?"

"Aye, he's always been a stubborn bastard, right enough."

"D'you mind? I might be ill, but I'm no' deaf," Logan told them. He indicated the front door of the nightclub with a glance that threatened to make his head start spinning again. "Now, can we hurry this up? The sooner we get started, the sooner we get it over with."

Ben regarded him for a moment, then leaned in closer to Shona and spoke in a loud stage whisper. "You sure he's not hungover? He was a right grumpy bastard then, too."

Shona smirked, and Logan dismissed them both with a scathing glare and a wave. "Aye, very good. Bugger off, the pair of you. And try and keep Palmer away from me, will you? I don't know if I can handle that bastard today."

Ben stepped aside, bowed slightly, and made a sweeping

hand gesture in the direction of the club. "M'lady," he said. "If you'd care to step this way."

Shona tipped an imaginary hat at the older detective, shot a final look of concern back at Logan, then set off towards the club's entrance.

Logan waited until they were both inside, before allowing himself to sag back against the car, and letting it support his weight. Since yesterday evening, the ground beneath him had felt soft and spongy, like a partially deflated bouncy castle. The car, on the other hand, felt reassuringly solid behind him, and he took a few moments to appreciate the feeling of it there at his back.

A few uniformed officers were wandering around, mainly keeping away the early-morning nosy bastards who slowed as they passed the cordon tape. None of them were looking his way, though. None of them were asking him questions, or looking to him for guidance. Not right now, anyway. Not yet.

He closed his eyes, swallowed back another rising wave of nausea, and enjoyed the peace and quiet.

He'd barely slept all night, and yet every attempt to get up had turned the bed, and the room, and the whole world around him into a spinning tornado that had forced him back under the covers.

The exhaustion was filling his bones now, weighing him down. He was sure he'd feel better if he could rest. Just a moment, that was all he needed. Just a moment alone to get himself together.

A voice chirped cheerfully in his ear, making him jump, and sending the world off-balance once more.

"Alright, boss?" it said. "You look like a big bag of shite!"

———

"Morning, Geoff," Shona said once she was kitted out in all the necessary protective gear and ready to get started.

Geoff Palmer stood in front of the door to the ladies' toilets with his arms folded. He had that *chewing a wasp* look on his face that everyone who knew him was only too familiar with. He was a right sour bastard at the best of times, and it seemed like someone had pished on his cornflakes today.

"*Is it* morning, Shona? Are you sure?" he asked. He pointedly tapped the wrist of his paper suit, presumably to indicate a watch he had on under there. "Because it feels like I've been standing twiddling my thumbs here for hours."

Shona maintained her smile. This, she knew, was a most effective way of winding Geoff up. Once upon a time, he'd have been fawning over her, pre-emptively accepting apologies she had no intention of making, and gladly excusing any imagined transgression she might have made.

That was before she and Logan had got together. Now, Geoff considered himself the wronged party, and he was making damn sure everyone knew it.

"It might feel like it, Geoff, but you haven't," Shona told him. "It's seven-forty. I got the call half an hour ago."

Palmer let out a derisory snort. "Half an hour? That's how long it takes you to get across Inverness, is it? What, were you on a skateboard?"

"God, I wish. Sure, a skateboard would be great, wouldn't it?" Shona told him. "Can you go a skateboard, Geoff?"

"No, I cannot!" Geoff spat, like it had been some sort of vile accusation he immediately felt the need to refute.

Shona patted him on the shoulder. Her smile hadn't shifted. Not once. "Ah, well, that could be a fun hobby for you. Maybe away and give it a go?"

"Of course I'm not—"

"Shift your arse, Geoff," Shona instructed, jerking her head to one side to indicate her preferred direction of his travel. "I'm trying to get inside."

"What?" Palmer scowled, then realised he was blocking the door and scuttled aside. "Oh. Fine. Be quick."

Shona pulled her mask down over her mouth, and her reply was a little muffled. "I'll be as long as I need to," she said, then she pushed open the door, and stepped into the ladies' bathroom.

Even through the mask, the smell caught at the back of her throat. Or, more accurately, the *smells*. There was an onslaught of them that forced her to take a moment to compose herself at the door.

The stench of bodily fluids was the big headline, but there was a lot going on below that. Soap. Deodorant. Perfume. Booze.

Death. She knew that one well.

There were a few tent-like numbered markers on the floor, and a couple of others by the sinks. Geoff's team had already gone over the area surrounding the body, though they wouldn't yet have investigated the body itself.

She had the pleasure of that particular task.

He was in the fourth of five cubicles. She didn't have to check the others. The blood pooling on the tiled floor told her where she'd find him.

"Ouch," she remarked when she finally saw him.

He had fallen between the toilet and the cubicle wall, and while she was strictly supposed to check for a pulse, she knew there was no point whatsoever in doing so. There was no chance that this man was alive. And, if he was, he almost certainly wouldn't want to be.

There was a hole where his groin should be. That was how it looked with his trousers on, anyway. She'd have to wait to get him back to the hospital to confirm for sure.

From where she was standing, though, his whole crotch area

appeared to be missing. A tattered mess of raw, bloody flesh was all that he'd been left with. The blood loss would've killed him within minutes. Five. Maybe fewer.

But every second of that time would've been spent in pain.

A few crimson handprints marked the walls, smeared downwards like he'd been trying without success to drag himself up. A toilet roll holder had been broken off. It lay in the puddle on the floor, the roll of paper puffed up and swollen with the blood it had absorbed.

The cubicle was a potential treasure trove of forensic evidence, so it would help nobody for her to disturb it unless it was absolutely necessary.

It wasn't. The colour and the texture of him—of his eyes and of his pale brown skin—had already told her enough for now. He'd been dead for hours. Four to eight, she'd estimate, though she'd have a better idea when she got him on the slab.

"I'm sorry," she whispered.

He was dead. Murdered.

And that meant there was work to do.

CHAPTER THREE

TYLER WAS STILL TALKING. He'd been talking for what felt like a very long time, though Logan couldn't recall a word that he'd actually said. It was possible there weren't any words, in fact, just a constant stream of chirps, cheeps, and other irritating noises designed to make his headache even worse.

Logan held up a hand. It left a flickering little trail in the air as it moved, and he scowled at it until it behaved itself.

"Stop, stop," he said. "Just... shut up."

Tyler stopped. He shut up.

But not for long.

"You alright, boss?" he asked. Unlike last time, there was a note of genuine concern in the question. "You don't look well."

"I'm fine," Logan said. "Just a cold."

"You sure?" the detective constable asked. He took a step closer and swam into some sort of focus. "Because you really do look like shite."

"So everyone keeps bloody telling me," Logan grunted. "I'm fine. Where's Sinead and Hamza?"

Tyler blinked. "Eh, I just told you that, boss."

"Well, tell me again," Logan said. "I wasn't listening."

"Right. Aye. They're in talking to the cleaners."

"Crime scene cleaners?" Logan looked past the DC in the direction of the nightclub. The whole building undulated like it was made of jelly, and he quickly averted his gaze. "The hell are they doing here already?"

"Eh, no, boss. The club's cleaners. They found the body."

"Oh. Right. Aye," Logan said. He stopped leaning on the car, wobbled unsteadily, and decided he wasn't quite ready to go anywhere just yet, and rested his weight against the reassuringly solid metal again. "Someone should go and talk to them. Get their statements."

Tyler hesitated. He looked back over his shoulder, hoping someone with more authority might be available to take over this conversation, but the only other officers nearby were all in uniform, and all busy with their own jobs.

"Aye. Sinead and Ham are doing that already," he said. "Remember? I just told you."

"Course I bloody remember!" Logan snapped, though he wasn't quite sure *what* he remembered, exactly. But he definitely remembered something.

The unwelcome noise that was DC Tyler Neish was interrupted before it could continue. Unfortunately, what interrupted it was even less welcome than Tyler.

"Jesus, is he back on the sauce or something?"

Palmer.

Shite.

There was no way he was letting that bastard see any weakness. He'd never hear the bloody end of it.

Logan detached himself from the car and stood unsupported. There was a bit of wobbling involved, but not so much that anyone would notice, he reckoned.

He blinked, and Palmer was suddenly standing right there in front of him in his white paper suit. The way his pudgy red face poked out through his hood's circle of elastic made it look like a giant plook in desperate need of popping.

Logan giggled at the thought of it, which drew confused looks from Palmer and Tyler alike.

Not that he noticed.

"The hell is wrong with him?" Palmer asked, addressing the question to Tyler like Logan wasn't even there. "He looks like a Jakey's first dump of the day."

"I'm no' a Jakey," Logan interjected, picking up on the few words that he could. The world was really starting to twirl now, the early morning clouds blurring across the sky like aeroplane trails.

"No, no, no. I didn't say you were a Jakey," Palmer clarified. "I said you were the shite from a Jakey's arse. That's how bad you look. Are you hungover? Is that..." He stepped in closer and sniffed.

The sudden movement towards him made Logan's eyes cross, and his head spin faster.

"Have you been drinking?" Palmer demanded. "Is that what this is? Are you—?"

The bullfrog in Logan's stomach grumbled again, and this time there was nothing he could do to stop it. He brought his hand up to his mouth, but the sheer force of the vomit forced it through his fingers, turning it first into a fine mist, then a follow-through splatter that coated the front of Geoff Palmer from chin to scrotum.

The retching lasted for just over a second. The silence that followed seemed to stretch into eternity.

"Fuck," Tyler muttered, which pretty succinctly summed up the general feeling at the time.

When Palmer finally found his voice, it came as a screech of outrage and disgust. "Jeeeesusssss!" he wailed, throwing his arms out to his sides like the vomit was acid, and he was trying to keep them from being burned. "Jeeeeesussss *Christ*! Look at me! Look what you've done!"

Logan leaned back against the car. There was no point trying to hide the fact that he was ill now. It was safe to say that ship had already sailed.

"God. Geoff. I'm sorry," Logan said.

"No you aren't!" Palmer wailed. "I bet you're bloody loving this! I bet this was planned! Wasn't it?" He jabbed a finger at Logan and Tyler in turn. "Both of you! I bet you both planned this. Didn't you?"

"Definitely not," Tyler said. He glanced down at Palmer's puke-splattered front, swallowed back something sour and unpleasant, then looked between both men and started ejecting words at random. "Look. I don't... I mean... What if...?"

"Everything OK here?"

The sound of DI Forde's voice drew a sharp laugh of relief from DC Neish, who then immediately retreated a pace to suggest that his involvement in this matter was done.

Ben arrived on the scene, considered all three men in turn, then said, "Alright, Geoff?" so casually it almost made Palmer explode with rage.

"What? What do you mean?! Of course, I'm not bloody alright! Look at me! I've got sick all down me!"

"Well, why have you done that, then?" Ben asked.

It was Palmer's turn to start stuttering. "What do...? I didn't... This wasn't..." He glowered at Logan and prodded at his chest with an accusing finger. "It was him! He did it! On purpose, I might add!"

"It wasn't on purpose," Logan said.

"Course it wasn't," Ben agreed. He moved as if to pat Palmer on the shoulder, then thought better of it. "I reckon you should go and get yourself a nice new paper suit, Geoff. Can't have you contaminating the place, can we?"

"I'm not the bloody one contaminating the place!" Palmer hissed.

"Geoffrey," Ben said, and while there was no obvious malice in the DI's tone, something about the look on his face made Palmer stop whining and start paying attention. "Go and get yourself cleaned up," Ben instructed. "Now."

Palmer's jaw moved from side to side like he was chewing on something rubbery and unpleasant. "Fine," he eventually spat. "I'll go get changed."

"Wait, hold on," Logan said. With some effort, he placed the hand he'd been sick into on Palmer's arm and wiped the worst of it off onto the SOC man's paper suit.

"Jesus!" Palmer spat, recoiling when he realised what was happening.

"You already had it on you," Logan pointed out. "I didn't think a bit more would make much difference."

"You're a bloody animal," Palmer told him, grimacing. He turned and started waddling away, his arms still held out like he was Christ on the cross. "And all of you mark my words, I'll be complaining about this."

"You're already complaining about this," Ben pointed out. "But no bugger's listening."

He watched Palmer go, Uniforms scurrying out of his path, eyes wide in horror.

Once he was convinced the SOC man wasn't coming back, he turned his attention to Logan. "Right. You. Home. Now," he said.

"I'm fine," Logan said, but there was no conviction in it.

He was done here, and he knew it. His best bet was to be gone by the time Shona came out, so he could at least avoid the worried looks and, more importantly, the *I told you so*s.

"OK, fine," he muttered, responding to a comment nobody had made. He fumbled in his coat pocket until he found his keys. "I'll go home."

"Oh no you don't," Ben said.

Logan stared at his empty hand, reasonably confident that there had been a set of keys in there just a moment before.

"You're not driving. Not in your condition," Ben told him.

"I'm perfectly capable of driving my own car," Logan insisted. He tried to slap the roof like this would somehow prove he was fit to drive, but despite the fact he was currently leaning on it, managed to miss making contact completely.

"Aye, no. You really aren't," Ben told him. "But don't worry, I've already found a driver to get you home."

He tossed the keys to his left. Tyler fumbled the catch, frantically juggled with them for a few seconds, then managed to grab them before they hit the ground.

"Good luck, son," Ben told him. Then, with a smug little smile, he tucked his hands behind his back, and walked away, whistling cheerfully.

Tyler looked from the keys in his hand to Logan's BMW, then up at the DCI himself. He swallowed and nodded, like he was steeling himself for some Herculean task.

"Right, then, boss. You best go round the passenger side," he said.

"No. No, way," Logan said. "We're not taking my car. I might be sick."

"Oh. Right." Tyler looked down at the keys again, like they might hold the answer to the question he was about to ask. "So, whose car are we taking?"

Despite everything—despite the nausea, the headache, the pool of sweat sticking his shirt to his back, and the fact that the whole world was tilting on its axis, Logan managed to smile. It was not, however, a smile you wanted to be on the receiving end of.

"Yours," he said. "We're taking yours."

CHAPTER FOUR

"I UNDERSTAND this must be very upsetting for you, Miss Sheen, but if you could try to answer the questions..."

Angela Sheen tore her eyes from her untouched mug of coffee, and practically snarled at the young female detective sitting across the table from her.

The police had taken over one of the small independent coffee shops just along the road from the nightclub, and both Angela and Josh had been taken inside for questioning—Josh by a South Asian man with a disconcertingly thick Aberdonian accent, and Angela by a woman who'd identified herself as Detective Constable Sinead Bell.

"Of course it's upsetting! It's very upsetting!" Angela replied, her voice wobbling a bit around the edges. "Have you ever seen a dead body before? One like that, I mean?"

Angela had given her age as thirty-six, and Sinead had been forced to double-check she'd heard correctly. If she was telling the truth, then not one of those thirty-six years had been kind.

Her hair was dark, but tendrils of grey had infected it, taking hold at the roots and spreading like some invasive species. Her skin was waxy, and flaked here and there with the tell-tale signs of eczema.

Where she looked oldest most, though, was in her eyes. They were ringed with red now, and bloodshot from crying. But that wasn't what aged them. What aged them was everything they'd seen, and everything going on behind them.

"I have seen similar before, yes," Sinead confirmed.

"Well, I mean, of course. Obviously. But you chose to. I didn't! That's your job. It's not my job!" Angela continued. "And I knew him, so that makes it worse! It's different when you know them. It's worse. You might've seen bodies before—all bloodied like that—but I bet they weren't your friends!"

Sinead had had enough of the pity party. "Actually, I was first on the scene when my parents were killed in a car accident," she stated matter-of-factly. "I found them both. So, I do understand what you're going through."

Had Angela not been sitting down, that would've taken the feet right out from under her. Sinead took some perverse satisfaction from the look of shock on the woman's face, then quickly capitalised on her stunned silence.

"So, you were friends, then? You and the victim?" she asked.

The look of shock on Angela's face remained. Only the reason for it changed. "What? No. I mean, no. Not really. He hired us. I barely knew him," she backtracked.

"Do you have a name?"

The other woman missed a beat. "Angela Sheen."

"Eh, no. Sorry. For him, I meant. Can you give me his name?"

"Oh. Yeah. Course, sorry. It's Mr Rani. Um, Dev. Dev Rani." She shot a quick glance to the other detective who was currently talking to Josh, and dropped her voice a little. "He's, eh, Indian or something. Pakistani, or... I don't know. Somewhere over there."

"Right. And he's the manager?" Sinead asked.

"Yes. Well, owner, I think. Or co-owner." Angela wrapped her hands around her mug, warming them. "There was a woman. Older. I only met her once, back when they hired us."

Sinead made a note in her pad. "Do you have a name? For her, I mean," she added, to avoid any further confusion.

"No. I mean, I probably heard it at the time, but I don't remember."

"OK, don't worry about it," Sinead said, smiling warmly. "You're doing great. And, listen, I know it's going to be hard, but I need you to talk me through everything that happened this morning."

———

At a table on the other side of the room, Detective Sergeant Hamza Khaled pointed to the doughnut on the plate in front of him. Or, what was left of it, anyway. It was salted caramel flavour, and still warm from the fryer, the icing on top all oozing and sticky.

"You sure you don't want one, Mr Holder?" he asked. "They're really good."

The man sitting opposite shook his head and confirmed for the second time that no, he was quite sure he didn't want one.

"You don't mind me eating, do you?" Hamza asked. "Didn't get a chance to grab something before I came out."

"No, fire on," came the reply.

Hamza picked up the doughnut, enjoyed another bite, then washed it down with a big glug of tea.

That done, he rubbed his hands together, gave a shake of his shoulders like he was warming up for something, then picked up the pen he had sat beside the open notepad.

"Right!" he announced, then he looked across to the other man. "Do you mind if I call you Josh? I always think it feels less formal. Puts people on edge a bit if we use last names."

"No. It's fine."

Hamza raised a thumb in thanks, and the other man acknowledged it with the thinnest of smiles.

He seemed like a young lad—far younger than his thirty-one years suggested. It wasn't just the size of him—five-six, he'd guess, and skinny with it—it was everything. He had a wide-eyed look to him, like everything was new, and he was seeing it all for the very first time.

He had been wearing a protective boiler suit when Hamza first met him, before the SOC team took it off him for testing. It had been emblazoned across the back with the logo of *Shine & Sheen*, the name of the cleaning company he worked for, and was about two sizes too big. A tightly tied belt had pulled the whole thing in around his waist so that he'd looked like a male backing dancer in a 1980s music video.

Now, he sat in a faded grey t-shirt with orange food stains down the front, and a pair of shapeless shorts that stretched down to his knees.

"So, rough morning, Josh," Hamza said. It wasn't a question, exactly—he already knew the answer—but the other man treated it like it was.

"Yeah. Not great," he admitted, and he squirmed in the chair as some recent memory resurfaced in vivid Technicolour. "It was... It was really horrible, actually. He was... Have you seen him?"

"Not yet," Hamza admitted.

"No. Right. Well, it's... there's a lot of blood. I'll warn you," Josh said. "He was like, sort of half on the floor, jammed in next to the toilet. In the ladies, too. That's weird, isn't it? I mean, what was he doing in there?"

"Not sure yet. Checking to see if there was anyone in there before locking up, maybe?"

"It was already locked up. We had to unlock it to get in," Josh told him, and Hamza scribbled that down. "But... the blood. God. I've never seen anything like it. I didn't know there was that much blood inside people. Did you know there was that much?"

"Well, again, I haven't seen it. But there's about ten pints. So, aye, it's a lot."

Despite the talk of death and gore, Hamza's eyes crept back to his doughnut. He really was hungry, and it was genuinely one of the most delicious things he'd ever tasted.

He resisted, and consoled himself with a quick sip of tea.

When he looked across to Josh again, he looked like he was fighting back tears. Hamza picked up a paper napkin from the table and offered it across.

"It's fine, Josh. Don't worry. It's a really upsetting thing you've seen."

Josh took the napkin and blew his nose into it. The *honk* he made—like the strained final note of a school trumpet recital—was so ridiculous and unexpected that Hamza had to bite his cheek to stop himself laughing.

"I just... I keep thinking..." Josh muttered. "If we'd been here last night, maybe we could've stopped it. Or, I don't know, helped him. Done something."

"There's no point in thinking like that," Hamza said. "It'll drive you mad."

Josh sighed. Nodded. "Yeah. Yeah, I suppose."

Hamza glanced down at his pad, then back to the man across the table. "What makes you think he died last night, anyway?"

Panic set up camp on Josh's face. His words tumbled out with barely a breath between them. "What? Well, it had to be, didn't it? The club was open. He usually leaves after cashing up, but obviously he didn't this time, and we came in first thing and found him, and he looked like he'd been dead for a little while, with all that blood everywhere, so I don't know, I just thought he must've died last night, but I don't know, maybe he didn't, it just seems—"

Hamza held up a hand to calm him. "You're right, Josh. It probably was last night. That all makes sense."

That seemed to ease Josh's panic a bit. He nodded and sat back, like he needed a breather.

Unfortunately, Hamza wasn't done with his questioning yet.

"Where were you last night? Out of interest."

Josh paled. "I was at home."

"Alone?"

"Uh, yeah. Online, though. On Twitch. You know, the..."

"I know what Twitch is," Hamza said. "You're a streamer?"

"Aye. Aye, I am!" Josh said. *Call of Duty*, mainly. Some *Minecraft*. Not got too many subscribers yet, but I had a few watching the feed last night. You'll be able to check it. You'll be able to see."

Hamza made a note. "OK. Good. Now, just one more thing, Josh," the DS said, leaving the point of his pen resting on the paper. "How would you describe your relationship with the victim?"

"Relationship? Non-existent," Josh said. "I mean, I saw him occasionally. In passing. But I don't tend to deal with the clients. Angela does that. I'd be surprised if he even knew my name."

Hamza was making a note of that when Josh spoke again.

"Can... can I ask you something?"

"Sure," Hamza said, looking up from his pad.

"How do you...? How do you deal with stuff like that? Blood. Death. That sort of..." His voice cracked, and he directed his gaze down at the table, unable to continue with his question.

Not that he needed to continue. It was a question Hamza had asked himself often enough.

"You just... you deal with it," he said. "It's not always easy, but you just get on with it. You get back to work. You carry on. You..." He looked to the ceiling, as if seeking spiritual guidance. "You're grateful that it isn't you lying there. Or someone you love. And you carry on."

Josh wiped his eyes on his sleeve, raised his head, and nodded. "Carry on. Right," he said. He smiled, but his eyes shimmered. "I've just... I've never seen anything like that before."

"Yeah, well," Hamza began, and there was a note of bitter resignation to the words. "You get used to it, sooner or later."

———

DI Forde stood in the centre of *Refuge's* dance floor, his hands still tucked behind his back, his neck craning as he took in his surroundings.

The place was a mess. Not just dirty—though it was that, too—but decrepit. Half of the seat cushions had been ripped, then inexpertly taped back together. The mismatched tables were scraped and scratched with names, and swear words, and crude drawings of genitalia carved into the wood.

There were a lot of lights, he noted. A *lot* of lights, all with different coloured gels covering the glass, and most of them pointing directly at the dance floor. Just the thought of them flashing and pulsing in time with the music—if you could even call the bloody racket they played in these places music—was starting to give him a sore head.

The soles of his shoes *clacked* as they pulled free from something sticky on the floor. He turned on the spot, still scanning the room, taking it all in.

The bar was a horseshoe-shaped thing that looked much grander than the rest of the place, with its curved wooden top, and brass foot rail that ran all the way along the bottom.

Metal shutters had been pulled down from the ceiling and

locked in place as a security measure. The SOC team hadn't been able to get access yet, though Ben thought it unlikely they'd find anything useful in there.

He looked up to the ceiling again, and this time found what he was looking for. A domed camera was fixed there near the bar, its beady eye watching—and hopefully recording—events going on below.

"Bingo," he announced to the empty room. Fingers crossed that would make life easier.

He turned at the sound of a door creaking open, listened to a brief conversation between Shona and one of the men in paper suits, then waited while she removed her protective gear and placed it in a waiting bag.

The bag would be sealed up, marked, and taken in with the rest of the material Palmer's crew collected, in case any forensic evidence had accidentally been transferred during Shona's work with the body.

He smiled at her when she emerged from the toilet corridor, and she diverted to come over and join him.

"How was it?" he asked.

"Nasty one," Shona told him. "Looks like his undercarriage has been put through a mincer. If you can imagine such a thing."

"I'm sure I can, but I'd rather not," Ben said. "We've sent himself home, by the way."

Shona frowned. "Jack? Shite, you didn't let him drive, did you? He tried to overtake a lamp post on the way here."

"No. Tyler's taking him," Ben said, and he was unable to hide his smirk.

"You're a spiteful and vindictive man, Benjamin Forde," Shona told him, which earned a laugh from the DI.

"I know! I don't even know which one I was trying to annoy. Still, two birds with one stone!"

Shona leaned back a little, and her eyes narrowed as she studied him. "You seem awfully cheerful."

"What? Me? No," Ben said, emphatically shaking his head. His smile, however, contradicted him. "Just full of the joys of life, I suppose!"

"Well, I'm glad to hear it. It suits you," Shona told him.

"Oh, before I forget. About Jack. There's something you should know," Ben began.

Shona tensed. "What? What happened? He didn't collapse, did he? Because he was swaying about this morning."

"No, no. He didn't collapse," Ben said. "He was sick on Geoff Palmer."

Shona blinked a few times, then stared. "Sorry, he what?"

"He was sick on Geoff Palmer."

"What do you mean?"

Ben shrugged. "Well, you know Geoff Palmer?"

"Yes."

"Logan was sick on him."

"*On* him?" Shona asked, apparently still not quite getting it. "He was sick *on* Geoff Palmer?"

"Right down his front," Ben clarified. "Like, *right* down his front. Boobs to balls."

"Jesus," Shona said. She whistled quietly through her teeth, then shook her head. "Geoff wouldn't have liked that."

Hamza's voice cut in before Ben could confirm or deny this. "Geoff wouldn't have liked what?" he asked, and there was a hopeful note to the question. None of the team were fans of Palmer. But then, it was unlikely that anyone who'd met him could stand the bastard.

Ben and Shona turned to see Hamza and Sinead crossing the dance floor towards them.

"Logan was sick on him," Ben explained.

Both of the younger detectives faltered, mid-step. "Sick on him?" Sinead asked. "On who? On Geoff?"

"Right down his front."

Sinead and Hamza swapped looks of surprise.

"What, on purpose?" Hamza asked.

Ben tutted. "Of course not on bloody purpose!"

"He's got the flu or something," Shona explained.

"We've sent him home," Ben added.

"Home?" Hamza asked. He and Sinead arrived in the middle of the dance floor and stopped beside the other pair. "Is he that bad?"

"He was sick on Geoff Palmer," Ben reminded him. Mostly, just because he enjoyed saying the words out loud. "So, aye, he's pretty bad."

"Wow. That's... I didn't know he could even get sick," Hamza said. "I thought he'd just, like, scare bugs off." He looked from Shona to Ben and back again. "You sure he didn't do it on purpose?"

"Well, I can't be a hundred percent, but they both looked equally surprised, so I'm guessing no," Ben said. He tilted his head in the direction of the toilets, steering everyone back to the job at hand. "Once Scene of Crime's done, we'll go in and check the scene before anything gets moved."

Sinead groaned, and rested a hand on her stomach. "Do you mind if I give the body a miss, sir?" she asked. "Feeling a bit ropey myself this morning."

"God, not you, too," Ben said. "Do you need to go home?"

Shona's eyes flitted from Sinead's face, and lingered on the hand on her belly for a few moments.

"No. No, nothing like that," Sinead insisted. "I'm fine. Just... I don't fancy getting up close to anything too, you know, full-on."

"Right. OK. Well, let me know if you start to feel worse," Ben said. "And, for the love of God, if you feel like you're going to throw up, at least aim it in Palmer's direction..."

CHAPTER FIVE

BY JUST AFTER LUNCHTIME, the Scene of Crime team had finished up, the body had been bagged, tagged, and carted away, and all the necessary measurements, photographs, and statements had been taken.

The nightclub was secured. The cordon tapes on the street were removed. And, within minutes, nobody passing by outside would've suspected what had been going on that morning.

The main Incident Room at Burnett Road station was now a hubbub of activity. Although, granted, much of that activity currently centred around the consumption of bacon and square sausage rolls, and the quaffing of hot beverages.

"Sinead, you can work up the Big Board for us, will you?" asked Ben. He indicated the roll on the plate in front of her—bacon, crispy, and with a tattie scone on top. "Aye, after you've eaten, I mean."

"No bother, sir," Sinead confirmed. She took a sip of tea, and eyed the roll like it was something to be conquered, rather than enjoyed.

"You not hungry?" asked Tyler. He was sitting across from

her, his feet on his desk, his own roll—square sausage, a wee daud of brown sauce—already all but devoured.

"Not really," Sinead said.

Tyler paused, mid-chew. His eyes crept down to Sinead's plate. "So, what? You not going to eat that?"

Sinead shook her head. "No, don't think so," she said, then she got halfway through asking him if he wanted it before he leaned over and plucked the roll from the plate.

"You sure you don't want a wee bit?"

At the next desk over, Hamza snorted. "Hear that? He's not even offering you the full thing back, just a bit."

"A *wee* bit," Ben corrected. "No' even a big bit."

Tyler smirked, and took a bite of the roll. "You two are just jealous you didn't grab it first," he said, crumbs tumbling out of his mouth as he spoke.

Sinead got up, collected her disposable cardboard cup, and crossed to where the Big Board stood in the centre of the room. It was empty, but that wouldn't last. As more and more evidence came in, she'd fill it up, making connections where any needed to be made, and even the odd leap of faith when required.

She had just set her cup down on the table beside the board when the doors to the Incident Room swung open, and Detective Superintendent Mitchell made her presence known.

"What's this I hear about DCI Logan?" she demanded. "Where is he?"

Mitchell was not a large woman, but she was an imposing one. Her crisp white shirt contrasted sharply with her dark skin, and she had an air of authority about her that made even the most seasoned officer stand up straight and take notice.

Sinead looked to Ben to handle the response, then to Hamza. Both men rather conveniently had their mouths stuffed full, though, leaving her no choice but to reply.

"He, eh, he went home, ma'am," she said, pulling her shoulders back. "He's ill."

"What do you mean, he's ill? We've got a live investigation," she said.

Sinead wasn't quite sure how one thing influenced the other, but she didn't dare say so. "We think it's the flu, or a bug of some kind," Sinead said.

"He was sick on Geoff Palmer," Tyler interjected, throwing his wife a lifeline.

Mitchell's head snapped in his direction, eyes narrowing. "I beg your pardon?"

Tyler swallowed his half-chewed lump of roll. "Oh. Aye. Sorry. He was sick on Geoff Palmer, *ma'am*."

Mitchell tutted. "No, I mean... What do you mean he was sick on Geoff Palmer?"

"From the Scene of Crime team," Sinead explained.

"Yes, I know who Geoff Palmer is, Detective Constable. I wasn't asking who he is." Mitchell shot withering looks at both DCs, then turned her attention to Ben, who was hurriedly chewing what he now realised was far too big a mouthful of square sausage and bread. "DI Forde? Please explain to me what they're talking about."

Ben pointed to his mouth, made some apologetic noises, then chewed frantically for what felt like a very long time. He forced the last remnants down with a swig of tea, thumped his chest a few times to unclog the pipes, then met the detective superintendent's impatient glare.

"He was sick on Geoff Palmer," he said, which didn't really help make things any clearer. But then, he reasoned, how much clearer could he make it? "I'm no' sure why people have such a hard time grasping the concept."

Mitchell blew out her cheeks. "I assume Geoff was furious?"

Ben tried to hide his smile behind his tea. "Aye. Aye, he was that alright."

The detective superintendent pinched the bridge of her nose and gave it a squeeze. "Well, at least that's something, I suppose," she muttered, before addressing DI Forde again. "How long will he be off?"

"No idea. Until he gets better, I suppose," Ben replied. "Though, knowing Jack—sick or not sick—we won't be able to keep him away for long."

"Yes. Well, unfortunately, I don't have the luxury of being able to make that assumption. We've got a live murder case of an influential, high profile victim."

A look passed around the team. Mitchell picked up on it immediately.

"You do know who he is, yes? Mr Rani?"

"He's, eh, he runs the nightclub," Ben said.

Mitchell sighed. "*And* he's a local independent councillor with the Highland Council," she added. Her gaze darted around the Incident Room, scrutinising them. Accusing them. "Please tell me you knew that."

None of the more junior officers spoke. None of them dared. It was left to Ben to throw himself into the firing line.

"We're still at the gathering information stage," he told her. "We'd have come to it shortly."

"Oh. Good. You'd have come to it shortly. That's alright, then," Mitchell said, and her tone was so barbed it practically drew blood. She gave them all another look. Most of them avoided meeting it. "This does not bode well for Jack's absence," she said. "Let's all pull our socks up, shall we? I want this killer found, and I want them found quickly. Is that understood?"

"Understood, ma'am," Ben said.

"I was asking all of you," Mitchell snapped, glaring at each of the officers in turn.

They all sat or stood up straighter, quickly nodded, and responded to say that they, too, understood the order.

"Good. Then jump to it," Mitchell said.

She clapped her hands once, like the *crack* of a starting pistol. The sudden sound propelled Tyler onto his feet as if he was standing for the national anthem. He looked at his legs in surprise, shuffled on the spot for a moment, then quietly sat back down again.

By the time he was seated, the door to the Incident Room was swinging closed, and a collective sigh of relief was released.

"Blimey. Someone got out of the wrong side of bed this morning," Hamza remarked, then he flinched when the door was pushed inwards. Everyone held their breath once more, only exhaling when a sturdy-looking man with a big broad grin rolled into the room in his wheelchair.

"Jesus Christ," said Dave Davidson, his smile faltering a little. "At least try to look pleased to see me."

CHAPTER SIX

DCI JACK LOGAN was having a lovely time. He lay in bed, stripped to the waist, eyes closed as Shona kissed him. She was being... unusually passionate. Not that he was complaining, of course. Her tongue was exploring his neck, his mouth, his ears.

His nostrils.

OK, that one was a little weird.

The darkness swam behind his eyes, as he rose towards the surface of consciousness, and light forced its way through his closed lids.

Shona was hairy. One of her paws dug sharply into his chest.

"Aw, for fu—" Logan grunted, batting limply at the small dog that was currently exploring his face with its tongue. "Taggart!" he said sharply. "Piss off. Enough!"

The dog slid off his chest and onto the bed beside him. Logan wiped the slobber from his face, then returned his hand to his forehead. Christ, he was burning up. That couldn't be good.

The inside of his mouth, despite Taggart's best efforts, was as dry as a badger's arse. His tongue felt like a mummy in a tomb, only one wrapped in sandpaper instead of bandages. He swallowed, and all the apparatus involved scraped around inside his throat.

Taggart watched in a sort of curious silence as Logan arranged himself onto his elbows. This took him some effort, and quite a lot of thought, as he tried to remember his body's basic operating procedures.

Once his head was off the pillow, Logan remained motionless for a few moments, gauging how he was feeling. The room wasn't spinning, exactly, but it seemed to be drifting around to the left in slow, lazy revolutions. This only applied to things he wasn't looking directly at. Stare at the door, for example, and it remained where it was, but the window came creeping closer.

Look at the window, and it froze like it had been caught in the act. The door, meanwhile, and everything else in the room, took the opportunity to try and sneak away.

Was this better or worse than the general spinning sensation of earlier? He had no idea. It was less nauseating, but it was making him a bit paranoid that, if he didn't keep a close eye on it, the door might fuck off completely, leaving him trapped.

He knew this was impossible, of course. He recognised that fact. And yet, he could feel the fear of it happening twisting like a knot deep down in his chest.

"Still sick, then," he croaked, and Taggart's tail wagged as if in agreement.

How long had he been asleep? He couldn't remember. In fact, he couldn't recall much about the morning, other than an edited highlight showreel in which a vomit-slicked Geoff Palmer featured quite prominently.

He remembered Tyler sitting beside him in a car. Not his own car, he thought, though he couldn't be sure. Sick or not, he wouldn't have let Tyler drive his car, would he?

He dimly recalled hobbling up the path, leaning on something. Something that made a lot of garbled noises. Something irritating.

Tyler again? Had to be.

And then...

And then...

What?

A conversation. One-sided. An instruction, maybe? Something he was supposed to do. Something important?

He closed his eyes, hoping that the door wouldn't seize the opportunity to make a break for it, and concentrated.

A face you wouldn't tire of slapping formed in the murk. The conversation had been with Tyler, then. Something about bed. Something about... staying hydrated.

Opening his eyes again, he adjusted himself so he could see the bedside table. There, like an oasis in the desert, was a bottle of water. Droplets of moisture clung to the outside, and when he reached for it, the plastic was cool to the touch.

Logan took it all back. Every joke at Tyler's expense. Every bad thing he'd said about him, every teasing word, every roll of the eyes, he retracted it all. The boy was a godsend. The boy was a bloody hero.

"Not that I'll ever say that out loud, you understand?" he rasped, and Taggart cocked his head in confusion while Logan slaked his thirst with the water.

There were a couple of pills on the bedside table, too, right next to the wet circle that marked where the bottle had sat. Logan assumed they were painkillers, tossed them both to the back of his throat, and sent them on their way with another glug of water.

It was then that he realised that a phone was ringing. Not only that, it occurred to him that it had been ringing for a while now. He'd been dimly aware of it, but his fever-addled brain had disregarded it. He'd had other things to worry about—a throat like old parchment and an amorous dog for starters—but now that he wasn't going to die of thirst, the ringing was being brought to his attention.

His mobile was in the pocket of his trousers, which lay in a heap on the floor beside the bed. He very much hoped that he'd taken them off himself without Tyler's assistance, but he couldn't be sure. He'd never know, either, because the last thing he was going to do was ask, and while Tyler might not be the sharpest knife in the drawer, even he wasn't daft enough to mention it.

The main problem at the moment—ignoring the fact that the window and door were still trying to sidle out of the room—was that the floor seemed an unfathomably long way away. Groaning with the effort, Logan flopped down onto his left side and stretched out his right arm, fingers splayed wide, as if he could summon the garment to his hand like some sort of trousers-based Jedi Knight.

The phone continued to ring. The trousers remained tantalisingly beyond his reach.

"How high's this fucking bed?" he grumbled to himself. And then he found out first-hand when he rolled off it, and landed with a *thump* on the floor.

He lay on his back, readjusting to this unexpected turn of events, and watching the light shade on the ceiling do the same crab-like scuttle as everything else in the room had been doing a moment before.

Only more so.

Taggart's head appeared over the side of the bed, tongue flopping, ears excitedly pricked up like he was sensing a new game.

"Don't you bloody dare," Logan warned him. And, to his surprise and relief, the dog didn't jump down and land on him.

The phone was still ringing. Where was voicemail when you needed it?

Logan didn't have the energy to turn, so he twisted an arm

up behind his back, grabbed a handful of material, and pulled the trousers out from beneath him.

The mobile was in the third pocket he checked. Technically, it was in the second pocket, but he unwittingly checked the other one twice.

The screen was dark. He poked and slapped at it, then put the phone to his ear.

"Hello?" he said. Then, more forcefully. "Hello!"

The phone kept ringing. He looked at the screen, and a nagging little voice told him it wasn't this phone that was ringing, but another one.

He ejected a series of obscenities and started hauling himself to his feet on the side of the bed, while mentally plotting the route to the house phone.

It was on a table in the hall. Shite. That meant tackling the stairs, which struck him as a disaster waiting to happen.

Maybe he could slide down them on his arse. It wouldn't exactly be a dignified descent, but there was nobody around to see, so what did it matter?

Aye, sure, the dog might be watching, but he wasn't exactly going to spread the word.

"The arse it is," he declared, then he threw himself in the direction of the bedroom door, and hoped it didn't choose that moment to bugger off elsewhere.

He was halfway down the stairs, carpet burns forming on the backs of his thighs, when he remembered the second handset in the bedroom, just five or six inches from where the water bottle and painkillers had been.

He let fly with another outburst of swearing, lost his footing on the next step, and slid down several stairs in a oner.

The wall at the bottom was pleasingly cool. Logan rested there a moment, his face, one shoulder, and part of his chest pressed against it. Then, with the din of its ring vibrating through his skull, he got up, stumbled to the phone, and tore it out of its dock.

"*What*?!" he hissed into the handset.

There was a pause, then a woman spoke. "Uh, is that Mr Logan?"

"Yes. Who's this?"

"Mr Logan," the woman continued, completely ignoring the question. "Did you know you could get up to three thousand pounds for your old windows, as part of a government-supported scrappage scheme?"

There was a *crack* as Logan's hand tightened around the plastic casing of the phone, and the LED display became garbled and indecipherable. Logan shouted at the handset, though none of the noises he made qualified as actual words.

He mashed all the buttons at once, ending the call, tried to fit the phone back into its docking station, then gave up after several failed attempts and settled for slamming it down on the table instead.

It rang again the moment he took his hand away. This time, he was ready for the bastard. He snatched it up, prodded the button to answer it, and roared a particularly hate-filled, "*Fuck off!*" down the line.

"Well, now," came the reply, and even through his fever-haze, Logan recognised Shona's Irish lilt. "I think *somebody* needs to do some brushing up on their phone etiquette."

CHAPTER SEVEN

THE BIG BOARD was slowly starting to come together. Once Dave had been brought up to speed and taken his usual spot at the Exhibits desk, everyone but Sinead had jumped on their phones or their computers, gathering together all the information they could about the victim, the nightclub, and anything else that they thought might be relevant to the investigation.

As their findings had filtered in, Sinead had written them up, and started laying it all out on the board. They'd now built the beginnings of a picture of the victim including his jobs—both of them—his home address, his family relationships, and the details of his partner in the nightclub business.

What they didn't have was any idea about who had killed him, or why. But then, it was early days.

It was still too early for the SOC report, and Shona hadn't yet sent over the results of the Post Mortem, so there wasn't much in the way of evidence to add to the board.

In fact, there was even less than they'd been hoping for.

"No CCTV footage from the club," Hamza announced. He made a clicking sound from the side of his mouth, then sat back with his hands on his head, visibly disappointed. "Someone from Palmer's team just emailed."

"Shite," Ben groaned. "What, none?"

"Hasn't been working for a while, by the looks of things," Hamza said. "The last recording on the hard drive is from weeks ago."

"Could someone have deleted the more recent stuff?" Sinead wondered.

Hamza shook his head. "Doubt it. These systems tend to overwrite the old stuff every few days. More likely, it just hasn't been recording anything since then. I could check it out, though."

"Aye, do that. Hopefully, we can get something useful out of it somehow. But it'll have to be later," Ben said, checking his watch. "I want you and Tyler to go to the hospital. Shona should be done with the PM shortly. I want you over there to go through it with her."

Tyler let out a pained sort of moan. "Aw, do I have to, boss? I don't like, you know, poking around at dead bodies."

"Well, don't bloody poke around at it, then," Ben told him. "You're going. Both of you. Sinead and I are going to go talk to the family. Uniform's already broken the news, so no saying what state they'll be in. Would you rather do that?"

Tyler had to begrudgingly admit that no, he wouldn't. Dead bodies you eventually got used to. Questioning grieving loved ones, in his experience, you never did.

Sinead was far better at it than he was. She was far better at it than anyone. He used to think it was because she'd been on both sides of the conversation, but he didn't believe that now. Now, he knew better. That ability, not just to empathise with a victim's family, but to console them, and offer them comfort, it wasn't a learned skill. It was innate. It was something that had always been in her, long before the tragedy that had taken her parents.

It was what he'd fallen in love with.

Well, that and her face, which he reckoned was also top-notch.

"Dave, you keep manning the phones, will you?" Ben asked. "And keep an eye on the inbox for Palmer's report. The evidence bags should start turning up shortly, too."

"Aye, I'll get them logged when they arrive, and do all that other stuff. No bother at all," Dave said.

Ben gave him an enthusiastic thumbs-up and a smile that was positively gushing. "That's the attitude. Good for you, son!" he chirped, then he sprang from his chair like a man half his age and rubbed his hands together like he was raring to get started. "We all fit, then?"

The other detectives regarded him with something like suspicion. He looked around at them, his smile losing just a touch of its dazzle. "What?" he asked. "What are you staring at me like that for?"

"Eh... Are you OK, boss?" Tyler asked.

"What? I'm fine. Aye. Why do you ask?"

"It's just... You just seem a bit... I don't know. *Chipper*."

"Chipper?"

"Aye."

"What's wrong with being chipper?" Ben asked.

"Eh, nothing. No. Nothing wrong with it at all," Tyler said. "I just... I don't..." He wrinkled his nose and shrugged. "Why?"

Ben pulled on his coat. "Do we need a reason to be cheerful?"

"Not me!" Dave chimed in from the corner.

Ben pointed to him. "See? Dave's happy."

"Dave's always happy," Hamza said.

"Apart from that time he burned his arsehole," Tyler reminded him.

Hamza conceded this point with a nod. "Apart from the time he burned his arsehole."

"Don't bloody remind me," Dave said, wriggling in his chair.

"You just seem... sort of... oddly *pleased* about something, boss," Tyler said. "There's nothing wrong with that or anything, it's just..."

"A bit disconcerting," Hamza said.

"Aye. Aye, that," Tyler agreed. "It's just a bit that. Especially when it's like, you know..." He pointed upwards and circled his finger, indicating the room around them. "...a murder."

Ben looked from DS Khaled to DC Neish, then wheeled around to where Sinead was pulling on her jacket. He held a hand out, like he was inviting her to dance.

"Shall we, Detective Constable?" he asked.

Sinead smiled and accepted the hand. "Aye, we shall," she said. "And don't listen to this pair of maudlin buggers, sir. They're just jealous that we get to do all the fun stuff."

"You bet we do!" Ben said. He clenched his free hand into a fist and shook it excitedly in the air. "Room full of grieving loved ones, here we come!"

CHAPTER EIGHT

HALF AN HOUR LATER, Hamza and Tyler stood down at the feet end of the recently deceased Dev Rani, waiting for Shona to return from making a phone call in the adjoining room. She had been rattling off the Post Mortem results when the phone had rung, leaving them both staring down in horror at the exposed corpse on the slab.

They'd both seen dead bodies before. Plenty of them, in fact. What they had never seen was one with quite so many stab wounds in such a confined area.

It had been a reasonably short blade, Shona had said, though the attack had been so savage that there were deep gouges in the victim's pelvic bone. Those were the only clue as to how many times the knife had been thrust into Mr Rani's crotch—their sheer number turning his genitalia into a tattered mush of flopping flesh.

"Is that what yours looked like?" Hamza asked. He was whispering, like a naughty schoolboy afraid the teacher might hear. "After your operation."

Tyler shrugged. "Dunno. I didn't look," he replied, also whispering. "Still haven't, actually."

Hamza tore his eyes from the ravaged remains of Dev Rani's family jewels. "Eh?"

"Can't do it. Can't bring myself to. Too scared," Tyler said. "In case it's all..." He nodded down at the body. "Like that."

"What do you mean? It's been months. Of course you've looked!"

Tyler shook his head. "No. Not even in the shower. I wear one of them big dog collar things. What do you call them? Cone of shame." He flinched at a painful memory. "Nearly drowned in it once. Filled right up. Thought my time had come."

It perhaps said more about Tyler than it did about Hamza that the DS couldn't be *completely* sure if the other detective was kidding or not. He watched him for a few seconds, eyes narrowed, then shook his head.

"Bollocks!"

"Bollock, technically. Singular," Tyler said. He tutted. "And of course it didn't look like that! Who do you think did the operation, Edward fucking Scissorhands?"

They both stopped whispering and stood to a sort of attention when the door to the mortuary opened and Shona returned. She stopped just inside the door, studied them both with suspicion for a second, then shook her head and continued into the room.

"That was Jack calling me back," she said, throwing a thumb back over her shoulder. "Says he's feeling a bit better."

"That's good," Hamza said.

Shona didn't look convinced. "I mean, he called me 'Mum' twice, so I'm not sure he's fully fighting fit *quite* yet. But he's dressed, he's eaten, and he's asking about the case, so I suppose he's headed in the right direction."

"Tell him we were asking for him," Tyler said.

Shona glanced at the door she'd just come through. "I will," she said. "I mean, I'm off the phone now, obviously. But, you know, should he call back, I'll make sure to pass that on."

She stopped at the opposite end of the trolley, put her hands on her hips, and furrowed her brow.

"Now, sorry. Where were we again?"

Hamza pointed to Dev Rani's desecrated crotch and swirled his finger in a vague circle. "This sort of area."

"Oh, right. Yes. His old lad there," Shona said. "Like I was saying, someone really went overboard with the old frenzied knife attack motif. Really had it in for his poor genitals. I'm thinking we're looking at about..." She positioned her forefinger and thumb a short distance apart. "Four inches, and lightly serrated."

Tyler frowned and glanced down at the damage. "What? His... willy?"

Hamza snorted behind his surgical mask.

Shona patiently shook her head. "The knife."

"Why the fuck would his knob be serrated?" Hamza asked. "He's not a mutant."

"Alright, shut up! I just forgot what serrated meant for a minute," Tyler added. He quickly tried to save face by asking the sort of question he reckoned proper grown-up detectives would ask. "Was that the cause of death? The stabbed goolies?"

"Using the technical terminology there," Hamza remarked. "Well done."

"Yes. Well, mostly," Shona said. "It was blood loss, predominantly from his groin. There's an artery in the inner thigh—"

"The femoral artery," Tyler said, nodding.

Shona and Hamza both looked at him in surprise.

"What?" he asked. "I do actually know some stuff."

"You didn't know what serrated meant a minute ago," Hamza reminded him.

"Anyway, that got severed," Shona continued. "Blood, blood, blood. Gush, gush, gush. Dead." She raised a finger. "But, that's not all."

She beckoned them over to a screen on the wall, tapped at a

few keys, and brought up a selection of thumbnail photographs showing the victim from more angles than either detective had any real desire to see. She prodded one with a finger, and it expanded to fill the screen.

"That's his lower back," she said. "Three puncture wounds, angled upwards, and as you can see, all pretty close together."

"Same knife?" Hamza asked.

"Yep. Think so. Same size and type, anyway," Shona confirmed.

"Angled upwards?" Tyler said. He stepped behind Hamza and mimed stabbing him in the lower back, bringing his hand up from around hip height and plunging the imaginary knife into the DC's lumbar region. "So, like that?"

"Yes, but steeper," Shona said. She caught Hamza by the shoulders and tilted him forwards.

"Don't mind me," Hamza muttered, but he allowed himself to be manhandled so he was bent forward at roughly a thirty-degree angle.

"I think he was bending over a little bit," Shona explained. "Not a lot, just like that. Then—stab him again."

Tyler played out the attack again, plunging the make-believe blade repeatedly into Hamza's kidney area.

"This is degrading," the DS said.

"Just building a picture, Sarge," Tyler replied. "It's important we get these things figured out."

Shona took Hamza by the shoulders and straightened him again. "There. You're grand," she told him.

"Can I stab him in the bollocks now?" Tyler asked, but Hamza very quickly shot the idea down.

"I don't think that'll be necessary. We get the gist," he said, turning back to the body. "Anything else we should know?"

"Couple of bruises," Shona said. "Based on the pattern, and what I saw of the scene, I reckon he was surprised from behind, stabbed in the back, then stumbled forward and walloped his knee on the edge of the toilet while trying to turn to face his attacker. I'd say he landed on the toilet first, was stabbed a few times there, then slid down to the floor where the attack continued."

"Poor bastard," Tyler said.

"Yeah, not a great way to end your night," Shona agreed.

"And health-wise? Anything of interest worth noting?" Hamza asked.

Shona shook her head. "Nope. Scar on the palm of the right hand that's maybe a couple of months old, but otherwise he was right as rain. Also, no evidence that he was a smoker, a heavy drinker, or a habitual drug user, though toxicology will need to confirm some of that. But, in my professional medical opinion, I reckon Mr Rani would've gone on to live a long and healthy life." Her gaze flitted, just briefly, to the body on the slab. "Were he not repeatedly stabbed in the cock and bollocks."

Both detectives winced, then thanked Shona for her help, and were soon relieved to be out of the mortuary and into the pathologist's substantially less corpse-filled office area where they could both breathe freely, and safely unclench their nostrils.

"I'll get the preliminary report sent over in the next twenty minutes or so," she told them, as they swapped the protective masks and gloves for their jackets. "And obviously I'll update it all as I hear back from toxicology and the like. Don't hold your breath on that, though. It could be a couple of weeks. They're busy. And short-staffed." She shrugged. "And, you know, an absolute bunch of lazy bastards. But don't tell them I said that last bit, for God's sake, or I'll never hear the end of it."

Neither detective had the faintest idea how they'd even go about contacting the toxicologists should they even want to, so they had no problems promising not to grass her up to them.

"How's Sinead doing?" Shona asked. "She feeling OK now?"

Tyler paused with one jacket sleeve on. "Aye. She's fine, I think," he said. He flailed around until he found the other sleeve and slipped his arm in. "Why?"

"Nothing," Shona said, just a fraction of a second too quickly. "She just... She'd mentioned she was feeling a bit queasy earlier."

Tyler shook his head. "Must've passed."

"Right. Yeah. Must've done," Shona said. She gave him a double thumbs-up, turned her fingers into guns, then pretended to shoot him several times in the chest.

If asked, she would be unable to fully explain why.

"Eh, right. Cheers for that," Tyler said, then he zipped up his jacket while Hamza opened the door, and both detectives headed out into Raigmore Hospital's labyrinth of corridors.

CHAPTER NINE

NEITHER BEN nor Sinead said a word until they were back in Ben's car. He had parked it around the corner from Mr and Mrs Rani's home, well out of sight, so they could sit there psyching themselves up before going to the house, and again afterwards while they processed and debriefed.

"That was rough," Ben said, staring ahead out of the windscreen. It had been raining, and the glass had misted up. He made no attempt to clear it yet. "The mother. I thought we were going to have to call an ambulance."

Sinead nodded. She let out a long sigh, breathing out some of her pent-up tension. Not all of it, though. Not by any means.

"Aye. She's heartbroken. His dad, too, though he was putting on a brave face. You could tell, though."

Ben agreed. "Aye. You could see it written all over him."

Dev Rani's parents hadn't been permitted much time to grieve. The family liaison officer had turned up on their doorstep less than four hours ago to tell them that their son was dead. Worse—that their son had been murdered.

Neither detective was a stranger to loss, but only Ben knew that particularly unique pain. Only he'd had someone he loved deliberately taken from him. Of the two of them, only he'd experienced that firsthand.

An image of Alice, his late wife, took form in his mind, and a sense of dread and guilt knotted up his stomach. He shut his eyes for a moment, ran a hand down his face, then pulled himself together.

The Ranis had still been in shock when Ben and Sinead had come to the door. The liaison officer—a uniformed sergeant with a bit of an old-fashioned schoolteacher vibe about her—had made the introductions, then gone to make tea while the detectives asked questions about Dev's life.

It had been the usual stuff mostly—grudges, enemies, debt, that sort of thing.

They'd insisted that he hadn't. He was a good man, popular with everyone. The family were Hindus, and both parents had strong views on gambling, which they claimed Dev had shared. His younger sister, Chanda, had seemed less convinced of that fact, but she'd gone along with it when asked.

"The sister. What did you make of her?" Ben asked.

Sinead took a moment to consider before replying. "She seemed... I don't know. Upset, obviously, but..." She shrugged. "Scared, maybe? I put it down to being worried about her parents—about what was going to happen—but, I don't know."

"You think she was hiding something?" Ben asked.

"Maybe. I don't think she was being completely open with us," Sinead said. "But then, she's just found out her brother's been murdered, and we come marching in questioning them about everything. So you're not really going to be on top form, are you?"

"That's true," Ben admitted. "Still, something seemed off. I think we should talk to her again."

There was a knock on Sinead's side window. They both turned to see Chanda Rani standing out there, shoulders hunched, her face distorted by the rain on the glass.

"That's handy," Ben said, then he jerked his head towards the back seat and shouted, "Door's open. In you come," so loudly that Sinead was momentarily deafened in her right ear.

The SUV's back rear passenger door opened, and Chanda gave a deep, shoulder-shaking shudder as she climbed in out of the rain.

Where her parents' dress sense—and the decor of their home—had been heavily influenced by Indian style and culture, Dev's sister had been wearing a *Metallica* t-shirt and black leggings when the detectives had turned up at the door.

She was still wearing the same outfit now, but with the addition of a pair of trainers bright enough to be visible from space. Without the benefit of a jumper or jacket, her whole body was shivering uncontrollably with the cold.

"Everything alright?" Ben asked, turning on the car's engine and cranking up the heater.

He and Sinead both twisted around so they were looking back through the gap between their seats. Chanda sat shivering in the centre of the rear bench seat, her bob of dark hair dishevelled by the wind. She was twenty, but could've passed for sixteen or seventeen if she ever felt like repeating the last couple of years of high school.

"Was there something you wanted to tell us, Chanda?" Sinead asked, once the girl had been given a few moments to warm up.

"Nah. I mean, yeah," Chanda said. Her accent was mostly from the north of Scotland, with just the slightest suggestion of her parents' Bengali inflection and cadence. There was a suggestion of North London about it, too, but that felt contrived and tacked on, like it was a deliberate attempt to appear more cosmopolitan. "Sorry to come at you like this. Out of nowhere, like. There was some stuff I didn't want to say in there. Like, in front of my mum and dad, or whatever."

"It's no problem at all," Ben assured her. "We appreciate anything you can tell us."

"I just want you to find who did it, an' that," Chanda said. Her bottom lip shook, and she looked down at the hands she had clasped in her lap. "Who killed Dev."

"We're going to do everything we can," Ben said. "And if you have something to tell us, it could really help a lot."

The girl kept gazing at her hands, saying nothing. The detectives swapped looks, then turned their focus back to Chanda.

"We can go somewhere else, if you like?" Sinead suggested. "A café, maybe, or the station, even, if you think that would—"

"What? No!" Chanda's head snapped up. "No, I don't want to go to no police station. Here's good. I just..." She sighed, and seemed to sink lower into the seat. "They didn't know him. Dev. My mum and dad. They didn't know him. Not like I did."

"No, well you were his sister. That's a special thing," Ben coaxed. "I'm sure he shared a lot of stuff with you."

"Nah. I mean, yeah. Some stuff. Not a lot, though," Chanda said. "He was well older. Like, eleven years. I was just his annoying kid sister." Her head lowered, and she looked furtively between them. "But he did tell me something."

"What was it he told you, Chanda?" Sinead pressed. "What did he say?"

The girl in the back took a deep breath. "My mum and dad, they're not strict or nothing. I mean, not properly. Not like some parents. But they expect certain things, you know? Like, they're OK with me—think they've pretty much given up—but they wanted Dev to marry an Indian girl. Kept trying to set him up with the daughters of their friends back in Bengal, or whatever. Saying he should fly over and meet them. That sort of thing."

"Like an arranged marriage?" asked Ben.

"Nah. Not really. Not proper, like. Just... it's what they wanted. He said they always seemed sort of disappointed if he started going out with white girls." She looked quickly to Sinead. "I mean, not that they've got a problem with white people, or anything. They're not like that. It's just, I think they always imagined him settling down and giving them loads of brown babies, an' that."

"He was in a relationship," Sinead realised. "A relationship that they didn't know about."

Chanda fidgeted in the seat for a few moments, then confirmed this with a nod. "Yeah. I never met her, but he told me her name. I wouldn't remember, but I took the piss out of it at the time."

Something choked her, and she looked down while she composed herself again.

"It's Cassandra. Her name. The girl he's been seeing. It's Cassandra."

"Do you have a surname?" Ben asked.

Chanda winced. "Nah. Sorry. He didn't say. But I reckon... It's a pretty unusual name, right? Can't be too many of them knocking around Inverness."

Ben offered a comforting smile. "No. No, there can't be many."

"I think she lived across the river. Greig Street. Think that's what he said."

"Great. That's very helpful, Chanda. You've done the right thing in telling us," Ben assured her.

"Well, I just... I thought you should know."

"We really appreciate it. Was there anything else you wanted to tell us?" Sinead asked.

"No. No, that was it," Chanda said. She reached for the door handle, and opened it just a crack. "Only that... He was nice. I mean, he could be a dick sometimes, yeah, but he was always nice really. And not just to me. To everyone. I don't know why anyone would want to hurt him. I don't know who'd do that to him."

"Well, I never like to promise too much, Chanda, but I can promise you this much," Ben said. "We're not going to give up until we find out."

Her mouth became a thin line, then wobbled at the bottom again. The door opened. The rain and the wind swirled in.

And like that, she was gone.

CHAPTER TEN

"DELIVERY FOR YOU."

Dave Davidson shifted his gaze from his computer screen, and acknowledged the female constable pushing the trolley with a big, welcoming smile.

"Alright, Nids?" he said, with not a little gusto. He'd walked the beat with Constable Beatrice Niddrie for a couple of years before his accident. They were of similar ages, had both grown up in the Highlands, and had got on like a house on fire from day one, thanks in part to their shared sense of humour and mutual love of chip shop pickled onions. "Long time no see. What you up to?"

"This," the constable said, indicating the trolley. "You?"

"This," Dave replied, gesturing to his desk.

"Nice. You've landed on your feet," Bea said. "I mean, not literally, obviously..."

Dave murmured something so quietly it was almost inaudible. Bea pulled an exaggerated frown, turned her head to reveal one of her hearing aids, then shouted, "WHAT? I CAN'T HEAR YOU!"

The door squeaked behind the constable, and Detective

Superintendent Mitchell poked her head around it, her expression pitched somewhere between concerned and annoyed.

"Is everything alright?" she asked.

"Uh, yes, ma'am," Bea said, drawing herself up to her full height. "Sorry, I was just..."

She couldn't lay her hands on the excuse part of the apology, so instead, she just hung her head a little and tried to appear suitably contrite.

"Yes. Well," Mitchell said. "Perhaps not so loud." She glanced around the room. "No DI Forde?"

"He's out interviewing the victim's parents, ma'am," Dave said.

Judging by the way her expression tipped all the way over into 'annoyed,' this was not what the detective superintendent wanted to hear.

"We've spoken about this in the past. He's supposed to be running the room, not gallivanting about. Not with his heart."

"He seemed in good health," Dave said, leaping to Ben's defence. "And with DCI Logan off sick, I think it was an all hands on deck sort of situation."

Mitchell clicked her tongue against the back of her teeth. "Well, fortunately, that won't be a problem much longer," she announced somewhat cryptically. She fired a sharp nod at both constables, told them to, "Carry on," and vanished back out into the corridor.

Dave and Bea managed to stifle their laughter for all of five seconds before it became too much to contain.

"You absolutely shat yourself there," Dave declared.

"Me? No chance. I was fine! I was like..." Bea shrugged and pulled a disinterested face. "*Yeah, whatever.* I was ice cool just then."

"I must be thinking of someone else, then," Dave said.

"Finally!" Bea said. She sighed and rolled her eyes. "So sick of you *only* thinking about me all the time. I swear to God, you're obsessed."

Dave laughed, though, if he were honest, he hadn't thought about her at all in several months. Now, sitting here talking to her, he couldn't for the life of him think why.

"Anyway, I bring gifts!" Bea said. "Check it out."

She waved her hands around above the trolley like she was going to make it disappear. Then, she gave it a half-hearted nudge forwards with a flat-sounding, "Ta-daa!"

"Nice presentation," Dave told her.

"Thanks. It is my gift to you," she said, bowing. "A big pile of evidence bags. Don't say I'm not good to you."

"It's like Christmas," Dave said.

Bea's eyes narrowed. "Are you building up to a joke about me coming down your chimney?" she asked. "Because that's sexual harassment, I'll have you know."

Dave ejected a laugh and shook his head. "Wouldn't dream of it, Nids."

"Right. No," Bea said. "Shame," she added, then she winked, and gave the handle she was clutching a light tap. "You don't get to keep the trolley, by the way, so hurry the hell up and get it unloaded. I can't stand here gassing all day. Some of us have got *actual* work to do..."

———

The earlier downpour had eased off to a drizzle by the time Ben's car drew up on Greig Street. It had taken just a cursory search of the Electoral Roll to find the address of one Cassandra Leigh-Taylor, and Sinead had done a little more digging on the way over.

She was an artist, albeit not a particularly successful one. She mostly hawked her wares on social media, to a largely luke-warm reception.

"No wonder no bugger's buying it," Ben had remarked, when Sinead had showed him one of her works while stopped at the Ness Bridge traffic lights. "That's shite."

"I think some people like that sort of thing," Sinead said, diplomatically.

"Rubbish! I mean, what is that even meant to be?" Ben had asked, tilting his head and squinting at Sinead's screen. "It looks like an arse on a stick."

"It's called 'The Ebbing Ways,' if that helps any?"

Ben's look of confusion became one of thinly veiled contempt. Then, the blasting of a car horn had told them the lights had changed, and Ben had raced to beat them before they could change back.

Now, as he and Sinead fell into step on Greig Street, their focus turned to more important matters.

"She probably doesn't know," Ben said. "What's happened, I mean. She shouldn't do. Nothing's been released about the identity yet, and if the family don't know who she is, they can't have told her."

"Word travels fast around here, though," Sinead pointed out. "There was a heavy police presence outside the club all morning. News could well have got back."

"Aye. Maybe. Watch for her reaction, anyway," Ben said. "That could tell us a lot."

There was a sound from somewhere inside his jacket. It was the sort of sound, Sinead thought, that accompanied the waving of a magic wand in a *Disney* movie.

"Bloody thing," Ben muttered, patting himself down. He eventually found his mobile phone, and held it at arm's length as he tried to read the screen.

"New message tone, sir?" Sinead asked. "It's good. It sounds quite... magical."

"I don't know how the hell it changed," Ben said. "It used to *beep-beep*, now it *tra-trings* like it's showering me in bloody pixie dust." He groaned. "Ah, shite."

"Problems, sir?"

"Mitchell. She's onto me," he said. "She wants me back in the office now. Says there's something urgent."

"I'll be fine here," Sinead said. "I can walk back across the footbridge when I'm done."

Ben looked along the row of flats, his eyes lingering on the door they'd been headed towards. The place looked harmless enough on the outside, but you never knew what lurked inside.

Especially with these bloody artist types.

"I don't know. You shouldn't be going in alone," Ben said.

"It's a house call, sir. I made them all the time when I was in uniform," Sinead reminded him. "It's fine. It's not a problem."

Ben looked from her to the door, then down at his phone. He sighed. "Fine. OK. But phone me the second you're done. If I don't hear from you within the hour, there'll be five big Bobbies kicking the door in."

Sinead smiled. "Sounds like a plan."

"Right, then," Ben grunted. He fished in his pocket until he found his car keys. "Better go and see just what's so important back at base."

———

Logan stood in the middle of the kitchen, in the middle of what he had come to think of as a series of diagnostic tests. They were pretty simple, as diagnostic procedures went, and largely involved variations on the theme of standing upright.

He'd discovered that standing fully straight posed no problems. He could stand fully straight for hours, if he had to. He could stand fully straight *forever*.

A slight incline forward was doable, too. He had ten, maybe fifteen degrees of leaning angle available to him before everything in the room started getting itchy feet. Another few degrees beyond that, and the spinning started in earnest.

From a fully standing position, he was able to sit down without too much difficulty, provided he kept his back straight all the way to the chair. Getting up was harder, and brought a vignette of twinkling shadows to the edges of his vision, but it passed after a second or two, with minimal desire to vomit.

His temperature was down a few degrees, he thought—though he had nothing to base this on but instinct—and overall he felt like he was on the mend.

The main issue now was the headache. It bored into his skull like a carpenter's drill, pushing down from above and forcing his head down so it was all but resting on his shoulders.

It had been a couple of hours since he'd necked the painkillers Tyler had left for him. Their effect had been minimal, but he wasn't due another dose yet. What had they been? Ibuprofen? Paracetamol? Whichever they were, he could safely knock back a couple of the other type, which might help take the edge off the discomfort.

He carefully lowered himself back down onto the kitchen chair, barked out a warning to Taggart not to jump straight into his lap like he had the last three times, then picked up his phone from the table.

His eyes felt dry as he tried to focus on the screen. Tiny pinpricks of pain poked at his retinas and burned like sand when he blinked.

"Tyler. Tyler..." he murmured, trying to will the phone to call the DC. You could order it to do so by voice these days, he knew, but he'd never taken the time to look into it, and he was damn sure that now was not the best time to do so.

He poked the screen a little more forcefully than intended, stared at the bewildering array of app icons for what felt like an eternity, but was actually just a very long time, then tapped the little picture of a telephone.

"There you are, you wee bastard," he said, spotting Tyler's name in the list of recent contacts. He took careful aim with his swaying finger, then pressed on the 'N' of 'Neish.'

It took just a few moments for the call to connect. Tyler's chirpy, "Alright, boss?" did nothing to ease Logan's headache.

"Tyler. It's me," Logan said.

"Eh, aye. I know, boss," Tyler said. "It says your name on the screen."

"Right. Good. Where are you?"

"Hamza's car, boss. We're headed back from the PM."

Logan heard Hamza's voice shouting from the background. "Hiya, sir."

"That was Hamza," Tyler said. "He says hiya."

"Aye, I heard," Logan grunted.

Tyler's voice became muffled. "He says he heard," he remarked. Then, more clearly, "How you feeling now, boss?"

"Better," Logan said. Technically, this was true, though it was very much relative. "Got a headache I can't shift, though. Need to take more painkillers. What were those tablets you left out on the bedside table?"

Even though the skull-splitting pain was making it hard to concentrate, he could hear the confusion in Tyler's voice.

"Tablets?"

"The pills," Logan croaked, rubbing his forehead with his free hand.

"Pills?"

"For fu— Beside the water. The two white pills. What were they? Paracetamol? Ibuprofen? What?"

"*Tic Tacs.*"

Logan's forehead furrowed into a series of lines. "What?"

"They were... They were *Tic Tacs*, boss," Tyler said. "Spearmint. I thought, you know, with you having been sick and everything, you might want to freshen up."

"*Tic Tacs*? You left...? Who the hell leaves two bloody *Tic Tacs* out for someone?"

"I only had five left," Tyler explained.

"Jesus Christ," Logan groaned. "So, I've had no painkillers, then?"

"None that I gave you, boss, no," Tyler said. "Might be worth taking some, though."

"Oh, you think so?" Logan replied, then he hung up the phone without another word, groaned, and stood up a little too quickly. Darkness sparkled. He swayed ominously.

And then, the kitchen's real colours returned, like the room's contrast had been turned back up.

Muttering unspeakable things about DC Neish and *Tic Tacs*, he set off for the medicine cabinet in the bathroom.

CHAPTER ELEVEN

THE WOMAN who answered the door to the flat on Greig Street was every inch the artist. Or possibly every inch the painter and decorator.

She looked like she'd thrown herself into the path of a flicked paintbrush. Her face was flecked with dots of blues and reds. Her fringe was pushed back away from her face by a pair of thick-rimmed glasses that she wore on her head, but this had done little to stop it from receiving the same spattering.

The dungarees she wore had a base of pale yellow denim, but was sprinkled with so many spots of other colours that she resembled a cake topped with *hundreds-and-thousands*.

Her hands were slicked with paint, and opening the door had involved the use of wrists and elbows.

"Yes?" she asked, taking Sinead in with a single up and down eye movement. "Can I help you? If you're selling something, it's a bad time."

"Miss Taylor?" Sinead asked.

"Miss *Leigh*-Taylor," Cassandra corrected. Her face and her tone softened. "Sorry, are you a customer? Are you supposed to be picking something up? Because I wasn't expecting anyone."

"Not a customer, I'm afraid, no," Sinead said. She produced her warrant card and held it out. "I'm Detective Constable Sinead Neish. I'm with the police."

Cassandra wiggled her forehead until her glasses fell into place. Like the rest of her, the lenses were dotted with paint.

"It says your name's Sinead Bell on this."

"Oh. Yeah. Sorry. I got married," Sinead said. "My husband works in the same department. It's less confusing if..." She decided that no further explanation was necessary, and looked past the artist into her flat. "Do you mind if I come in and have a word?"

"It's about Dev, isn't it?" Cassandra asked. It almost sounded like an accusation. "That's why you're here."

"Uh, yes. Yes, that's right," Sinead said.

"I knew it. I knew this would happen. It was only a matter of time."

"Sorry?" Sinead asked, caught off guard by her reaction.

Cassandra exhaled sharply, raised her eyes to the ceiling, then shook her head and stepped aside.

"Fine. Well, in that case, you'd better come in so we can talk properly," she said. "I have got a *lot* to tell you."

———

Sinead sat on a two-seater couch so small she reckoned it barely qualified as a one-and-a-half seater. It was down the window-end of an open-plan space that was one part living room, one part dining area, and three parts art studio.

Calling it an 'open plan space' was being quite generous. It was a room. And not a particularly large one, at that.

Cassandra's latest artwork was propped up on an easel just five or six feet away from where Sinead was sitting. It was a big, imposing piece, full of dark, muted colours that made Sinead think of depression. If that was what the artist had been aiming for, she was bang on, because just being stuck in a room with the bloody thing was making Sinead suicidal.

Of course, there was also the possibility that it wasn't an artwork at all, and Cassandra had just been wiping paint off her brushes. At this point, Sinead had no real way of knowing for sure.

The walls were mostly adorned by similarly bleak works, all in the same style. There were a couple of framed posters, too, both advertising different productions by a local amateur dramatics group. Both had taken place at Eden Court, by the looks of it. Neither poster was particularly professional looking, or pleasing to the eye, so presumably, Cassandra had some involvement in them for her to have stuck them up on her wall.

From the room next door—the kitchen, Sinead thought—there came a rattling, the sound of a tap gushing for a second or so, then footsteps announced Cassandra's return through the uncarpeted hallway.

She bumped the door open with her backside, then offered Sinead a mug with a sticky blue handprint wrapped almost all the way around it.

"Hold it by the handle or you'll get paint on you," Cassandra instructed. "Sorry, it gets everywhere."

"No bother. Thanks," she said, accepting the cup and taking a sip.

Cassandra took a drink from her own equally paint-slicked mug. Then, to Sinead's dismay, she indicated the canvas on the easel.

"What do you think?"

Sinead looked at the painting and reacted with a look of surprise, like she'd somehow failed to notice it until now. "Oh! It's... big, isn't it?" she said.

"Compared to what?" Cassandra asked.

"Compared to..." She grasped for an appropriate response. "...a smaller painting."

Cassandra regarded the canvas with a look that implied this comparison had not previously occurred to her. "And?"

"And what?"

"What about the content? What about the painting? What do you think?"

"It's, eh, it's nice," she lied. She was grateful that Logan wasn't here, so she didn't have to hide her face when he gave his answer to the question.

Or, God forbid, Bob Hoon.

Cassandra clearly wasn't impressed by her latest masterpiece being written off as 'nice,' but Sinead took the wheel and steered the conversation onto more familiar ground.

"So. Dev Rani," she said, reaching into her jacket pocket for her notebook. "You said you had information to share?"

Cassandra made a snorting sound, like a bull getting ready to charge. "Oh, you can say that again. Have you met her?"

Sinead hesitated. "Met who?"

"His girlfriend!" Cassandra replied, and she screwed up her face like the milk in her tea had turned sour.

"I thought... I thought you were his girlfriend?"

"Was. Yes, *was*. Past tense," the artist spat. "You think I'm hanging on in there, after I found out about her? After I found out what he is?"

"Eh, I think we might be talking at cross purposes here—"

"What did he tell you? How much did he say?" Cassandra demanded. "Did he tell you she's just turned seventeen? Hm? Did he tell you that? But it's been going on for months. Maybe longer. I don't know. Maybe she was fifteen when it started. Fourteen. *Twelve*! Nothing would surprise me."

Sinead looked around for somewhere to sit her cup, and decided the floor was the best bet. Cassandra had no floor coverings in any part of the flat that Sinead had seen so far, instead opting for bare, natural floorboards—skelfs, rusty nails, and all.

"No, eh, he hasn't told us anything, Cassandra."

"Well, make him. Squeeze it out of the dirty sick bastard!"

"No, you don't understand," Sinead continued. "Mr Rani... Dev... I'm afraid he's dead."

Despite the weight of it, the word hung there in the air between them. Cassandra waved a hand sharply, like she was swatting it away.

"What? I don't... How d'you mean?" she asked.

Sinead leaned forwards on the couch, her hands clasped. A sympathetic gesture.

"He was attacked," she said, omitting the details. Maybe, if Sinead was lucky, Cassandra would fill some of them in, incriminating herself in the process.

"What? Where? When?"

So much for that plan. Sinead decided to go ahead and take the bull by the horns.

"Sorry to ask this, Cassandra, but do you mind telling me where you were last night?"

"Last...?" The artist looked momentarily confused, then her eyes widened in shock and horror. "Wait. Jesus! You think I killed him?"

Sinead shook her head. "No. No, of course not. But in an investigation like this, we need to account for everyone's whereabouts. It helps us build up a picture of the victim's final hours. It would be really useful to know if you'd interacted with Dev in the last day or so."

"No. No, I haven't seen him for days," Cassandra replied. "And I definitely didn't kill him!"

"No phone calls? Texts?"

The artist hesitated for a moment before replying. She was considering her answer, but Sinead couldn't tell if she was simply trying to remember the facts, or coming up with a way to obfuscate them.

"No," she said, which didn't really seem worth the wait.

"No? Nothing at all?" Sinead pressed.

Cassandra pulled a rickety dining chair out from under a table, leaving a blue handprint on the wood. She sat down heavily, like her legs had been struggling to hold her up, then shrugged.

"I called him, yeah. Last night."

"What time?"

"About, I don't know. Nine? Half past, maybe. He didn't answer. I didn't really expect him to. I didn't leave a message."

"Why were you calling?"

"Just..." Cassandra looked down at the tea in her mug, and gave it a swirl. "I don't really know. I'd had a few drinks."

"Out? Or here?"

"Here."

Sinead made a note. "On your own?"

Cassandra nodded, then panic agitated through her. "But my neighbour saw me. Colin. Upstairs. I spoke to him. He'll be able to tell you."

"I believe you, Cassandra," Sinead said, but she made a note, then asked, "Colin...?"

"Um... Um..." The artist clicked her paint-covered fingers, searching for the name. "I can't remember. I just know him as Colin. I mean, I know it—his surname, I do know it—it's just..."

"I understand," Sinead said. "This is a very stressful time for you. You're doing great."

She flipped to a clean page on her pad, placed the point of her pen against the paper, then paid very close attention to the woman sitting across from her.

"Now, a wee minute ago you called Dev a 'dirty sick bastard.'" She watched the lines of Cassandra's face. The shape of her shoulders. The movement of her hands. "Would you mind telling me why?"

CHAPTER TWELVE

IT WAS JUST after four when Sinead returned to the station on Burnett Road, and found almost the full team back at their desks in the Incident Room, with the exception of DCI Logan.

The rain had picked up when she was halfway back, but she didn't even take time to peel off her jacket before breaking out the big news.

"Dev Rani was at it with a seventeen-year-old," she announced, dripping in the doorway.

Everyone sat up a little straighter, rapidly trying to process this juicy new nugget of information.

"At it?" asked Ben. "Like... *at it* at it you mean?"

Sinead peeled off her wet jacket and hung it on the rack by the door. "His girlfriend certainly reckons so. Or, ex-girlfriend. She found their texts on his phone last week. Pretty full-on, she said."

"Why was she checking his phone?" Tyler asked.

Sinead gave her hair a shake to flick off some of the moisture, then pushed it back off her face with her hand. "She got suspicious. Said he was being secretive. She knew his PIN for the phone, so she looked through it while he was sleeping one night."

"That's a bit invasive," Tyler said.

Sinead had been making her way to the Big Board, but stopped by her husband's desk. "That's what you're taking out of this?"

"Well, no, but..." Tyler shrunk down into his seat. "I'm just saying. It's a bit sneaky."

"So's texting high school kids to ask for naked pictures," Sinead said. "In fact, I'd say that's a bit more than sneaky."

Tyler swallowed and nodded his agreement. "Aye, that's worse, right enough."

"Hold on, hold on!" Dave chimed in from the corner. He fished around in a box on the floor beside him, then produced a plastic evidence bag and held it up for the others to see. "One mobile telephone. *Samsung*. Property of the deceased. Any use?"

"Nice," Hamza said, springing up and taking the offered package. He turned it over in his hands, studying it. "Might struggle to get into it, though."

"Yeah, well, like I said..." Sinead fished her slightly damp notebook from her bag and raised it aloft like it contained some holy scripture. "His ex-girlfriend had the PIN."

"Great work, Sinead!" Ben told her, as the DC tore the page with the PIN from her notebook and passed it to a visibly eager Hamza.

DS Khaled got excited by tech stuff. If there was a laptop to be investigated, or a server to be checked, he was all over it. A mobile phone could be a treasure trove of evidence, and he'd just been given the key to the chest.

"What else did you get from her?" Ben pressed. "How did she seem?"

"She's a bit weird," Sinead said. "I think she'd probably

think of herself as a bit sort of ethereal or something, but she isn't. She seemed genuinely shocked when I told her that Dev was dead. But then, I think she's part of the *Highland Players* group."

"What are they?" Tyler asked. "Swingers or something?"

Sinead rolled her eyes. "No, dear. They're actors. It's an am-dram group."

"Oh right, aye. Gotcha."

Ben turned his chair to face the Big Board, where Sinead had started writing something on a *Post-it Note*. "You think it might've been a performance? Her being surprised?"

"I don't know," the detective constable admitted. "If it was, she's a better actor than she is an artist."

"Aye, but that's no' exactly saying much. *I'm* a better actor than she is an artist," Ben said. He looked back over his shoulder at the others, his face contorted in distaste. "You should see the arse on a stick she did. Bloody awful."

Hamza, who had sat down to go through Dev Rani's phone, suddenly stood up again. "Whoa. Whoa. Got it. She's right. About the seventeen-year-old. I mean, I haven't seen it say that she's seventeen yet, but... his ex is right." He scrolled quickly through dozens of messages, then gave a non-committal sort of tilt of his head. "I think."

"What do you mean? What does it say?" Sinead asked. She slapped a note up on the board that simply read, 'Grooming?'

Hamza took his seat again, his eyes still glued to the screen. "He's... I don't think he's..."

"Spit it out, mate," Tyler said. "We're on the edge of our seats here."

Hamza blinked. "Hm? Sorry. Aye." He scrolled a little further. "He's not egging her on, he's knocking her back. I mean, there are hundreds of messages, but they're mostly all from her. Some of it's pretty racy stuff."

"What, like pictures?" Ben asked.

"Well, no. I mean, maybe, I don't know. It looks like he's deleted a few picture messages. The app says there was a photo received, but that it's been deleted. It's more what she's saying," Hamza said. He swiped at the screen, caught a flash of an image, then scrolled back. "Here's one of her. Fully clothed. School uniform, I think."

"Course. Nonces love that stuff," Tyler said.

"I don't think he's a nonce, though," Hamza replied.

"OK, well technically not if she's seventeen, but still..."

"No. I mean, you've got to scroll for ages to find any of his replies, and they're mostly telling her to stop. But..." He pinch-zoomed in on the left breast of a blonde-haired girl who was flashing a two-fingered peace sign to the camera.

"Alright, steady, mate," Tyler said, looking over his shoulder. "She's only seventeen."

"Shut up," Hamza said, zooming in further until a logo on the girl's jumper filled the screen. "What school's that from?"

"Looks like a load of flames," Tyler pointed out.

"I've seen it before," Hamza muttered. "I'm sure of it."

"Millburn Academy."

The rasp of the voice from the doorway caught them all by surprise. They turned to see Logan come shambling into the room, a veneer of sweat bringing a polished shine to his forehead.

He had decided against the traditional shirt and big coat combo, and was instead kitted out in a pair of grey jogging bottoms and a t-shirt that had been stretched out of shape, most likely over a number of years.

"Jack? What are you doing here?" Ben demanded, rising from his chair. "You're meant to be at home."

"Aye, well, I'm not," Logan replied. "I'm fine. Just needed a bit of rest." He shot Tyler a disparaging look. "And a couple of bloody *Tic Tacs*."

He made his way to his desk, felt around behind him for his chair, then stiffly lowered himself onto it.

"Oh aye, you look in tip-top shape, right enough," Ben remarked.

"School uniform. Flames on the logo. It's Millburn Academy," Logan said, ignoring the dig.

"How do you know that, boss?" Tyler asked.

"It's Olivia Maximuke's school," said Logan. "We were there last year."

"Shite. Aye, that's it," Hamza said. "Millburn Academy."

"See? That's why you need me here," Logan told them. He scowled at the room in general, and flapped the neck of his t-shirt back and forth. "It's roasting in here. Can we turn the heating down?"

"Heating's not on, sir," Sinead said. "Are, eh, are you sure you shouldn't be in bed?"

"I'm quite sure," Logan insisted.

"Does Shona know you're here?" the DC continued.

Logan's brow creased, like he was trying to work out the answer to some complex mathematical puzzle. "No," he eventually concluded. "No. I should probably let her know." He took out his phone, placed it on the table with an air of resignation and defeat, then puffed out his cheeks. "You let her know, will you, Sinead?" He gestured to the phone. "I can't be dealing with that bloody thing."

"Eh, aye. Aye, no problem, sir," Sinead said, taking out her own phone and tapping at the on-screen keyboard.

Meanwhile, Logan turned to Hamza, glazed over for a few seconds while the world caught up, then focused again. "Why were you asking about Millburn Academy?"

Hamza held up the phone for Logan to see. The DCI spared it a momentary glance, but not a second longer than that.

"The victim, Dev Rani, it looks like he was having some sort of relationship with a girl at the school," the detective sergeant informed him.

Logan's lips moved, like he was repeating the sentence to himself in an attempt to better understand it. "Jesus Christ," he finally remarked. "What age was he?"

"Thirty-five, boss," said Tyler, after a quick check of the board.

"And he was shagging a schoolgirl?"

Hamza shook his head, but the movement was hesitant. Uncertain. "I don't... I'm still going through the messages, but so far I'd say no. She's the one driving all the contact." He scrolled through a few more texts, then stopped. "I mean, here's one from him. It comes after, like, a dozen from her over a few days, saying she wants to be with him. Kisses. Stuff like that. His just says, 'You need to stop this. Please. You need to find someone your own age. I'm not interested. Sorry.'"

"Sounds pretty clear cut," Ben said. "That doesn't read like he's leading her on."

"But how did it even start?" Sinead asked. "How did she get his number? Why is she texting him this stuff in the first place?"

Hamza scrolled back to the start of the messages. It took a while.

"Bugger," he muttered. "Must've got a new phone or something at some point. It sort of starts in mid-conversation. Nothing to say how they met."

"You got a name, though?" Logan asked.

"First name, just," Hamza told him. "Eva. And her number, obviously. Might be able to get more details from that."

"Or we could phone her," Ben suggested.

Logan shook his head, and immediately regretted it when it felt like his brain started sloshing around in his skull.

"No. Let's not alert her," he instructed. "Get onto the school. Get her details."

"It'll be shut, boss," Tyler said, checking the clock.

Logan groaned. He didn't have the energy to explain or give instructions, so he just sort of glowered at Tyler and hoped that he could somehow convey it all through telepathy.

DC Neish glanced around at the others as Logan continued to stare at him, shuffled uncomfortably in his chair, then rolled in closer to his PC.

"But, I could probably track down the headteacher and ask them," he suggested.

Logan's eyelids scraped across his eyes as he blinked in surprise. Bloody hell. It had worked.

"Aye. Do that." He jabbed at his phone like a disinterested cat with a dead mouse. "Someone get onto Olivia Maximuke, too. See if she knows the girl."

"They're in different years, aren't they?" Sinead asked.

"Aye, but she's a right nosy wee cow," Logan said. "She might be able to tell us something. If not, get her to ask around. Teenagers talk to each other. More than they'll talk to any of us lot, anyway."

"Are you sure we can trust her, boss?" Tyler asked. "After, you know, everything?"

"I'm asking her about a girl from her school, no' bringing her on board as a bloody consultant," Logan barked. "We're no' giving her her own login for HOLMES."

Tyler held his hands up in surrender. "Aye, fair enough. You're the boss, boss."

Logan grunted. "Aye. Well." He ran a hand down his face and sighed. "It was a good point you made. I shouldn't have taken your face off. When we talk to her, let's be sure and no' tell her anything we're not happy going public."

"Right you are, sir," said Sinead, picking up his mobile. She swiped the screen, then showed the camera Logan's face. It took a little longer than usual for the software to recognise him. But then, he wasn't exactly looking his best.

"OK, that's me, I'm in. I'll get onto her now," Sinead said, turning away with the phone.

"Good. Right. Tyler, find the headteacher. Hamza..." Logan gestured vaguely at the DS. "...keep doing whatever it is you're doing. And someone—anyone—do me a favour and bring me a big glass of water and two of every kind of painkiller you can find."

CHAPTER THIRTEEN

IT DIDN'T TAKE LONG to get the full name and address of Eva MacLean. She lived on Denny Street, just around the corner from the prison, in a mid-terraced house that stood out from those around it like a cancerous cell.

Olivia Maximuke had been a dead end. She'd said she was dimly aware of Eva's existence, but knew nothing about her beyond that. Sinead felt uncomfortable asking the girl to do some digging, but fortunately, Olivia had volunteered and had promised to report back if she heard anything.

She was, Sinead supposed, a decent enough kid. If you ignored the gangster father, history of drug dealing, and attempted murder of her mother's ex-lover.

"This place is a shocker," Tyler remarked, peering out at the house through the windscreen of his car. There was a decent number of parking spaces available on the street, but he'd pulled up a few doors down from the house so they could get the lay of the land without arousing suspicion.

The street seemed nice enough. The front gardens were small, but most of them were neatly kept, with the exception of the one they were most interested in. That hadn't just been left to go to ruin, but had become a sort of dumping ground for bits of old car engines, old wooden pallets, and a washing machine that lay on one side like it was trying to catch some shuteye.

The clock had barely struck five, and there were a good couple of hours of grey daylight left, but almost all the curtains had been closed, the only exception being one of the two upstairs windows. That window, unlike the others, was also slightly ajar.

"These would've been expensive houses, too, I reckon," Tyler said. "They've got them fancy double doors. And the rest of them look nice."

"They do, aye," Sinead confirmed.

"I bet they've got a dog," Tyler said. "I bet they've got a big dog. Big angry bastard."

Sinead conceded that this was a possibility, but promised she'd protect him.

"Aye, you'd better," Tyler told her, then they opened the doors, got out of the car, and made their way towards the house.

The barking started when they were halfway up the path. "I told you. What did I say?" Tyler groaned. "I told you there'd be a dog."

Sinead rang the doorbell. The barking intensified, and then a roared command drowned the animal out.

"Fucking shut up!"

The dog stopped barking at once. A door inside the house slammed, then footsteps thundered along the hall until Tyler was convinced he could feel the ground shaking.

The door was opened, and there stood something from a nightmare. Quite a specific nightmare about large semi-naked overweight men with bad tattoos and angry faces. Not a nightmare Tyler had been troubled with in the past, but one he felt was now certain to crop up in the future.

"You Jehovahs?" the brute in the doorway demanded.

He really was a very large man, Tyler thought. The smell of

old sweat seemed to radiate from him, mixed with undertones of tobacco and cheap lager.

"You can fuck off with that shite," he informed them, then he opened the door wider so he could give it a particularly forceful slam.

It was Sinead who got over the shock of him first. She produced her police ID before he could complete his manoeuvre.

"Mr MacLean?"

"Who's asking?"

"I'm Detective Constable Bell, and this is my colleague, Detective Constable Neish."

"Ah, fuck. What do *you* want?" barked Mr MacLean, who'd clearly have far preferred his initial assumption about them to have been the correct one. "Who's been complaining now? Is it that fat bitch across the road?"

Tyler glanced back over his shoulder, like he might catch a glimpse of the woman in question. Presumably, she'd have to be some size before this guy could make derogatory comments about her weight. She could be a hippo in a dress, and it'd still be a case of the pot calling the kettle black.

"No. Nothing like that, Mr MacLean," Sinead said. "We're actually hoping to have a word with Eva." She tried to look past him into the corridor, but he was blocking all of it. "Is she home?"

"Eva? What the fuck do you want to talk to her for? She's done nothing."

"No, we know. We'd just like to talk to her about... a friend of hers."

"What friend?"

"It'd be better if we spoke to her directly," Sinead told him. "Is she in?"

The man in the doorway scratched his bare belly and sniffed. "No. No, she's not. I don't know where she is," he said.

"Do you know when she'll be back?" asked Tyler.

Mr MacLean shifted his gaze to him. "Fuck me, it speaks. I thought you were mute. No. I don't know when she'll be back, alright? She's a teenager. She doesn't tell me nothing."

"Right. I see," said Sinead. She tilted her head so one ear was pointing upwards. "It's funny, though. I can hear music coming from that bedroom. Dua Lipa, I think."

"So? She left music on. Like I say, she's a teenager, she's a law unto her fucking self."

Sinead stepped back suddenly and looked straight up at the window. Through the glass, she made eye contact with a blonde-haired teenage girl, who was too slow at trying to duck out of sight.

"Yeah. Turns out she's in after all, Mr MacLean," Sinead told him. She smiled. "Must've snuck up the stairs without you noticing. Teenagers, eh?"

The half-dressed behemoth glowered down at her, jaw and fists clenched. "You got a warrant?" he asked. "If you don't have a warrant, you can't just—"

"It's fine, Dad."

Footsteps plodded down the staircase somewhere further along the hall. They triggered more barking from the dog, and another male voice—not dissimilar to that of the giant in the doorway—bellowed at it to, "Shut your hole!"

Muttering, Mr MacLean shifted aside and made room for his daughter. She was, in many ways, his physical opposite. Hair colour, height, tattoos, beard length and male pattern baldness—none of them matched. She was painfully skinny, too, as if her dad had been nicking the food off her plate, or somehow absorbing all her calories by osmosis.

She looked older than seventeen. The hair and make-up helped, of course, but it was her eyes that really sold it. They were eyes that had seen a lot more than her years should suggest. She could've easily passed for twenty. Maybe twenty-five.

"What do you want?" she asked, all bravado and false confidence.

Sinead didn't look at Eva's father, but the next words out of her mouth were largely designed for his benefit. "Maybe we could speak privately."

"Anything you lot have got to say, you can just go ahead and fucking say it," Mr MacLean told them. Eva appeared neither to agree nor disagree with this sentiment. She just stood there, arms folded, waiting.

Sinead shrugged. "OK. We're here to talk to you about Dev Rani."

Eva's cocky expression faltered. Her dad's vast, tundra-like forehead furrowed.

"Who?" he asked. Then, when neither of the detectives answered, he turned to his daughter. "Who they talking about?"

Eva ignored him. "Did he send you?"

"No, Eva. No, he didn't send us," Sinead told her. Just like with Cassandra, she watched for the reaction. Noted it. "I'm afraid that's not why we're here."

Eva searched Sinead's face, eyes darting faster and faster as her brain raced ahead, figuring out the rest of the conversation, anticipating where it would lead and concluding that she didn't like where the finish line lay.

"OK. I'll talk to you," she said. She fixated on Sinead, ignoring her Goliath-like father beside her. "But not here."

"What? Why not? What the fuck's this all about?" Mr MacLean demanded. He caught Eva by the upper arm, his hand so large it practically wrapped around the limb twice.

"Dad, don't!" Eva protested, struggling to pull herself free. "Let me go."

"I'll let you go when I'm good and fucking ready. What's this about? What have you been up to?"

"You heard her," Tyler said. He drew himself up to his full height. Given the size of the other man, and the advantage afforded to him by the step, this put Tyler at barely above nipple height. He pressed on, undaunted.

Well, a bit daunted, but doing his best not to show it.

"Let her go, Mr MacLean," he ordered. "Now."

"Who the fuck do you think you are, you little shit?"

"I'm a police officer," Tyler said. "And unless you want to wind up on an obstruction charge, I suggest you respect your daughter's wishes and let her come with us. Is that understood?"

For a moment, it looked like the brute might reach over and rip Tyler's head straight off his shoulders, but then he grimaced, let go of his daughter's arm, and stepped back from the door.

"Good call," Tyler said.

"She won't be long," Sinead said, stepping aside to let Eva pass.

"Yeah, well, she'd better not be." Mr MacLean bellowed after his daughter as Sinead and Tyler led her up the path away from the house. "You're going to have a lot of fucking explaining to do, lady. A *lot* of fucking explaining."

The door closed with a slam. The dog started barking again, and was silenced by angry shouts from two near-identical voices.

Sinead and Tyler said nothing until they had deposited Eva in the back of the car, and shut her in.

"That was impressive," Sinead said. "Standing up to him like that."

Tyler grinned. "It was, wasn't it? I really put him in his place and showed him who was boss, didn't I?"

"You did," Sinead said.

"I know! I really did!" Tyler agreed. "And I don't even think he noticed I was totally shiteing myself!"

Sinead smiled at him across the roof of the vehicle. "What a hero," she said, then they opened their doors and slid into the car's front seats, watched all the while from the window of the house they'd just left.

———

Tony MacLean watched the car with his daughter inside pulling away from the kerb and driving off down the street.

"Who was that, Dad?" a voice, not unlike his own, asked from behind him. It triggered another fit of barking from the dog that made Tony grind his teeth together and ball his pudgy fingers into fists.

"Never you fucking mind," he grunted, watching the tail lights of the car disappearing around the corner. "And shut that fucking dog up before I shut it up for good."

CHAPTER FOURTEEN

THINGS WERE LOOKING UP. Logan's headache had stopped drilling through his skull, and now seemed content to just lurk behind his eyes. It voiced its objections when he tried looking in any direction that wasn't straight ahead, but this was still a notable improvement.

The dizziness was on the wane, too. He could successfully move from a seated to a standing position without his inner ear performing a triple somersault.

He was able to think more clearly than he'd been doing all day. As a result, the main thought that was currently occupying him was, "Why the fuck am I not still in bed?"

Coming into work had felt important a couple of hours before. It had felt necessary. There was no way they'd cope without him, he'd told himself. He owed it to them all to drag himself into the office.

But the fact of the matter was, they seemed to have been doing just fine without him.

Not that he'd ever admit such a thing out loud, of course.

"We've got statements through from the door-to-door of the businesses and flats around the nightclub," Hamza

CITY OF SCARS   87

announced, clicking a message in the inbox. He quickly scrolled through and skimmed what was written there. "Doesn't look like anyone saw or heard anything useful. Uniform's collecting CCTV footage, though. Might show us something."

Ben, who had been out of sight behind his computer, got to his feet. "Were you no' going to go check out the club's cameras?" he asked DS Khaled. "See if you can figure out why there's no recent footage."

Hamza and Logan both sat in silence, staring at the older man with matching expressions of surprise. Ben looked back at them, frowning.

"What?" he asked.

"Am I still seeing things, or is that a bow tie you've got on?" Logan asked.

Ben adjusted the tie. It was a dark purple, the colour of a recent bruise. "It's a dickie bow, aye," he said. "What's wrong with it?"

"You look like a magician," Logan told him.

"What's the occasion, sir?" Hamza asked.

Ben shrugged. "Can a man no' put on a bow tie without there being some sort of special occasion?"

The other two men looked at each other. They both shook their heads and replied in unison. "Naw."

Ben sighed, but it was good-natured. A smile played across his face, like he'd secretly been hoping they would ask. "I'm going to the theatre."

There was silence for a moment, while this was contemplated and processed by the others.

"The theatre?" Logan asked. "Like... with a stage?"

"Well, I've no' got dressed up to go to a bloody operating theatre," Ben replied. "Aye, with a stage. Eden Court. I'm off to see a show."

"Nice one, sir. What show?" Hamza asked.

"You know we're dealing with a murder case, aye?" Logan interjected. "You know a man's dead?"

"I do. And he'll still be dead tomorrow. Besides, I've done too many hours already this month. I'm owed a night off, I've been at it since after seven this morning, and you've got it all in hand," Ben told him.

"Aye, but we always work stupid hours," Logan said. "It's no' a nine-to-five job."

Ben laughed. "That's true. And, funnily enough, that's just what I'm off to see."

"What is?" Logan asked.

"*9 to 5*," Ben said. "The Dolly Parton thing."

"Oh, nice one!" Hamza said. "I've heard that's really good."

Logan's face contorted like his pain had returned with a vengeance. "What is it? A musical?"

"Aye," Ben confirmed.

"Like... with singing?"

"Aye. And dancing. I think."

"Why are you going to a musical?" Logan asked. "Did you lose a bet?"

Ben adjusted his tie. "If you must know, I'm going on a date," he announced.

"So that's why you've been looking so pleased with yourself all day!" Hamza realised. "Nice one, sir."

"And you're trying to put her off by taking her to see that shite, are you?" Logan said. "Smart move."

"It's not shite. It's got really good reviews," Hamza said. "Amira quite fancies it, actually."

"Who's this date with?" Logan demanded.

Ben tapped the side of his nose. "Never you bloody mind," he said, then he checked his watch, raised a finger while he counted down the final few seconds until half five, then declared himself done for the day.

"Aye. On you go. Part-timer," Logan called after him.

"Don't wait up, gentlemen," Ben told them. Then, with a wink and a tip of an imaginary hat, he backed out through the swing doors, and the sound of his whistling rang out through the corridors.

"Did that just happen?" Logan asked, squinting at Hamza like he wasn't sure even the detective sergeant was real. "He did just leave to go on a date, aye?"

Hamza chuckled. "Aye. He did. Good for him, I say."

"He can't half pick his bloody times, can he?" Logan remarked. He turned his whole upper body so he could look at the door while keeping his nausea to a minimum. "The big question now is, who the hell's he going on a date with?"

———

Tyler had just led the way into the reception area of Burnett Road station when he flinched in fright at the sight of the woman standing before him. He stopped so suddenly that Sinead and Eva MacLean had to swerve to avoid walking right up the back of him.

"Shite. You've not transferred up here, have you?" he asked, cautiously eyeing the older woman. She wore a look of utter contempt on her face. But then, she always did. It was her default expression.

Moira Corson, the dour, spite-filled receptionist from the polis station down in Fort William, gave Tyler a look up and down like she was only now clapping eyes on him for the first time.

"And you are?" she asked.

"What? What do you mean?" Tyler asked. "You know who I am."

"No, I don't," Moira insisted.

"Aye, you do! You've spoken to me loads of times."

Moira's nostrils flared. She shook her head. "You obviously didn't make much of an impression," she told him.

"DC Neish. I've been down in Fort William for a few cases." He swung his thumb between himself and his wife. "We both have. You make us fill in all the paperwork."

"Every time," Sinead added.

"Without fail. And we always moan about it," Tyler concluded.

Moira regarded them both down the length of her nose. "Yes," she said, after some consideration. "Yes, you look like the type who'd complain, right enough. You've got the look of a whinger about you."

"What? I'm not a whinger! You're just a pain in the—"

Before he could finish the sentence, and the conversation could tip over into an argument, a voice called out from over by the lifts.

"Moira! There you are!"

Sinead and Tyler both watched as Ben practically skipped across the foyer. He didn't notice them until he was much closer, and his sprightly approach suddenly became slower and more sombre.

"Eh, hello," he said, offering Moira his hand. "Good to see you."

Moira peered down at the offered hand like it was caked in shite, then met his eye. "Is that you ready? I've been waiting here for almost fifteen minutes."

"Eh, hello, sir," Sinead said, and Tyler gave the DI a little wave.

"Alright, boss?"

Ben turned to them, feigning surprise. "Oh! Detective Constables! I didn't see you there," he said, lying through his teeth. He smiled, and there was a sort of hopeless desperation about it that made Sinead leap to his rescue.

"We just bumped into Mrs Corson," Sinead said. "But we

need to go and have a word with Eva here. Would you mind helping her out?"

Ben looked from Sinead to Moira, then back again. He gave a nod. "Of course. No bother. I'll sort her out."

"You'll do nothing of the bloody kind!" Moira protested.

"Not... Not like..." Ben said, and his cheeks became a shade or two redder.

"Right. God. Let's go," Tyler said, side-eyeing Sinead. He gestured ahead for her and Eva to lead the way, then scurried along behind them.

When he glanced back, Ben and Moira were walking towards the exit, and the spring in DI Forde's step had returned.

"I think," Tyler announced to nobody in particular, "I'm going to pretend none of that just happened."

CHAPTER FIFTEEN

WHEN TYLER and Sinead made it back to the Incident Room, Dave Davidson was returning from a lunch so late it was technically dinner. He saluted them as he wheeled his way through the doors they held open, then whistled below his breath as he rolled on over to his desk.

He nodded to Logan on the way. "Still alive, then?"

"Aye, just about," Logan confirmed. "You fed and watered?"

"Just about," Dave said. "Canteen was shite the day, but..." He patted his belly as he pulled up at his desk. "Keep me going for a bit."

"Good. We're going to be burning the midnight oil," Logan told him. "Unless anyone else has any plans to go gallivanting off on a bloody date?"

Tyler and Sinead stepped into the room and let the doors swing closed behind them.

"Date, boss?" Tyler asked. "What do you mean?"

"DI Forde has abandoned ship to go to the bloody *theatre*, would you believe?" Logan spat. "To see—wait for it—a musical."

"*9 to 5*," Dave added. "The Dolly Parton thing."

"Oh. I've heard that's quite good," Sinead said.

Tyler reached around behind him like he might find something there to lean on. When he didn't, he caught Sinead's arm and held onto that, instead.

"Ben's off on a date? What, now? Right now?"

"Aye." Logan's gaze darted between both DCs. "Why?"

"I just... We just..." Tyler said. "We just saw him. Downstairs. And..."

"And we were wondering where he was off to," Sinead said. She turned to her husband and gave him a pointed look. "Now we know. Don't we?"

"Eh? Oh! Aye," Tyler replied, sounding for all the world like he was just listing off vowels. "Aye, now we know," he confirmed, though the thousand-yard-stare he wore said that he wished they didn't.

"We've got Eva MacLean in an interview room, sir," Sinead said, changing the subject. "She didn't want to talk at the house. Think she was worried about her dad hearing. No great surprise, he seemed like a bit of a bruiser."

"I put him in his place, though," Tyler said. He shoved his hands in his pockets, sniffed, and shrugged like it was no big deal. "Showed him who was boss."

"What, did you text him my picture?" Logan asked.

Tyler frowned. "No, I mean I—"

"I know what you meant, son," Logan said. He stole a look at Sinead, who nodded to confirm that Tyler's account of events was accurate.

For a second—half that, maybe—Logan actually looked impressed. But then, all those head and eye movements caught up with him, and he diverted his concentration back to not throwing up.

"You alright, Sinead?" asked Dave, peering at her over the top of his screen. "You look a bit... peaky. You're not going to start spewing, too, are you?"

Logan grunted. "You heard about that, did you?"

"Oh, aye. I very much heard about it," Dave replied, grinning from ear to ear. "I don't think there's anyone in the station who hasn't heard about it, actually. Everyone was talking about it in the canteen. All the Uniforms. Couple of CID boys. Doris."

"Who the hell's Doris?" Logan asked.

"On the till," Dave said. "Blue rinse."

"The deaf one? How the fuck did...?" Logan began, then he squeezed the bridge of his nose and decided this wasn't worth the headache. "Anyway, we weren't talking about me, we were talking about Sinead." He looked up from his chair to where DC Bell stood. "You feeling OK?"

"Fine. I'm fine, sir, aye," Sinead said. "Just... been a long day, and no end in sight. But I'm not sick.

"Lucky you." Logan shut his eyes until the room stopped birling around him. "You two going to be OK talking to the girl, then?"

"No bother, boss," Tyler said. "She seems well up for it. Talking, I mean, not..."

"Going by her texts, she was up for a bit of the other, too," Dave pointed out.

Before Tyler and Sinead could so much as turn to leave, one of the doors behind them swung open, and Detective Superintendent Mitchell returned to the Incident Room. She glanced around at everyone, before spotting Logan behind his desk. She left her gaze to linger there, clearly surprised but doing a very good job of not showing it.

"You're here," she told him.

"Well spotted, ma'am," Logan said. He didn't have the energy to add his usual note of sarcasm to that final word, so it sounded more sincere than usual.

"You're not supposed to be here," Mitchell told him. "You're sick."

"Aye, well, it seems maybe I'm the only one who's noticed, but a man's been murdered," Logan told her. "And since you let DI Forde carry on with his night off, it's a good job I'm here or we'd have no SIO."

"Yes, we would," Mitchell told him.

Logan blinked. It felt like tiny razor blades dragging across his eyeballs. "Hamza? He's a good officer, but he's a sergeant, and a relatively new one at that. I hardly think—"

"Not DS Khaled," Mitchell said, interrupting him. "Where is he, by the way? I'd have preferred him here for this."

"He's away checking CCTV at that nightclub," Logan said. "Here for what? What's going on?"

"When I heard you were sick, I reached out to one of the other MITs, to see if anyone was free to come and give us a hand," Mitchell explained. "And, as luck would have it, an old friend of yours had some availability to do just that"

"An old...?" Logan's brain wasn't firing at full capacity, but it was stirred enough to trigger a rush of adrenaline that made his balls retract and his stomach drop down to meet it.

He felt the rush of the fight or flight response, but was in no fit state to go running anywhere.

Aw, shite. This was going to complicate things.

The other swing door opened, and a list of formers came strutting in.

Former colleague. Former drinking partner.

Former lover.

"Team," Mitchell began, staring deliberately at all of them in turn. "I'd like to introduce you to Detective Chief Inspector Heather Filson."

Heather raised a hand in a half-hearted wave. "Alright?" She focused her attention on Logan, then leaned in closer to the detective superintendent. "God, you're not wrong," she remarked. "He does look like a sack of shite."

Logan got to his feet, acknowledged the new arrival with a

brief nod and a muttered, "Heather," then asked the detective superintendent if he might have a word in private.

The request was shot down immediately. "You shouldn't even be here, Jack," Mitchell told him. "DCI Filson is SIO on this case until you're back fighting fit. Then, she'll continue in a supporting role for as long as she's available."

"I'm here until you need me, Jack," Heather said.

She still had the same haircut as she had last time he'd seen her—cut short, slicked into a side parting. It was a man's hairstyle, but she wore it like it had been hers first.

She was dressed in a red and black checked shirt, and a pair of jeans so tight that Logan thought she could surely only have been sewn into them. She was tall for a woman—four or five inches taller than Mitchell, and a couple clear of Sinead. She had a swagger about her, too, that came from being brought up with four brothers and then surrounded by thousands of male polis colleagues.

"Right, well, I'll leave you all to it," Mitchell said, checking her watch. "And I'll expect a progress report in the morning."

"Yes, ma'am," Filson said before anyone else had a chance to open their mouths. "I'll make sure that's done."

Nobody spoke. Nobody moved. Not until Mitchell had left, and the door had *thunked* closed behind her. Even then, Tyler, Sinead, and Dave all watched on, mute and motionless, as the two DCIs faced off.

"I appreciate you coming all this way, Heather," Logan said. "But you've had a wasted trip. I'm fine. Everything's in hand."

"I'm not here to step on your toes, Jack," Filson replied. She was smiling, but it was a predatory thing, like a front-on view of a rapidly approaching Great White Shark. "I'm just here to support your team while you recover."

"I don't need to recover," Logan said.

Filson looked him slowly up and down. "Yes, well, Chuki thinks otherwise."

"Chuki?" Logan snorted. "You two are on first name terms now, are you?"

Filson pulled a look of mock surprise. "What, you aren't? I mean, I know Chuki... Sorry, *Detective Superintendent Mitchell,* is technically our superior officer, Jack, but she's actually lovely when you get to know her. You should make the effort." A smile tugged at one corner of her mouth. "I know how good you can be at connecting with colleagues when you put your mind to it."

Tyler quietly cleared his throat, and both DCIs turned to see him pointing towards the door.

"Eh, Sinead and me should go and talk to Eva," he said, eyes darting between both officers, but heavily favouring Logan.

"Who's Eva?" Filson demanded. She didn't even bother addressing the question to Tyler, and aimed it at Sinead, instead.

Sinead looked to Logan like she was seeking his permission. He gave it with an almost imperceptible raising of his eyebrows.

"She's a schoolgirl. Seventeen. We, eh... We think she was in some sort of relationship with the victim," Sinead said.

"What, sexual?"

"We don't know yet."

Filson tutted. "Well, we should find out. Considering the guy was knifed in the cock, I'd say there's a good chance it's sexually motivated, wouldn't you?"

"Uh, yeah. Yeah, good chance," Sinead agreed.

"Good. Right, I'll come in with you," Filson said. "What was your name?"

"Uh, Sinead."

"Sinead what?"

"Sinead Nei— Bell. Sinead Bell. DC Sinead Bell."

Filson left an uncomfortable pause before responding. "DC Sinead Bell *what*?"

It took a second. Sinead all but snapped to attention. "Oh! Ma'am. DC Sinead Bell, *ma'am*."

A grin spread across Filson's face. "Nah. Just winding you up. Heather's fine." She looked around at them all. "I don't want you to think of me as the boss. I want you to think of me as a colleague. A colleague who, right now, just happens to be in charge." She pointed to Logan. "That goes for you, too, Jack. Like I say, I'm not here to step on your toes. I'm just... I'm wearing your shoes. They're my shoes. Temporarily. That's all."

She made a clicking noise with her mouth like she was summoning a horse, then indicated for Sinead to lead the way to the door. "Right, after you. No idea where I'm going in this place, although..." She shot a disparaging look at the room around them. "...sure it won't take me long."

Sinead set off towards the door. Filson put a hand out to block Tyler when he moved to follow. "Whoa there, *Disney Junior*. Where do you think you're going?"

Tyler blinked. "*Disney Junior*? What's...?" He shook his head, dismissing the question, then pointed after his wife. "I was... I thought I was coming in to do the interview?"

"What, you think we can't handle it, or something?"

"What? No, I—"

"Do you think it needs three of us?" Filson asked.

"Eh, no, but—"

"You think a teenage girl is going to open up about her sexual relationships with a man in the room?"

Tyler squirmed on the spot, like he had itching powder in his underwear. "I mean... I suppose..."

"No. Exactly," DCI Filson told him. "So, how about you pop off and make us a brew? Coffee for me. Black, one sugar." She looked to Sinead. "You?"

Sinead hesitated. "Um, no. No, I'm alright."

"Fine. Suit yourself," Heather said. She pointed to Tyler. "Crack on. And you..." Her attention turned to Logan. He was still standing beside his seat, rocking ever so slightly back and forth. "Pack up your stuff and piss off home. You're making the place look untidy."

The two women walked out of the Incident Room, leaving the men to wonder exactly what the hell had just happened.

"Right, so, who are we talking to?" Heather asked. "Fill me in, but you can take lead on the interview and I'll hang back."

"You want me to lead it?" Sinead asked, shooting the DCI a brief sideways glance.

"Aye. I'm sure you're more than capable," Filson replied, then she swerved to allow another woman past, before slowing to a stop as their eyes met. "Hey. Hang on. I know you. You're the pathologist."

It took Shona Maguire a moment to recognise the other woman, then something like alarm went darting across her face. She knew Logan's history with Heather Filson. Or, as much of it as she'd care to know, anyway. The headlines, but none of the nitty-gritty details.

"Yes. That's right," Shona said. She smiled politely, then turned to Sinead. "Jack in there, is he?"

"Uh, yeah. Yeah, he's in there. Insists he's fine."

"Aye. I'll bet," Shona replied. Then, stealing a final look at Filson, she turned and headed into the Incident Room.

Heather watched the door swinging closed, then sucked in her bottom lip. "Actually, I might sit this one out. Let's go back to the original plan, you and wee plastic hair in there do the interview." She rolled up her sleeves, and rolled her head around until her neck went *crick*. "Before I jump into the case, I should really get DCI Logan to fill me in…"

CHAPTER SIXTEEN

HAMZA SAT in the back office of *Refuge*, scrubbing at high-speed through hours of footage from the club's security camera system, and idly tapping a pen on the edge of the desk.

The room was compact and cosy, with foam on the walls to dampen the sounds of the club. It probably didn't make a whole lot of difference when nights were in full swing, but now, when the place was already quiet, the insulation seemed to drink in and deaden even the sound of Hamza's breathing. The effect creeped him out a bit, and had only lessened when he'd opened the office door a crack to break up the lines of the soundproofing.

There were four cameras in the club—two covering the dance floor, one at the bar, and one in the entrance foyer that also took in a little bit of the street outside whenever the front doors were opened.

It was a refreshingly high-quality system. Not only was the footage in colour, the resolution was sharp enough that it was possible to identify the actual features of people on the screen, instead of having to squint at the usual blurry blobs that may or may not have represented human beings.

The last footage was from just under three weeks ago. It ended midway through a busy Saturday night, all four cameras stopping recording one after the other, roughly a minute or so apart.

Not a system crash, then, or they'd all have gone down at once.

The one at the bar had stopped first. The image frozen on-screen now showed a couple of people Hamza didn't recognise, and one that he did.

Two harassed looking members of staff—one male, one female, both in their twenties—were taking orders and serving drinks to a three-deep mass of punters all trying to squeeze their way to the front.

The third person in the footage—the one Hamza knew— was Dev Rani, the murder victim himself. He was standing off to one side, his phone pressed to one ear, a finger jammed into the other as he tried to block out the noise of the club.

Scrubbing back through the footage, Hamza saw him wander into shot with the phone already raised to the side of his head. Searching through the other camera angles hadn't revealed his approach to the bar, so it was impossible to say based on the CCTV whether Dev had been making a call or receiving one.

A check of his phone back at the office might give him the information. Whether it would help in any way remained to be seen, but given the timing, there was a chance.

Making a note of the details so he'd remember to check them later, Hamza turned his attention to the other screens.

None of them, as far as he could tell, showed anything of interest to the investigation. The dance floor cameras showed a mass of mostly young and quite sweaty bodies all twisting and gyrating. Meanwhile, a circle of lecherous looking men, all ten to fifteen years older, circled them like a moat, nursing their drinks as they tried to identify an easy lumber.

So, pretty much like any other Inverness nightclub Hamza had ever been to, then.

The final camera, out in the foyer, was perhaps the least interesting of them all. The entranceway was mostly empty, except for a couple of hefty looking bouncers in black jackets. They were big lads, one older than the other. They looked similar, although that was probably deliberate, given their matching shaved heads and identical attire.

Still, facially there was a likeness. Brothers, maybe?

Whatever, the older one was standing with his hands buried in his pockets, while the younger one was scrolling idly on his phone. It was eleven-fifty-three, according to the timestamp on the footage, but there were no punters coming or going. Everyone who wanted to be in, it seemed, was already in.

"Right. So, why haven't you been recording, then?" he asked the equipment.

Rather than wait for the answer he knew wouldn't come, he started to dig around in the system settings. He'd never used this particular software before, but most computer programs were the same on some level. Most decent ones, anyway.

Aye, you got some mad ones where the user interface was counterintuitive and the menu options didn't make sense, but generally speaking these things were similar enough that if you could find your way around one, you could find your way around most of them.

This particular piece of software wasn't the most straightforward he'd ever come across, but nor was it anywhere close to the worst. A few minutes of clicking, some experimentation with the right mouse button, and a cursory glance at the menu hierarchy, and he felt like he'd got the gist of all the basic functions.

The system settings were a different story. Hamza got the feeling that two or more different bits of software had been merged after an acquisition at some point, and all the back-end settings screens had just been mashed together to make one ridiculously long and complicated one.

Several of the options seemed to perform the same function, dozens of the toggle buttons were greyed out for no discernible reason, and nothing was grouped together into any sort of logical order.

What was worse was that this was the 'simple settings' screen. Any attempt to click through to the 'advanced' section resulted in the software throwing a hissy fit and spamming the screen with a dozen different instances of the same runtime error.

Had that error been what stopped the footage being recorded? Possibly, but unlikely. It didn't seem to be affecting the current feed from the cameras, and was instead confined to just the settings screen.

He was on his third read-through of all the checkboxes and toggle switches when he spotted the anomaly. There were three very similar options scattered through the settings. Two had been switched one way, and one the other. Depending on the code hierarchy behind the scenes, this was either completely irrelevant, or key to working out what had happened.

Hamza toggled the odd one out. He heard the high-pitched whine of a hard drive firing up, and watched a small red dot light up in the bottom left corner of every camera feed.

He switched the on-screen button back, and the light went out.

Bingo.

Someone had turned the recording functionality off, but left the cameras themselves running. Anyone watching the screens would have been able to see more or less everything going on in the club, but none of the footage would be captured and stored.

It could have been an innocent mistake, of course. Dev Rani, or one of the other staff members with access to the office, could have got confused by the settings and simply messed up.

But if they hadn't—if someone had deliberately stopped the cameras recording days before Dev had been murdered—then there was more planning to the attack than a frenzied stabbing in a nightclub toilet would suggest.

If the killer had deactivated the CCTV, then the murder was no random act of violence. It was organised. Pre-meditated. Planned, perhaps several weeks in advance, by a killer who knew what they were doing.

From outside the office, Hamza heard the creaking of a door, then the *clunk* of it being closed. He held his breath, listened, waited to see what would happen next.

A voice. Male. Low and murmuring. Nobody he recognised. Nobody he knew.

Shite.

He took out his phone, and grimaced when he saw the 'no service' message. Even in the city centre, there were some patchy areas of mobile signal. Here, in a soundproofed room on the ground floor of an old sandstone building, he was standing in a blackspot.

The footsteps were approaching across the dance floor, by the sounds of things. Hamza checked the screens behind him, but saw nobody on any of the screens.

That didn't make sense. There was definitely somebody out there, and unless they were vampires, they should definitely have been showing up on the camera.

Whoever it was, vampire or not, they were almost upon him. He decided it was best to take the bull by the horns, so he pulled his ID from his wallet, stepped out of the office, and was immediately floored by a flying tackle from somewhere on his right.

CHAPTER SEVENTEEN

TYLER AND SINEAD hurried out of the Incident Room, and didn't look back.

A moment later, the doors opened again, as Dave Davidson frantically wheeled himself out of harm's way.

"I'm not sitting in there for that," he announced, overtaking them. "I must be due another break by now."

"I'd take your time," Sinead called after him. She and Tyler both shot worried looks back in the direction of the room they'd just left. "I don't see it easing up in there for a while."

There had been no arguments or raised voices when DCI Filson had returned. No slapping or hair pulling. There had just been obvious flirting, fake smiles, and tension so thick you could practically chew it.

Heather had decided it would be a good idea to introduce herself properly to Shona, and had then proceeded to interrogate her not just on the victim's Post Mortem, but on her credentials as a pathologist.

At the same time, she'd made sure to sit close to Logan, and had a real knack of tying little parts of Shona's responses into both the DCIs' shared history.

"Reminds me of that guy who got his tadger cut off by his wife's girlfriend."

Or...

"Remember that guy who got his balls ripped off on that barbed wire fence when we were chasing him? That was a laugh."

Or even...

"Jack and I used to hit the clubs back in the day, didn't we? Used to get properly smashed, so we did."

Even when Logan had properly introduced Shona, DCI Filson didn't let up. If anything, it made her double down, rolling her chair a little closer to Jack's, and widening her smile just a little further.

It didn't help that Logan still wasn't sure how best to describe Shona. Not 'girlfriend,' not 'partner,' for reasons he'd gone over in his head several times before. Instead, he'd just fumbled out a vague, "We live together," and trusted that Heather could fill in the blanks and back off.

And she could. Of course, she could.

She was just choosing not to.

It was around this point that Tyler and Sinead had grabbed their notepads and fucked off out of the room, leaving them all to it. Neither had missed the jealous look from Logan as they'd abandoned him, and both suspected they hadn't heard the last of that.

"You think they're all going to still be alive when we get back?" Tyler asked.

"Alive? Yes," Sinead replied. "In one piece? I'm not so sure."

They stopped at the door to the interview room where they'd left Eva MacLean waiting far longer than expected.

"Ready?" Sinead asked.

Tyler confirmed that he was, then reached for the door handle. Sinead stopped him just before he could turn it.

"I look alright, don't I?"

Tyler blinked, caught off guard by the question. "What? Yeah. Course. You look amazing. As always. That's why I married you." He quickly backtracked. "I mean, that's not the only reason I married you, obviously."

"That would be quite shallow," Sinead told him.

"Exactly, yes! I also married you for your personality. Which is, you know... top class."

"You've got such a way with words," Sinead said. She ran a hand down her face. "It's just, Dave said I was looking a bit ropey."

"Yeah, but Dave sees you from your bad angle," Tyler said. He quickly bit his lip, but the horse had already bolted.

"What do you mean *my bad angle*?" Sinead asked him.

Tyler tried to laugh it off, but the tilt of Sinead's head and the raising of her eyebrows told him he wasn't getting out of it that easily.

"No, I mean... nobody looks good from a low angle, do they? You're all chins."

"I'm all chins?!"

"Not you! Everyone! I mean, except you, even!" Tyler babbled. "You're not all chins. You're barely one chin!"

"So you're saying my face has got no definition?" Sinead demanded.

Tyler's mouth formed a series of shapes like it was testing out responses, but he was unable to settle on any of them. It was only when he saw the upwards curved shape Sinead's mouth was making that he was able to speak.

"You bitch," he scolded. "You totally had me going for a minute."

Sinead leaned over and kissed him on the cheek. "Thanks," she said.

"For what?"

"I actually was feeling a bit ropey, but seeing the panic on your face there perked me right up," Sinead said. She winked, opened the door, then flashed the girl sitting at the table an apologetic smile. "Sorry for keeping you, Eva. I promise this won't take long..."

———

Logan's head ached. His ears, too. There was also a throbbing behind his eyes that refused to shift, a scratch at the back of his throat, and all his hair follicles felt like they were being repeatedly electrocuted.

Only one of the two women in the room seemed to have noticed, or cared. It was a shame, then, that she was the one he was having to disagree with.

"You need to go home," Shona told him. "You shouldn't be here."

"He's fine. He should stay," DCI Filson countered.

Logan regarded her, eyes narrowed. "You've changed your tune. You were telling me to piss off five minutes ago."

"Yeah, well, I realised that we need you on this one," Filson replied. "I'm not up to speed on any of it. I need you to, you know, *fill me in.*"

Shona muttered something below her breath, but so quiet that only she was aware of it.

"She's got a point," Logan said, much to Shona's surprise. "And honestly, I'm fine," he insisted. "Whatever it was, it's on the way out."

Heather took great pleasure in agreeing. "See? Told you. You get to know him well enough, and you can see it on him. He's grand."

"No. He is not *grand,*" Shona insisted. "You need to rest and get your strength back, Jack. DCI, um..." She flicked a disparaging look in Heather Filson's direction. "...I've forgotten her name. She can stand in for you until you're better, then you can step straight back in. And she can leave."

"No. It's fine. I'm in no rush," Heather said, partly reclining in the office chair she had claimed as her own. She was loudly chewing on a piece of gum, and Shona's nostrils flared in time with every *squelch* it made between the other woman's teeth. "It'll be good to catch up with Jack. It'll be a *pleasure*, in fact. Just like old times."

"Aye, well, there's always email. Besides, I'm sure you've got your own work to get back to," Shona sniped. "A boyfriend. Or... boyfriends, maybe?"

Heather stopped chewing just long enough to grin and shake her head. "No. Single and ready to mingle." She fired a very deliberate look in Logan's direction, before meeting Shona's gaze again. "Just like old times."

Before Shona could respond, Heather sprang to her feet so suddenly it made the pathologist take a worried step back, and drew a hissed, "Jesus," from Logan in the seat beside her.

"I've just had an idea!" the female DCI declared. "Food."

Shona and Logan both frowned. "Food?" they said at the same time.

"Yeah. Food. As in a meal. As in dinner," Filson clarified. "It'll help you feel better. Chicken kebab and a pint. Best remedy known to man."

"He doesn't drink these days," Shona was quick to point out.

"Oh." Heather looked over her shoulder at Logan, then back to Shona. "Maybe that's the problem, then. Dehydration."

Shona tutted. "Well, obviously he *drinks*. Just not alcohol."

"But he does eat kebabs?" Heather probed. "You haven't robbed him of that, too?"

"I didn't rob him of anything," Shona cried. "He wasn't drinking when I met him."

"Well, he was drinking when he left me, and, if I'm being honest, he was more of a laugh then than he is now!"

"Oh, well, sorry if he's not a rollercoaster of fun! He's sick! That's why he needs to go home!"

"I've known him longer than you have, and he needs to be here!"

"Yes, well, I live with him now, and I say—"

"Jesus Christ, will the pair of you shut up?" Logan groaned, pressing his fingers to his temples and trying to rub away the growing tension and gnawing pain. "I am in the room, you know? I'm capable of making my own decisions."

He got himself to his feet using the chair for support, waited for the momentary sensation of weightlessness to pass, then turned to Shona. "Honestly, I'm fine. I love that you're worried, but I'm OK. I promise."

The next part he addressed to DCI Filson.

"Heather, stop being an arsehole. It's a no to dinner, but if you're going to hang around, then we can sit down and I'll take you through everything we've got so far. But no flirty comments, or snidey wee jokes, or any of that shite, alright?"

Heather chewed her gum, still grinning. After a few seconds, she nodded. "Whatever you say, Jack. You're the boss."

Logan sighed at the way she made those two sentences sound so suggestive, but chose not to comment. Instead, he turned back to Shona with a hopeful look. "Happy?"

"Not really," Shona said. She shot daggers in Heather's direction, then blew out her cheeks. "And, I mean... You probably should eat something."

"I know, right?" DCI Filson interjected. "That's what I said. Food. Eat. Best way."

Shona ignored her and took a step closer to Logan. "We could go and grab something quickly. You should keep your strength up."

Logan grunted. Shrugged. Whatever kept her happy. "Fine. Aye. We can go across the road and get a fish supper or something."

"OK, we'll do that," Shona said.

"Great!" Heather cheered. "I am *starving*."

Shona frowned. "No, I didn't mean—"

"Ah, to be sure now, hold that thought!" Heather said, adopting an Irish accent so thick it almost qualified as a hate crime. "And give me a minute to fetch me feckin' coat!"

CHAPTER EIGHTEEN

"WHAT THE BLOODY hell are you doing, Tim?"

The man who had tackled Hamza to the ground stopped slapping at the fallen DS's face long enough to spit out a response.

"I'm apprehending this thieving bastard! What does it bloody look like?!"

Hamza seized the opportunity to drive an elbow into his attacker's solar plexus, and savoured the sound the guy made when he realised that breathing was not currently an option.

"Police!" Hamza spat, twisting away from the other man's grip and scrambling up onto his knees.

An older woman with blonde hair that was streaked with hints of grey, tutted and gestured down at the figure who was now *goldfishing* on the floor, his eyes wide, his mouth popping open and closed as he struggled for air.

"See? See what you've done, Tim? Police. He's not a burglar, he's police."

"Detective Sergeant Khaled," Hamza said, still all business. He stood, and jabbed a finger in the woman's face. "Who are you? What are you doing here?"

"I own the place," the woman told him.

"Right. I see," Hamza said, lowering his finger. "Well, this is a crime scene."

The woman rolled her eyes. "Fine. Well, I own this *crime scene*, then. I'd been led to believe you were done, so we came to check the damage." She hissed down at the man on the floor. "For God's sake, Tim, will you stop bloody whinging and get up? You're a bloody embarrassment."

Her tone softened considerably when she turned her attention back to the detective sergeant.

"I can only apologise. He thinks he's bloody Giant Haystacks sometimes!"

"Who?" Hamza asked.

"The wrestler? Big hairy lad." She waved a hand, and Hamza caught a glimpse of several expensive-looking rings. "Probably before your time."

She was English, he thought. From one of the more affluent parts. Bath, or Windsor, or somewhere like that. The accent was vague enough, and interwoven with enough of a Highland twang, that it was difficult to pinpoint.

There was definitely an air of wealth about her. It was in the way she looked, how she dressed, and the way she spoke to her male companion like he was a lowly stablehand, or perhaps a disobedient dog.

He looked to be roughly the same age as she was, and had come dressed like he thought a tennis match might be sprung on him out of nowhere. His white shorts, while technically in his size, looked far too small and tight for Hamza's liking. They had ridden right up the crack of his arse while he was rolling on the floor, and were now shoved in there so deep it would take a team of Sherpas and a Saint Bernard to fetch them back out.

"I didn't catch your name," Hamza told the woman.

"I didn't throw it," she replied, then she flashed a showy smile, and offered her hand like she expected him to kiss it.

"Maude. Maude Willington-Smythe. No doubt you've heard of me."

That last part wasn't a question. She wasn't modest enough for that. It appeared to genuinely surprise her when Hamza said that he had no idea who she was, and it immediately became a source of some amusement.

"Ha! You hear that, Tim? He hasn't heard of me, would you believe?" With the same hand she had offered out to him—and which he'd pointedly ignored—she tapped Hamza lightly on the arm. "Don't you worry. It's not your fault. I'm sure we move in quite different circles. It's really not an issue," she insisted, though she tried again, just to be sure. "Maude Willington-Smythe, Lady of Glencoe? No? No. It's fine. Honestly, don't worry yourself about it one bit."

"I wasn't," Hamza assured her. He gave his chin a thoughtful stroke. "Lady of Glencoe?"

"Laird and Lady of Glencoe, actually," wheezed Tim, shambling unsteadily into a standing position. He was still clutching his abdomen, and warily eyeing Hamza's elbows. "We're husband and wife."

Hamza knew he should let it go. It wasn't worth it. It was petty. He was better than that.

Ah, fuck it.

"That's one of those titles you can buy online, isn't it?" he asked them. "For, like, thirty quid?"

Laird and Lady alike both just stood there looking back at him for a few seconds, fixed smiles on their faces.

"Yes, well," Maude eventually said, and she flashed that showy smile again. "It's just a bit of fun, really. The money goes to helping create nature reserves, so all for a good cause." She leaned in closer, like she was sharing some terrible secret. "Tim and I are very fond of nature. Aren't we, Timothy?"

"We're very fond of nature," Tim confirmed, and there was

something about the way he said it that made an otherwise innocuous sentence sound alarmingly sexual.

"Right. Um, good. OK," Hamza said. "Since you're here, I'd like to ask you both a few questions."

He patted his pockets, searching for his notepad, then realised he must have left it in the office.

"Why don't you two take a seat at one of the tables, and I'll be right with you?"

"Oh, must we?" Tim asked. "We've got a lot on this evening."

Hamza looked down at the other man's tennis outfit. "Mixed doubles?" he asked.

The comment sailed straight over Tim's head. "I'm sorry?"

"Doesn't matter. Go sit down. I'll be right with you. This won't take long," Hamza said. Then, before either the Laird or the Lady could offer any further objections, he returned to the office to collect his notepad.

He had just picked it up when movement on one of the monitors caught his eye. It showed the dance floor, and the area directly outside the office. He and Tim were both on the ground, wrestling, as Maude berated her husband for the attack.

The footage, which was supposed to be a live feed from the cameras, was running a couple of minutes behind.

"How the hell is that happening?" Hamza wondered.

His mind raced with the possibilities—and the connotations—but he pushed them down. That was for later. Right now, he had a couple of old poshos to go and interrogate.

When he emerged from the office, he found Maude sitting in a booth on her own. Before he could ask where her husband was, Tim appeared behind him, holding a glass of clear liquid in each hand.

"No ice, I'm afraid," he announced.

"Oh, for goodness' sake," Maude protested, with an air of

exasperation that suggested this was by far the worst thing that had ever happened to her. "Honestly!"

Tim sniffed both drinks, then set one down in front of his wife. "Gin and tonic. Lemonade for me." He thrust the glass out towards Hamza. "Smell. See? Not drinking. In case you were going to try and arrest me before I got in the car. It's a soft drink."

Hamza put a hand on Tim's wrist and firmly, but politely, pushed the glass away from his face. "What are you doing?" he asked them.

Laird and Lady both looked at their drinks, then Tim tapped his palm against his forehead. "Apologies. Where are my manners? Would you care for something?"

"No. No, I would not. This is still a crime scene," Hamza told them. "You shouldn't be helping yourself to the contents of the bar."

"Well, they *are* mine, so..." Maude began, then she hurriedly took a sip of her G&T in case it was taken from her.

"You sure you don't want something?" Tim asked, jabbing a thumb back over his shoulder. "Are you driving? Do you drink alcohol? Are you allowed? You know, between being in the police, and..." He gestured at Hamza and made some lightly racist eyebrow movements. "...everything?"

Again, it was petty, but Hamza plucked both glasses from their hands, turned away, and set them both down on the next table along.

"It's potentially evidence," he told them, in a tone that brooked no argument. "If you want a drink, you can get one elsewhere once we're done."

"Seems rather vindictive," Tim objected, which earned him a sharp look from the detective sergeant.

"Might I remind you, sir, that you assaulted a police officer a few moments ago? You're already skating on some pretty thin ice, so I really don't think you want to add tampering with evidence to the mix, do you?"

Tim swallowed, and it almost looked like he was working up the courage to offer a comeback, but a withering, "Stop embarrassing me, Timothy!" from Maude quickly knocked any such notion out of him.

Hamza motioned to the side of the booth that Maude was sitting on, and instructed Tim to join her. Maude, who had plonked herself slap bang in the middle of the padded bench-style seat, muttered her objections as she was forced to slide along to accommodate her husband.

Hamza waited until they were both in place, then took his seat opposite, set his notebook down on the table, and twirled his pen around his fingers.

"Right, then, if we're all ready," he said. "Let's begin."

———

"Do I need a lawyer?"

It was the first question out of Eva MacLean's mouth once Sinead and Tyler had sat down across from her. Tyler assured her she didn't, but Sinead took a more measured approach.

"Unless you think you need one?" she asked.

"I haven't done anything wrong," Eva said.

Sinead smiled. "Then, you should be fine."

"How much do you know?" the girl asked.

She didn't seem to be afraid of the two detectives, or of the situation in general. Quite the opposite. She sounded confrontational, like she was the one with accusations to hurl at them.

"Most of it," Sinead bluffed, not sure what Eva was getting at, but very keen to find out. "But we'd like to hear it in your words. Get your side of the story."

"My side?" Eva snorted and crossed her arms over her chest.

She had looked skinny when they'd first seen her at her house, but here, under the harsh fluorescent lighting, she was positively skeletal. An eating disorder, Sinead thought. Had to be. Either that or she'd literally been starved.

"OK, my side. We fucked. He ghosted me. The end. Alright? That's my side." She pointed to the notepad Tyler had opened on the desk. "Write that down. Want me to spell it for you? F-U-C—"

"I've got it, thanks," Tyler told her.

"So... for clarification, Eva, you're saying that you were in a sexual relationship with Mr Rani?" Sinead asked.

"Well, that's what 'fucked' usually means, isn't it?" the teenager spat back.

"Not necessarily," Tyler interjected. "Can mean tired. Or broken. Or just, like, in big trouble. Like, 'The ship's sinking! We're all fucked!' or, 'There's a train coming! I'm totally fucked!' or..." He caught the looks from both women, and any further definitions dried up in his throat. "But, aye, in context, I suppose, there's really only one..."

He scribbled something on his pad, cleared his throat, then gave Sinead a nod. "Carry on."

"How long did the relationship go on for?" Sinead asked.

"Who said it's stopped?"

Sinead and Tyler swapped glances, as they silently agreed on how to play it from here. She didn't know that Dev was dead. Or she was pretending not to. Either way, they wouldn't break the news. Not yet. Not until they knew more.

"OK. So, can you tell us when it started? The relationship."

Eva shrugged. "Dunno. It's not like I marked the date in my diary or anything."

"Roughly," Sinead said. "A month? A year? When would you say it started?"

Another shrug. "About a year. Yeah. About that. Or, actually, just before Christmas. So bit less."

"And how did you meet?" Sinead probed.

"The club. His place. I was drunk."

Tyler checked his notes. "You'd have been sixteen?"

"Yeah. So?" Eva scowled, her defences going up. "Nothing else to do round here, is there? Anyway, like I said, it was Christmas."

"So, you met at the club," Sinead said. "Then what?"

"Then we went to his office and fucked."

"Just like that?"

Eva's face flushed red, but more through anger than shame. "Yeah. So?"

"He's quite a bit older than you. I'm just surprised," Sinead said.

The girl laughed drily. "Jesus. You sound just like him. That's what he said. 'I'm too old for you. It's not right.'"

Sinead nodded. "And was that before or after he had sex with you?"

"After. When he found out."

"Found out what?" Tyler asked.

"How old she was," Sinead said, answering on Eva's behalf. "Right?"

Eva shifted uncomfortably on the hard plastic chair. "It wasn't like I lied to him, or anything. He just didn't ask."

"You were in the club. He must've assumed you were over eighteen."

"That's not my fault, is it?"

"How did you get in?" Tyler asked. "I mean, you look older than you are, but you'd want to make sure nobody stopped you getting in. You have a fake ID in case you got jarred?"

Eva tutted and rolled her eyes. Though her arms were already folded, she somehow conveyed the impression that she was folding them *even more so*.

"I'll take that as a yes," Tyler said, making a note.

"Take it however you like, mate," Eva told him, and the

wild-eyed stare she gave him made it look like she was squaring up for a fight. "I don't care, do I?"

"And after Mr Rani found out you were only sixteen," Sinead continued, ignoring the escalating tension. "What then? Did the relationship continue?"

"You mean did we fuck again?" Eva asked. "No. No, he bottled it. Got all paranoid and told me not to tell anyone. Properly begged me not to. Said it could ruin him."

"And did you? Tell anyone?" Sinead asked.

Eva ran her tongue across the front of her teeth like she was checking she'd brushed them, then gave a single shake of her head. "No."

"And why not?"

Across the table, Eva shrugged. It wasn't the same *petulant teenager* sort of shrug as before, but something altogether more genuine. For the first time since the detectives had first set eyes on her, she actually looked close to her real age.

"Just because."

"But you must have been furious with him," Sinead said. "Using you, then tossing you aside the way he did."

"It wasn't like that."

"We saw the texts between you. The way he was ignoring you. You said yourself at the start of this conversation, he was ghosting you."

"He's got a reputation to protect," Eva insisted. "He's on the council."

"You're making excuses for him," Sinead said. "Why? Why didn't you tell anyone what had happened? Why didn't you tell people about the relationship?"

"I just didn't!" Eva snapped. "Alright? I just didn't."

"Were you using what had happened against him, Eva?" Tyler asked. "Were you blackmailing him?"

"What?!" the girl spluttered. "No! No, I'd never do... Did he say that? Is that what this is about? I'd never do that!"

"Why not? I might," Sinead said. "See, I remember being sixteen. I remember how important everything feels. How much more painful everything is. Even the little things. But this? Something as big as this? If someone had used me and tossed me aside like that at sixteen, I'd want to make him pay."

"Yeah, well, I don't care about that stuff."

"Why not?" Sinead demanded.

Eva's arms unfolded like a snake uncoiling itself from around her. Her hands slammed down on the table, shaking it. "Because I love him, alright?" she screeched. "And I know that's pathetic, and shit, and I know it makes me sound like some daft wee girl with fucking hearts in my eyes, but..." The fire burned out. The rest of the outburst came out like a sigh of resignation. "But, it's not that. I just... I love him. Fuck knows why. But I do. And I think... I think he loves me, too. Or, I don't know, could."

She ran a hand through her hair, blew out her cheeks, then spent another few seconds composing herself.

"So, if he's in trouble because of me, he shouldn't be. I was sixteen, so it was legal. And he didn't know. He thought I was older. And after he found out that I wasn't, nothing happened. I swear. Even though I wanted to, he wouldn't. He told me to find someone my own age. He said he was sorry. He's not a bad guy. Seriously, I know him, and he's not. He was... He was nice."

She stared past the detectives but kept talking, like she was figuring something out for the first time.

"I think that's why I like him. I tried to offer it up to him on a plate, but he was too nice a guy to take it. He's..." Her voice cracked. Her focus shifted back to Sinead and Tyler. "He's a good guy. He's caring. He's not done anything wrong."

Tyler and Sinead's eyes met again. An agreement passed silently between them.

It was time.

"Mr Rani's not in any trouble, Eva. That's not why you're here," Sinead said.

Across the table, Eva's eyes narrowed in confusion. "He's not? Oh. So... what, then? Why am I here?"

"I'm sorry to have to tell you this, Eva," DC Bell replied. "But I'm afraid I've got some bad news."

CHAPTER NINETEEN

IT HAD BEEN A LONG SHIFT. Mary had been on her feet
since before lunchtime, taking orders, arguing with the kitchen
staff, and running about after some of the day's more...
demanding diners.

Table thirteen sprang to mind. Four young lads. Shower of
drunken arseholes. The sooner they were off the premises, the
better.

They weren't her problem at the moment, though.

She had just over an hour until she was finished. Sixty-
seven minutes until clocking off, and it couldn't come soon
enough.

She'd hoped the time would pass quickly. She'd hoped for
an easy final hour.

The people at table six, however, had other ideas.

At least one of them was with the police. The big one. She
recognised him from the other times he'd nipped across the
street for an order of bacon and square sausage rolls to take
away. He'd always been polite, if a bit gruff, and he'd usually
tipped, which was unusual for takeaway customers.

And, to be fair to him, he wasn't the problem tonight. The problem was the two women he was sitting with.

"Just order something," the one sitting next to the detective said. She was Irish. Possibly police, too, though she didn't have the same air of authority about her, unlike the other woman.

She was rocking a short side-parting, and was dressed a bit like a cowboy who'd lost his horse. Mary was no expert on such things, but she was getting strong lesbian vibes off her. And yet, even in the few minutes that Mary had been standing there, the woman had shot three or four lascivious looks at the detective sitting opposite.

These had not gone unnoticed by the Irish woman sitting beside him, who had become increasingly annoyed by each one. She was trying not to show it, but you deal with people all day long, and you start to notice these things. And Mary had been dealing with people for a very long time.

"I'm easy," the short-haired woman said.

"Yes, well, we've established that," the Irish one replied below her breath. "But what are you going to eat?"

"Just whatever. I'll have what you're having." There was a darting of the eyes towards the only man at the table. "I mean, I'm sure we've got similar tastes."

"Oh, for God's sake..."

Mary raised her pencil like she was trying to get a teacher's attention. "Will I give you a few more minutes and come back?"

"No! God, no, don't go," the policeman said, and there was a pleading look in his eyes. "It'll be worse if you're not here."

Mary looked around at the restaurant. It was after six now, and the place was filling up. "It's just... there are other customers waiting, so..."

The detective groaned like he was in pain, then passed back his laminated menu. "Just give us the fish platter and three plates, will you?"

"What, we're sharing?" the Irish woman yelped.

The detective's sigh went unheard by everyone but Mary. "Make that two platters. But can you leave the whitebait off one?" he asked. "I can't deal with eating anything that's got a face right now."

Mary made a note. "You want something else instead? More calamari? Or chips?"

"I..." The policeman's mouth hung open for a few seconds, then he shrugged. "...don't care. Just that, thanks."

"I'll get that for you," Mary said.

"Great. Any idea how long it'll be?" the detective asked, and that pleading look was there in his eyes again. "Any chance it could be pushed up the queue?"

Mary slid her pencil into the spiral of metal at the top of her pad. "Leave it with me," she told him, and she winked. "And I'll see what I can do."

———

Hamza was starting to think he should've interviewed the Willington-Smythes in different rooms. Or maybe, judging by the way they kept sniping and picking at each other, on different continents.

The questioning would certainly have gone by much more quickly. Though, he had to admit, their bickering was throwing up a few points of interest.

When he'd asked Maude what her relationship with the deceased was, she'd insisted it was strictly professional. Tim's eyes had rolled at that, though, and when Maude had demanded to know what he was getting at, his attempts to brush the question off had eventually given way to a hissed, "Not for want of bloody trying!"

"Oh for goodness... Forgive my idiot husband, Detective Sergeant," Maude had said, and this time she'd been the one rolling her eyes. "Any time he sees me having a conversation with a man, he assumes I'm trying to have it away with them. He probably thinks I'm mentally undressing you as we speak, in fact."

"Nothing would surprise me," Tim said.

This earned him a tut, a sigh, and a mumbled remark along the lines of, "Just because you haven't got it in you to perform..."

"I can perform, Maude!" her husband snapped. "I can still perform perfectly well!"

"Oh? Who with, Timothy? Hmm? Who with? Because it most certainly has not been with me!"

Hamza had cleared his throat at that point, reminding them both that he was in the room. Then, when they'd stopped debating their respective levels of sexual appetite and activity, he'd moved the conversation on.

Maude Willington-Smythe, as Hamza had initially assumed, came from a wealthy background. Her husband, Timothy Willington-Smythe—better known to friends and family as Tim Smith—was a plumber by trade, though not a particularly good one, judging by the levels of debt his company had racked up before Maude had stepped in and wiped the slate clean.

She had taken great pleasure in informing Hamza about that incident, while her husband silently fumed on the seat beside her.

They had agreed that, given her status and ancestry, she would keep her own surname and append his to the end. 'Smith,' however, was far too common, so she tweaked it to make it more acceptable.

Investing in the nightclub had been her idea. She'd met Dev Rani through his work on the council, and her role of turning up to any events in Inverness that called for rich people to stand around wearing hats and looking important.

They'd somehow wound up on a panel together at an event held by the local Chamber of Commerce, had got chatting afterwards, and Dev had mentioned that he was trying to get a new club off the ground.

Maude had told him she was in possession of a portfolio that was in desperate need of diversifying—another phrase which, to Hamza's ears, sounded unsettlingly sexual—and things had snowballed from there.

Now, she had a sixty-percent stake in the business, and while she insisted Dev had never earned himself a place on her very select list of friends, they had, "A happy, and often close working relationship."

"Oh, I know you bloody did," Tim muttered sullenly. "You don't need to tell me that. Very close."

Maude forcibly ejected a loud, impatient sounding sigh, then twisted on the seat so she could glare at her husband. "You do understand what you're doing, yes? You're not honestly that stupid are you?"

The look of confusion on Tim's face suggested that, actually, yes, he was *precisely* that stupid, and possibly even more so.

"What am I doing?" he asked. "What are you on about?"

"Scorned husband. Jealous partner, unable to satisfy his wife, takes a bloody revenge on her younger lover." Maude tore her eyes off Tim just long enough to aim the next sentence in Hamza's direction. "Which he wasn't. But for the purposes of this explanation."

Hamza was interested to see how this played out, so waved at them to continue.

"You can see why that might paint you in rather a dim light in front of the detective here, Timothy, yes? You do see why that might be cause for some raised eyebrows? Hmm?"

Panic contorted the lines of Tim's face. He shook his head, and held a hand up in a 'stop' motion to Hamza, like this might be enough to prevent him leaping to any erroneous conclusions.

"No. No, I didn't do that. I didn't kill him. I couldn't. I mean, I could. There's no reason why I... If I wanted to. But I didn't! I don't! I wouldn't do a thing to him. To anyone! And I didn't. Not to anyone. But especially not to him." He smiled weakly. "I mean, I hardly knew the bloke. I wouldn't recognise him if he walked in here right now."

"Well, I'd imagine him being dead would be something of a giveaway," Maude remarked, then she slapped her husband's hand down. "You can stop now, Timothy. I think you've made your point. Anyway, you can barely bring yourself to carve a bloody goose. I'm sure the detective constable doesn't seriously believe you're capable of something like murder."

"In my experience, people are capable of some surprising things, ma'am," Hamza said. "But no, I'm not considering either of you as suspects at this time."

Tim frowned. "At this time? What, so you might change your mind later?"

"Oh, shush, Timothy. It's just a thing they say." Maude checked her watch, then looked around at the club. "Would I be right in assuming we won't be getting the place open this evening?"

Hamza half-smiled, like he thought she might be joking, then shook his head. "No. Definitely not."

"What on Earth is taking so long? What's involved in these things?" Maude demanded. "I mean, you've had all through the night, then most of today. Surely you're done by now? Opening up is..." She produced a crumpled tissue from her sleeve, and dabbed lightly at her eyes. "It's what Dev would have wanted."

Hamza sat forward, his arms resting on the table. "Hold on. Wait a minute. Go back. What did you say?"

Maude hesitated. "Which part?"

"You said we had all night."

"Well, yes. Why? What's so strange about that?"

"The body was only found this morning," Hamza explained.

"Was it? Oh." Maude's eyes drew an imaginary box in the

air in front of her, like she was working something out. "Well, why was that the case? I was told the cleaners found him."

"They did," Hamza said. "This morning, when they came in."

"Well, then what the bloody hellfire was going on there, then?" Maude demanded. "Because the buggers ought to have been here last night."

CHAPTER TWENTY

LOGAN WAS REGRETTING THIS. He wasn't actually sure what 'this' was, exactly, but whatever it was, he was regretting it.

He'd known this would happen. The moment that Mitchell had brought DCI Heather Filson into the Incident Room—a few seconds before that, in fact—he'd seen his future playing out.

Heather had deliberately tried to make Shona think that something was going on between the two DCIs while Logan was down in Glasgow earlier in the year. She'd answered his phone when Shona had called, and strongly implied that the two of them were engaging in drink and debauchery.

Logan hadn't known a thing about the conversation until he'd got back to Inverness and Shona had, with some cajoling, spilled the beans about all of it. He'd assured her that nothing had happened, and she'd believed it.

And that, he'd hoped, was an end to it.

Those hopes had been dashed an hour ago when Heather had come striding on in through his station's front door. Now, the best he could hope for was that neither of the women killed the other.

If it came to a straight fight, odds were that Heather would emerge the victor. She was bigger, stronger, had gone through hand-to-hand combat training, and—having spent most of her polis career on the streets of Glasgow—was experienced in both the giving and receiving of brutal acts of violence.

Logan reckoned the smart money would be on Shona, though. She might not have any of the things going for her that DCI Filson had, but she had a frighteningly thorough understanding of human anatomy, and a rock-hard constitution when it came to blood and innards.

Not that it would come to anything like that, though. Not that their sniping would dissolve into violence.

Surely?

"So. Inverness," Heather said, and there was something taunting in the way she spoke even those two words.

She'd tried to get a beer, but the restaurant didn't have a licence to serve alcohol, so she'd settled for a coffee so strong she could've stood her spoon up in it. She took a sip of it, then motioned around her with the mug, indicating the city beyond the walls.

"It's smaller than I remember," she said. "I mean, it's been a while since I've been up this way—why would I, right? You know what I'm saying? What's this place got that the central belt doesn't?"

"Fewer arseholes?" Shona said, and for a moment she looked shocked that she'd voiced the thought out loud.

"Fewer everything," Heather retorted. "I mean, I know you call it a city, but is it, though?" She wrinkled her nose. "Is it really? Isn't it just a nice, quaint little town with ideas above its station?"

She looked very deliberately at the chocolate milkshake sitting on the table in front of Shona.

"I mean, yeah, they do some nice children's drinks, but it's a bit far from the action for you, isn't it, Jack?"

"Jack's happily settled here," Shona informed her, then she maintained eye contact while eating a spoonful of whipped cream from the top of her drink.

A sly grin played across Heather's face. "That what you've done is it, Jack?" she asked. Her eyes crept to Shona and stayed there. "Settled?"

Logan rubbed his temples. "Oh, for fu—" He let out a sigh so heavy that it appeared to shrink him an inch or two. "Can we cut this out?" He jabbed a finger in Heather's direction. "I like it here. A lot. So quit being an arsehole. And Shona, don't let her wind you up."

"She's not winding me up," Shona said, though this was patently false.

"She is. That's what she does. She winds people up. Annoyingly, it makes her a good copper."

"Thank you," Heather gloated.

"It also makes her an absolute pain in the arse to be around," Logan continued.

There was a crash from around the corner, in another area of the restaurant. A plate. Cutlery. A drunken cheer followed, and the waitress who'd taken their order went hurrying past to investigate.

"That's not how you used to describe me, Jack," Heather practically purred.

Logan glowered at her. "Aye, it is. That's how I've always described you. To your face. Oh, and Shona knows, by the way. About us. About our... I'd call it a relationship, but that's a stretch. I told her about it. She knows. So you can stop your wee teasing act, pretending you've got a big secret. She knows."

"She'd rather not know," Shona added. "But she knows."

That took the wind from Heather's sails a bit. She'd been

leaning forwards, elbows on the table, but now her weight slumped back onto her chair.

"Tch. You two are no fun," she said, then she looked around for the waitress. "Where's the food, I'm starving?"

"Nah, love, we're not. No chance. It was shit."

All three people sitting at Logan's table turned to see a smirking lad in his late teens or early twenties come striding around the corner, the harassed-looking waitress scurrying along behind him.

Three other lads followed at their backs, all sniggering and whispering like mischievous schoolboys. They'd been drinking. You could see it in their movements, and the volume of the ring-leader's voice.

"You can't just walk out," the waitress said. "You need to pay!"

"Do we fuck!" the first lad countered. "The chips were cold. The food was shite."

"You ate it all! If there was a problem, you should've said."

The lad stopped and eyeballed her. He was a head taller than she was. Practically a third her age. The ferocity of his look made her shrink back, like she was bracing herself for a slap.

"I'm fucking saying now, alright?"

The lad failed to notice the sound of chair legs scraping on the vinyl floor behind him. Logan started to rise, unsteadily, but Heather put a hand on his arm.

"Please, let me," she said, and before Logan could answer, she bounced to her feet, tapped the lad on the shoulder, and stood there smiling as he shambled around to face her. "Alright?"

"What?"

Heather leaned in closer, and asked the question louder, and more slowly. "Are you alright?"

"Who the fuck are you?" the lad grunted, looking her up and down. His face lit up like he'd been struck by a bolt of pure comedy genius. "You a lesbo, or something?" He turned to the waitress. "She your girlfriend?"

He spread his index and middle finger into a V-shape, pressed them either side of his mouth, then flicked his tongue around, while making groaning noises. "You two give it that, do you?" he sniggered. "Couple of fucking—"

He was halfway through that sentence when his head hit the table. Logan's reactions were slow, but Shona had swooped in and moved the coffee cups and milkshake a split second before face-to-Formica contact had taken place.

"Ah, ah! What the fuck?" the lad wailed. An elbow dug into the back of his neck. His right thumb was forcibly introduced to his shoulder blade. "Stop! Fuck, stop! You'll break my arm!"

Heather's reply was a gleeful whisper. "I know. That's the idea, pal," she told him.

With the ringleader down, it fell to the other three members of his little group to do something. One of them—the biggest—was nudged forward by his mates.

"Leave him alone!" he barked, his hands balling into fists.

"I wouldn't, son," Logan warned. "It won't end well for you."

The murmur of conversation and clinking of cutlery that had filled the restaurant had fallen away into silence now, as everyone turned in their seats to see what was going on. Another waitress had rushed to stand beside the first, while a man in a white shirt and tie—a manager, presumably—hung back at the counter, stretching to see what was going on while trying not to be noticed.

The big lad clearly wasn't the brightest of the bunch, because he ignored Logan's warning and closed in on Heather with two big strides.

He had just completed his second step when the heel of DCI Filson's boot connected with the inside of his knee, and he went down like a puppet whose strings had all been cut. She had not, as far as anyone watching was aware, turned to look at her would-be attacker at any point.

Down on the floor, the big lad let out a guttural sort of wailing sound that rose up all the way from his toes. Competing instincts made him grab for his injured knee, but also avoid touching the damaged area, so he sort of clutched the air around it, instead, his eyeballs almost popping out of their sockets.

The other two drunks appeared to sober up quite quickly then. Neither of them moved a muscle. Neither of them dared.

"Right, here's what's going to happen," Heather announced, still pinning the first lad to the table. "You're going to pay your bill. You're going to pay for any breakages. And you're going to give a generous tip to..."

She looked back over her shoulder at the waitress.

"Mary."

"To Mary. And I mean a *very* generous tip. Like, a tip that's going to make us all collectively let out a gasp. You know, like them feel-good stories you read on the internet, about waiting staff being left life-changing sums of money?"

The lad beneath her squirmed and sobbed. She gave him a shake and wrenched his arm higher.

"That wasn't a rhetorical question, pal. *Do you know them feel-good stories you read on the internet about waiting staff being left life-changing sums of money?* Yes or no?"

"Yes! Yes!"

"Good. Well, that's what we're aiming for, alright? That's the sort of range we're looking at. Is that clear?" She kept the pressure on, but turned to the two lads who had thus far managed to remain unhurt. "You two. Hoddart and Doddart. Stop standing there like a pair of dildos and get your wallets out. We're all waiting to be moved by your generosity."

"You, eh, you can't do this," one of them voiced. "This is... this is blackmail."

"Assault," the other volunteered.

"We'll... we'll call the police."

Heather's smile was a frightening thing. Usually, a smile would light up a face, but this one somehow darkened it. "You're in luck, lads! DCI Logan. Would you do the honours?"

Logan had already removed his warrant card from his pocket in anticipation. He waved it around so all four of the lads got an eyeful, albeit sideways in the case of the one still being pinned by Heather.

"So, your choices are we arrest you all, I break this gentleman's arm, or you pay your bill and leave that generous tip we discussed. It's your call."

"We'll pay! We'll pay!" sobbed the lad beneath her. "Just... please, stop. It hurts!"

Heather caught him by the hair and hauled him upright, his arm still trapped halfway up his back.

"Good choice," she said. "Now, I'll escort you through and stay with you until you make your transaction. Alright?"

Without waiting for an answer, she shoved him towards the counter. Behind them, the two smaller lads helped the larger one back onto his feet—or, more accurately, his foot—and they went hopping and hobbling after their disgraced ringleader.

Shona tutted and rolled her eyes. "She bloody loved that, didn't she?"

"She did, aye," Logan confirmed. "Every minute."

A familiar face entered the restaurant and did a double-take as the group of lads and their captor passed him.

"Hamza?" Logan called, beckoning him over.

Hamza took a moment to spot the DCI at the table, then came hurrying over. "Eh, alright, sir?" he asked. "What's all that about?"

"Just some lads being arseholes," Logan explained. "DCI Filson has it under control."

"Aye. I see that," Hamza said. "Who's DCI Filson, though?"

"You don't want to know," Shona told him.

"Mitchell brought her in to assist," Logan said. "She'll be gone tomorrow."

"Oh. Right," Hamza said. "Fair enough. Your, eh, your phone's off. I've been trying to get hold of you."

"Shite. Must've turned it off when I went for a kip," Logan said, searching his pockets. "What's up?"

"Just back from the club. Checking the security cameras."

"And?"

"Tampered with weeks ago," Hamza said. "But that's not the most interesting bit. I also ran into the owner. Or co-owner. Her husband, too. And, well, Sinead and Tyler have made some headway with Eva MacLean..."

Logan could've hugged him. All that new information, all those developments—he couldn't very well sit here eating at a time like this, could he? Not when there was work to be done. Not when there was a murder to solve.

And he'd been so enjoying the atmosphere, too...

"Damn it," he muttered, and it almost sounded convincing. "We're going to have to call a team meeting to go over it all, aren't we?"

"Uh, yeah. Yeah, I think that would be best, sir."

"Right, go get set up. I'll be right over," Logan told him, then he called out to him as he was nearing the door. "Oh, and Hamza?"

"Sir?"

"Do me a favour, and ask them if they can do our food to go..."

CHAPTER TWENTY-ONE

SHONA HAD SEEMED ALMOST as relieved as Logan was to call a halt to dinner. She'd taken her boxed-up share of the fish platter—most of it, since Logan wasn't particularly hungry —swapped dirty looks with Heather, then driven home to let Taggart out for a no-doubt much needed pee.

"Does she do that to you, too?" Heather had asked, as they waited for the lights at the crossing to change and the dual carriageway traffic to come to a stop.

"Do what?"

"Dictate when you can have a piss?"

Logan looked at her wearily. "Aye. She draws up a schedule," he replied, then he tutted. "Of course she doesn't. And she's gone now, you can stop."

Heather smirked, then reached inside the box she was carrying, plucked out a chip and tossed it in her mouth.

She chewed in silence while they waited for the lights to change.

"God, those lads were right," she remarked, her face contorting. "That does taste shite."

By the time Logan and Filson reached the Incident Room,

they'd both ditched their food, and were trying to remove grease from their fingers using the two tiny napkins they'd been provided, which had all the absorbent properties of a plank of wood.

"Alright, boss?" Tyler asked as the DCIs took their seats. He glanced at Heather, then added a hesitated. "..es. Bosses. Alright, bosses?"

"Don't give her the satisfaction, son," Logan told him. "DCI Filson is a guest here. I'm still in charge."

"That's not what Mitchell said," Heather reminded him. "You're not even supposed to be here."

"Aye, well, I am. So, you're free to leave anytime you like."

"I'm just starting to enjoy myself," Heather told him.

"Makes one of us," Logan muttered.

Sinead, who was making some finishing touches to the Big Board, caught the looks from Tyler and Hamza. Both men looked as uncomfortable as she felt, and even Dave—who was generally unfazed by most things—was keeping his head down and studiously cataloguing some further exhibits that had come in from Geoff Palmer's team.

"Right, where are we?" Logan asked. "What's the latest?"

"Actually..." Heather raised a hand to block Sinead's response. "Let's recap from the start. Catch me up. We were supposed to be doing that at dinner, but that didn't happen."

"Maybe if you'd shut your mouth for two minutes..." Logan countered.

"Tell me about the vic," Heather instructed. "Who is he?"

Sinead looked to Logan for approval. He tutted and shrugged, which she took as permission.

"His name's Dev Rani. Minority shareholder and manager of *Refuge*, the nightclub where he was found murdered. He's also on the Highland Council. Ward thirteen, Inverness West."

"What's his record like on the council?" Heather asked. "Any controversy, or made himself any enemies?"

"Not that we can see, no," Sinead replied. "Seems to have been pretty well thought of. Anyway, the nature of the attack suggests—"

"Something more personal than professional," Filson finished. "Yeah, noticed that."

"I wondered if maybe it was race-related," Hamza ventured. "Mr Rani had made a few complaints of racially motivated harassment in the past."

"What sort of stuff?" Heather asked. "Anything violent?"

"No. Abuse on social media. A few drunken comments from punters. Some graffiti in the club toilets." Hamza shook his head and shrugged. There was a weariness to both gestures. "Nothing unusual."

"Did it strike you as a racist attack?" Heather pressed.

"Not... not really," Hamza admitted.

"No. OK. Given the nature of the injuries, I'd say sexually motivated. Anyone disagree on that?"

Sinead joined Hamza and Tyler in looking at Logan. He shook his head. "She wasn't asking me. What do you think?"

It was Hamza who offered a response again. "Uh, depends what you mean," he said.

"Go on," Heather prompted.

"Well, do I think someone took sexual satisfaction out of it? No. I don't think so. It would've been over too quick," Hamza ventured. "But, that doesn't mean there was no sexual motivation behind it."

"You mean like someone out for revenge for something?" Tyler asked. He tipped his head towards his wife. "Because that's what we were thinking. His girlfriend was raging with him, wasn't she? Because she thought he'd been cheating on her with someone underage."

"And was he?" Logan asked. "How did you get on with the girl?"

"She says they did have sex, sir, yes," Sinead confirmed.

"She was sixteen at the time, but she claims he thought she was older. When he found out, he put a stop to it."

"Aw, what a bloody hero," Heather said, making no attempt to hide her sarcasm. "What was he, mid-thirties?"

"Thirty-five," Sinead confirmed.

"Thirty-five and shagging wee lassies," Filson continued. "Aye, that'll get you into trouble, right enough."

"Her dad's a right scary bastard, too," Tyler added. "I half thought he was going to stab *me*, and all I did was knock on his door."

"And did he know?" Logan asked. "About Dev and his daughter?"

"Don't think so, boss," Tyler admitted. "When we asked Eva, she said she'd never told him, and when we mentioned Dev's name at the house, he didn't seem to know who we were talking about."

"Still, worth digging around," Logan said. "See if there's anything interesting in his background."

"I can get on that," Dave announced. "Finished checking this stuff in, so I'm at a bit of a loose end, anyway."

"Nice one," Tyler said. "Cheers for that."

"Nae bother!" Dave said, and he turned his attention to his computer screen.

"Could it have been the girl herself?" Heather wondered. "If she was into him, and he rejected her, that might've prompted some mad as fuck bollock stabbing."

"I mean... maybe. But, I don't think so, no," Sinead replied. "She didn't know Dev was dead. Or she certainly acted like she didn't, anyway. Completely broke down when we told her. Didn't get much out of her after that, and ended up getting Uniform to take her home once she'd calmed down a bit."

"She said she loved him," Tyler added.

Heather put her fingers in her mouth like she was going to make herself throw up. "Oh, God, spare me the nausea of a lovesick teenager," she groaned, then she waved a hand vaguely in the direction of the Big Board. "What about the scene? What's the report on that saying?"

It took a second for the sudden change of conversational track to shunt into place in Sinead's head, then she rattled off the details she'd written up for the board earlier that day.

"No sign of forced entry. The doors were locked, but the back one locks automatically when pulled shut from the outside, so we're thinking the killer went out that way. No CCTV out there, and no passing traffic, so it would've made it easy to slip away unnoticed. Especially at that time of night."

"You checked cameras on the streets around there?" Heather asked.

Sinead looked almost embarrassed by the question. "Uh, well, there aren't any," she said.

Heather's frown had a hint of amusement to it. "Sorry? But it's the town centre, isn't it?"

"City centre," Logan corrected. "And yes. But we don't have the same CCTV coverage up here as down the road."

"Evidently," Heather said. "So, we've got no footage of anyone approaching or heading away from the club at any point?"

"No," Sinead confirmed. "We could ask for dashcam footage. That's proven useful before. It was late, but... taxis, maybe?"

"What about inside the club? They must've had security, right?" Heather asked. She looked expectantly around at the team. "You do actually have access to video technology up here, yes...? I'm not introducing new concepts you've never heard before?"

"No, ma'am. You're not," Hamza assured her. He'd spotted Logan's jaw clenching and his shoulders squaring off, and had jumped in quickly before an argument could completely derail proceedings. "There's actually a pretty solid system in place in the nightclub. One of the better ones I've come across."

Heather rubbed her hands together. "Nice! So, what have we got on there, then?"

Hamza hesitated, before taking the plunge. "Nothing."

DCI Filson's hands dropped down into her lap. "Nothing? What do you mean?"

"Someone had tampered with the system. Not recently, either. Couple of weeks back. Knew what they were doing, too, I'd say. It was pretty clever."

"Oh, good. Well, I'm glad you're impressed," Heather told him, and there was a note of reproach mingled in there somewhere. "How does it help us nail the bastard?"

"It, eh, it doesn't," Hamza admitted, then he rallied and stood his ground. "Although, it tells us the killer's tech-savvy, which is something."

"If it was even the killer who did it," Heather countered. "Could've been a staff member with their fingers in the till. Might have been the victim himself, trying to cover something up. You're telling me someone messed with the security system. Fine. But unless you can prove who it was, then don't waste my time. Alright?"

Hamza nodded. It was a slow and wary thing, like he was worried he might trigger something explosive. "Aye. OK. I'll keep digging."

"Good. You do that. And, you be sure to keep me posted, Detective Sergeant," Heather told him. "But for now, what I'm hearing is that we've got sweet fuck all in the way of footage. From anywhere. That correct?"

"Um, yeah. Yeah, that's right," Hamza confirmed.

"OK, so... fingerprints? DNA? Anything on that front?" DCI Filson asked.

"Oh aye, loads," Tyler said. "Prints and DNA from about

four hundred punters and staff. It would take months to sift through it all."

"And the budget's not there for that," Logan said. "Not without a damn good reason."

Heather made a low grumbling sound. Budgetary issues were not unique to the Highlands. She'd had avenues of investigation closed off to her several times before on the basis that she couldn't justify the cost.

"Jesus." She put her hands on her head and studied the board. "Staff been interviewed?"

"Yeah, they would have been," Sinead confirmed. "Uniform took statements."

"Any of them see anything?" Logan asked.

"Doubt it, boss. Uniform would've flagged it if there was anything they thought was important," Tyler said. "Want me to take a look, though?"

"Why are you even asking me that?" Heather said before Logan could open his mouth. "Yes. Of course. Check. Because, right now, it looks to me like we've got a whole lot of fuck all else to be going on with."

While Tyler jumped into his seat and started to type, Hamza cleared his throat. "Actually, that's not quite true," he volunteered. "I went to the club to check the footage, but I got interrupted by..." He flipped open his notepad and squinted at his untidy handwriting. "...Timothy and Maude Willington-Smythe."

"Who are they when they're at home?" Logan asked.

"She's old money, sir. Owns a big estate in Moray. Passed down for generations."

"Oh. One of those bastards," grunted Logan, who had an instinctive disliking for toffs, particularly those who'd been handed their wealth and status on a platter.

"The husband was a plumber," Hamza continued. "He's making an effort to fit in with her lifestyle, I think, but he looks pretty out of his depth. She definitely wears the trousers."

"I feel like I'm reading the bloody society pages of a newspaper here," Heather interjected. "Who are they in relation to old Billy-No-Bollocks in the bogs?"

"Uh, aye. Sorry. She put most of the money up for the club," Hamza explained. "Couple of hundred grand, she tells me."

Logan whistled through his teeth. "Big investment. Were they friends before then or something?"

Hamza shook his head. "Not really. They'd just met at a couple of Chamber of Commerce things, and had got talking about the nightclub business."

"That's a big chunk of cash to give to a stranger to start a club," Heather said. "Sure there was nothing else going on between them?"

"She says not."

DCI Filson tutted. "Aye. Well, she would, wouldn't she? What did the husband say?"

"Actually, he said... Well, suggested, that Maude and Dev were having some sort of relationship. He seemed pretty adamant, actually. It was only when his wife pointed out that he was risking making himself the prime suspect that he shut up about it."

"Do you think he was right?" Logan asked.

"I don't know, sir."

"Gut instinct?"

"Gut instinct...?" Hamza sucked in his cheeks, then shook his head. "I'd say I think he believed it, but I couldn't make a call on whether he was just being paranoid or not."

Sinead sat on the edge of her desk. "What did she look like?"

"Uh, bit... bigger," Hamza said. "Heavy build. Good few years older. And a bit, sort of, horsey-looking. Long face. Serious teeth."

"Based on the two women we know he was in a sexual relationship with, she doesn't sound like his type," Sinead said.

"No, she'll have gone through puberty," Heather remarked.

"She's maybe not his traditional type," Logan said. "But, if she was game, and he thought his source of funds might start drying up, his 'type' might be pretty flexible."

"She doesn't sound very flexible, boss," Tyler said, looking up from his computer and grinning. The smile quickly evaporated in the heat of Heather's glare, and he hurriedly ducked back down out of sight behind his monitor.

"It doesn't matter if they were shagging or not," Heather pointed out. "If the husband believed it, then that's motive. That makes him a suspect, along with... who else?"

It was clear from the way she asked the question that she already knew the answer. This was another test. Obviously, she'd learned a lot from Logan over the years.

Sinead was first to put forward a name. "Cassandra, his ex. She was furious with him."

"Eva, I suppose," Tyler said. "Spurned teenager with a broken heart."

"Or her dad, if it turns out he knew about their relationship," Hamza added.

Tyler winced. "Aye. Wouldn't fancy being on the wrong side of that conversation," he admitted.

"So, who do we bring in first?" Logan asked.

"One other thing," Hamza said. "Might not be anything, but the owner—Maude—she thought the body had been found last night."

"How do you mean?" Logan asked. "She knew about it in advance?"

"Oh. No, sir. Just... she'd been told the cleaners found it. The cleaners normally come in after closing and do their stuff then."

Logan blinked. It was slow and methodical. He was feeling

significantly better than earlier, but his inner ear was still grumbling whenever he made any sudden movements, and he didn't want to chance setting it off.

"So, why wasn't that the case this time?" he asked. "Why the change?"

"Don't know, sir," Hamza admitted.

"They didn't say anything about it when you interviewed them?"

Sinead and Hamza swapped synchronised looks and shakes of the head.

"Not a thing, sir," Sinead told him.

"To be honest, I'm not sure Maude was exactly up to speed with the day to day running of the place, so she might have been wrong," Hamza said. "But I thought it might be worth checking up on, out of interest."

"Eh, speaking of things worth checking up on..." Tyler announced. He gestured to his screen like he was inviting them all to read it, then went ahead and told them what it said. "Got a statement here from one of the members of the bar staff. Says that Dev's ex came to the club yesterday and they had a big shouting match in his office. Proper barney, it says here."

"Is this..." Logan's eyes flitted to the Big Board. His nausea levels didn't thank him for it. "...Cassandra Leigh-Taylor?"

"He doesn't give a name, boss, but the guy mentions in his statement that he thinks she's an artist, so must be," Tyler said.

"What were they arguing about?" asked DCI Filson.

"Doesn't say," Tyler replied. "They couldn't make out the words, could just tell it was a big argument."

"The office has soundproofing on the walls," Hamza explained.

"That's a bit creepy, isn't it?" Tyler asked. "Bit serial-killery. What's he done that for?"

"It's a nightclub," said Sinead. "Probably about keeping the sound out, rather than keeping it in."

"Oh. Aye. Aye, that makes sense," her husband agreed.

"And she didn't mention this argument to you?" Logan asked Sinead.

"No, sir. She said she tried calling him last night, but that she hadn't seen him in days."

Heather sprang to her feet. "Well, looks like we know who we're bringing in first!" she said, looking around at the others. "Who wants to come with me to bring her in?"

Nobody answered. Nobody volunteered. Heather shrugged, and with a point and a snap of her fingers, selected Sinead.

"You. With me," she instructed.

"Are we no' jumping the gun a bit here?" Logan asked. "We're not even sure it was her. We've got one witness who couldn't even tell us her name."

"Good point," Heather said, and this time she jabbed a finger at Hamza. "Get onto the guy who gave the statement. Get him to give you a description. Show him a picture if you can find one. I want to know for sure it was her."

"Eh, right, aye." Hamza nodded, then turned in his chair to face his screen.

"Good. Everyone else better go chug some caffeine." Heather pulled on a puffy black jacket and fastened the zip all the way to the top with a swift, sudden jerk. "Nobody's leaving here tonight until we nail this bitch!"

CHAPTER TWENTY-TWO

THE RAIN that had ushered them from the car to the theatre front door had dulled to a light drizzle by the time the show came to an end. It was the sort of rain that visitors to the Highlands might find irritating, but which locals would fail to notice. It wasn't so much *background* rain as *baseline* rain—the level of rain to which all other instances of weather could be compared.

While, to the non-native, it was clearly raining, to those who'd been brought up in the area, it wasn't. Aye, it was raining, but it wasn't *raining*. This wasn't *rain* rain. Rain was the next step up on the scale, followed by 'raining heavy' and 'pishing down.'

Everything below the baseline was usually met with surprise, and accompanied by the conversational phrase, "Still, at least it's dry," as if this were some sort of miracle that nobody could quite allow themselves to believe, much less get used to.

Ben wasn't technically native to the Highlands, but he had lived there for years, and had spent most of his life in the similarly precipitationally blessed west coast. Moira was a Highlander born and bred, and had spent much of that time in and around Fort William. To her, even *rain* didn't count as rain, and she wouldn't entertain the thought of a waterproof jacket or brolly until they were through 'pishing down' and deep into 'blowing a hoolie.'

The inside of Eden Court theatre had been stiflingly warm by the time all the singing and dancing was over, and the cool drizzle was not unwelcome when Ben and Moira shuffled out as part of a slow-moving caterpillar of theatre patrons squeezing its way through the front doors.

They stepped clear of the crowds once outside, and both looked genuinely confused by the half-dozen or so umbrellas that were raised by the punters around them.

"Well, that was quite a show," Ben remarked. "I mean, I will say, I don't know what they were all moaning about. Working nine-to-five sounds like a bloody dream. No night shifts. Scheduled breaks. They don't know their luck."

"Aye, that's young people for you," Moira said. "Scared of a hard day's work."

"Still. Good show, though," Ben said. He rocked on his heels, nodded slowly, then agreed with himself. "Aye. Good show."

He usually had a pretty decent handle on small talk. He was able to chat freely to most people, regardless of their age, status, or even whether or not they'd recently murdered someone.

Normally, he could chat away to Moira quite the thing, too. But then, they were usually arguing. She was an easy woman to disagree with, and he enjoyed their back-and-forth. The one thing they had previously enjoyed together had been a ludicrous magazine filled with horrifying 'true life' stories. They'd both got a laugh at that, and it had been a refreshing change from their bickering.

Tonight was different, though. Felt different. Tonight, small talk was a struggle.

"Did, eh... did you enjoy it?"

Moira clutched her handbag and contorted her face like she was struggling with a stubborn bowel movement. "I didn't like it."

"You didn't?"

Moira shook her head. "No. Not really."

Ben snorted. "My arse!"

"I beg your pardon?"

"I saw your toes tapping away, you lying old bastard," Ben said, calling her out. "I heard you humming along."

"OK, fine. Some of the tunes were quite catchy," Moira admitted.

"And you were laughing," Ben said. "Which, I have to say, I didn't know you could do."

"Of course I can laugh!" Moira snapped. "I'm not a... non-laughing robot."

"Aye, because they're definitely a thing," Ben mumbled below his breath.

"And I did quite like when they were plotting murder," Moira added. "We've all done that, haven't we?"

"What, made plans to murder a boss?" Ben asked. He was about to deny this, then he thought about former Detective Superintendent Bob Hoon for a few moments. "Aye. Aye, I suppose so," he confessed.

"Right. Well. I suppose I'll get a taxi to the hotel."

"Aye. Right. Well, if you think... Aye, I suppose that's..." Ben looked over to the road, like he might find a cab waiting there with its light on. When he didn't, he reached into his jacket and took out his phone. "I can call one. Or I could give you a lift. I don't mind."

Moira's mouth tightened like it had just filled up with vinegar. "I think a taxi would be more appropriate."

"Aye. Aye, of course," Ben said, nodding his agreement more wholeheartedly than he'd intended. "I'll just have to find a number, since I don't really use taxis round here, so I'm not sure—"

"Unless..."

Ben looked up from his phone. "Unless?"

Moira's body was stiff. Her jaw was clenched. She clutched her bag like it was a shield with which she might protect herself.

"Unless you know somewhere to go dancing?" she said.

"Dancing?" Ben glanced back at the theatre window, and the poster for the show they'd just seen. "What, like...?"

"Oh, yes. Exactly like that," Moira said, and sarcasm oozed from every syllable. "Hang on and I'll do some cartwheels and a jumping splits while I'm at it, will I? You can watch my hips just going flying off into the distance."

Ben chuckled at the image, then chewed his bottom lip for a while as he thought. The flood of people leaving the theatre was now a trickle. The drizzle had dissipated completely, so it was officially no longer raining in any sense of the word.

"Dancing?" he said, and he tried very hard not to smile. "I'm sure we can find somewhere."

Moira's only reply was a curt nod. Ben tucked his hands into his pockets, then angled the arm closest to her outwards—just enough that she'd notice it, but not enough that he couldn't deny he'd meant anything by it if she started giving him grief.

To his surprise, she hooked her own arm through the gap, and he felt her weight against him.

"It's a bit of a walk back across the bridge into town," he told her, as they set off. "You sure you're going to be OK?"

"I'm not a bloody invalid," Moira told him. "And I'm not the one with the dicky ticker. It's you who should be hanging onto me."

Ben laughed. "Aye. Fair point," he said, then he looked up at the sky overhead. Stars were appearing as the rain clouds parted. "Still, at least it's dry," he remarked.

"Aye," Moira agreed, as they fell into step on the pavement.

"At least it's dry."

———

Hamza stood in the car park at Burnett Road, jigging on the spot to keep warm as he listened to the voice on the other end of the line. He'd come out without his jacket, and the evening air had a real chill to it.

On the other hand, at least it wasn't raining.

"I know. I know, I told Kamila we'd finish the story tonight," Hamza said. He rubbed his forehead with finger and thumb. "Yeah, I know she'll be fine with you doing one, it's just... I'd promised we'd do that one."

He listened. Nodded. Smiled. "No, I know you will. And... thanks. It's just..." He sighed. "Tell her I'm really sorry, will you? Tell her we'll carry on tomorrow, and we'll stay up all night to get it finished, if we have to."

He listened again, then laughed. "Aye, we'll keep our voices down so you can get your beauty sleep. Not that you need it!" he added hastily, then he flinched like his wife had thumped him one through the phone. "As if I would say such a thing!"

Hamza laughed, then he leaned back against the bonnet of his car and looked up. Even with the light pollution from the city, stars sparkled like precious gems on the black silk cloth of night. He watched them sparkling and listened to his wife's voice in his ear.

"I love you, too, Amira," he told her. "I'll try and not wake you up when I get in."

They said the last of their farewells, then Hamza returned the phone to his pocket, shivered like he could chase away the cold evening air, then hurried back inside the station.

He took the stairs two at a time, the sudden burst of cardiovascular exercise getting his blood pumping and helping to warm him up so that by the time he arrived back in the Incident

Room, he was no longer suffering from the nipple chafe that had plagued him for the previous several minutes.

He entered the room to find Tyler standing by the Big Board, a pad of *Post-it Notes* and a pen in hand.

"Watch you don't mess with her system," Hamza warned, as the door swung closed behind him. "Not sure your marriage would survive."

"Aye, I know," Tyler said, appearing genuinely concerned by the potential consequences of what he was about to do. "Just... we got some new info. The boss said I should update it."

Hamza noticed the empty chair that had previously been occupied by Logan.

"Where is he?"

Tyler looked towards the private office at the back of the room. Technically, it was where Logan was supposed to set up camp, but the DCI had always preferred to sit out here with the rest of the team, and the office was rarely used.

Now, the blinds had all been drawn, and the door was firmly shut.

"Said he was going to make a few phone calls. Not going to be long, apparently."

"Oh. Right." Hamza stared at the door for a while, like he could somehow see through it. "He having a kip, do you think?"

"No he is not!" came a muffled reply from inside the office, and Hamza and Tyler both ducked like they expected a projectile to come crashing through the glass.

"Sorry, sir!" Hamza called back, then he tiptoed to his seat and motioned to the stationery that Tyler was clutching. "What's the latest, then?"

"It was Dave who dug it up," Tyler said, indicating the constable in the corner.

Dave lowered his head as if accepting a medal from the Queen. "Nae bother," he said.

Hamza looked from one to the other. "Well? What was it?"

Tyler opened his mouth to explain, then closed it again and motioned for Dave to do the honours.

"It's your man," Dave began. "Tony MacLean."

Hamza's brow furrowed, like he couldn't place the name. "Tony MacLean?"

"Eva's dad," Tyler clarified.

"Eva the seventeen-year-old? Right, aye. What about him?"

"He's got a record," Dave said. "Quite an impressive one, actually. Lot of violence. Assaulting police officers, resisting arrest... and I'm pretty sure his CV will have 'Breach of the Peace' listed under 'Hobbies.'"

"I mean, none of this is surprising if you've seen him," Tyler said. He nodded to Dave. "Tell him what else."

"He's got a court date next month on an assault charge," Dave continued. "He leathered shite out of a young guy. Nineteen. Said, and I quote, 'This is what you get for trying to fuck my daughter.'"

"Bloody hell," Hamza muttered.

"Aye. So, we know he's overly protective when it comes to Eva. That's what he did to a guy roughly her own age who he thought was just *trying* to shag her," Tyler said. "What do we reckon he'd do to an older guy who had been at it with her?"

"Stab him repeatedly in the cock and bollocks?" Hamza suggested.

"Doesn't seem beyond the realms of possibility, does it?" Tyler said.

Hamza swivelled in his chair so he was looking straight at the Big Board. "No. It doesn't," he agreed. "We bringing him in?"

"Boss wants us to do a bit more digging first. See if we can find any connection between him and Dev before we make a move," Tyler replied. "Besides, Sinead and the scary new woman should be picking up Dev's ex-girlfriend..." He checked his watch. "Right about... now."

CHAPTER TWENTY-THREE

CASSANDRA LEIGH-TAYLOR WASN'T ANSWERING her door or picking up her phone. The lights were off in her ground floor flat, and there were no obvious signs of life inside.

DCI Heather Filson and DC Sinead Bell waited by her front door, which opened directly onto the street. Sinead had her mobile to her ear, and could hear Cassandra's landline ringing out inside the flat.

"Still nothing," Heather said, and it was more of a statement than a question. She tutted, returned to one of the flat's two front windows, and cupped her hands against the glass, trying to find a clear view of the inside.

A set of Venetian blinds had been drawn, but not quite all the way, so it was possible to see a couple of feet into the room, as long as you had excellent night vision, and didn't mind exclusively looking at the floor.

"Should I keep trying?" Sinead asked.

"Don't bother. She's not going to answer," Heather said. "And the ringing is really starting to get on my tits."

"I can try her mobile again," Sinead suggested.

Heather shrugged. "You think sixth-time-lucky, maybe?

Sinead looked at her phone. "She's not going to answer, is she?"

"Nope. I'd say that's pretty unlikely at this stage."

There was a rattle of metal as Sinead checked the door handle again. Still locked. No surprise there.

"We could try and get a warrant," she said. "And I can see if we can get a location ping from her mobile. If she's done a runner, we can maybe track her that way."

"Aye, maybe." Heather shuffled sideways and stood on her tiptoes, trying to see more of the room through the glass. "Actually, no. Changed my mind. Call her again, will you? Her mobile."

Sinead did as instructed. She shifted her weight from foot to foot as she waited for the call to connect.

"It's ringing," she announced.

"Shh." Heather urged. She froze like a meerkat, one ear cocked towards the glass. "I hear it. It's in there. It's on vibrate."

"What? Are you sure?" Sinead asked, joining the DCI by the window. She removed the phone from her ear, then listened, her head tilted just like Heather's. "Oh! Yeah. I hear it buzzing, it's..."

Through a gap at the edge of the blinds, she saw the glow of the phone's screen. It was dim, and if the room hadn't been in near-total darkness, she wouldn't have spotted it.

"I see it," she announced. "It's lying there on..."

She stopped. No. Not *on*. It wasn't on something.

It was *in* something.

A hand, lying motionless on the floor.

"Shite. I think... I think she's there. Cassandra. She's... unconscious. Or dead. I don't know, she's not..."

Sinead ducked at the sound of shattering glass, then spun to see Heather jamming her arm through a broken glass pane in the front door.

"Jesus. You don't hang about," she remarked.

"Nope. Occupant in danger. Perfect excuse," Heather said, and by the time she'd finished replying she had already undone the catch and gone barging on into the flat.

The smell hit Sinead as soon as she entered. It was the taste of old coins and dental procedures. Copper, snagging at the back of the throat.

She felt her stomach twitch, and her feet slow. Heather had already gone racing into the living room and flicked on a light. Her gasp of shock reached all the way back to the front door and dragged Sinead onwards through the thickening stench.

The first thing that Sinead saw when she entered the room was Cassandra Leigh-Taylor. She lay on the floor, surrounded by empty wine bottles, snoring lightly with her phone in one hand, and a paintbrush in the other.

"Well, she's alive," Heather said. She was kneeling next to the sleeping woman, checking her breathing and her pulse rate. "Just pished, I think." She thumbed open one of Cassandra's eyelids and watched how the pupil reacted. "Maybe wasted, actually. We'd better call an ambulance."

"Right. On it," Sinead said.

Before she could make the call, she saw the second thing of note in the room. It was brought to her attention by DCI Filson, who pointed it out with a sharp nod of her head.

"That's some painting she was working on, eh?"

A canvas was propped up on the big easel Sinead had seen earlier. The artwork could be described as 'abstract,' but might equally have been called, 'demented.'

The canvas had been covered with wild, swinging daubs of red. They hadn't absorbed into the surface well, and ran in thick rivulets down its front, pooling in the base of the easel, and dripping through the narrow gaps.

"Aye. It's some painting, right enough," Sinead agreed.

She picked up a large plastic container with the lid missing.

Moving the tub in a circle, she gave the red liquid inside it a cautious swirl around. Her mouth soured at the familiar coppery smell of it.

"Except, I really don't think this is paint."

———

The sound of a phone ringing made Logan open an eye. The, "Fucking hell!" from Tyler made him stop reclining in the chair and sit up straight.

He hadn't been sleeping. He didn't think so, anyway. He'd just retired to the office so the painkillers he'd recently necked had a chance to kick in. Had he leaned back in his chair and shut his eyes? Yes. Had he fallen asleep? No. Definitely not.

He wiped a string of drool on his shirt sleeve, glanced around surreptitiously like he was worried someone might have seen this, then hauled himself to his feet.

By the time he made it out of the office, Tyler was hanging up the phone.

"What's happened?" the DCI grunted, sounding for all the world like someone who had just been woken from a pleasant and much-needed nap.

"That was Sinead, boss. They found Cassandra Leigh-Taylor out of the game in her living room. Ambulance is there now. They're not sure if it's drink, drugs, or a meal deal of the two," Tyler said.

"Oh. Right," Logan said, a little disappointed. The shock in Tyler's voice had promised more. "Is that it?"

"Not by a long shot, boss," Tyler said, bouncing like an excited puppy. "Turns out, she was working on a new painting. It was there on the stand thingy when they arrived."

"Easel," Hamza said.

"What? Oh, aye. That."

Logan felt his headache creeping back. He sighed. "Well, I'm sure that's big news for art collectors, son, but I don't see why we should give a flying—"

"It wasn't paint, boss," Tyler said, practically *squeeing* with glee. "That she was using to paint with, I mean. It wasn't paint." He looked around at the faces of the three other men, making sure he had their full attention. "It was blood."

"Blood?" Hamza asked. "As in...?"

"As in the red stuff that comes out when you cut yourself, aye," Tyler replied.

"Do we know whose blood it is?" Logan asked.

"Not yet, boss. As far as the girls can tell, Cassandra wasn't injured or anything, so probably not hers. Not unless she's kept it knocking around for a while, anyway."

Logan had more questions about the gruesome discovery, but first there was another important issue to address.

"Did you just call Sinead and DCI Filson 'the girls?'" he asked.

Tyler hesitated. "Eh, I'm not sure, boss. Maybe, aye."

Logan winced and cast a brief look towards the door to make sure neither woman was standing there listening in.

"For your own safety, son, I'm going to strongly suggest you don't include DCI Filson and the phrase 'the girls' in the same sentence again," he said, his voice low and secretive. "If she heard that, your arse would be out the window. And I don't mean in a metaphorical *you'd be in big trouble* sort of sense. I mean your literal arse would be out the actual window, quickly followed by the rest of you."

"Eh, aye. Right you are, boss," Tyler said. "Sorry."

Logan dismissed the apology with a wave of a hand, then lowered himself down into his chair. "Right. The blood. What's the score?"

"Uh, OK. So... the, eh, ladies..."

"That's not much better, son," Logan interjected.

Tyler took a moment to organise the next sentence in his head before coming out with it. "Sinead and DCI Filson..."

"There we go," Logan said.

"They've asked us to get Scene of Crime over there. They're going to secure the scene once the paramedics have gone, then Palmer's team can go in and do their thing."

"Blood could be from an animal. No saying it's anything dodgy," Hamza said. He considered this statement for a moment, then added, "I mean, it's weird either way, obviously. But it might not be connected, is what I'm saying."

"No, could be nothing," Logan agreed. "Was there anything in the PM about there being less blood than expected at the scene?"

Tyler, Hamza, and Dave all exchanged blank looks, then DS Khaled answered. "Nothing that I saw, sir. Maybe worth asking Shona?"

"Aye. Aye, I'll give her a ring," Logan said. "In the meantime, get Palmer and his lot over to the address. I want to know as soon as possible whether that blood is human, and if it matches Dev Rani's blood type, so tell them not to stand around with their fingers up their arses."

Hamza picked up the phone and started to dial. "I'll maybe leave off that last part," he said. He listened to the ringing from the other end of the line. "Unless it's Palmer, obviously. Then I'll say it."

He ran his tongue against the back of his teeth, checked his watch, and waited for someone to pick up.

A few seconds later, there was a click, and Hamza swapped the handset from one ear to the other. "Geoff?" he said. A smile tugged at the corners of his mouth, and his gaze flicked over to where the DCI sat. "Detective Chief Inspector Logan has asked me to pass on a request..."

———

Sinead stood outside Cassandra Leigh-Taylor's flat, inhaling fresh air. Her eyes were closed, but the swishing blue lights of the ambulance brought colour and texture to the darkness.

She listened to the driver's door closing, and the rumble of the engine turning over, then opened her eyes in time to see the vehicle pulling away from the kerb. There had been a roll of cordon tape on the rear floor of DCI Filson's car, half-hidden by empty *Coke* bottles and petrol station sandwich wrappers.

Between them, they'd cordoned off the pavement around the front of the flat, and also blocked access to the small garden area out the back. Technically, this was shared with the neighbour upstairs, but judging by the state of it, and the length of the grass, nobody had made use of it in a very long time, so it was unlikely that he'd have grounds to complain.

"You alright?"

Sinead jumped a little when she realised Heather was standing beside her. "Oh. Sorry. Yeah. Just getting some air. Smells in there."

Heather glanced back at the door. "Aye. Aye, I suppose so."

"Stuff like that doesn't usually bother me, but... I don't know. Hope I'm not coming down with DCI Logan's bug."

"What, man flu?" Heather asked. "Since when do we ever have time for that?"

Sinead smiled. "Fair point." She side-eyed the older officer. "You've, eh, you've known him for a while?"

"Who, Jack? Aye. Twelve years, maybe. Fifteen." She sniffed. Shrugged. "I can't say I got it when he decided to move up here. I mean, what's this place got that Glasgow doesn't?"

Sinead's reply came out slowly, like she was testing the floor beneath her for fear that she might fall right through.

"Maybe it's not what it's got," she ventured. "Maybe it's what it doesn't have."

Heather frowned. "What do you mean?"

"I mean... I got the impression there were some bad memories," Sinead replied. "The whole Mister Whisper thing. And I'm sure other cases, too. I think... I think maybe this was a way to put all that behind him."

Heather scraped her teeth across her bottom lip before replying. "A fresh start?"

"Something like that, yeah."

"Aye, well. Alright for some," Heather said, and there was a coldness to it that lingered in the air between them.

"Eh, sorry if that caused offence or anything..." Sinead said, sensing the chill.

"Offence? No. God. Takes a lot more than that to offend me," Heather said. She looked back over her shoulder again at the flat behind them. "And, I have to say, I thought he'd come up here for a quiet life, but you get some messed up shit going on up here, don't you?"

Sinead laughed at that. "God, yes. We had a guy calling himself the Iceman freezing people to death for a while. Beheadings. Occult stuff in Loch Ness..."

"Jesus, seriously?"

Sinead nodded. "Then there was one guy who thought we were all living in a computer game..."

Heather snorted. "Bollocks! Now you're ripping the piss."

"All true! I swear."

"Fucking hell," Heather muttered, and she looked up and down the street as if she might see some of these cases playing out somewhere. "Must be something in the water. Mind you, we've had some right weird bastards down the road, too. One guy had a *Sooty* glove puppet—you know, the wee orange bear thing off the telly?"

"I'm aware of his work, aye," Sinead confirmed.

"It was telling him to kill women," Heather revealed. "Whispering to him, he said. The puppet. *Sooty*. Creepy as hell." She shrugged. "I mean, it wasn't actually whispering to him, obviously, he was just mental, but still. Only case I've worked where, as well as being prosecuted for murder, the killer got served a cease and desist by *CITV*."

Sinead laughed again. They both looked out across the darkened street, the cordon tape flapping in the breeze behind them.

"It's a fucking ridiculous job, isn't it?" Heather remarked.

"Aye," said Sinead after a moment's pause. "Aye, I suppose it is."

They stood there silently for a while, each lost in their own thoughts. Finally, Heather checked her watch. "It's late. No point both of us standing around here waiting for Scene of Crime to turn up."

"No. Suppose not," Sinead agreed.

Heather reached into her pocket, found her car keys, then handed them over. "Take my car. Just leave it at the station."

Sinead gratefully accepted the keys. It had been a long shift, and the cold of the pavement wasn't helping her aching feet.

"Are you sure?" she asked.

"Aye. Just don't crash it," Heather said. "I mean, not that anyone would probably notice, it's pretty banged up as it is."

Sinead smiled. "I'd spotted a dent or two, right enough."

"Is that it? Obviously, you weren't looking very closely," Heather said, then she indicated the bridge at the end of the street with a jab of her thumb. "I just walk this way, do I?"

Sinead blinked in surprise. "Sorry?"

"To get to the station," Heather said, backing away in the direction she'd pointed.

"Oh. So you're...?" Sinead stole a look at the car keys in her hand. "So, I'll stay here, and...?"

"Yeah. Like we said, no point us both standing here," Heather replied. "So... it's this way?"

Sinead nodded. She smiled, but it was a thin and insipid thing. "Aye. Aye, it's that way," she said.

And then, with a raised thumb and a wink, DCI Filson turned on her heels, and set off across the river, leaving Sinead to stand guard of Cassandra Leigh-Taylor's flat, all alone.

CHAPTER TWENTY-FOUR

SHONA MAGUIRE SAT on the couch, the index finger of her left hand raised while, with her right, she attempted to balance a dog treat on Taggart's nose. The dog, for its part, was practically going cross-eyed as it tried to focus on the tiny T-bone steak shaped snack on his snout.

"OK, Tag. So, wait..." Shona said, withdrawing her right hand while keeping her finger raised. "*Waaa-ait...*"

Taggart did not wait. He ducked his head, and snapped his jaws around the treat the moment it slid off. His tail thumped happily on the floor and he sat up, straight and proud.

He liked this game.

"No, you're supposed to..." Shona began, then the ringing of her mobile stopped her. "We're going to come back to this," she told the dog. "You're not getting off that easily."

She checked the name on the screen, prepared herself for news—bad or good, she wasn't sure—and answered.

"Jack. Hello. You OK?"

"Aye. Aye, feeling better," Logan replied.

"Feeling better in general, or better than you were earlier?" Shona pressed.

"Either. Both. Whichever one stops you worrying," Logan told her. "Anyway, I've got Heather here to tend to all my needs."

Shona's eyes widened for a moment, before the penny dropped. "You're hilarious."

"Aye, I thought so," Logan agreed.

"She still around, then?" Shona asked, trying very hard to sound like she couldn't care less either way. "Not gone back to Glasgow yet?"

"She's still around somewhere, aye," Logan said. "Out with Sinead. Made a bit of a find, actually. You might be able to help us out with it."

Shona sat forward. Taggart's gaze followed her, then very deliberately went to the bag of treats sitting on the arm of the couch, politely drawing her attention to them. "What is it? Another body?"

"Oh. No, no, nothing like that," Logan said. "I wanted to check up on the last one. Dev Rani."

"He's still dead, as far as I know," Shona said.

"Shame. Make life a lot easier if he suddenly came to," Logan said. "It was his blood I was interested in."

"His blood?"

"Specifically, the amount of it. You saw him there on the toilet floor. You got a good look at him?"

"I mean... aye. He was obviously dead, so I tried not to compromise the scene, but... Why?" Shona asked. "What do you want to know?"

"You think he had the right amount of blood?"

Shona's lips moved silently as she replayed the question, hoping it would make sense the second time around.

It didn't.

"Do I think he had the right amount of blood?" she asked. "I mean, no. Obviously not."

She heard Logan's chair creaking, and could picture him

sitting forward in it.

"He didn't?"

"No. Otherwise he wouldn't have bled to death."

There was another squeak of leather and metal, and she imagined him sitting back again.

"Aye. No, I mean, between the body and the surrounding area. The amount of blood at the scene. Did it strike you as too little?"

"There was loads," Shona told him.

"Aye, but do you think that was his full body's worth of blood? Could someone have... taken some?"

"What, like a vampire?" Shona asked.

"Or a crazy woman with a plastic tub," answered Logan.

Shona blew out her cheeks. Taggart gave a brief growl that sounded not unlike a clearing of the throat, and once again tried drawing the pathologist's attention to the bag of dog treats beside her.

"It depends," Shona said.

"On what?"

"On how big the tub is. I mean, it's hard to say for sure, but I don't remember thinking, 'This isn't much blood,' when I walked in. In fact, I thought the opposite of that. Was it a full ten pints, though? I don't know. But I doubt it was far off it."

"But it could've been nine pints, say?"

"Yeah. Could've been. Geoff might be able to give you a better idea," Shona said.

"Aye. Maybe," Logan said. "He's heading out to check a flat for us the now. I'll get someone else to ask him later. After the spewing incident, I don't imagine he'll be talking to me yet."

"Or ever again," Shona said.

"I should be so bloody lucky," Logan replied.

Down the line, Shona heard the sound of a door swinging open, and some muffled conversation. She recognised Tyler's voice, and what she thought was a woman's, too.

"That's... the others back," Logan said, demonstrating a surprising degree of diplomacy. "I'd better see where we are."

"Right. Yeah, of course. If you need me for anything else..."

"I won't. We should be fine," Logan said.

"Right. OK. Cool." A thought occurred to her. "You haven't got your car. I can come pick you up. I mean, when you're ready."

"No, don't worry about me. Just you head to your bed. Don't wait up. It could be a late one. I'll get Uniform to drop me off when we're done."

Shona hesitated. "OK. Well, if you're sure..."

"I have to go," Logan said. The voices behind him had raised a little. "I'll see you later."

"Yeah," Shona began, then the line went dead. She kept the phone to her ear for a few moments, then lowered it. "See you later."

———

"You just left her there? On her own?"

Tyler was on his feet, his head tick-tocking between DCI Filson and the door behind her, like Sinead might come traipsing through it at any moment.

Logan replaced his desk phone in its cradle, then swung his chair around to face the drama.

"Well, yes," DCI Filson replied. She seemed confused by the question—or maybe by the fact that a junior officer was asking it in that tone.

"You left her on her own," Tyler stressed. "Outside the house of a suspected murderer?!"

Heather nodded. "Yes. Though, if it helps with whatever this hissy fit is that you're having, the suspected murderer isn't inside."

"That's not the point!" Tyler insisted.

"And what is your point exactly?" Heather demanded, lunging closer. "I know you two are married—I mean, fuck knows how that's allowed, but I'm choosing to ignore it—but that's not your wife standing guard out there. That's a detective constable of police. And a very capable one, from what I gather."

Tyler started to reply, but Filson immediately shouted him down.

"Would you be OK out there?" she asked. "Would you be able to cope on your own?"

"Well, aye. Course."

"So, what's the difference? Same rank. Why can't she stand out there? Because she's a woman?"

"No, because..."

"Because what?"

Logan decided to intervene before Tyler could be turned into a smear on the floor.

"He's just concerned that DC Bell might be... anxious about being left alone," he said. "She's had a bit of a rough time of it lately."

"Haven't we all?" Heather asked, wheeling around to face her fellow DCI. "Isn't that the job? Turn up, have a shite time, clock out, and hope you've made a difference somewhere. Is that not what we all signed up for?"

"She was drugged and kidnapped. Almost sexually assaulted, and nearly killed," Hamza said, joining the discussion.

Heather looked over at him and hesitated. "I mean, aye, that's not ideal," she conceded, then she rallied. "But she's not a bloody invalid. She's a good officer. She's capable, and certainly no bloody less so for being a woman. Wrap her in cotton wool and all you're doing is smothering her. Is that what you want?"

"Well, I mean, no. Obviously," Tyler admitted. "It's just... What if something happens?"

"Then she'll deal with it," Heather said. She looked around at the three male detectives, Dave having had the sense to keep his mouth shut. "Or have I completely misjudged her?"

"No. You haven't," Logan said. He nodded to Tyler. "She'll be fine."

"Aye. Well. She'd better be," Tyler said. He said it quietly, though, and quickly sat down before Heather could take issue with it.

Logan rocked back in his chair while he waited for Heather to shrug off her jacket.

"So, a painting in blood?" he asked, once she'd taken her seat. "Sounds like a fun night."

"Yeah, didn't see that coming," Heather confessed. She pulled one leg up beneath her and ran a hand through her hair. "Cassandra's being taken to hospital for tests. Uniform's going to keep an eye, and we'll haul her over the coals tomorrow. You get in touch with Scene of Crime?"

"They're en route," Hamza said. He checked his watch and stifled a yawn. "Should be there by now."

"Good," Heather said. She shrugged nonchalantly, like she was brushing off praise that nobody had actually offered. "Looks to me like we've got our prime suspect, then. Unless you lot manage to royally fuck it up, we should get everything wrapped up tomorrow."

"And I suppose that'll be you leaving, then," Logan said, and Heather couldn't fail to notice the lack of question mark at the end. It wasn't a query, but a command.

"We'll see," she replied.

"Because there's all that stuff with Tony MacLean, too, boss," Tyler said.

Logan could've throttled the daft bugger. He glowered at him to be quiet, but by then the damage was done.

"What stuff?" Heather asked, perking up. "The girl's dad? What's happened?"

Between them, Tyler and Dave filled her in on Tony MacLean's criminal record, assault on a teenager he believed was making moves on his daughter.

"Pretty suss, eh?" Tyler said, once they'd finished.

Heather nodded contemplatively. "Yeah. Pretty suss. We planning on bringing him in?"

"Not yet," Logan told her. "I want more background on him first, and we'll see how things play out with your blood painter. If we get a match for Dev Rani, she's the focus. If not, we'll see about having a chat with Mr MacLean."

"Bagsy not doing that interview, boss," Tyler said. "Anyway, probably best if I don't."

"Why not?" DCI Filson asked.

Tyler shrugged. "Just don't think we'll get much out of him if I'm there. I think I get on his nerves a bit."

Heather sniffed. "Right." She looked Tyler up and down. "In that case, I'm assuming you don't do many interviews, then...?"

Tyler stared blankly back at her, a twitching of an eyebrow suggesting he was trying to work out if he'd just been insulted or not.

Before he could come to any sort of conclusion on the matter, Sinead entered through the swing doors, and he leapt to his feet like his chair had catapulted him out of it.

"Sinead! You're back!" he cheered, hurrying over to her.

"Eh... aye," Sinead said. She glanced around the room like she was missing something. "Shouldn't I be? Scene of Crime and Uniform both arrived..."

"No. I mean, aye. I mean, I'm just glad you're alright," Tyler told her.

Sinead tossed the car keys to Heather, who snatched them from the air and slapped them down onto the desk beside her in a single arm movement.

"I'm fine," Sinead said.

"Are you sure, though?" Tyler pressed.

"Yes."

"Aye, but really?"

"Jesus, Tyler! I'm fine!" Sinead said, and her voice was like the cracking of a whip.

Taken aback, Tyler muttered, "Alright, alright. I was just worried."

Sinead ran a hand down her face, sighed, then arranged her features into something softer. "Sorry. It's just been a long day."

Logan inserted himself into the conversation by standing up suddenly and tapping at his watch. "You can say that again. We've done all we can for tonight."

He realised he'd stood up a little *too* suddenly, and placed the tips of the fingers of one hand on the desk beside him to counteract the sudden urge to sway and fall over.

"Everyone go home. Get some rest. We'll meet back here in the morning and pick it up."

"Nice one, sir," Hamza said as, behind him, Dave hurriedly shut down his computer before the DCI changed his mind.

"Aye, cheers, boss," Tyler agreed. He warily side-eyed his wife. "I think a rest'll do us all good."

"You need a lift home, sir?" Sinead asked, fighting back a yawn.

It was good of her to offer, Logan thought, given that her face and body language were both willing him to say no.

"You're fine. I'll get Uniform to drop me off," he told her.

"Ah, now, we can't be having that. I'll take you," Heather announced.

She got to her feet, swung her keys around on her finger, then pointed to where Logan had hung his jacket on the back of a chair.

"Get your coat, Detective Chief Inspector," she instructed. "You've pulled."

CHAPTER TWENTY-FIVE

SHONA MAGUIRE WOKE WITH A START, scowled at
the early morning sun streaming in through a gap in the
curtains, then checked the clock on the bedside table and saw
that it was just after half six.

A jumble of half-formed memories arranged themselves,
with some difficulty, inside her head. She remembered coming
to bed. Reading for a while. Checking her phone half a dozen
times for any word from Jack.

OK, maybe a dozen times.

He hadn't been home by the time she dropped off, and she
had no memory of him coming to bed during the night.

A jolt of panic cut through the worst of her early-morning
bleariness. What if his sickness had worsened? What if he'd
collapsed? What if—?

He snored in the bed behind her and shifted in his sleep.
Shona breathed out all the panic she'd sharply inhaled, then got
out of bed and tiptoed into the hall, her moment of worry
having been replaced by a sudden urge to pee.

She pushed down the handle of the bathroom door, then

collided with it when she tried to step through and it refused to budge.

Stepping back, she gave the door an indignant look. "What the feck is this now?" she muttered, then she tried the handle again.

Locked. Definitely locked.

There was something happening inside, she thought. Running water. A *lot* of running water.

"Oh, God!"

It must be a leak, she decided, though had she been more fully awake, a number of other alternatives might have occurred to her.

As she was not, she went stumbling back into the bedroom, grabbed a coin from the pocket of the trousers she'd abandoned on the floor, and hissed out a, "Jack! The bathroom's flooding!"

He groaned out a response, but she was already out of the room again, prising the coin into the slot on the bathroom door handle, and wrenching it around so the locking mechanism went *clunk*.

A cloud of steam came out to meet her as she barged in. Rather than find a partially collapsed ceiling and a puddle on the floor, she set eyes on something much, much worse.

"Eh, do you mind?" asked DCI Filson from the shower. "Some of us are naked here."

————

Logan sat on the end of the bed, while Shona paced back and forth in front of him. He was feeling better. Or, he had been for the first handful of seconds after opening his eyes, at least. Now, the headache was creeping back in.

"No, but, you don't understand, Jack. She wasn't just naked," the pathologist whispered. "She was *naked* naked. Like, I saw... I saw everything. Absolutely everything, Jack. *And* it was on fecking purpose. I mean, it had to be. Nobody showers in that position." She shook her head, like she was trying to dislodge the image from where it had taken root in her brain. "I didn't even know it was possible to get into that position, and believe me, I've seen some poor messed up bastards in my time."

"I'm sure she didn't do it on purpose," Logan assured her.

"I saw arse, tits, and chuff all at the same time, Jack!" Shona cried, while still somehow keeping her voice to a whisper. "The whole lot, all at once! I mean, how is that even possible? How could her lower half be facing in two directions at the same time? Is she an octopus? Did she bring a mirror in there with her? It doesn't make sense."

"I'm sure you were just confused," Logan told her, which did not go down particularly well.

"Confused? Oh, I was that, alright," Shona ranted. "I was very confused as to why your naked ex-lover was soaping herself up in the shower in the first place. And I mean, like, *properly* soaping herself up, Jack! Like, way too much, in all the nooks and crannies. You're in a shower, you big gobshite, you're not throwing a foam party."

She stopped pacing so suddenly that it took Logan a moment to realise, and another for his eyes to backtrack until they found her.

"Wait. Was that bitch using my face cloth?!"

Logan stood up. He waited a moment to see if yesterday's dizziness and nausea were lying in wait to surprise him, but if they were then neither chose to make their move.

"I'm sorry. I should've warned you, but you were out for the count when we got in," he explained. "She gave me a lift back. It was late, she hadn't got a hotel sorted, and so I said she could sleep on the couch."

The assortment of expressions that crossed Shona's face suggested she would still quite like to argue about this, but she clearly concluded that it wasn't worth the effort.

"It's fine," she said. "I just got a shock, that's all. And, you know, almost pissed myself, which wouldn't have been a good look."

"No," Logan agreed. "That's never a winner. And, again, I'm sorry. I should've asked."

"It's your house," Shona reminded him. "You don't have to ask my permission."

Logan wrapped his arms around her and pulled her in close. "Aye. I do."

She smiled, then put a hand on his chest. "Well, thank you. But it's fine. I might not like her, but it's a work thing. I get it. I don't mind her being around. Honest."

"If it's any consolation, I think she'll be heading back down the road today."

"Oh, thank God for that!" Shona replied, feigning a relief so great that only Logan's arms around her kept her from falling over. "But, just so we're clear, you owe me a new face cloth."

"Deal," Logan agreed.

He leaned down, and she stretched up, and their lips met in a peck.

"You look better," she told him.

"Aye. Feeling better," he said.

"Grand. You hungry?"

Logan's stomach rumbled in response. "I'm sure I could force myself to eat something, aye," he said.

Shona detached herself from his embrace. "Right you are, then. I'll go see what I can do us for breakfast."

"What was that?" asked a voice from out on the landing.

Heather nudged open the door and leaned in, her bare shoulders glistening with moisture, her short hair tousled and towel-dried. She had a towel wrapped around her like a dress, concealing all her more intimate areas.

Albeit just barely.

She grinned at Logan, while looking straight through Shona like she wasn't even there.

"Did somebody mention breakfast?"

———

Heather had firmly rejected Shona's offer of blueberry baked oats on the basis that she literally couldn't think of eating anything worse. Instead, she'd raided Logan's fridge, and was now in the process of plating up.

There hadn't been all the necessary components for a Full Scottish, but she'd made do with some bacon, a bit of square sausage, a couple of eggs, some shrivelled mushrooms, and half a tin of *Heinz Baked Beans*.

Plus toast, obviously. It wasn't a proper fry-up without toast. She'd have done fried bread, but there hadn't been enough room in the pan. Besides, she was trying to eat more healthily these days. Hence the beans.

Even when she sat down at the table across from him, Logan remained committed to his blueberry oats. Even though he wasn't a big fan of blueberries. Or oats, for that matter. Nor was he overly fond of the Greek yoghurt piled on top of the dish, although he did enjoy the wee splash of maple syrup on the side.

"You sure you two don't want any?" Heather asked, horsing a mushroom and a chunk of sausage into her mouth. "There's more bacon."

Down on the floor, Taggart watched her like a hawk, his big brown eyes following every movement of the fork, his tongue hanging down halfway to the floor.

"I'm fine, thanks," Shona said. "Very kind of you to offer though. I know food's not cheap these days…"

"Jack?" Filson asked. She tilted the plate in his direction, and the beans oozed tantalisingly up onto the translucent white of a fried egg. "Can't tempt you?" She teased him with a lop-sided smirk. "You always loved it when I made you breakfast."

"Oh, for God's sake," Shona muttered.

Logan shook his head, perhaps just a touch too firmly. "No. I'm fine. This is good. I'm enjoying this," he said, pointing with this spoon to the dish on the table before him.

And he was. Or... he usually would be. Neither he nor Shona were exactly skilled cooks—he'd always valued quantity over quality, and her idea of haute cuisine was a limited edition *Pot Noodle*—but they'd recently discovered that baked oats were a thing, and had been experimenting ever since.

The results had been mixed—their savoury phase, for example, was very short-lived—but incorporating blueberries into the mixture had worked out nicely, and they'd both very much enjoyed the final product.

And yet, the smell of Heather's fry-up was intoxicating. She'd cooked the whole thing in butter, with just a splash of oil to stop it burning, and Logan would swear he could feel his arteries hardening every time he breathed in.

They sat in uncomfortable silence, listening to the clinking and scraping of Heather's cutlery on the plate. She had a way of eating bacon that involved stabbing it with a fork, bringing it close to her mouth, then sort of hoovering it up, making as much noise as possible. Every time she did this, Shona's nails dug grooves in the tabletop, and Taggart's anticipation levels shot through the roof.

She'd made herself coffee. Hadn't bothered to ask anyone else, of course. She hadn't drunk any yet, but Shona knew—she just bloody *knew*—that she'd slurp it. Loudly.

"You still feeling shite?" Heather asked Logan.

"No. Better," Logan replied.

"Nice one."

The silence returned. Well, except for the clinking, scraping, *schlup-schlup-schlup* of limp, fatty bacon being inhaled, and the occasional sound from the dog as he attempted to draw attention to what a good boy he was.

Shona's eyes followed Heather's hand as it reached for her coffee mug. One of them twitched as she watched the mug being raised to the other woman's shiny, grease-coated lips.

Shluuuuurp.

"I knew it," Shona said, so quietly that nobody heard her above the sound of Heather drinking.

There was a knock at the door, and Shona sprung to her feet, desperate to be away from the table. Taggart, who usually went into a bit of a barking frenzy at the sound of the door, remained rooted to the spot. Some things were more important than intruders.

Sausages, mostly.

"I'll get it," Shona announced.

She hurried through to the hallway, and saw a dark outline through the frosted glass of the front door. It was someone around her height, dressed quite officially, Shona thought. It didn't matter. Right then, there was almost nobody on Earth she wouldn't take over DCI Heather Filson.

She unlocked the door, opened it, and was confronted by a teenage girl in a school uniform.

"Alright?"

"Olivia!" Shona said, unable to hide her surprise.

Out on the step, Olivia Maximuke tapped her forehead in salute. "You remember, then," she said, and there was a note of accusation to it.

Shona's relationship with Olivia Maximuke could generously be described as 'complicated.' It had started with a fake abduction, bloomed into an unusual sort of friendship, before another abduction—a real one this time, with Shona as the victim—had sort of put a dampener on it.

Despite everything—despite her brief stint as a drugs dealer, her attempted murder of her mum's boyfriend, and the fact that her father was a notorious Russian gangster who had almost killed Logan's entire team—Shona was convinced that Olivia was, at heart, a good kid.

And Logan, perhaps even more surprisingly, agreed.

Mostly.

"You've, eh, wow. Hello," Shona said. "It's been..."

"Ages, I know," Olivia confirmed. She shrugged and pulled her schoolbag higher on her shoulder. "Thought, you know, with everything that happened, you probably wouldn't want me hanging around."

"No," Shona said, then she gave herself a shake. "I mean, no. That's not... Yes. I mean... You're always welcome, Olivia. Whatever happened... All that stuff, it wasn't your fault."

Olivia shrugged again, but said nothing. She had grown since Shona had seen her last, and yet somehow looked smaller.

"You've had your hair cut," Shona remarked.

Olivia ran a hand through her short, shaggy crop of hair, pushing it back to show off that one side of her head was shaved down almost to the scalp.

"You like it?"

"It's... adventurous," Shona said. "So, you know, that's one in the plus column for it."

Olivia grinned. "Yeah, my mum hates it, too." She threw a glance past Shona into the hall. "Is the big man in?"

"Oh. Um, yeah. Yeah, he's in," Shona confirmed, then she stepped aside as Olivia invited herself inside. "He's just through... Yeah, that way."

She leaned out, looked in both directions along the street like she was worried someone might have been watching, then closed the door and scurried after Olivia as the girl went striding into the kitchen.

"Who's this?" she and Heather asked at almost exactly the same time.

Taggart, who was starting to suspect no breakfast goods

were coming his way, sidled over to Olivia and began sniffing around her feet.

"You've still got the dog!" Olivia declared, as if this would be news to them.

Logan chewed hurriedly on something decidedly bacony and un-oat-like, then forced it down with a swallow. He shot the most fleeting of guilty looks in Shona's direction, then turned his attention to the girl.

"What the hell are you doing here?" he grunted.

Olivia dropped her bag on the floor, pulled out the chair across from where Shona had been sitting, then plonked herself down on it. Taggart immediately sat by her side, and she patted him under the chin.

"That's charming, that is," Olivia replied. "Come here to do you a good deed, and that's how you greet me."

Heather twirled the end of her fork in the newcomer's direction. "Sorry, who is this?"

Logan sighed. "Olivia Maximuke, DCI Heather Filson. Heather. Olivia."

"Oh, she's a cop? Phew," Olivia said. "Thought maybe I'd walked in on the horrible aftermath of some weird sex thing."

"Jesus!" Shona cried. "Definitely not!"

Heather glossed right over the notion. "Just telling me her name doesn't really tell me who she actually..." she began, then her brain made the necessary deductive leap, and a frown creased the lines of her forehead. "Wait, Maximuke? Not as in..."

"As in Bosco, aye," Logan confirmed.

"He's my dad," Olivia said. "Don't worry, I think he's an arsehole, too. I'm nothing like him."

She tossed something that Taggart snapped from the air, and Heather looked down to find the last chunk of square sausage—the bit she'd been saving for last—missing from her plate.

Olivia smirked as the dog happily chewed. "I'm way better."

"You're also meant to be staying out of trouble," Logan reminded her. "So, what do you want?"

Olivia scowled, and looked across the table to where Shona was taking her seat. "Jesus, what's his problem?" she asked, then she turned to Logan. "You called me, remember? Last night. Well, one of your little minions did. Said you'd told them to."

Some vague, far off memory niggled away at the back of Logan's brain, but refused to allow itself to be pinned down. "Oh, right. Aye," he said, playing it cagey. "And?"

"And, I asked around," Olivia said.

Logan nodded, still none the wiser. "Good," he said. "And...?"

"And it turns out that quite a few people knew about it."

Logan hadn't stopped nodding from the last time, so decided just to keep going. "Did they?" he asked.

"Sorry, I'm lost," Heather said. "Who knew about what?"

Olivia studied her with barely concealed contempt.

"It's fine. You can tell her," Logan urged.

"You sure?" Olivia asked, still scrutinising the female DCI. "She looks shifty."

"It's probably the eyes," Shona said. "They're a bit beady."

"Yeah. Maybe,' Olivia said, then she sighed and—to Logan's relief—rattled off a summary of her findings. "Eva MacLean. She'd told loads of people that she was shagging that dead guy. Before he was dead, like."

"Right. Aye," Logan said, his faint, fevered memory of the day before creeping back to him. "Eva. Yes. So, she wasn't keeping that to herself, then?"

"No. Definitely not. Loads of people knew," Olivia said. "I didn't, because she's a couple of years above me, but pretty much everyone in her year did."

The DCIs swapped looks.

"Possible her dad knew, then," Heather said.

"Aye. Could've heard rumour of it, anyway."

Olivia drummed her hands on the table. "See, this is where you need me," she said. "Because that's not the half of it."

"There's more?" Logan asked.

"There's *waaaay* more. There's, like... Well, there's just one thing more, but it's huge. It'll make you, like..."

She waggled her fingers to mime her head exploding, complete with sound effects, then crossed her hands on the table in front of her and smiled expectantly at all three adults.

"Well?" Heather asked. "What is it?"

Olivia looked across the table to Shona. "Is she being serious?"

"Yes," Heather said, answering before the pathologist could say a word. "What do you have to tell us?"

"I mean, I can't just give it away, can I? Information like this?" Olivia said. "Worth a fortune, something like this."

Heather dropped her knife and fork onto her plate and tensed like she was getting ready to grab for the girl. Logan stopped her with a look, then reached into his back pocket for his wallet. "How much?"

"More than you can afford," Olivia told him.

Logan stopped, confused. "What? Well, no other bugger's going to pay you for it. It's not like you can go out and find a higher bidder."

"Maybe I can," Olivia said, shrugging. "You don't know what it is."

"Why are we entertaining this?" Heather demanded through gritted teeth. "Just tell us what you know, kid."

Olivia returned her attention to Shona. "I don't think much of your new friend," she said.

"We're not friends," Shona replied.

"Don't blame you," Olivia told her. She drummed her hands on the table again, then made her offer. "I'll swap. I'll tell you what I heard, but..." She skipped a beat, like she was steeling herself. "...a movie night. Like... like before. Popcorn. One of your stupid films. Like, I don't know, *Lethal Weapon 6*."

Shona snorted. "Well, we can't do that."

Olivia's eyes widened, even as the rest of her face crumpled in betrayal. "Oh. Right..."

Shona quickly shook her head. "No, I mean they only made five. *Lethal Weapons*. So, we can't watch that. But we can watch something else. Anything. Whenever. Definitely."

Heather looked between them both, her eyebrows almost smushing together above her nose. "Wait. Are you... are you pals with a twelve-year-old?"

"I'm fifteen," Olivia told her. "Nearly."

"Oh." Heather picked up her mug and took a slurp of her coffee. "Well, that's perfectly normal, then."

"And that's it?" Logan asked. "That's what you want? A movie night, and you'll tell us what you heard?"

"Yes," Olivia confirmed. "But you're not allowed to be there. For the movie night. No offence."

"It's my bloody house!" Logan pointed out.

"Take it or leave it, Jack," Olivia said.

"It's *Detective Chief Inspector*," Logan told her.

Olivia patted his arm, then winked. "Come on, Jack, we're all friends here." She jabbed a thumb in Heather's direction. "Except her, obviously. Now, do we have a deal?"

"Fine. Yes. Just tell us what you bloody know," Logan instructed. "And it had better be good."

Olivia rubbed her hands together and leaned forward like she was about to do a particularly impressive magic trick. "Right. You braced for this?" she asked them.

"Just spit it out," Heather told her. "My patience is wearing—"

"Yeah, yeah. Keep your hair on, Glenda, I'm getting there."

Heather blinked. "Glenda? Who the fu—"

She abandoned the question when Olivia launched into her big reveal.

"Right, so, Eva's one of the hot girls in her year. There's loads of lads after her. I don't see it myself, she's insanely skinny, but apparently, that's what boys go for."

"Because boys are idiots," Shona felt compelled to add. "You don't need to starve yourself for them to like you."

Heather sighed. "Do you mind? She's making a statement."

"Well, excuse me for trying to prevent her from developing an eating disorder," Shona snapped.

"Right. Well, good job, Mother Teresa," Filson fired back. "But, can we get back to it now, d'you think?"

"Go on, Olivia," Shona said, folding her arms sulkily. "But you take your time."

Olivia shot Logan a sideways look. "Have they been like this all morning?"

Logan dipped his head in a subtle nod. "And yesterday."

"Nae luck," Olivia told him. "Anyway, they're all after Eva. The guys. And there's a couple of older lads who've really been trying their luck. And get this—one of them got a kicking off her dad! Just for trying it on with her. Her old man found out, and gave the guy a proper shoeing."

Heather tutted. Logan sat back in his chair.

"We knew that," Filson told her. "We knew that yesterday."

"Did you?" Olivia asked, the wind in her sails dropping slightly.

"Aye," Logan confirmed. "We did. He's awaiting trial."

"Oh. Right. Fair enough," Olivia said.

"So, your movie night's off," Heather told her.

Shona quickly shook her head. "Eh, no. It's not, actually. She's welcome anytime."

"It's his house!" Heather snapped, pointing across to Logan.

Logan held his hands up like he was trying to deflect the statement, or at least distance himself from it.

"Here, don't drag me into this!" he protested. "It's *our* house. I mean, technically it's mine, but..."

"I didn't tell you about what he did to the other boy."

The arguing stopped. All three adults turned slowly to look at the almost-fifteen-year-old girl sitting at the table with her fingers steepled in front of her.

Heather opened her mouth like she was going to ask the obvious question, but Logan got in there just before her.

"What other boy?"

Olivia shook her head like she was disappointed. "I said a couple of older lads had been sniffing around her." She held up two fingers, like she was flicking him the V, then folded the index finger away, leaving the middle one standing. "One of them got a kicking. That still leaves the other one."

She waggled the finger at Logan for a few moments more, then turned it so Heather could enjoy the benefit, too.

"I'm guessing by the looks on your faces that you don't know about him?" Olivia asked.

"No," Logan admitted.

"Steven Sangster. Sixth year. Face like a dog shit sandwich, but he's on the football team, and he's got a car, so apparently that makes up for everything." She shrugged and shook her head, like she couldn't quite work this out, then continued. "You know about him?"

Logan had to admit that the name hadn't come up, and pressed her to tell them what she knew.

Olivia grinned, enjoying the moment. Savouring the power. She cracked her knuckles, eyeballed all three grown-ups in turn, then dropped her voice into a dramatic whisper.

"Right, well, strap yourself in," she said. "Because what I'm about to tell you? It's going to change *everything*..."

CHAPTER TWENTY-SIX

IT WAS AN HOUR LATER, and Logan stood on Tony MacLean's front step, waiting for the bastard to answer the door. He'd called Tyler and told the DC to meet him at the address, since he'd already met the man, and would be able to identify him.

Assuming, of course, he ever opened the door.

"Must be sleeping. Curtains are all shut," Logan said, stepping back onto the path and casting his gaze across the front of the house. Moss had taken hold wherever it could, so the building looked like it had some sort of fungal infection.

"Nah, boss," Tyler said, stifling a yawn. "It was like this yesterday, too. I think they're just lazy bastards."

Logan glanced around at the overgrown garden, and the mounds of discarded junk that filled its corners. "Aye, you can say that again."

Tyler's yawn got the better of him. The attempt to suppress it only made it longer and more powerful, and Logan looked him up and down while he waited for it to be over.

"What's wrong with you?" he asked. "Late night?"

"Early morning, boss," Tyler said. "Sinead's been getting up about half five every morning lately."

Logan appeared equal parts horrified and bewildered. "What, on purpose?"

"Aye. No." Tyler scratched the back of his head and yawned again—a smaller one, this time. "I don't know. She says she just needs the toilet, then doesn't see the point in going back to sleep. Woke me up this morning. And, you know, someone had us burning the midnight oil last night..."

A thought struck him. A terrible, awful thought.

"You, eh, you heard from DI Forde this morning, boss?" he asked. "Any word on how his hot date went?"

"No. Dread to think."

Tyler shuddered, and tried very hard to shut down the mental images that started to swirl together in his mind.

"Aye," he muttered. "Aye, same here."

Logan approached the house's double front doors, hammered a fist on one of them, then bellowed, "Mr MacLean, I know you're in there."

Tyler watched the door and listened for a few moments, breath held. Then, he shot a sideways look at the DCI. "Do you?"

"Do I fuck," Logan admitted. "He could be anywhere."

"He might well be in bed," Tyler said, backtracking on his earlier remark. "Didn't strike me as an early riser."

"It's half-nine," Logan said.

Tyler shrugged. "I put him down at maybe an eleven-fifteen sort of guy. You still haven't actually told me why we're bringing him in, boss. Has something come up?"

Logan studied the doors, like he was considering shouldering them off their hinges, but clearly decided against it.

"Aye, you could say that, son. You know he leathered shite out of the lad he thought was after his daughter?"

"Yeah, boss. He's been charged for that one already, though," Tyler said.

"True. But what he hasn't been charged for is Steven Sangster."

Tyler looked from Logan to the door and back again, his frown deepening.

"Who?"

"Another lad in Eva's school. Sixth year boy. Been trying his luck with Eva, apparently," Logan explained. "So, one night, Eva's old man grabs him off the street, bundles him into the back of a van, whips his trousers off him, and holds a knife to his bollocks."

Tyler's eyes widened. "Shite. Seriously, boss?"

Logan nodded. "Aye. Said he was going to slice them off."

Tyler shifted his weight uncomfortably, until he was almost crossing his legs.

"Oof. Sounds pretty suss, boss," he said, wincing. "And a hell of a coincidence."

But Logan wasn't finished.

"There's more," he said. "He told the boy to spread the word. To tell all his pals. Anyone attempt to fire it up his daughter, and they'd find themselves missing their tackle."

"Bloody hell," Tyler ejected. "And did he believe him? The kid? Did he think he was actually going to go through with it?"

"Apparently, aye," Logan said. "I mean, whether you believe him or not, a man's got a knife to your bollocks, you're probably no' going to call his bluff. But, aye. He certainly kept well out of the daughter's way after that."

A text *bleeped* on Tyler's phone, and Logan returned his attention to the house while the DC checked his messages.

Another round of hammering brought no stirring from within. Logan was just contemplating going around the back when a startled, "Fucking hell!" from Tyler distracted him.

"What is it?" he asked, glancing at the phone in the younger detective's hand. "What's happened now?"

"Eh, just an update from the office, boss," Tyler announced. "The blood that Cassandra Leigh-Taylor was painting with yesterday?"

"What about it?"

Tyler stole another look at his mobile, like he was double-checking his facts, like he couldn't trust his memory, like he couldn't risk getting this one wrong.

"They think it's Dev Rani's."

———

Cassandra Leigh-Taylor was suffering. That much was clear.

She sat across the table in the interview room with her head lowered, like there was a heavy weight or a sharp spike pressing relentlessly down on the top of her skull.

Her hair was lank and greasy, her skin a shade of grey, and she didn't just have bags below her eyes, she had *luggage*.

It had been alcohol, the hospital said. A *lot* of alcohol. When she'd woken up, she'd said that she'd taken an overdose of painkillers, but blood, urine, and kidney function tests hadn't backed that up, and there had been nothing found at the scene to suggest she was telling the truth.

Looking at her now, she'd probably have given her eyeteeth for a couple of Paracetamol, but neither of the detectives sitting across from her was about to offer any up. Not without her earning them.

She'd been handed into police custody shortly after 7 AM, and had apparently kicked up quite a fuss while being manhandled through the corridors of Raigmore Hospital.

Upon being checked in at the station, she had demanded her lawyer, but then refused point-blank to provide his or her name. She had seemed pleased with herself then, like this was some brilliant masterstroke that would prevent her being interviewed under caution, then had kicked off again when the duty solicitor was brought in to provide legal counsel.

From there, things had become desperate. She'd announced that she was too sick to be interviewed, before ramming her fingers down her throat in an attempt to make herself vomit.

She'd claimed Diplomatic Immunity and then, in the very next breath, and for reasons not immediately clear, denied being a Russian spy.

For a while, she had just broken down into tears, sobbing inconsolably in the corridor outside the interview room, insisting her legs were too shaky for her to take another step.

It was only when DCI Filson had rocked up and warned her to, "Cut the shit," that she'd miraculously pulled herself together and plodded into the interview room with the air of a child who'd just been caught with her hand in the biscuit tin.

Now, the pantomime seemed to be over for the most part. Only the hangover remained.

The formalities had been taken care of first—recording started, introductions made, warnings given. The usual.

Cassandra had scowled through most of it, her eyelids opening and closing slowly, like they were being operated on some sort of manual setting. With some prompting from the duty solicitor—a portly, dishevelled gent named Oliver Coots, who always looked to be in a state of alarm—she had begrudgingly stated that she understood, and the interview proper was able to commence.

"You're in luck today, Cassandra," DCI Filson told her. "Two Detective Chief Inspectors for the price of one. I hope that makes you feel special."

"Not really," Cassandra replied, and her voice ground like sandpaper inside her dry, aching throat.

"Why do you think you're here, Cassandra?" asked Logan.

She scowled at that. Or, scowled more than she had already been. "You tell me."

"No, see, I know why you're here," Logan told her. "I'm asking you why *you* think we've brought you in."

"I haven't done anything," the artist insisted.

Logan shrugged. "OK. You don't want to answer that one," he said. He smiled at her, and there was something bloodcurdling about it. "Maybe I'll have more luck with this one. Why did you kill Dev Rani?"

"Oh, yeah. Here we fucking go," Cassandra muttered. "I didn't kill him."

"No?"

"No."

The DCIs turned to look at one another. Heather shrugged. "Good enough for me," she said, starting to stand. She only stopped when Logan put a hand on her arm.

"Let's not be so hasty here, Detective Chief Inspector," he told her.

Heather frowned. "What? You reckon she's not telling us the truth?" She stared across the table at the suspect, looking genuinely hurt. "You're not lying to us, are you, Cassandra? You wouldn't do that, would you?"

Cassandra looked less than impressed by whatever show this was the detectives were putting on. "No. I'm not lying," she insisted.

"She says she's not lying," Heather said.

"Ask her about the blood," Logan replied, keeping his gaze firmly fixed on the woman on the other side of the table.

"Oh. Aye." Heather sat down again. She interlocked her fingers on the table in front of her, like she was offering up a lazy prayer. "Tell us about the blood, Cassandra."

Cassandra rolled her eyes, revealing a tangle of fine red lines through the whites. "Of course. The blood. That's what this is about."

"What, you having a container filled with your ex-boyfriend's blood on the same day he bled to death?" DCI Filson asked. "Aye, funnily enough, that has raised a few eyebrows around here this morning. Hasn't it, Detective Chief Inspector?"

"Very much so," Logan confirmed. "You'd be hard pushed to find an eyebrow out there that's not currently halfway up a forehead. You see, everyone's wondering the same thing."

"What the fuck is she doing with a jug of a dead man's blood?" Filson finished.

Much as Logan hated to admit it, he and Heather still worked well together in interviews. They'd established a rapport and a rhythm years ago, and it was easy to slip straight back into it now. It wasn't Bad Cop and Good Cop—one wasn't shouty, while the other was sweet. Nothing as obvious as that.

It was more a sort of juggling act, passing questions and comments between each other in such a way as to keep the suspect on the back foot, while always being ready to follow the other's lead and change tack at a moment's notice. From the outside, it looked effortless, but it had taken time and practice to get right.

"That is what they're asking, aye," Logan said. "So, Cassandra, what can we tell them? How can we clear this mess up?"

"Sorry, sorry, can I just..." The solicitor leaned forward, awkwardly inserting himself into the conversation. "To be clear, we don't yet know if it's the victim's blood. All we know is that it's the same type, not that it's—"

"It's his blood," Cassandra said.

The solicitor stopped talking, and for a moment, even *his* eyebrows raised in surprise.

"Oh," he said. "Right," he said. "Well, in that case... I suppose just... carry on."

"OK. So, it's his blood," Heather prompted. "Mind telling us how you came to be in possession of such a large quantity of it? Because, I don't know about DCI Logan here, but I am very excited to hear the explanation."

"*Very* excited," Logan agreed, though his face didn't back this up.

"Well, it's obvious, isn't it?" Cassandra spat.

DCIs Logan and Filson swapped looks. "Aye. I mean, I can think of one very obvious explanation, right enough," Logan said.

"No. Not that. I've told you, I didn't kill him," the suspect insisted.

"Then how did you end up with a pint of his blood, Cassandra?" Heather demanded, the lightness fading from her voice. "And I'd advise you to think very carefully about the next words out of your mouth."

"How do you think I got it?" Cassandra asked. She glared at first Heather, then Logan, but didn't leave long enough for either to respond. "He gave it to me."

CHAPTER TWENTY-SEVEN

DETECTIVE INSPECTOR BEN FORDE was whistling to himself as he crossed the Incident Room, a mug of steaming coffee in one hand, a Tupperware box the size of a small loaf of bread in the other.

There was a spring in his step, although it wasn't translating well to the rest of his body, which was being forced to hobble and limp along in an attempt to keep pace.

Tyler, Sinead, and Hamza all watched in silence as he set the plastic box down on Sinead's desk, pulled off the lid, then gave them all an encouraging wink.

"On you go. Get stuck into that," he instructed. "It's proper stuff. Homemade. None of your rubbish."

Hamza leaned across and lifted a sheet of kitchen towel away to reveal a stack of finger-length golden biscuits.

"Shortbread, sir?" he said.

"Made by my own fair hands," Ben said, then he resumed his whistling, shuffled over to his desk and, with some mild physical discomfort, sat down.

"Um... date go well, sir?" Sinead asked.

"It did, thank you, Detective Constable. It went very well."

Ben tapped the side of his nose. "Let's just say, I even woke up stiff this morning!"

"Jesus." Tyler flinched. "Too much information, boss."

"What?" Ben stared blankly back at him for a moment, then recoiled. "No' like that, you dirty bastard! Get your mind out of the gutter. Sore, I mean. My legs. Well, my legs and most of the rest of me, in fact."

"Why, what happened, sir?" Hamza asked. "Did you have a fall?"

Tyler grinned. "You need to watch your hips, boss."

"Shut up! No, I didn't have a fall. I'm sore from the dancing."

Sinead smiled. "You were dancing, sir?"

"Rocking and rolling all night long!" Ben confirmed. He took a sip of his coffee, then shrugged. "Well, until about half ten, but that's late enough for me these days."

"Good on you, sir. We going to be hearing wedding bells?" Hamza asked.

Tyler's eyes widened in alarm. "What? No. Surely not?" he spluttered. Then, when the others turned to look at him, he added, "I'm just saying, there's no point rushing into anything, I mean. Not at your age."

"What do you mean, at my age?" Ben asked. "I'll have you know, there's life in the old dog yet."

"Aye, no. I know, boss. I just mean, like, maybe you should take your time?"

"At *my age,* we can't afford to take our time, Detective Constable. At *my age,* we have to seize the day. We can't go pissing about." He knocked back a big swig of coffee, leaned over and pinched one of his shortbread fingers from the box, then turned to the Big Board. "Now, who's going to bring me up to date?"

Hamza and Tyler both volunteered Sinead at almost precisely the same time.

"You'll just be better at it," Tyler said when she shot them both a questioning look.

"Aye, you know your way around the Big Board better than we do," Hamza added.

"I mean, I can't argue with either of those statements," Sinead said.

And so, it was down to her to do the honours, and she spent the next few minutes talking Ben through all the latest developments in the case, from Hamza's encounter with the Willington-Smythes, to the arrest of Cassandra Leigh-Taylor.

While Sinead rattled through the recap, Hamza slid his chair sideways so he was sidled up close to her husband.

"What's your problem?" he asked, keeping his voice low so the others wouldn't hear.

Tyler shook his head. "Nothing."

Hamza narrowed his eyes, like he was trying to read the junior officer's mind. "Bollocks. There's something," he said. "About the date. You're being weird. There's something about the date you're not telling me. Do you know who it was with?"

Another shake of the head from the DC. When he replied, "Nope," it came out as a high-pitched squeak that made both Ben and Sinead momentarily turn to see what was going on.

Hamza and Tyler both stared at Tyler's monitor, like they were studying something written there, and waited for the others to turn back to the board.

"OK, fine," Tyler whispered. "But you can't tell anyone."

"I won't," Hamza said. "Spill."

Tyler listened to make sure that Ben and Sinead were fully engaged in conversation, then whispered something far too quietly for Hamza to hear.

"I have no idea what you just said," the DS whispered out of the side of his mouth.

Tyler tutted. He picked up a sheet of paper and held it in

front of his mouth, blocking the sound from travelling in the direction of the Big Board.

"His date was with Moira."

Hamza's eyebrows dipped. "Moira?" he mumbled. "Moira who?"

"Fucking..." Tyler gave a jerk of his head. "Moira."

Hamza's jaw dropped. "What, not *Moira* Moira?"

"Aye. Moira Moira. That Moira."

"Fort William Moira?"

"Fort William Moira, aye."

"The Paperwork Witch of the West?"

Tyler sunk down into his chair. "Keep your voice down," he mouthed. He raised his volume until it was just about loud enough to be audible by the detective sergeant sitting right beside him. "He might hear us."

Hamza gazed at a spot somewhere in the middle distance. Clearly, he was having trouble getting his head around this.

"Aye, but *Moira* Moira?"

"Stop saying her name," Tyler pleaded. "I bet that's how you summon her. Say it again and she'll probably appear behind us with a meat hook, and a load of filing for us to do."

They both smiled at the joke. Then, separately, they both stole glances back over their shoulders.

"What are you two whispering about?"

They both faced front to find DI Forde and Sinead standing over them.

"Eh, nothing, boss," replied Tyler, once he'd finished almost jumping out of his seat. "Ham was just helping me with something on the computer."

"That's right," said Hamza, reaching across and taking control of Tyler's mouse. "So, you just... click. On the thing. And... that's it."

"Click on the thing." Tyler gave a single nod. It was the sort of nod that Hollywood heroes gave before rushing into battle, equal parts solemn and gung-ho. "Got it."

"Christ, even I could've figured that one out," Ben remarked.

He took a sip of his coffee, regarded them both with quiet suspicion, then shrugged. "So, Jack and Heather are doing the interview. What are the rest of us up to?"

Hamza rolled himself back over to his desk, relieved by the change of subject. "We've been trying to hunt down Tony MacLean, sir," he said. "Doesn't seem to be anyone at the house, and Eva didn't turn up for school today."

"We've put a shout out on his car reg, so Uniform's keeping an eye," Tyler continued. "We thought, what with Cassandra in for questioning, it wasn't worth going overboard on the search yet. They might just be at the shops, for all we know."

Ben nodded. "Aye," he said, then he helped himself to another bit of shortbread. It crunched as he bit the end off. "What do we know about Mr MacLean? Not the criminal record, or the threatening to cut a lad's goolies off. In general."

"We know he's a big lad," Tyler said. "Aggressive."

"Doesn't like Tyler much," Sinead added.

"So, a decent judge of character, then," Ben remarked. "Go on."

When none of the other detectives volunteered any more info, Ben prompted them with a few suggestions.

"Where's Eva's mother? Is it just the two of them? Does he work? Could he be at work now, maybe?"

"Eh, no. He's unemployed," Hamza said. "Claiming disability benefits for a back injury for the past seven or eight years."

"Before that?"

"We, eh, we don't know, boss," Tyler admitted. "Does it matter?"

Ben shrugged. "Everything matters, son. The more we

know, the better." He took another swig of coffee and another bite of shortbread. "And his wife? She's not around?"

"No, sir," Sinead told him. "We asked Eva when we had her in. Apparently, her mum walked out on the family when she was young."

"How young are we talking?"

"Eva doesn't remember her," replied Sinead.

Ben sucked air in through his teeth. "That young, eh? Poor kid."

"Poor kids, actually, boss," Tyler said, picking up the thread. "She's got a brother. Mark. Few years older. Bit of a recluse, she says. Rarely leaves the house. Usually only with the old man."

"We confirmed that with his old school," Sinead said. "Once we found someone who remembered him, that is. He dropped out in second year. There were loads of wrangles with the council over it. Uniform got called in, but no charges were brought against Tony, who said that Mark was being..." She made air quotes around the next words. "...'home educated.' And those quotes were his, by the way, not mine. They were in a letter Tony sent to the council. After that, they were just left to get on with it."

"He got any past convictions? The son?"

"Nothing, sir. Apart from the issue with the school, he's never even been questioned for anything."

"Odd that he's not in the house, though," Ben said. "He's no' much of a hermit if he's gone gallivanting about the place."

"I'd be surprised if Tony MacLean had done it, boss," Tyler said. "Killed Dev Rani, I mean."

"Are you just saying that because we've got a woman with a tub of his blood sitting in the interview room?" Ben asked.

Tyler gave a chuckle. "Well, that helps, aye. But it was his reaction when we mentioned Dev's name. He said, 'Who?' like he'd never heard of him."

"He could've been faking it," Hamza suggested. "Pretending not to know."

"Aye, he could've been," Tyler admitted. "But, I don't know. He didn't seem bright enough. It was instant—like, immediate. It was just right out of him. He wouldn't have had time to think about it. It just, I don't know, it seemed like a genuine reaction."

"Unless he'd been expecting the knock at the door," Ben reasoned. "And had already figured out how he was going to respond to mention of the victim's name."

Tyler's eyes darted left and right, like he was quickly reading something floating in the air in front of him.

"Shite. Aye," he muttered. "Maybe it's that. Maybe he did do it!"

"Well, that was a quick turnaround," Ben said. He tossed the last piece of his shortbread finger into his mouth and chewed. "I want him found. The whole family. If this falls through with the vampire queen through there, I want Tony MacLean cued up ready for us to run with."

"Want me to get onto the phone networks and see if we can get a ping on them?" Hamza asked.

"I could check Eva's social media," Sinead suggested. "See if she's said anything, or uploaded any photos."

"Do whatever you need to," Ben said. "Just find out where they are." He took his seat again. "And, if any of you happen to see me nodding off at any point this morning, gonnae give me a wee nudge?"

———

"He gave it to you?" Logan said. "He gave you a pint of his blood?"

Across the table, Cassandra Leigh-Taylor shook her head. "No."

"But you just said—"

"He gave me half a pint. The other half in the container is mine."

DCIs Logan and Filson both sat back in their chairs. It wasn't intentional—they hadn't coordinated it—but they moved like members of a synchronised sitting team, their timing impeccable.

"Yours?" asked Heather.

Cassandra held up a hand, like she was hailing a cab. There was a scar on the palm of her hand. It wasn't recent, but it also didn't look all that old, like it had only healed in the last couple of months, and was still bedding in.

"It's a thing I do. With all my... lovers," Cassandra said.

Logan frowned. "What's a thing you do?"

"A bloodletting," the artist explained.

Logan looked at Heather, who could only offer a shrug in response.

"Aye, I'm afraid you're going to have to give us more than that," he said. "What do you mean, 'a bloodletting'?"

Cassandra let out an impatient sigh, like she was being forced to explain something painfully obvious. "Whenever I get into a new relationship—a sexual relationship, I mean—then, sooner or later, my partner and I both draw blood."

It was DCI Filson's turn to look confused. "Sorry, you're saying this like it's a normal thing to do. You're saying... what? You cut yourself? On purpose?"

"Yes," Cassandra said. "Exactly. Then, I mix our blood, and use it as an artistic medium."

Time seemed to stretch as the detectives sat staring at her. Even the solicitor, Logan noticed, had a look of bewildered disgust on his face.

"Doesn't that hurt?" the lawyer asked, then he remembered his place and quickly apologised for butting in.

"No, it's fine," Logan told him. "I was wondering the same thing."

Cassandra sighed again. "Well, of course it hurts. What would be the point, if it didn't hurt? All true art is suffering."

Heather shrugged. "Aye, well, I saw some of your paintings in your flat, right enough, and I felt like I was suffering through a few of those."

The remark was met with an indignant scowl, but Cassandra didn't reply. Instead, she looked over at the door, then to the duty solicitor, and asked, "So, is that us done?"

"No it is bloody well not," Logan barked. "You expect us to believe that Dev gave you half a pint of blood?"

"Well, that's what happened, so..."

"He didn't think that was weird?" Heather asked.

"Of course he thought it was weird," Cassandra replied. "But, unless we've slipped into some sort of totalitarian police state, doing weird stuff isn't illegal. Check his hand. There'll be a scar, like mine. Ask any of my ex-partners. They'll be able to tell you."

"That's a lot of blood," Logan pointed out. "Half a pint? From a cut hand?"

"The hand is symbolic," Cassandra explained. "The first few drops come from the hand, then I have a kit to draw out the rest."

Logan grunted. "Of course you do."

"Bottom drawer, bedside cabinet," Cassandra said. "I'm sure you've already found it."

Much as Logan hated to admit it, her story was plausible. Batshit crazy, yes, but plausible all the same. These artist types were always up to weird shit like this, and he'd seen mention of a scar on the victim's hand on the report.

He hadn't seen anything about a bloodletting kit in any bedside cabinets, but then he hadn't looked at the SOC team's findings yet, and he suspected he'd find it listed when he did.

A change of approach was in order.

"You told Detective Constable Bell that you tried calling

Dev the night he died, but hadn't spoken to him. Is that correct?" Logan asked.

Despite her raging hangover, Cassandra had seemed pretty sure of herself until now. At the mention of the call, though, she suddenly looked less confident. Both detectives sat forward, as if sensing blood in the water.

"That's right."

"Did you leave a message?"

Cassandra didn't say anything, but shook her head.

"And why were you calling?" Heather asked.

"I was drunk."

"You seem to get drunk a lot, Cassandra," Heather asked. "I've seen people do some wild stuff when they're drunk. Sometimes, they get so pissed, in fact, that they can't remember half of what they did."

"I told you, I didn't kill him."

"But what if you did?" Heather asked. "What if you got so smashed off your tits that you killed him, but can't remember?"

"Is that why you broke out the paintbrushes?" Logan asked. "So you'd have an excuse for having his blood everywhere?"

"God, that's clever," DCI Filson said. "Well done, Cassandra. That's really smart."

"No! That's not... I didn't kill him. I was in my flat all night," Cassandra insisted. She rubbed her head, trying to dull the raging pain.

"And you phoned him?" Logan said. "Just the one call?"

"Yes. Just one. He didn't answer, and—"

"You didn't leave a message. Right," Heather said. "We've actually got his phone records. And, well, they back up your story."

"Good. Right. Well, there you go," Cassandra said.

Logan opened a slim cardboard folder on the desk in front of him, produced a single sheet of paper from inside, and slid it across the table.

"What's this?" the solicitor asked, tilting his head back so he could peer through the lower half of his bifocals.

"That's the statement you made to DC Bell, Cassandra," Logan said, addressing the suspect directly. "Can you confirm that for the recording?"

Cassandra's eyes flitted down to the page, but she otherwise didn't move. "Looks like it," she confirmed after a few seconds.

"Thank you," Logan said. "In it, you state that you hadn't seen Mr Rani 'for days.' You remember saying that?"

Cassandra shrugged. "Yes. I said something like that."

"No, not something like that. You said exactly that," Logan told her. He spun the page back towards him and read it aloud. "'No. No, I haven't seen him for days.' That's what you said when DC Bell asked if you'd seen him recently. Those were your exact words."

"OK. Fine. Those were my exact words. So?"

It was DCI Filson's turn to tag in. "So, how do you explain the fact that on the day Dev was murdered you were seen at the club by a member of staff who insists that the two of you were arguing in Dev's office?"

"I explain it by saying that he's talking shit," Cassandra fired back.

Filson raised an eyebrow. "Who said it was a he?"

Cassandra stumbled over her reply. "It's... It's just a figure of speech. *He or she* is talking shit. That better?"

Logan went for the Hail Mary move. Whatever her response, they could learn a lot. "Club's CCTV can place you at the scene, Cassandra," he said, then he watched and studied her response.

Did she know that the system had been tampered with? Did she know there were no recordings from that day, or any other day in the past few weeks?

Apparently, not.

"OK. Yes. Fine. I went to see him," she admitted.

"The day he died?" Heather asked.

"Yes. Yes, the day he..." Cassandra swallowed. "And yes, we argued."

Logan tapped the sheet of paper on the table. "Why didn't you say that to Detective Constable Bell?"

"Because it was none of her bloody business!"

The air around Logan seemed to crackle, like his growing anger was generating static electricity. "See, that's where you're wrong, Cassandra. A man is dead. That makes it our business. Now, I'm going to give you some advice. It's going to be the best advice anyone's ever given you, so I'd advise you to pin back your lugs and listen. OK? Ready?"

Cassandra clenched her jaw and stared at him, her blood-shot eyes blazing with defiance.

"Cut the shit," Logan told her. "That's my advice to you. Cut the shit. Drop the bloody attitude. Because, right now, you're dangerously close to being charged with murder, and you're doing nothing to help yourself. I mean, if I was you, I'd be spilling my guts, trying to make sure everyone knew I didn't do it. You wouldn't be able to shut me up."

He leaned closer, his voice becoming graver, and more stern.

"I certainly wouldn't be incriminating myself by lying to the polis."

"Or just being a bit of an arsehole," Heather added.

"True," Logan agreed. "Because, I can't speak for DCI Filson, but right now, I actively *want* you to go to jail."

"Nothing would give me more pleasure," said Heather.

"See? That's how unlikeable you're making yourself, Cassandra," Logan told her. "So, again, cut the shit, drop the attitude, and let us help you stay out of prison, eh?"

Cassandra shot a sideways look at her appointed solicitor, cleared her throat, and spent a few seconds adjusting herself in her chair like she was trying to find a comfortable position.

Only then, once she'd settled down again, did she nod.

"Good," Logan said, his tone instantly becoming lighter. "Let's start with the meeting in his office then, shall we? Why were you arguing?"

"Because he was having sex with a child," Cassandra said. There was a bitter edge to the words. The words that came next, however, were softer. Quieter. "And... because I wanted to tell him about the abortion."

"Abortion?" Heather asked. "What abortion?"

"My abortion," Cassandra said. The earlier defiance was gone. Her eyes were fixed on the table for the most part, only occasionally flitting up to briefly meet the detectives' gazes. "Our abortion, I suppose."

"You were pregnant?" Logan asked. "With Dev Rani's baby?"

"Yeah. Not then. It had been taken care of when I went to see him at the club," she replied. "But before that, yes."

"Did he know you were pregnant?"

Cassandra gave a single shake of her head. "I was... I would've told him earlier. But, I'd found out about his fling with the schoolgirl by the time I knew, and how could I tell him then? And how could I bring a child into the world with a father who's a fucking paedo? I couldn't. I just... I couldn't."

She lowered her head further and ran a sleeve across her eyes, wiping away the tears that were forming there.

"Do you need a minute, Cassandra?" Logan asked, which earned him a look of surprise from Heather, who jumped in before the artist could answer his question.

"So, you aborted the baby? Then, you went to the club to tell him. Why?" Heather demanded. "What were you trying to achieve?"

Cassandra's head rose quickly, some of her earlier fire roaring back. "To make him see. To make him realise what he'd done. What he'd lost when he went off shagging a... a child!"

"You wanted to hurt him," Heather pressed. "You wanted to make him pay for betraying you like that. For humiliating you. You wanted to punish him."

"Yes!"

"You wanted to punish him so badly that you aborted the baby you were carrying inside you," Heather said.

Cassandra paused, sensing the rapidly approaching trap.

"You wanted to hurt him so much that you ended a life. You ended your own child's life, just to get back at him."

"No, I mean... It wasn't the right time. I wouldn't have... Even if he hadn't, I couldn't have kept..." She looked imploringly at the solicitor beside her, but he had nothing to offer. "You're twisting it. I didn't get rid of the baby to hurt Dev, I just... I went and told him about it because I knew it would hurt him. I'd have had the abortion anyway."

Heather's teeth were dug in deep now, though, and she wasn't giving up that easily. "No. That's not what you said, Cassandra. You said you had the abortion because you couldn't face bringing a child into the world whose father was, and I quote, 'a fucking paedo.' That's what you said."

"I know that's what I said!" Cassandra yelled back. "But that wasn't all of it! I'm not ready for a kid. I can't afford a child! I can barely pay rent, and..." She sniffed. Sighed. Looked away. "Maybe if it had been different. If Dev and I had still been together. If we had a future. Then, yes. Maybe we'd have kept it. But we weren't. We didn't. So, I couldn't. I didn't."

Logan cut in before Heather could continue.

"How did he react? When you told him?"

"He..." Cassandra's bottom lip wobbled. Her eyes filled with tears, but this time she made no effort to wipe them away. "...didn't give a shit. He... He..." Her voice fractured, becoming a whisper. "...*thanked* me."

Even Heather felt the sting of that one. "Jesus," she muttered.

"Said his parents would have never understood. Said he had to think of his political career, too, and that I'd done the right thing."

"And how did that make you feel, Cassandra?" Logan asked. His voice was gentle. Friendly. Coaxing. "Did it make you feel angry?"

She swallowed, looked down, and nodded. "I didn't kill him," she insisted. Her gaze crept back up until she met Logan's eye. Her voice, when she spoke again, was a thin, reedy whisper. "But I did do something I probably shouldn't have..."

CHAPTER TWENTY-EIGHT

"NOT AT WORK TODAY, VIK?"

Vikram Ganguly had barely slid his front door key into the lock when the top of his neighbour's head popped up above the fence. It was quite a high fence, and Vikram had installed it for a reason.

And that reason was Ernie Peele, the seventy-something now peering down at him from on high.

Ernie was nice enough in his own way, he was just something of a nosy bastard. He was also somewhat racist, although Vikram was sure the old man would vehemently deny this if questioned.

"Racist? Never! I was always nice to him," he'd undoubtedly say. "Always handed him in my old clothes. We were about the same size, and they were barely worn. Like new, some of them."

The fact that Vikram earned well over three times the national average and had an extensive wardrobe of designer clobber never seemed to occur to old Ernie. And, when Vik had pulled up in a brand new *Mercedes* a few months back, his ashen-faced neighbour had said that, provided he returned the car to its rightful owners, he would say nothing about the matter to the police.

"You know me, Ernie. Always working," Vikram explained. "Just working from home today."

Even after four years of living next door, the accent still caused the old man problems. His lips moved in a near-silent whisper, like he was unravelling the code of what Vik had just said.

"Oh. Oh, right," Ernie said. He looked as if he disapproved, like working from home wasn't real work, at all. "And you can just do that, can you?"

Vikram smiled back at him, showing his teeth. The work he'd had done on them had cost a lot, so he liked to show them off. "I'm the boss, Ernie. I can do what I like."

Ernie laughed. "Aye. At least until your old mum comes over again. Eh?" he cried, delighting in his own joke.

"Oof! Yeah, you can say that again!" Vik replied. He turned the key in the door, and eased it open. "Anyway, best get to it. You take care, Ernie. OK?"

"You too, son. You, too," Ernie replied. He lowered out of sight as he stepped off the stool he had placed on the other side of the fence, then reappeared again almost immediately. "Oh, and I've got a couple of lovely jumpers through here. Not a mark on them. Like new, they are. Do you a trick, they will. I'll swing over with them later."

Vik didn't waste his breath arguing. The old man meant nothing by it. And better some misplaced charity than a brick through his window.

"Much appreciated, Ernie," he said, then he hurried inside, and closed the door behind him, blissfully unaware of what was to come.

———

"We've got a hit," Hamza announced, standing up so suddenly his chair went rolling backwards until it knocked against the Big Board.

Ben, who had been fending off a wave of tiredness by standing in front of the board with a fresh cup of coffee, almost jumped out of his skin at the *thud* of the chair's impact.

"Jesus!"

"Sorry, sir," Hamza said. "Got excited. Uniform's just caught sight of Tony MacLean."

"And?"

"He's in Merkinch. Headed to a gym, by the looks of it."

"I bet it's not a nice gym," Tyler said. "I bet they don't do spin classes, or yoga, or whatever. It'll be rough as fuck. All big beefy guys like him, getting even beefier."

The remark made Hamza hesitate for a moment, as a thought niggled at him. "Is he a big guy?"

"Bloody right. He's massive," Tyler said. "I mean, proper huge. Like a guy out of a comic."

"He's not *that* big," Sinead said.

"He bloody is!" Tyler insisted. "I'm amazed it took Uniform this long to find him. I'm pretty sure you'll be able to see the bastard from space."

Sinead rolled her eyes and shook her head for Hamza's benefit. "He's not that big."

"Have we got a picture of him?" the DS asked her.

Sinead checked the board, blinked in surprise, then turned her attention to her computer. "Aye. Saw a mugshot earlier. Meant to print it off. Losing focus today. One sec."

She sat at her desk and set about procuring the photo from the files. Tyler, meanwhile, sat back in his chair with his hands behind his head. "Merkinch isn't far. We going to go bring him in? If so, bagsy not being the one to do it. It's Hamza's turn."

"Aye, well, I outrank you, so I'll just delegate," the detective sergeant reminded him. "By which I mean, I'll make you go."

Tyler was outraged. "No chance! You can't do that! He can't do that, can he, boss? If you tell him to go, he can't just sack it off onto me, can he?"

Hamza grinned. "Course I can. Chain of command, Detective Constable."

Ben held his hands up, urging calm. "Nobody's going anywhere. Not yet. We don't have enough on him to pull him in. And, anyway, we don't even know what's going on next door yet. For all we know, she's signing her confession right now. So, until—"

"She didn't do it."

They all turned to find Detective Superintendent Mitchell standing in the doorway, holding one of the swing doors half-open.

Ben frowned. "Ma'am?"

"The ex. In the interview room. She didn't do it. I've been watching on the camera feed. They're going to let her walk. They'll have to. We've got nothing on her."

The rest of the team all exchanged looks of disbelief.

"What? But... the blood?" Sinead said. "She had his blood. How did she explain that?"

Mitchell tutted. "I don't have the energy to explain," she said.

It was clear from her demeanour that she was disappointed. Cassandra had seemed like a dead cert for a conviction, and her hopes of getting this case wrapped up quickly were now in jeopardy.

"DCI Logan will fill you in on the details, I'm sure. But, unless she breaks down and signs that confession you mentioned, DI Forde, we'll be letting her go." The detective superintendent looked across the faces in the room. "So, if you've got someone else in mind, I suggest you get working on them."

With a single curt nod to be shared among all of them, she

left, and the *thu-thunk* of the door flapping back into place seemed to echo in the silence of the Incident Room.

"Well... shite," Ben muttered. "Looks like maybe we'll be calling on Mr MacLean, after all."

Tyler groaned. "But, like you said, boss, we don't have enough on him yet. We should take our time. No point rushing into anything. And, as *I* said before, I really don't think he knew the guy."

"Aye, but you changed your mind on that," Hamza reminded him.

"Yeah, well... I'm changing it back."

While they were talking, Sinead got up from her desk, crossed to the printer, and tapped her foot while she waited for the page to be churned out through the rollers.

Once the machine had completed its *whirring* and *clunking*, she took the page, checked it to make sure that it had printed correctly, then walked over to the Big Board with it and pinned it up beside a *Post-it* with Tony MacLean's details written on it.

"Hold on," Hamza said, when he saw the mugshot. "That's him? That's Tony MacLean?"

"That's the bastard, aye," Tyler confirmed. "Doesn't do him justice, though. He looks to normal scale there. If we had an A3 printer, his head would be more life-sized."

"Why?" Ben asked, glossing right over Tyler's contribution. "You recognise him?"

Hamza nodded. "Aye. I mean, maybe. I'd have to check, but..."

He stepped in closer, studying the image. It was only a headshot, and facing straight on, but the similarities were there. Not just there, in fact, but *obvious*.

The bald head. The shape of the brow, which implied some serious Neanderthal ancestry. The piggy little eyes. The downward turning of the mouth.

It was him. He was almost certain.

"I, eh, I can't be a hundred percent, sir," Hamza told him. "But I think I saw this guy on the CCTV from the nightclub."

"Bit old to go clubbing, isn't he?" Sinead said.

Ben raised a warning finger. "Here, don't you start. You're never too old to go dancing, you know?" he said, although most of the muscles in his body would beg to differ.

Hamza shook his head. "No. No, I don't mean like that. He wasn't there for the dancing." The DS looked back at the picture again. It was him. He was sure of it. "He was one of the bouncers."

Tyler took a second to process this. "What? But that would mean—"

"He knows Dev Rani," Sinead said. "He was lying."

"The bastard!" Tyler ejected. He quickly tried to save face. "Mind you, I had my suspicions."

"Your arse," Ben said.

"You sure it's him?" Sinead asked. "He's down as claiming benefits, not working."

"Could be a cash in hand gig," Hamza replied. "And I reckon it's him, yeah. Based on his record, I don't think he's above a bit of benefit fraud, either."

Ben clapped his hands and rubbed them together. "Right, we've got motive. We've got a connection with the victim. And, we know he's not only attacked someone trying to have it away with his daughter, he's threatened to cut another one's goolies off."

"That enough to bring him in, boss?" Tyler asked. "We still don't know if he knew that Eva and Dev had been at it."

"Aye, we do," announced Logan, striding into the room.

"We do, boss? Since when?"

"Since Cassandra Leigh-Taylor just told us she messaged Tony on Facebook the night that Dev died, to tell him what her ex-boyfriend had been up to with his wee girl."

"And there we have it!" Ben announced. "All the evidence we need to bring the bastard in!"

"We found him yet?" Logan asked.

"Gym in Merkinch, sir," Sinead told him. "Uniform spotted him going in about twenty minutes ago."

"They still there?"

Hamza shook his head. "No. They got called away to an accident on the Kessock Bridge."

Logan snatched up his coat and thrust an arm into a sleeve. "Right, Tyler, Hamza, you two are in one car. DCI Filson's checking Cassandra Leigh-Taylor out of the building, so I'll grab her and she'll be with me," he said, barking out the words in a manner that left zero room for discussion. He pointed to Ben and Sinead. "You two, stay here. Anything new comes in, get on the phone to one of us right away."

"Will do, Jack," Ben replied.

Logan waited approximately three-fifths of a second, then clapped his shovel-like hands together. The resulting *bang* ricocheted around the room like a gunshot.

"Well, come on, then!" he boomed, making both Hamza and Tyler grab for their jackets. "Let's get this bastard before he gets away."

CHAPTER TWENTY-NINE

TYLER HAD BEEN RIGHT. The gym was not the sort of place that held spin classes, yoga sessions, or any other exercise regimes that might be considered 'on trend.' Instead, it was a place where large, muscular men went to become even larger and more muscular, usually while glowering at themselves in mirrors, and grunting strings of hot saliva out through their gritted teeth.

If that was the sort of thing you were after, then this place was perfect. And, judging by the number of triangular men striding in and out through the front door, a lot of people were indeed after that sort of thing.

"Look at the size of him," Tyler remarked. Despite the fact he and Hamza were sitting in the detective sergeant's car some thirty feet away from the man he was referring to, he spoke quietly, barely moving his mouth, worried the giant outside might hear him. "How much do you think he weighs?"

Hamza looked ahead through the windscreen, and gave the wipers a quick flick so they cleared away the pebble-dash of raindrops that had formed there while they were parked on the road along from the gym, waiting for Logan's orders.

The gym was one of several fitness businesses, tucked away on an industrial estate, where all the buildings were protected by tall metal fences with sharp, spiky tops.

To say the guy who had just emerged from inside the gym was built like a brick shithouse felt wrong. If anything, brick shithouses were built like him.

He wore a tight T-shirt—although, Hamza imagined, all T-shirts would be tight on him, regardless of their size—but his physique wasn't built for show. He didn't have the slender lines of an action hero, or even the sculpted bulk of a bodybuilder. This was a man who had favoured sheer brute strength over physical appearance.

He had the build of a mountain gorilla, with a chest like a whisky barrel, and a neck like an *incrementally smaller* whisky barrel. The only part of him that looked in proportion with the rest of the human race was his head, and so it appeared comically undersized plonked on top of the rest of his body.

"In stone or in kilos?" Hamza asked.

"Doesn't matter. The answer's the same either way," Tyler told him. "Too much. That's what he weighs. Way too much."

They both watched the man crossing the street. He didn't look to see if there were any cars coming first. But then, he didn't need to. When you were that size, the world bent itself around you.

"You reckon you could take him in a fight?" Hamza asked.

Tyler sucked air in through his teeth. "How long have I got to prepare?"

"An hour."

"Jesus, is that it?" Tyler grimaced. "Am I allowed weapons?"

Hamza shook his head. "No."

"Shite. What about other equipment?"

"Like what?"

"I don't know," the DC replied. He shrugged. "Like a time machine and Bruce Lee's phone number?"

"No. You've got one hour. That's your lot. No weapons."

"Does he know I'm coming?" Tyler asked. He watched the brute go striding off down the street, and could've sworn he felt the ground tremble. "Not that it'd make much difference, mind you."

"So, you don't think you could take him in a fight, then?"

"Of course I couldn't! I mean, look at the bastard! He could probably blow in my general direction and I'd be flat on my back." Tyler shook his head and settled back into the passenger seat. "I'd have to rely on outsmarting him."

Hamza sat watching the detective constable for several seconds, then turned to face front again. "Ah, well, that'd be you fucked, then."

"Cheers for that. Cheeky bastard," Tyler said. He joined the DS in looking ahead at the gym.

It had only been a couple of minutes since DCIs Logan and Filson had gone inside. They'd decided not to wait for Uniform to provide backup since, for all they knew, Tony MacLean might not even be still in there.

Besides, MacLean might be a big bugger, was so was Logan, and DCI Filson didn't look like she'd take any shit, either. Between them, they were confident that they could bring Tony in. Assuming, of course, that he was there.

Should it all go wrong, however, then Tyler and Hamza were Plan B. They were faster on their feet than Logan, and should—in theory—be able to chase MacLean down.

Quite what the fuck they'd do when they caught him, however, was another matter entirely.

"You think they're getting a hard time in there?" Tyler asked.

"How do you mean?"

"Well, what if they're in there, and everyone's sort of standing around them, like, cracking their knuckles and stuff?

Or, you know, like, that thing where you pull a belt really tight until it creaks? What if they're doing that?"

Hamza tutted. "I'm sure nobody's creaking belts at them. And it's a private gym in Inverness, it's not a break yard in an American mega-prison. I'm sure it's all perfectly civilised, and they'll be bringing MacLean out any minute now."

It was then that the front door of the gym was thrown open with enough force to buckle its hinges. A large, bald man wearing a sweat-stained grey T-shirt and elasticated jogging bottoms came thundering out, his face an unhealthy shade of purple-red, the rasping of his breath audible even from inside the car.

Tyler groaned, as both detectives hurriedly unclipped their seatbelts. "You were saying?"

———

Two minutes earlier, Logan and Filson approached the man on the lat pull-down machine, flanking him on both sides as they closed in. He was facing the machine, so had his back to them, and didn't notice them until Logan called his name.

"Tony MacLean?"

Tony paused, mid-pull down, the muscles in his shoulders all bunched up and tensed. He didn't turn to look at the detectives, but checked out their reflections in one of the mirrors across the room.

"Who's asking?"

Logan made the introductions, stressing the 'Police Scotland' part. Rather than asking the question again, he rephrased it as a statement.

"You're Tony MacLean."

Tony relaxed his arms, letting the counterweight on the other end of the chain pull them back up to the starting position.

"Yeah," he said. He pulled the bar back down again. There was an impressive amount of weight loaded onto the other end, Logan noted, and the effort drew a grunt from the man in the chair. "So, what if I am?"

"We'd like to talk to you, Mr MacLean," Heather told him.

For the first time since the detectives had arrived, Tony turned his head. He took in DCI Filson with a slow, deliberate look, and didn't bother to hide his contempt. "You're talking to me now. See our lips moving? That's us talking."

Heather looked over the behemoth's bald head to where Logan stood. "Oh, he's funny. You didn't tell me he was funny."

"I didn't know," Logan said. "You're just full of surprises, aren't you, Mr MacLean?"

"You don't know the fucking half of it, sunshine." MacLean grimaced, still heaving away at the machine.

Logan was about to reply when he caught the concerned look from DCI Filson. "Jack," she said, glancing past him just as Logan felt the rubber mat he was standing on shift slightly, like some enormous weight had been applied to it in very close proximity.

"You alright, Dad?"

Logan turned to find another Tony MacLean standing behind him. That was his first instinct, anyway. It took him a few seconds to spot the differences.

This one was younger, the skin of his face smoother and less ravaged by the potholes of old acne. He was smaller, too, but not by much. A few percentage points, maybe. A little less height, an inch or two narrower at the shoulders. Nothing you'd notice if you weren't standing directly between them.

"Fine. Piss off," Tony barked. He was back to staring ahead now, and addressed his doppelgänger via the mirrored wall. "It's under control."

"Aye, you're right, Mr MacLean," Heather told him. "It's very much under control. Just not yours."

"What are you doing to my dad?" the younger MacLean demanded.

He was dressed almost identically to his old man, in the same saggy grey outfit that had been darkened across the chest and under the arms by pools of sweat.

"We're just going to ask him a few questions, son," Logan replied.

From his seat on the pull-down machine, Tony let out a deep, resonating snort. "Like fuck you are," he retorted, exhaling as he let the bar pull his arms straight upwards once again.

It was too good an opportunity to miss. With a practised flick, Heather opened her foldable handcuffs, and fastened one side around one of Tony's wrists. It was a big wrist, and she felt a twinge of doubt that the cuff would be big enough, but it secured with a *click* and she gave him the speech while she grappled with the other hand.

"Tony MacLean, I am arresting you on suspicion of the murder of Dev Rani—" she began. That was as far as she got before an explosion of movement from the man in the chair sent her staggering backwards, thrown off-balance.

Tony reared up, roaring and lashing out with his shackled arm like an enraged *King Kong*. He turned, hands grasping for the female detective, but the stool of the pull-down machine was between his legs, and while his top half twisted, his bottom half was unable to follow along, and he flapped in panic as he fought to keep himself upright.

All the fuss was starting to draw the attention of the other gym users. There were eight or nine of them, not counting the MacLeans, all but one of them male. Most of them, with the exception of the guy lumbering along on the treadmill, had stopped what they were doing.

They all watched as Logan grabbed Tony's flailing arm by the handcuff, and violently wrenched it up and back. Tony was forced to choose between bending over or breaking his arm. He chose the former, and when his feet tangled in the workings of the gym equipment, he fell forwards onto the rubber mat.

It wasn't a dignified fall. Despite the size of the man, the tumble wasn't like the felling of some majestic oak. It was awkward, and clumsy, and painful. He threw out his free arm to protect himself, but his weight and the speed of his fall meant his face quickly impacted on the mat, drawing a hiss and a bubble of bloodied spit from his lips.

Logan grabbed for the fallen man's free arm, but hands pulled at the bottom of his coat, dragging him away before he could secure the other cuff. The younger MacLean spun like a hammer-thrower, sending Logan into a scuttling sideways stagger.

"Mark, don't!" Tony cried from down at floor level. He thrust his free hand out in Heather's direction and half-begged, half-ordered her to cuff him. "I'll come. It's fine. I'll come."

But Mark didn't hear. Wasn't listening. He bellowed like a banshee as he released his grip on the detective's long coat, and Logan could do nothing but stumble desperately, trying to stay on his feet.

He'd been kidding himself, he realised. Whatever bug had been in his system the day before hadn't left. Not fully, at least. Not yet. The floor became sludge, and the ceiling became the wall, and all sense of up or down or left or right went out the window.

He landed on his shoulder. To start with, anyway. Momentum carried him on into what was surely a contender for the least graceful forward roll the world had ever seen.

"For fuck's sake, Mark, cut it out!" MacLean roared.

"Jack, you alright?" Heather asked, grappling with the prisoner's other wrist. He may have offered it up to her, but his attempts to reach his son was making it difficult to secure him.

"Fine," Logan replied, arms shaking as he heaved himself up onto his knees.

"Mark, no!"

Heather followed Tony's gaze, and hissed out a warning that came too late. A foot caught Logan a powerful kick to the head, and the few laws of physics that he'd still been clinging to evaporated like the early morning dew.

The room folded in on him, the air inside it becoming thick, and hot, and sour. Droplets of blood burst like paintballs on the scuffed mat beneath him, then his hands sunk into the floor like the whole thing had turned to treacle.

Tony MacLean erupted upwards, shrugging Heather off like she wasn't there.

A hand grabbed Logan by the back of the neck. He swung wildly with a fist, and hit something solid with enough force to draw a cry of pain.

There was a shout from elsewhere in the gym—the booming, "Oi!" of a reluctant Good Samaritan who hoped that no further involvement would be necessary. It did not escape Logan's notice that the voice was that of the only woman in the place.

So much for all the big strong men.

Lady Luck was obviously smiling on her, because just that single syllable ignited panic in Mark MacLean. He aborted his second kick, stared in mute horror at his seething, red-faced father and the female detective catching her balance on the lat pull-down machine, and then he did the only thing he could think of.

He ran.

CHAPTER THIRTY

DETECTIVE CONSTABLE TYLER NEISH had voiced his feelings about running before. He was, it was fair to say, not a fan, and yet he seemed to spend a disproportionate amount of time either haring towards or away from things, depending on what the situation called for.

Given the option, he preferred running after things. This was generally better than the alternative. It was simple maths—if something was running away from him, then it was probably afraid. If something was running after him, then it almost certainly was not.

Today, though, as he sprinted between two warehouse-sized buildings on an industrial estate in one of the less refined areas of the city, he reckoned the running could go either way. Yes, he was currently doing the chasing, but if the big bastard lumbering along ahead of him suddenly realised his size advantage, the script could be flipped pretty damn quickly.

That was why it was vital to catch him soon. Now, ideally, before the fleeing suspect came to his senses and turned around.

He had jumped clear of the car before Hamza, and had launched himself into the chase while the DS was still pissing about with the locks. He could hear Ham behind him now, but he was a good bit back, and falling further behind. He didn't have all Tyler's running experience, of course, so he could hardly be blamed for not being able to keep pace.

Up ahead, MacLean glanced back over his shoulder, then grabbed the handle of a wheelie bin he was passing and threw it to the ground. The wind whipped at the metal cans and plastic bottles, rattling them across the alleyway, the bin itself almost completely blocking the passage.

"Ooh, shit!" Tyler yelped, then he launched himself into a flying leap, hurdling over the bin with his eyes wide and his arms waving.

He landed in a spilled mound of mixed recycling, stumbled off-balance for a few steps, then picked up the pace again. MacLean had vanished around a corner up ahead. He could fairly shift for a big lad, but he'd been slowing, the effort of the chase taking its toll.

Tyler knew these streets well. Like most officers in the Highland capital, he'd spent a good chunk of his beat days in and around Merkinch, and could map it in his head quite effectively.

It was cut off from the rest of the city by a couple of bridges. If the suspect went by the road, they were a good three-quarters of a mile away from either one. If he took shortcuts, it would be less, but not by all that much. Not enough that exhaustion and shortness of breath wouldn't get the better of him.

Which meant that Tyler, who was confident he could run further and faster than the fleeing ox, was going to catch him. There would be no escape for the bastard.

Great.

The DC skidded around the corner at the end of the alley-way, and found himself in a loading area for the warehouses on either side. Stacks of wooden pallets loomed like towers beside the huge, roll-up doors. Vans, trucks, and a forklift had been parked haphazardly around the loading bay. He couldn't see drivers in any of them.

Nor, for that matter, could he see MacLean.

He spun on the spot, looking both ways along the road that ran past the back of the buildings, shielding his eyes against the strengthening rain. He'd assumed that the suspect would make a break back towards the town centre, but what if he was smarter than that? What if he'd hung a right, instead, and headed deeper into Merkinch?

Or, what if...?

Behind DC Neish, a tower of wooden pallets creaked, then slowly began to topple.

"You OK?" asked Heather, side-eyeing Logan as they led Tony MacLean out of the gym. MacLean wasn't fighting them. If anything, he was leading the way, hurrying outside to try and catch a glimpse of his son.

Logan screwed his eyes shut, then dabbed at his nose with a paper towel, and at the cut on his cheek from where a size fourteen trainer had made contact. Both times, the paper came away bloodied.

"Fine. Had worse," Logan grunted.

He squinted against the rain, and looked over at Hamza's car. Empty. No sign of the younger MacLean, either.

"Shite," he spat.

"Where is he?" Tony demanded. "Where's Mark?"

"Right now, I'd imagine he's being huckled to the ground by two of my officers," Logan said. He didn't add the "Hopefully," out loud.

"They better not fucking hurt him!" Tony warned, his voice rising in sync with his anger. "He's a good lad. He wouldn't harm anyone."

"Aye, well, my face would beg to bloody differ," Logan told him.

"He panicked, alright? He just... He got scared." Tony's building rage seemed to hit a wall, then it dissipated. "He's on the spectrum. Autistic. He doesn't... He freaks out sometimes, that's all. He's not a bad kid. He's just..." MacLean shifted on the balls of his feet. Despite his bulk, he suddenly looked smaller. "He panics. He gets into a flap. And then he reacts."

"I'd say maybe he *over*reacts, Mr MacLean," Logan said, indicating his cheek. "Wouldn't you?"

Logan had expected the response to be hissed through gritted teeth, or accompanied by a swinging kick, maybe. Instead, it was quiet. Pleading. Vulnerable, almost.

"Please. Just... just please don't hurt him."

Heather shoved the giant in the centre of his back, urging him towards Logan's car. "We'll do whatever's necessary to bring him in," she said. "If we're all very lucky, maybe he'll agree to come quietly..."

———

"Tyler!"

The shout from Hamza made DC Neish turn, and he immediately became aware of movement on his right. Quite a large movement. Coming towards him.

"Jesus fuck!" he yelped, covering his head with his hands and throwing himself sideways just as the pallets came crashing down on the spot where he'd been standing. The ground reverberated with the thunder of splitting wood.

With the tower now fallen, Mark MacLean was revealed. He rocked from foot to foot, eyes darting between the detectives, but never quite finding them.

His lips were moving, but whatever he was whispering was too quiet for Hamza or Tyler to hear.

"Mr Mac—" Tyler began to boom, then he frowned and shot Hamza a sideways look. "Hang on, is this even the right guy?"

Hamza, who had been blessed with enough foresight to grab his extending baton from the boot of the car before joining the chase, looked the shuffling suspect up and down.

"He's younger than he looks in his picture," he admitted.

Tyler groaned. "Shite. Have we chased the wrong guy? The boss'll go bananas if we've chased the wrong guy."

"He did run away," Hamza pointed out. "And he did try and crush you to death."

These were both fair points, Tyler thought. The suspect wasn't running away or attempting to murder him now, though. Instead, his rocking had become more pronounced, and his whispering had become a low, regular murmur.

"Two. Twenty-two. Twenty-two. Twenty-two."

"Eh... you OK, sir?" Tyler asked.

MacLean flinched like he'd been struck, then went back to darting his eyes left and right. His hands, which were jammed down by his sides, flexed and contracted their fingers in time with his counting. If you could call it counting, given that he wasn't exactly making a lot of progress.

"Twenty-two. Twenty-two. Two. Twenty-two."

Tyler looked to Hamza, who shrugged. They had both dealt with their share of suspects with mental health issues. A good half of the call-outs back in their Uniform days ended with referrals to Social Work Services, in fact.

Every case was different, of course. Every stew of psychosis was unique. But you quickly learned to read the signs, and right now the signs were written large and clear.

Hamza tucked the baton behind one of his legs, out of sight, but still primed and ready. Mental health issues or not, the suspect looked to be as strong as an ox, and he'd already demonstrated a willingness to use violence, albeit through the medium of falling pallets. If he kicked off, they'd need all the help they could get.

"You alright, mate?" Tyler asked, inching closer to the much larger man. "I think we all got a bit carried away there, eh? No harm done."

MacLean's eyes flitted to the fallen pallets. They had landed in a sort of triangular heap, like someone was preparing a bonfire.

"Don't worry about them," Tyler told him. Another move closer. Another inch. "They were stacked way too high, anyway. They were bound to fall. Pretty sure stacking them that high's illegal, isn't it, Hamza?"

"Pretty sure, aye," Hamza agreed, not taking his eyes off the shuffling suspect.

"So, you did us a favour, really. Cheers, for that. I'm Tyler, by the way. That's Hamza. What's your name?"

The younger MacLean gritted his teeth. "Two. Twenty-two. T-twenty-two."

"That's a good number, that," Tyler told him. "Like two wee ducks."

Mark's mantra skipped a beat. His gaze crept to Tyler, and the DC froze, mid-step.

"Two. Two," MacLean whispered. "Two wee ducks. Twenty-two wee ducks."

Tyler smiled. "That's a lot of wee ducks," he said. "Old Mummy Duck'd have her hands full with that lot."

He looked back to Hamza and pulled a face that quite succinctly asked the question, *What the fuck am I talking about?* Hamza's response was an equally confused shrug, and a shake of the head.

"Wings."

Both detectives turned to the suspect.

"Sorry, mate. What was that?" Tyler asked.

Mark looked down at his feet, like a naughty schoolboy

getting the bollocking of a lifetime from the head. "Not hands. Wings full," he mumbled, then he stretched his fingers out wide and went back to whispering. "Wing-fulls. *Wings full*. Wing-fulls."

Tyler let out a laugh. Not too loud. Not too sudden. "Haha. Aye, you're right. They don't have hands, do they? Ducks? Except..."

He looked back over his shoulder at Hamza again. "Does Donald Duck have hands?" he wondered, then a glare and a nod of the head from the DS drew his attention back to MacLean. "Right, aye. Sorry."

He stole another step forward, closing in. The suspect spotted this, and fell silent, like he was holding his breath.

Hamza's grip tightened on the baton. Tyler seemed to sense this, and held a hand out, down low, urging calm.

"You're alright," he said, fixing MacLean with one of his more convincing smiles. "You're OK. We're all just chatting here. What's your name, mate?"

The younger man stared at Tyler's feet for what felt like a very long time. Then, with a shrug of his hulking shoulders, he mumbled out, "Mark. It's Mark. I'm Mark. Mark."

"Mark! Great. How you doing, Mark?" Tyler asked, his smile broadening like he was greeting an old friend. "I don't know about you, but I'm knackered after all that running. You want to come back with us and we'll get a seat? Maybe go get a cup of tea and a biscuit, and get all this sorted out, eh?"

"Where's my dad?"

"Your dad?" Tyler asked. The penny dropped. "Is your dad Tony? Tony MacLean?"

Something lit up in the lad's eyes. He nodded. "Tony, Tony, Tony MacLean."

"Aw, magic," Tyler said. "We can bring you to him now, if you like? He's probably looking for you."

Mark brought both hands up suddenly, and it took all

Tyler's self-control not to jump back and scream. The MacLean boy's hands grabbed at the air, like he was squashing the enormous breasts of a nine-foot-tall woman.

"He's freaking out," Hamza warned, readying the baton.

"He's fine. He's fine, he's just stressing," Tyler said. "He just needs a minute to—"

There was a clattering from the alleyway at Mark MacLean's back. A rush of movement. The *whumming* of a baton.

"Wait, no!" Tyler cried, but the warning came too late.

Mark wailed like a wounded animal, and buckled at the knees. He shuddered violently, like some inner conflict raging inside him was shaking its way to the surface.

A knee to the back of his thigh forced him down further, down onto his elbows, down onto the cold, dirty tarmac.

"Cuffs," barked DCI Filson, thrusting a hand out to Tyler while pinning the suspect with the other. "Give me your cuffs."

"We had that. You didn't need to do that," Tyler protested. "We had it under control."

"Didn't look like it from where I was standing," Heather shot back. "Cuffs, Detective Constable. That's a bloody order."

Tyler hesitated. Sighed. Shook his head. "We were dealing with it," he muttered, producing his handcuffs from his pocket and holding them out to the DCI. "You really didn't have to do that."

"I'll be the judge of that," Heather said.

Down on the ground, Mark MacLean's lips moved as he silently mouthed his mantra of twos, and a tear fell onto the tarmac.

CHAPTER THIRTY-ONE

THE MACLEANS WERE TAKEN to the station in separate cars, and kept apart through the check-in process, despite Tony MacLean's demands to see his son. Logan and Filson handled MacLean senior, while Tyler and Hamza handled escort duties on Mark.

"You OK?" asked Hamza, as he and DC Neish led the younger MacLean along the corridor in the direction of the interview rooms.

"No' really," Tyler admitted. "She was bang out of order."

After he'd been cuffed, Mark had come quietly. Too quietly for Tyler's liking. He had stopped responding to questions. He wasn't even chanting his numbers anymore. He had, for all intents and purposes, turned mute.

"I think... I think she thought he was going to take a swing at you," Hamza reasoned.

"Aye, but he wasn't," Tyler said.

Hamza looked up at the silent giant limping along between them. Mark was staring straight ahead, with a vacant, empty gaze that focused on nothing in particular.

"No. No, I don't think he was," he admitted.

A door opened ahead of them, and DCI Filson emerged, accompanied by a barked complaint from the suspect she was leaving to stew in the room.

"There you are. About time. Put him in two," she instructed, then she turned away and headed for the Incident Room.

"Eh, I'm going to stay with him," Tyler said.

Heather stopped. Turned. "What?"

"I'm going to stay with him," Tyler said again. He cleared his throat. "Ma'am."

"Why?"

"Because... Well, because he's scared."

Heather snorted. "I don't give a shit what he is. He's a suspect. He assaulted an officer." She jabbed a thumb over her shoulder. "Stick him in two. Alright? We'll get to him when we get to him."

She made for the Incident Room again. Tyler cleared his throat, and straightened himself up. "No, ma'am."

This time, DCI Filson didn't just turn, she came striding towards them like she was closing in to attack. Tyler stood his ground. Hamza shot him a darting sideways look, then matched his body language.

"What did you say, Detective Constable?" Filson demanded.

"I said, no, ma'am," Tyler reiterated. "He's a vulnerable adult."

"Vulnerable?" Heather snorted. "He didn't seem very vulnerable when he was throwing DCI Logan across the room."

"That's irrelevant, ma'am," Tyler said. His heart was hammering away inside his chest, but he wasn't going to show it. He refused. "He's a vulnerable adult, so we have a duty of care."

"Jesus Christ," Filson sighed. She looked Mark MacLean up and down, then turned her attention to Hamza. "And what about you, Sergeant? Do you agree with this idiot's assessment?"

"I do, ma'am," Hamza said. He puffed himself up, and managed to grow an extra half-inch in height. "And, I'd appreciate it if you didn't call DC Neish an idiot."

Filson glowered at them both like she might win the argument through sheer willpower alone. But then, to their surprise, she let out a long, exhausted sounding sigh, and nodded. "You're right. That was out of order. Please accept my apologies, Detective Constable."

"No bother, ma'am," Tyler said, still standing to full attention.

"If you think Mr MacLean here needs your... support, then fine. You can sit in with him."

"Cheers, ma'am," Tyler said.

"But, if he tears your arms off and beats you to death with them, that's on you," she added, turning away once more.

"I want to let him see his dad, ma'am."

Filson stopped.

Filson sighed.

"Don't push it, Detective Constable."

"Just for a few minutes. I think we'll get more out of both of them if they see each other," Tyler insisted.

"And, what? Give them a chance to get their stories straight at the same time?"

"DC Neish and I will be with them the whole time, ma'am," Hamza said. "I'll take responsibility."

"Oh, you'll take responsibility? For what? Blowing the whole case?"

"We'll be there the whole time," Hamza said.

"And we'll be five minutes, ma'am," Tyler insisted. "That's all."

Filson raised a finger and stabbed it at both detectives in turn. "Aye, well," she said. "You'd better be."

———

"Looks like a sore one, Jack," Ben remarked. He was bent over, studying the face of the seated DCI like he was scoping out a second-hand car he was considering buying. "He's caught you a beauty there."

"It's fine," Logan told him, reapplying the paper towel to the cut on his cheek.

"You should maybe get it cleaned up properly," Ben continued. "Don't want it going septic on you."

"It's a graze. I hardly think it's going to go bloody septic," Logan said. He spotted an empty plastic container sitting within reach on the DI's desk and picked it up. "What's this?" he demanded, peering in at the sad wee collection of crumbs clinging to the kitchen roll that lined the bottom. "Was that shortbread? Did you bring in shortbread?"

"Eh, aye. Aye, I did. It is. I mean... it was," Ben said. "But, we ate it."

"Speak for yourself," called Dave from his desk. "You'd polished it off before I got here."

"*We'd* polished it off," Ben protested. He looked over at Sinead, who could only shake her head. Ben winced. "Shite. OK. Well, I needed to keep my energy levels up. Late night."

"Oh, aye. That's right. The date," Logan said.

"The date!" Ben confirmed. He rocked on his heels and smiled expectantly at the DCI. "You no' going to ask how it went?"

"Absolutely not," Logan told him.

"Well, I'm going to tell you, anyway," Ben said. "It went very well."

"OK. Well... good," Logan said. "I'm glad to hear it." He turned his attention back to his screen, but couldn't help himself. "So, is it... I mean, are we talking, like... romance?"

Ben took a moment to consider this. "I'd say we're talking the possibility of romance somewhere down the line."

"Aye, well, no' too far down the line, I hope," Logan said. "How much line do you think you've got left?"

Before Ben could answer, the doors of the Incident Room were thrown wide, and DCI Filson entered like a Wild West sheriff come to clean up the town.

"Do you know your DS and DC just disobeyed a direct order?" she demanded.

Logan chewed his bottom lip in contemplation for a while, then nodded. "Aye, sounds like them, right enough. What have they done now?"

Heather flopped into the closest office chair to his and swivelled to face him, slouching down with her legs splayed wide in a classic 'manspreading' position. "They insisted on letting Mark MacLean see his dad."

"Why'd they do that?" asked Ben, getting in on the conversation. "I mean, they must've had a good reason..."

"Vulnerable adult, duty of care, blah, blah, blah," Heather replied.

"So... they were right, then?" Logan asked.

DCI Filson shrugged. "Never said they weren't."

"You fairly heavily implied they weren't, though," Ben pointed out. He smiled, but not with a lot of conviction. "Hello, by the way. Long time no see."

Heather nodded. "Aye. Hello," she said, equally as unenthusiastically. She aimed the next part squarely at Logan. "Do they all give backchat like this?"

"Constantly," Logan said.

"And you stand for that?"

"Well, I try not to, but they just ignore me," Logan said. He shrugged. "Still, seems to work out fine."

"Jesus," Heather muttered, her eyes narrowing as she scrutinised his face. "You *have* changed."

"Aye. Well." Logan slapped his thighs and stood up. "We all have to, sooner or later. Now, let's go talk to Tony

MacLean, will we, so we can wrap this up and you can go home?"

———

Tony MacLean was trying very hard to hold himself together, but with little success. Tears were brimming, his bottom lip was trembling, and the words he managed to eject were a croak, all ragged and tight.

"You're alright, Mark. You're going to be alright, it's fine. It's fine, son."

"Dad, I don't want to. I don't want to," his son replied, then he began to whisper below his breath. "Two. Two. Twenty-two."

The room was full now. DCIs Logan and Filson had joined Hamza, Tyler, both MacLeans, and a harassed looking young female solicitor who was doing her best not to get involved. The junior detectives had been instructed by Filson to take Mark next door.

Mark, however, had other ideas. He had plonked himself down in the chair beside his dad and was gripping the table so hard that his knuckles had turned white. His head was shaking out a firm refusal, and had been since Logan and Heather had entered the room.

Mostly Heather.

"What's with the numbers?" Logan asked.

"It's just a thing he does," Tony said. "It just... It calms him down."

"What, this is him calm, is it? I knew it was a bad idea letting him in here," Filson said. She jabbed a finger in Mark's direction, making him flinch. "Either he walks out of here now, or we call for some constables to come in and drag him out."

Mark's headshaking intensified. "No, no, no, no, n-no, no, two, twenty-two."

"Jesus!" Tyler ejected, the word slipping out before he could stop it. "I don't think saying something like that to him is going to help, do you?"

"Uh, yes. Yes, steady on," the solicitor murmured, though it was so quiet and half-hearted that nobody in the room even noticed.

"Excuse me?" Heather demanded, turning on Tyler.

Tyler's weight shifted from one foot to the other, like he was preparing to run. "I just think—"

"Think what, Detective Constable? What do you think?" Heather barked.

Logan stepped in before things could escalate any further. "What do you think would help with this situation, DC Neish?"

Tyler looked momentarily terrified by the pressure he had suddenly found himself under, then he met Tony MacLean's eye. MacLean was still a big bugger, but he looked a lot less scary now.

"What if..." Tyler began, then he perked up as inspiration struck. "What if Mark stays here and hangs out with us, and you two take his dad next door for... a chat?"

Tony nodded, seizing on the suggestion. "You'd be alright with that, wouldn't you, buddy?" he said. "You'd hang out with..."

"It's, eh, Tyler. And he's Hamza."

"You'd be alright hanging out with Tyler and Hamza, wouldn't you?" Tony asked, and there was a softness to the question that seemed utterly out of place coming from those lips on that face.

Mark released his grip on the table. He wiped his eyes on his sleeve, then stood up with such urgency that even Logan took half a step back.

"It's OK. I'll go," he announced. Then, without a look back, he marched over to the door and stood facing it, his fingers flexing in and out.

"Good. I'm glad that's settled," said the solicitor, who was once again roundly ignored by everyone else present.

Tyler met Tony's eye again, and offered a smile of consolation. "We'll, eh, we'll make sure he's OK."

"Yeah. See that you fucking do," Tony told him, though the cracking of his voice at the end robbed the warning of much of its power.

Logan and Filson waited for the junior detectives to lead Mark out, then took their seats across the table from Tony. Logan turned in his chair to look at the solicitor lurking beside the door, though it was Heather who spoke first.

"You sitting down, then? We'd like to crack on, so we can get Mr MacLean here charged with murder, and get home in time for dinner."

"Yes. Well..." The lawyer stole a glance at the door, and let it linger there for a while, like she was hoping backup might arrive.

When it was clear that it wasn't going to, she sighed below her breath, clutched the handle of her briefcase with both hands, and joined them at the table.

"I suppose we had best get started."

CHAPTER THIRTY-TWO

SINEAD TURNED AWAY from the Big Board at the sound of Hamza entering the Incident Room. She smiled, looked past him for anyone following, then asked, "Where's Tyler?"

"He's staying in one of the interview rooms with Mark MacLean," the detective sergeant explained. "I was just going to sort out a solicitor and see if we need to get Social Work involved."

"I can do that, if you like?" Sinead suggested. "Dave's got something that came in for you."

"Nice one, ta," Hamza said. He turned to see Dave Davidson holding aloft an evidence bag.

"Came in about twenty minutes ago. One of Palmer's guys delivered it."

Hamza took the offered bag and turned it over in his hands. There was a small black square of plastic inside, about half the size of a mobile phone.

"What is it?" he asked.

"Some computer thing, he said," Dave explained. "To do with security cameras?"

"Oh, shite. Aye, of course," Hamza said, realising what he

was holding. He angled the back and saw two ports where HDMI cables could be inserted, one on either side of the box. "It's some sort of relay. Probably got a small hard drive inside."

"Um... OK," Dave said. "If you say so."

"So, what does one of them do, then?" asked Ben, idling his way over with his freshly filled mug of coffee in hand.

"Um, I won't know properly until I do a bit of research, but I'd imagine it's what was causing the delay on the security system in Dev Rani's club. The way I reckon it works is that the live feed goes in here, and the..."

Hamza noted the glazed expression that was working its way across DI Forde's face, and set the evidence bag down on his desk.

"Doesn't matter. I should probably look into it before I jump to any conclusions."

"Whatever you think yourself, son," Ben told him, but his relief was clear for all to see.

Hamza sat in his chair and rolled himself in close to the desk. Before he could pick the evidence bag up again, Sinead let out a sudden, "Oh!" that made him look her way.

"You alright?" he asked.

"Yes! Sorry, just... Amira called."

Hamza's brow creased with concern. "Amira? Is everything OK?"

"Yeah. Yeah, fine," Sinead said. "She'd tried your mobile, but wasn't getting you."

"What?" Hamza stood up again and patted his pockets in growing panic. Then, he tutted and sat down again. "Shit, I chucked it into the little dookit in the car before we chased Mark MacLean. Must still be there."

"Right. Aye. Well, she was just asking if you could give her a ring. Wanted to know if you were going to be home for dinner," Sinead said. "Apparently, your daughter's asking..."

Hamza groaned. He ran a hand through his hair and

scratched his head. "Right. Yeah. I've been promising to finish a story with her all week." He looked down at the device on his desk and sighed. "I'll give her a call. We'll do it tomorrow. She'll understand."

"Your arse," Ben told him. "These are precious days, son, and they don't hang around forever. We've made good progress today. Chances are, we've got our killer through there right now."

"Aye, but we did think that earlier, sir," Hamza said.

"True," Ben was forced to admit. "But either way, we can spare you for one night. Get on the phone to your missus, and let her know you'll be knocking off at five."

"Eh... wow. OK. Cheers, sir!" Hamza said, lighting up. His eyes were soon drawn to the Incident Room doors, and his burst of optimism quickly faded. "But what about...?"

"Never you mind about Jack. If he's got a problem with it, he'll have to go through me," Ben assured him. "Alright?"

"Uh, yeah. Alright!" Hamza replied. "Thanks again, sir."

"No bother. Now, go get your phone, give Amira a ring..." Ben pointed to the evidence bag on the desk. "...then have a poke around with your doohickey until it's time to clock off."

He sat down at his desk, feeling pleased with himself, and raised his coffee mug like he was making a toast.

"Everything's safely in hand!"

———

It was a big bag. Hessian. Too big for a couple of jumpers, even if they were in good nick. Ernie had rummaged in the wardrobe until he'd found a couple of old shirts, too. Nothing special—not as good as the jumpers—but perfectly wearable.

And what did he need shirts for these days, anyway? It wasn't like he went anywhere. Not since Elsie had passed.

In fact, the last time he'd worn a shirt had been at her

funeral. That was his good white shirt, though. These two weren't as good as that one, but they were fine. More than adequate.

He stopped by the kitchen and popped a wee tub of soup into the bag on top of the clothes. Homemade. Leek and potato. Nothing exciting, but he was sure Vikram would appreciate the gesture, and Ernie had always been a firm believer that you did what you could to help those less fortunate than yourself.

Vikram had been having some work done in the back garden. The old fence was being taken down and a series of much taller posts had been cemented into the ground, ready for new panels to be added, roughly the same height as those out front. The panels hadn't arrived yet, though, which meant Ernie could walk from his back door to his neighbour's in fewer steps than it would take to walk along his own front path.

He switched the bag from his right hand to his left, knocked out a cheerful rhythm on the door's frosted glass, then retreated back a step and waited.

And waited.

He sang a few random tuneless notes to himself—"*Dye-dee-dee*"—then rapped his knuckles on the door again.

"Hello? Vik? It's Ernie. I've brought those jumpers."

That should do it.

He cleared his throat. Rolled his shoulders. Waited.

And waited.

Jesus. What was keeping him?

Ernie tried the handle. He was sure Vikram wouldn't mind. It was just being neighbourly, after all.

It took a bit of effort before the handle *clunked* down. It gave way suddenly, drawing a little yelp of surprise from Ernie.

He edged the door open enough to poke both the bag and his head around, and called out to announce his presence.

"Vik? It's me. It's Ernie," he called. Then, in case that wasn't enough, "From next door. I've brought you those jumpers."

He held the bag up and waggled it, presenting it to the empty kitchen.

Ernie had never been in Vikram's kitchen before, and the smell of spices almost knocked him on his arse. He should've expected it, of course. Vikram was originally from Bangladesh—it had been one of the first things Ernie had asked him after he'd moved in—and while he was no expert, Ernie was pretty sure they were all into curries over there.

He suddenly had some doubts about just how appreciated his leek and tattie soup would be, but there was no going back now. Vikram could always add spices to it, if that's what he wanted. Some chilli, or a pinch of curry powder, or whatever.

Apparently, people were doing some *very* imaginative things with ginger these days. None of that was Ernie's cup of tea, of course, but each to their own. Who was he to judge?

"Hello? Vikram? You there?"

The house wasn't silent. If it had been, he'd probably have set the bag on the kitchen worktop and headed home. Left it as a wee surprise.

But there was music coming from an adjoining room. Ernie's house was a mirror image of this one, which meant that the music was coming from the downstairs bedroom, which Vikram had turned into a home office, despite Ernie's warning that this was a bad idea. The box room upstairs would have been better suited. It wasn't huge, but it was big enough for a desk and a chair, and would have given Vik a lovely south-facing view along the street, with plenty of sunshine throughout the day.

Not that it was any of Ernie's business, of course, but it really was a much better use of the layout.

Closing the kitchen door, Ernie followed the sound of the music. It had an exotic, foreign sound to it, all jangling and banging, and a warbling voice he couldn't identify as male, female, or something between the two.

Because you never knew these days, did you? You couldn't just assume someone was one or the other. You weren't allowed.

So his grandchildren kept telling him, anyway.

Not for the first time, he wondered what his Elsie would have made of it all.

Stepping out into the hallway, Ernie's attention was drawn to the floor. Instead of a nice soft carpet, he found himself walking on sanded and varnished wooden boards.

"Poor bugger," he whispered to himself. "Hasn't even got a rug."

The door to the bedroom office appeared closed as he approached it, the music seeping out through the gap at the bottom—a gap, it occurred to him, that wouldn't have been there if Vikram's budget had stretched to even the most basic of floor coverings.

"Don't worry, just me!" Ernie announced, knocking on the door.

It creaked inwards, and he realised that it hadn't been closed at all. Not properly. Not all the way.

"I've brought you them two jumpers," he said, holding the bag in front of him like it was a lantern leading the way. "And I've popped a couple of shirts in, too, in case..."

The rest of the sentence died in his throat.

The hessian handle slipped from his grip.

And two good jumpers, a couple of decent shirts, and half a tub of leek and potato soup spilled out onto the slick red puddle on the floor.

———

This was not Tony MacLean's first time in a polis station interview room. Once his son had been taken away, he'd quickly regained his composure, and despite the seriousness of the charges he was facing, he didn't appear in the least bit concerned.

The same could not be said for his solicitor. Her name was Jemmah—the 'h' on the end was apparently important enough for her to spell it out for the benefit of everyone else in the room —and she had drawn the short straw at the law firm that represented the MacLean family.

Logan could imagine them literally drawing straws, too. He couldn't imagine anyone would willingly spend time in Tony MacLean's company if they could possibly avoid doing so. They'd barely been in the room fifteen minutes, and Logan was already sick of the sight of the bastard.

Certainly, Jemmah-with-an-H didn't seem to be having a great time. Something about her demeanour reminded Logan of the TV series that Shona had been making him watch on one of the higher-numbered *Sky* telly channels.

He'd been aware of *Quantum Leap* first time around, but had never watched an episode until Shona had essentially forced him to. It was about a time traveller from the far future, who would leap back into the bodies of people in the past, usually at the most inopportune or embarrassing of moments.

With her wide-eyed stare, lack of preparation, and failure to demonstrate even a basic understanding of the legal system in general, Logan reckoned the lawyer could very well have been the show's protagonist, Dr Sam Beckett, once again finding himself in a predicament completely beyond his understanding and personal skillset.

"You alright, there?" Logan asked, as she fiddled with the combination lock of her briefcase.

It was the fifth or sixth time she'd done so, and whenever either detective had asked if she needed a hand she'd instantly returned the case to the floor and acted like nothing had happened.

This time was no different. She slid the case down at the

side of her chair, clasped one hand around the other like she was shielding her cards from a wily poker opponent, and nodded slowly as if listening to something interesting.

Quantum Leap. Logan was bloody sure of it.

"Is there something in the case you need?" Tony MacLean demanded. Clearly, he was getting as fed up with her footering as the detectives were.

"Hmm?" asked Jemmah, with a sort of rising intonation that suggested she had no idea what he was on about.

"You keep pissing about with that case," Tony snapped, not prepared to let the subject drop. "Have you got your fucking lunch in there, or something? What do you need?"

The solicitor quietly cleared her throat. "Just... just a pen."

"Jesus Christ," DCI Filson muttered. She pulled a pen from her pocket and slammed it on the centre of the table. "Here. Use that."

"Thanks. Thank you!" Jemmah gushed, grabbing the implement and removing the lid. "I'll give you it back at the end."

"I don't give a shit," Filson said. "Can we continue?"

"Yes. Continue," Jemmah said, like she was the one giving the orders.

"Right, Tony," Logan said. "You were just about to tell us where you were between the hours of eleven PM on Wednesday and four AM on Thursday. I'm assuming all that buggering about with the briefcase has given you ample opportunity to cast your mind back. I mean, I know it won't be easy to think that far back—it was the night before last, after all—but it's important that you try."

"Sorry."

Both detectives turned to look at Jemmah, who was raising an index finger like she was trying to catch the attention of a waiter.

"This pen's not working."

"For fu—" Heather rolled her eyes. "It is. Scribble it on the pad."

Jemmah scribbled it on the pad.

"Oh, yes. That's it now. Thanks."

Beside her, Tony MacLean ran a hand down his face and groaned, as if only just realising he'd been saddled with a right useless bastard.

"I was in bed, wasn't I?" he said, answering the detective's question.

"I don't know, Tony. Were you?" Logan asked. "And, more importantly, can anyone back that up?"

"Yes, I was. And no, they can't," Tony retorted.

"Not even your kids?"

"My kids don't come to bed with me."

Logan made a noise like the start of a chuckle, but which didn't really go anywhere. "Well, I suppose that's something."

"You leave my fucking kids out of this," Tony warned.

"No can do, Tony," Heather said, stepping in. "See, your daughter—Eva—we think she's key to all this."

"Where is she, Tony?" Logan asked.

Tony's expansive brow creased. "Where's who? Eva? How should I...? What time is it? She's at school." His gaze flitted from one DCI to the other. "Isn't she?"

Logan checked his watch. "School's done for the day, Tony. But, either way, she wasn't there. She didn't show up."

"You what?" MacLean sat forwards so suddenly his solicitor flinched and let out a shrill little cheep of fright. "What do you mean? Where the fuck is she?"

The worried look on his face was real, Logan would swear to it.

He didn't know. He had no idea where she was.

"When did you last see her?" Heather asked, clearly coming to the same conclusion.

"This morning. When she left for school."

"She said that was where she was going?" Logan asked. "She said she was going to school?"

"Yeah. Well, I mean... I don't know. I was in bed," Tony admitted.

Heather tutted. "God. Father of the year, eh?"

"She's seventeen, not fucking seven," MacLean spat. "She gets herself out to school, doesn't she? Doesn't need me hanging over her shoulder. Doesn't fucking *want* me doing that."

Heather rose from the table. "I'll go get a shout put out, see if we can get eyes on her," she told Logan. Then, for the benefit of the recording: "DCI Filson leaving the room."

Logan said nothing until the door had been closed again, then continued. "Right, Tony, so you say—"

The solicitor raised her hand to attract his attention. "Should we... should we wait for her to come back?"

Logan sighed. "No. I'm quite alright to continue."

"Is that allowed?" Jemmah wondered.

"Jesus Christ. What do you mean, *is that...*? Have you done this before?"

"No. Well, yes. Well, I've sat in on a couple," the lawyer explained. "But this is my first time in the hot seat, so to speak."

"You're not in the fucking hot seat, sweetheart," Tony snapped. He prodded himself in the chest. "I'm in the fucking hot seat. So up your fucking game, eh?" He met Logan's eye, and a moment of shared disbelief passed between them, before he turned on Jemmah again. "Is there no' anyone else they could've sent? Someone with a bit more fucking experience?"

"Not really," Jemmah said. "I won't be your actual solicitor if it goes to trial or anything."

"Aye, too fucking true you won't be!" Tony agreed. "I wouldn't trust you to represent me if I'd had an accident at work, never mind for a fucking murder case!"

Jemmah appeared momentarily taken aback. "Bit harsh."

"Funny you should mention that, Tony. Work," Logan said.

"According to your records, you're not currently in employment. Is that right?"

Tony locked eyes with him again. This time, there was no moment of empathy between them, just something hard and confrontational.

"No comment."

"What? Really?" Logan scoffed. "It's not exactly a difficult question. You're unemployed. Right?"

"No comment."

Logan shrugged. "Fine. Well, for the sake of clarity... You're down as claiming Universal Credit. You and Mark both, in fact. So, fine. There we are. We've established that you're unemployed." He smiled, but it was a mirthless thing. "Except, see, this is where things get a bit confusing for me. This is where I'm hoping you can help clear something up."

Logan glanced down at the notepad in front of him.

"A few minutes ago, when we asked you what your relationship was with Dev Rani, you said you didn't know him. You said, you'd never heard of him, and never heard Eva mention him. You remember that? It was literally just five minutes ago."

"Course I remember," Tony said. There was venom in the reply, but a hint of dread, too. He knew what was coming. He had to.

"Good. Great," Logan said. "Except, here's the thing that confuses me about that. You *do* know him."

"No, I don't."

"Come on, Tony! Don't piss about here. We both know you know him."

Across the table, MacLean shook his head, shrugged, but said nothing.

"Fine. We'll play it like that. Will I tell you how you know Dev, Tony? You know Dev because you work for him."

MacLean's forehead creased again. "You what?"

"Your wee cash-in-hand job. Weekends at *Refuge* nightclub. On the door. That ringing any bells?"

Tony shifted his not inconsiderable weight in the chair. It let its objections be known in a series of creaks and groans.

"No comment."

Logan sat forward and clasped his hands on the table. "Right. It seems to me, Tony, that you're concerned about being done for benefit fraud here. Let me make something crystal bloody clear for you, right here and now. It'd be a *dream* for you to be done for benefit fraud. Considering what you're facing, a charge of benefit fraud is pie-in-the-sky fantasy stuff. It's a fucking lottery win. *EuroMillions* rollover jackpot. If you leave here and all you're getting done for is a dodgy Universal Credit claim, you'll be the luckiest bastard walking the face of this Earth."

He gave that a few moments to sink in, before continuing.

"So, let me ask you again. Were you working the door at *Refuge*?"

"You don't have to answer that," the solicitor said.

This seemed to be even more persuasive an argument than the one that Logan had made. If that useless bastard was advising silence, then maybe it wasn't in his best interests.

"Yeah. Sometimes," he said.

Logan slapped the table and smiled. "There we go! Wasn't so hard, was it?"

"But, just every once in a while. Not on the regular," Tony added. "Just... if they were short. They'd call us in."

"You and Mark," Logan said. It wasn't a question—they'd looked at the videos and spoken to one of the bar staff, who'd confirmed it.

"Yeah," Tony said. "Me and Mark."

"Good. We're making progress," Logan said. "So, now we've established that you know Dev Rani."

Tony shook his head firmly. "No. No. I don't. I mean... I do now. I see where you're going with it, and everything. But I've never dealt with him. I didn't know his name. He was just some Pa—" He managed to stop the slur before it got out. "What is it you call them now? Indian? Asian? I don't fucking know where he's from, and didn't know his name, because we never dealt with him."

"Come on, Tony. I thought we were making progress there. You don't expect me to believe that, do you? You telling me you work somewhere and you don't even know who your boss is?"

"He wasn't my boss," MacLean insisted. "I dealt with Big Marty."

Logan checked his notepad and found the name of the barman who'd confirmed the identity of the bouncers on the CCTV footage. "Martin Byron?"

Tony nodded. "Yeah. Marty. He would call us in, sort us out with cash at the end of the night. Anyway, like I said, it was once in a blue moon. Not regular. I'd never spoken to the boss guy. He always sort of kept out of our way."

"Aye, well, can't exactly blame him for that," Logan said. "After everything with your daughter."

There was that frown of confusion again. Logan wished it didn't look so damn convincing.

"What you on about?"

"We know you know about their relationship, Tony," Logan said.

"Relationship? What do you...?" He seemed to swell. Grow larger. "What fucking relationship? What are you talking about?"

"We're doing this again, are we?" Logan sighed. "We know you were told about it. Cassandra Leigh-Taylor showed us the message she sent you the night Dev was murdered. And see, the thing about Facebook, Tony, is it tells you when a message has been read. So we know you saw it."

"Who the fuck is Cassandra Leigh-Taylor? *Facebook*? I've

not got Facebook," Tony spat back. He threw himself forwards in his seat so his bulk shook the table. "What are you fucking saying? That dirty fucker and my Eva?"

"We saw the message, Tony," Logan said, but even as the words came out of his mouth, there was doubt.

Had they checked the profile? There had to be more than one Tony MacLean in the world. Cassandra had said she was drunk. Were they certain she'd sent the message to the right guy?

"No, no. This is... This is fucking bullshit," Tony spat. "Not Eva. Not with that dirty fucking... No. No way. You're lying! You're fucking lying! I want to see her. I want to talk to her!"

"They don't know where she is," Jemmah reminded him, which drew a roar so furious that she dropped her borrowed pen.

"*Well, they'd better hurry the fuck up and find her!*"

The door opened behind Logan. Heather entered, but only halfway. "DCI Logan. A word."

Logan grimaced. "Right now?" he asked. "We were just starting to get somewhere."

"Yes. Right now," Heather said, and something about her tone—everything about her tone—told him not to argue.

"Don't you go anywhere, Tony," he said, pushing back his chair and getting to his feet. "This conversation is *to be continued.*"

He announced his departure, then paused the recording, and joined Heather out in the corridor.

"What's happened?" he asked, not beating around the bush.

"You know your man, Dev, with the hole where his cock used to be?" Heather asked.

Logan tutted. "Obviously."

"Aye. Well. Surprise!" Heather replied. "We've only gone and found another one..."

CHAPTER THIRTY-THREE

THE SCENE WAS ATTENDED. Palmer's team was called in. Hamza phoned home to say he wouldn't be back for dinner, after all.

Logan and DI Forde had stayed with Tony MacLean. They would keep the pressure on, see if they could break him down. Tyler was still keeping Mark MacLean company until someone could come and relieve him, so DCI Filson had gathered up DS Khaled and DC Bell, and they'd all headed to the crime scene in her car.

"Just shove that stuff aside," she'd told Hamza as he clambered into the back, and he'd dutifully tried to make room for himself amongst the mess of discarded food wrappers and old newspapers.

There was a lingering odour of something rotting somewhere, so by the time they'd reached the address out in Culloden, he was desperate for some fresh air.

Uniform had already arrived and blocked off most of the street. None of the assembled sergeants and constables recognised DCI Filson, but they all responded quickly to her barked orders, instinctively sensing that she was in charge.

A door to door was ordered. It was a residential street in the early evening. Someone must have seen something.

"Is that the detectives? Are you the detectives?" called an elderly man, who had until that point been in conversation with two female constables. He raised an arm and waved, like he was hailing an old friend across a crowded bar.

Heather didn't falter as she marched right past him, but dispatched Hamza to deal with him instead. "You, go see if that's our witness," she told the detective sergeant, then she indicated Sinead with a jerk of her head. "You, with me."

Hamza didn't bother to argue, and split off from the others without a word. Sinead hurried to keep up with Heather's much larger strides, then both women were forced to stop when a man with the face of an angry gerbil threw himself into their path.

"Whoa, whoa, whoa, there!" Geoff Palmer cried. The sudden lunge had made his white paper suit ride up, and he took a moment to hook the elasticated hood back under his chin. "Who are you, and where do you think you're going?"

"DCI Heather Filson. This is—"

"I know who she is. I've seen her before," Geoff said, and his sneer of distaste said he hadn't liked what he'd seen. "It's you I don't know."

"Well, let's keep it that way," Heather said, immediately getting the measure of the man. She nodded past him to the front door of the house. "What have we got?"

Palmer looked her up and down like he was sizing her up for something. It was best not to think about what. Then, when his mental calculations were complete, he shrugged, rustling the paper of his protective outfit.

"Not sure yet. We're waiting for the pathologist to finish."

Heather's gaze flitted across the front of the house. She moved her weight from one hip to the other. None of this went unnoticed by Sinead.

"The pathologist?" Filson muttered. "You mean—?"

"Oh. Great. It's you."

Both detectives and the giant gerbil turned to see Shona Maguire stepping out of the house and stopping on the doorstep.

"Where's Jack?" Shona asked.

"He's not here."

Shona sighed. "And yet, you are. I thought you'd be gone by now."

Heather's mouth adjusted itself into something that looked like a smile, but had none of the sentiment behind it. "Nope. Still here."

"Well, hopefully not for long," Shona retorted.

Geoff Palmer, whose head had been tick-tocking left and right during the exchange, let out a breathless sounding giggle. "Careful, ladies! Let's not start a catfight!" He grinned. "Or, at least wait until I've got my camera!"

"Oh, fuck off, Geoff!" Shona said, then she looked horrified by her outburst and slapped a hand over her mouth to stop anything else offensive slipping out.

Heather, on the other hand, had no such qualms. "Yeah. Fuck off, Geoff," she said. "Go and dust some grass for fingerprints or something."

Palmer's smile fell away. He made an adjustment to a tie that he may or may not have been wearing beneath his paper outfit. "You can't talk to me like that..." he began, then he recoiled when Heather clapped her hands together right in his face, and pointed to somewhere far, far off on her left.

"Yes, I can. I just did. We all heard it. Now, go. When we're looking for some light misogyny, we'll give you a shout. Alright?"

The Scene of Crime man ejected a series of short stammering sounds, but none of them came to anything. Instead, he turned suddenly as if someone had called his name, said,

"What?" in the general direction of one of his team members, then nodded and went waddling over to join them.

"That the guy Jack was sick on?" Heather muttered, watching Palmer go.

"That's him, yeah," Sinead confirmed.

"Ah, well. Good enough for the snidey wee bastard." She turned her attention back to Shona and started towards the door. "Right, you going to show us what we've got?"

"What? Now?" Shona asked. She shook her head. "No. That's not my job."

"Eh, aye it is. You help us solve murders. That's your job," Filson told her. The DCI wasn't slowing, so Shona had no choice but to shuffle backwards into the house to avoid a collision.

"No, *actually*, my job is to determine the details of the death, not—"

"Yeah, yeah. Where is he?" Heather demanded, stepping over the threshold.

"No!" Shona cried. She pointed to the DCI's feet. "Shoe coverings!"

Heather rolled her eyes. "Oh, Jesus. You're one of them. OK, fine."

She held a hand out, like she expected Shona to provide her with the necessary protective gear. Shona, however, just shook her head.

"I haven't got any."

"Well, why not?"

"Because it's not my job to provide you with them!"

Heather pulled a face that could best be described as *whiney little bitch*. "That's not my job, that's not my job!" she chirped, in a dense Irish accent. "What is your job, exactly?"

"I'm a fecking pathologist," Shona spat back. "Do you want me to spell that for you?"

Sinead cleared her throat. "Eh, here. I've got some," she

said, producing shoe coverings and gloves from her jacket pocket.

"Great. Someone's on the ball," Heather said, snatching them off her.

"Just what I was thinking," Shona agreed. "Good on ye, Sinead. Nice to see another professional at work."

Heather maintained unwavering eye contact with the pathologist as she shoved first one foot, then the other, into the bright blue plastic shoe coverings.

"There. Happy?"

"Not really," Shona said. "Now, maybe if you'd click your heels together three times and say, 'There's no place like home...' then we might be onto something."

Heather scowled, then beckoned for Sinead to follow with another jerk of her head, albeit a more forceful one than last time.

Sinead, however, hung back. "Eh, do you mind if I don't come in?"

"See? Professional," Shona said.

"Why not?" DCI Filson demanded.

"I just... I don't know. I haven't been feeling great, and the smell of blood has been turning my stomach a bit lately. I don't know why."

Heather snorted. "What, seriously?"

"You really don't know why?" asked Shona, though with far less venom than the detective.

Sinead looked at them both in turn, her head shaking. "No. No, it's just—"

"Jesus Christ," Filson muttered. "You're pregnant."

Sinead's mouth experimented with a few possible responses, but didn't quite manage to formulate any. Nothing more interesting than, "What?" anyway.

"It's obvious. You're pregnant," Heather repeated. She

glanced back at Shona. "I mean... right? It is obvious, isn't it? I don't know her, and even I can tell."

Shona gave a shrug that was intended to be non-committal, but fell short. "Well, you can't just diagnose pregnancy by..." She nodded. "But, yes. You're definitely pregnant."

Sinead stared at them both like she was waiting for the punchline. Going by their silence, she'd be waiting a long bloody time.

"Pregnant?" she said, then the volume of her voice startled her and she dropped it down into a whisper of denial. "No. No, I can't be pregnant."

"When were you last on the rag?" Heather asked.

This drew a disapproving, "Jesus!" from Shona, who then posed the same question, but in a less unpleasant way. "When was your last period?"

"I don't know. Like... not long ago," Sinead said. Her eyes darted from side to side as she went rifling through her memory banks, then she let out an, "Oh!" as the memory came back to her. "Just after that case down by the lighthouse."

"So..." Shona gave a slow, encouraging nod, waiting for the penny to drop.

"Shit! That was two months ago."

"Three," Shona corrected. "Well... closer to three-and-a-half."

"*Three-and-a-half*?!" Sinead gasped. "How can it be three-and-a-half? It can't be three-and-a-half! I'd have noticed. How can I not have noticed?"

"Right, calm, deep breaths," Shona said, stepping down onto the path. "Let's not freak out."

"No. I'm not. No, but... Pregnant! I'm *pregnant*?"

"Um..."

They all turned to see Hamza standing just inside the front gate. He looked like a rabbit trying to stare down a rapidly approaching juggernaut, while knowing full bloody well who the victor was going to be.

He gestured vaguely over his shoulder with his pen. "Uh, the... guy. I spoke to the guy. He, eh..." The DS blinked several times, like he was coming out of a trance. "Pregnant? Really?"

"Shh! Shut up!" Sinead hissed, hurrying over to him. She caught him by the front of his jacket, her eyes like two ping-pong balls of panic. "You can't say a *word* about this. Alright? Not a word, until I know for sure. Not to Tyler, not to anyone. But especially not Tyler."

Hamza wasn't sure whether to nod or shake his head, and he ended up doing both simultaneously, which meant his head just sort of moved around in tight concentric circles. "Aye. I mean, no. I mean, I won't say a word."

"Promise!"

"I promise! I won't. I'll..." He mimed zipping his mouth shut. "I'll keep shtum."

Sinead realised that she had the detective sergeant's jacket all bunched up in her fists. She released her grip, smoothed the waterproof fabric back down, then nodded.

"Thanks. I just... I need to make sure before I say anything."

"Pretty sure we passed a chemist on the way in," Heather announced.

"It's just up on the corner," Shona confirmed.

Sinead turned to them, frowning. "I can't just... What am I meant to do? Go pee behind a bush?"

"We're at a house," Heather pointed out. "I'm sure it's got a toilet."

It was Shona who pointed out the obvious flaw in that plan. "The house is an active crime scene. There was a murder. Maybe you heard...?"

That caught the DCI's interest. "It's definitely murder then?"

"Well, either that or he caught his tackle in his fly three

hundred times in quick succession," Shona said. "Yes. It's a murder. So it's a crime scene."

Heather tutted. "Alright, alright. God, keep your hair on." She looked around, spotted the elderly man that Hamza had just been talking to, and gave him a wave. "Hey! Old fella!"

Ernie Peele heard the shout and saw the wave, but clearly didn't recognise himself in the DCI's description. He looked back over his shoulder like he might see the 'old fella' in question standing there. Then, when he didn't, he pointed to himself. "Who are you talking to? Me?"

"Yeah, you. Of course, you," Heather confirmed. She jabbed a thumb in a mortified Sinead's direction. "You mind if my colleague here goes for a piss in your bathroom?"

An assortment of Uniforms, crime scene investigators, and nosy neighbours all turned to look in the detective constable's direction, and though she tried very hard to turn herself invisible, she was largely unsuccessful.

"No, it's OK!" she called. "I can... I can hold it."

She turned back to the house and pulled another pair of shoe coverings from her pocket.

"I've changed my mind," she announced, blushing so hard that even her ears turned red. "Let's go and take a look inside."

"I thought you were feeling sick?" Heather said.

"Aye. Well," Sinead muttered, trudging past her. "Better sick than bloody mortified..."

Hamza remained frozen on the path while Heather, Shona, and Sinead all headed inside the house. He started to move to his left, stopped, then looked around like he'd forgotten where he was.

"Eh, right..." He said, gesturing back over his shoulder. "I'll just... Right."

Then, he picked a group of uniformed officers, headed in their direction, and tried to make himself look busy.

———

"Oh, God."

Sinead, who had been quite gung-ho about entering the room, now stood back by the door, one gloved hand over her mouth, her eyes looking everywhere but at the body on the floor.

"I see what you mean," Heather said to Shona. "He'd have to go some for that to be self-inflicted. Straddling a chainsaw, maybe."

"It's the same as the last one," Shona said. "Multiple stab wounds."

"Same weapon?"

"I don't know."

DCI Filson shot the pathologist a sideways look. "Not very good at your job, are you?"

Shona tutted. "Yet. I don't know *yet*. I'll have to get a closer look."

Heather gestured to the bloodless corpse on the floor. "Knock yourself out."

Shona patted her coat. "Right. Hang on, I'm sure I've got an MRI machine on me here somewhere..." she said, then she shook her head. "Oh. Wait. No. Looks like I'll have to use the one back at the hospital."

Filson didn't bother to reply. Instead, she squatted down at the edge of the blood puddle. It had mostly seeped in the other direction, towards the window, suggesting the wooden flooring had a slight slant to it.

The only thing of note about the window itself was that a set of metal blinds had been pulled closed across it, blocking the view of the back garden.

The victim had been seated when he was attacked, judging by the bloodstains and the gouges on the seat of the padded chair that lay on its back, half-hidden beneath the computer desk.

"Killer came in through the door. Rolled the chair back, stabbed down from above. Overhead, knife pointed down. Like Psycho in the shower scene," Heather reasoned.

"Norman Bates," Shona corrected.

"Sorry?"

"The shower scene. His name's not Psycho. That's the name of the film. His name is Norman Bates."

"Oh, well, I beg your pardon. I stand corrected," Heather said with a scowl. She turned her attention back to the body and the chair on the floor. "I think he pulled him right back. Tipped him all the way over."

"That's... possible," Shona begrudgingly admitted. She pointed to a series of red rivulets on the front of the victim's shirt. "They're running upwards, so I think he was on his back at the time, but still seated."

"Estimated time of death?"

"Recent. Within the last couple of hours."

Heather nodded and stood up again. "Fits with what the neighbour said when he phoned it in." She glanced around them. "There's a lot of blood spray."

"Yeah, frenzied knife attacks tend to do that," Shona said.

"The killer would've been covered in it."

Sinead seized on the opportunity to back out of the room. Her saliva glands had been working overtime since she'd entered the house, and it was taking all her effort to keep swallowing the stuff back without drowning in it.

"Not seeing anything out here," she remarked.

"What, nothing?" Heather asked.

Shona shook her head. "I had a quick look, too. Didn't see anything. Geoff's lot might find something, though." She glanced at the open front door. "We should go and leave them to it."

"In a minute," Heather said. She joined the other two woman in the hall and squatted again to check the flooring. "No, you're right. I'm not seeing anything, either. It should be traipsed all through here."

She stayed crouching down, but looked ahead through the open doorway. "Busy street out front. What's the back like?" She clicked her fingers, prompting one of them to answer. "Anyone?"

"How should we know?" Shona asked. "We don't live here."

With a tut of annoyance, Heather sprang to her feet and headed through an open door into the kitchen. The back door stood wide open, and a uniformed constable who was stationed on the garden path almost lost all bladder control when Heather prodded him in the back.

"Shit! Sorry! Yes! Hello, eh...?" He was new, Sinead thought. She didn't recognise him. And, judging by the vacant expression he wore as he looked across the faces of the three women, he didn't recognise any of them, either. "...ma'ams," he concluded, playing it safe.

"Was this door open?" Heather demanded.

The question seemed to completely befuddle the young constable. "Eh... when? Now?"

"No, not now. I can see it's open now," Filson told him. "When you got here. Was it open?"

"Um, yes, ma'am." His gaze flitted past her again to the other two. "*Ma'ams*. I think so. I just... The sarge, he just told me to stand here and not let anyone in."

A look of doubt crept across a face that looked almost too young to shave.

"Although... he didn't say anything about letting anyone out..."

Heather pointed to the gate at the other end of the path. The root of a tree had formed a bump below the tarmac, and the bottom of the gate was wedged against it, keeping the gate held half-open. It let out onto a few feet of long grass, and beyond that, a line of trees that marked the beginning of Culloden Wood.

"And that? The gate. Was it open like that?"

"Eh, aye. Yes, ma'am. *Ma'ams*. I, eh, I think so."

Heather's eyes narrowed. "You think so, or you know so?"

"I... No, I know so. It was definitely open. Just like that. I'm nearly... No, I'm sure. It was. Deffo." He shook his head, chastising himself. "Definitely," he corrected. "It was definitely like that when I got here. I came in that way, now that I think about it."

DCI Filson closed her eyes, just for a moment, muttered a, "God help us," then marched past the constable and along the path.

When she reached the end, she turned and called back in the direction of the house. "You coming, then, Detective Constable?"

Shona drew in a breath, then flashed Sinead a sympathetic smile. "Rather you than me," she said.

"Ha. Yeah. Thanks," Sinead said. She positioned her hand over her belly like she was about to lay it there, but then let it fall back to her side. "And, eh, you won't say anything about—"

"No," Shona said. She tapped the side of her nose, and winked in quite a theatrical way. "Your secret is safe with me."

CHAPTER THIRTY-FOUR

LOGAN AND BEN were almost back to the Incident Room when Tyler caught up and fell into step behind them.

"Alright, bosses?" he chirped. "How's it going?"

"Shite," Logan said. "You?"

Tyler shrugged. "Aye, well, that's a social worker turned up to talk to Mark, and the duty solicitor's hovering around, too. Thought I could safely leave them to it."

"You get anything out of him?" Ben asked.

Tyler puffed out his cheeks. "His top fifty favourite *Pokemon*," he said. "Not sure that'll help us build a case against his old man, though."

"Aye. Well, I'm no' so sure there's a case to build," Logan said.

"What? How d'you mean?" Tyler asked, but Logan left the comment hanging as he and Ben pushed open the doors of the Incident Room, and all three men almost tripped over Dave coming the other way.

"Aha! Good stuff. I was just coming to look for you lot," Dave announced. "We've found Eva MacLean. Her phone network caved in and gave us her location."

"Good. Where is she?" Logan asked.

"She's at home."

"At home?" Ben echoed. "Since when?"

"Since about half four," Dave told him. "We've got all her movements for the day."

Logan scratched his cheek. The injury he'd sustained from Mark MacLean's toe-punt to the head didn't hurt, exactly, but it was really starting to itch.

"I don't suppose she's been out at a house in Culloden, has she?"

"That would make life easier," Ben added.

Behind them, Tyler frowned. "Culloden? Why, what's happened at Culloden?"

Logan grunted. "Of course. You don't know, do you?"

"Know what, boss?"

"We'll explain on the way," Logan said, then he beckoned for Dave to hand over the printout that was resting on his lap. "So... what? She was just hanging about in town?" he asked, once he'd scanned the page.

"Looks like it," Dave confirmed. "I managed to cross-reference a couple of the pings with CCTV at the Eastgate, so it checks out. She was there with another girl. Reckon they were probably just skiving off school."

"Aye. Looks like it." Logan passed the paperwork to Ben. "Get Uniform to go over there and question her. See what she has to say for herself."

"Will do, Jack."

"And better go and tell her old man."

Ben nodded. "I'll do that, too."

Logan stepped around Dave's wheelchair, then stopped and sighed. "In fact... Get onto Cassandra Leigh-Taylor. Check out the Facebook account she sent that message to. If he's telling the truth—if it wasn't him—then let him go."

"Let him go, boss?" Tyler asked. He looked from Logan to Ben. "What have I missed?"

"I'm not really up on the old Facebook, Jack. Dave, maybe you could give me a hand with that?"

Dave raised two thumbs, Fonzie-style. "No bother."

"Tell MacLean not to leave town, though," Logan said, grabbing his coat. He pointed to the cut on his cheek. "There's still a conversation to be had about this."

"Added to the list, Jack," Ben said.

Logan glowered at Tyler, who was still standing just inside the doorway, looking completely confused by the conversation.

"Well, hurry up, then!" the DCI barked. "Get your jacket. We haven't got all bloody day!"

———

The ground beyond the victim's back garden was lumpy and uneven, and had been softened by all the recent rain. It was the sort of ground that, had they stepped on it, it would've *squelched* and gripped their feet, and their hope was that it would've done just that to anyone who'd recently fled that way in a hurry.

A thin layer of concrete ran along the length of the back fences, separating the gardens from the grass and the forest beyond. Around the size of a kerbstone, it wasn't wide enough to be a path—not even remotely—but by holding onto the fences and putting one foot in front of the other, Heather and Sinead were able to use it as one. This way, they could scope out the area without compromising any footprints or other forensic evidence.

"You think the killer came this way?" Sinead asked, picking her way along the concrete tightrope.

"What do you think?"

Sinead looked to her right, into the darkening shadows

beneath the pine trees and birches. Culloden Wood had some popular walking routes running through it that could be busy at weekends, or in the height of summer. Right now, though, on a drizzly weekday in late September, there wouldn't be many people around. Far fewer than there would be out on the streets, anyway, and the forest offered far more opportunities to hide.

"It would make sense," the DC said. "Could come and go without being seen."

"It's how I'd do it," Heather agreed. "You know, if I'd repeatedly knifed a man's dick off." She looked back over her shoulder. "And, between you and me, I won't say I've never been tempted."

Sinead laughed. Not because the comment was particularly funny, but because it seemed like the expected thing to do.

"I'm not seeing any blood out here anywhere," she said, switching the direction of the conversation. "You?"

"No. Nothing," Heather said. She stopped just past the next gate—the third one along from the victim's—and shuffled herself around on the concrete. "Might as well head back and let that crime scene shower do their poking around."

"Right. Yeah."

Sinead clambered awkwardly around, using the fence for support, until she was facing the other way. Heather, for whom patience didn't seem to be a strong point, was snapping at her heels by the time she had turned, and Sinead could practically feel the DCI breathing down her neck as she led the way back to the scene.

The light misting of rain that had been moisturising the area was steadily being replaced by a much heavier variety. They could hear them approaching through the woods—big, fat droplets that rattled off leaves and *thunked* against the grassy forest floor.

Any forensic evidence that might be out there in Culloden Wood wasn't going to last long.

"So. Up the duff, then," Filson announced, at a volume several decibels higher than Sinead would ideally have liked.

"Uh, yeah. I mean, maybe. I suppose I'll have to... I don't know. Do a test?"

Heather laughed. It sounded teasing. Almost cruel. "Liar!"

Sinead looked back at her, frowning. "Sorry?"

"You don't need a test. You already know. You can feel it, can't you?" Filson said. "All the little changes. Things you can't even explain. You can feel it happening. Like, subatomic level stuff."

Sinead faced front again. She picked her way on along the concrete, grasping each third or fourth fence spar to stop herself losing her balance. She couldn't argue with the DCI. Not really. Not with any sort of conviction, at least.

Things *had* felt different, even before the other two women had suggested she was pregnant. She'd known. Or... no. No, that wasn't quite right. She'd suspected, but she'd dismissed the suspicions before they could go anywhere. She hadn't allowed herself to think about it. Thinking about it made it real.

And, if it was real, then things got complicated.

"Do you have children?" she asked.

The reply took a little longer than expected to arrive. "No," Heather said.

"Oh. Right," Sinead said, unable to hide her surprise. "It's just, you sounded like you knew what—"

"I don't have kids," Heather said, shutting her down.

"OK," Sinead said, and while she felt like she should be apologising for something, she felt that might open a whole other can of worms.

"I take it it wasn't planned?" Heather asked

"Um, no. No, we hadn't... I mean, we've spoken about it," Sinead said. "But not with, like, a timeframe in mind or anything. We just always thought, like... further down the line, maybe. *Definitely*. We did want kids. We *do*. Just..."

"Not necessarily right now?"

Sinead put a hand on her belly, like this might somehow prevent what she was about to say from being heard by the collection of cells forming within.

"I just... It's tricky. I've got my little brother who lives with us, he's not long started high school, and he already gets bounced around all over the place far more than I'd like. And, I mean, Tyler..."

"Is a ludicrous man child?"

"Would make a great dad, is what I was going to say," Sinead continued, but she smiled at the description. It was, after all, not wholly incorrect. "I just... I don't know how he'll react about it being now. So soon."

She ran her hand across her stomach, then picked up the pace, suddenly wishing she hadn't allowed herself to get into this conversation.

"I'm sure it'll all be fine, whatever happens," she said, then she shot a worried look back over her shoulder. "You won't say anything, will you?"

Heather shook her head. "No. I won't say anything."

Sinead stopped so suddenly that the DCI almost walked right up her back. "Seriously, though?" the DC said. "I can't... I need a bit of time to... I can't have Tyler knowing. Not yet. Not until I know for sure."

"You already know for sure."

"Yes. No, but... Please," said Sinead, shuffling around on the concrete strip. "I need to know you won't say anything. I don't know you very well, so—"

"I was pregnant."

Sinead stopped talking. "What?"

"When I was fifteen. I... got pregnant."

"Um. Oh."

"I know what you're thinking. *What a slut.*"

Sinead stared back in horror. "What? No. I wasn't thinking that!"

"Yeah. Well. You'd be the first. Anyway, for some completely fucked up reason, don't ask me to explain now, I wanted to keep it," Heather said. She had a faint, not-quite smile on her face—a false and intangible thing. "But my parents talked me out of it. Well, 'talked' isn't quite the right word, but... Aye. And they were right, of course. It was for the best. Keeping it would've been mental."

Sinead wasn't quite sure what the right response was. In the end, she settled on the one that at least *felt* right.

"I'm sorry."

Heather gave a shrug. "There. Now we both have secrets." She held a hand out for Sinead to shake. "I'll keep my mouth shut about yours if you do the same for mine."

"Deal," Sinead said, and they shook on it.

"Right, now let's get a shifty on," Heather ordered, pointing to the next gate along. "It's about to start pissing down. And, I want a chance to wind up Jack's bird again before she leaves."

Sinead let out a laugh at that. "You're a terrible person."

Heather grinned. "Aye," she said. "Tell me about it."

"And she's nice. Shona," Sinead said. "She's *really* nice. She's lovely."

"Well, of course she is!" Heather said. She winked. "That's what makes it fun."

———

Sadly, by the time Heather and Sinead returned to the house, Shona Maguire had already headed to Raigmore Hospital to prepare for the arrival of the body. Logan, Ben, and Tyler were all now on the scene, coats and jackets done up against the cooling evening air, and the increasingly heavy rain.

When Sinead spotted Hamza talking to Tyler she shot over

to join them, her eyes blazing out a warning to the detective sergeant.

"Alright, Sinead?" Hamza called, straightening like he was in the presence of a much senior officer. "I was just filling Tyler in on the door-to-door."

"Were you?" Sinead demanded.

Tyler pulled an amused, rubbery sort of frown. "Eh... aye," he said. He looked his wife up and down. "You alright?"

"Why wouldn't I be alright?" Sinead asked, and a significant percentage of the question was aimed in Hamza's direction.

"Eh..." Tyler risked a sideways glance at DS Khaled. "I don't know. You just seem..."

"What?" Sinead asked. "I seem what?"

"Stressed," Tyler said. "You seem stressed. Does she seem stressed to you, Ham?"

Hamza shook his head. There was no way he was siding with Tyler on this one. "No. No, not particularly," he said.

The answer surprised DC Neish. He looked from his wife to his friend, and then back again, before shrugging and putting it down to an overactive imagination.

"Fair enough. Must just be me, then," he said.

"Right, you three. Get over here," Logan ordered, summoning them with a wave of a hand.

They hurried over, heads down to help shield their faces from the strengthening downpour. Hamza quickly pulled ahead, leaving Tyler and Sinead trailing a few steps behind.

"You sure you're alright?" Tyler asked.

The worried look Sinead wore quickly gave way to a smile. "I'm fine. Fine. It's nothing. Honest," she said, then she picked up the pace and picked a spot to stand between Logan and Ben, shielded from any more whispered questions.

"Right, here's the situation," Logan said, raising his voice to be heard above the whistling wind. "Palmer's team is combing the house and garden, starting with the room the body's in so we can get it shifted for Shona to start the PM. Uniform is going to run a search through the woods out back, and there's a team continuing to knock doors."

He ran an arm across his face, wiping away the droplets of rain that were forming on his eyebrows and the end of his nose.

"So, my question is, does anyone feel the need to stay here?" he asked. "Or, are we all in favour of fucking off back to the office where it's dry?"

"Probably get more done in the office, boss," Tyler said.

Hamza zipped his jacket all the way up to his chin and nodded inside his hood. "Easier to coordinate things from there."

"Thank Christ for that," Logan said, pulling open the door of his BMW. "Everyone back to the station, then. We'll pick it up from there."

"Should we, eh, sort out a bite to eat, sir?" Hamza suggested, the rumbling of his stomach audible above the roaring wind. "If we're going to be pulling another late one?"

"I'll go pick up some sandwiches," Heather suggested.

Logan eyed her suspiciously, but she pretended not to notice.

"Sandwiches? Is that it?" said Tyler, sounding more than a little disappointed. He quickly turned away from Heather's scowl and addressed Logan. "I could grab us a chippy, boss."

"Aye, that sounds more like it," Logan agreed. "A wee fish supper and a pickled egg wouldn't go amiss."

Heather shrugged. "Right, well, I'm still going for sandwiches. DC Bell?"

Sinead looked surprised by the sound of her own name. "Um, ma'am?"

"You come with me. Show me where the supermarket is." Heather was already backing towards her car, searching her pocket for her keys. "Anyone else want a sandwich? No? No.

Fine. Suit yourself. With me, Detective Constable. Chop-chop!"

Sinead shot furtive looks at the rest of the team, swept a strand of hair back behind her ear, then went hurrying after DCI Filson.

The others watched, squinting in the rain, until both women got into Heather's car and closed the doors.

"The hell was that about?" Tyler wondered.

"Eh, no idea mate," Hamza said, after just a moment of hesitation.

"Aye, something very strange going on there," Logan muttered. "I mean, who the hell chooses *sandwiches* over the chippy?"

CHAPTER THIRTY-FIVE

SINEAD SAT in the car outside *Tesco* at the Inshes Retail Park, listening to the rain rattling against the roof.

She'd offered to run in for the sandwiches, feeling that it was much more a DC's role than a DCI's, but Heather had insisted on going personally. She had no idea what she fancied, she'd said, and wouldn't know it until she saw it.

It had been a good ten minutes since she'd gone running, head down, across the car park. Given that the sandwiches were right at the front of the shop, she was apparently having a hard time making her selection.

The moment the DCI had left the car, Sinead had been straight out with her mobile, and had rattled off a text to Tyler with her chippy order.

Haggis supper. Curry sauce.

The reply had come back just a few seconds later.

Since when did you like curry sauce?

She'd stared at the screen for a while, trying to come up with a reply. The fact of the matter was, she'd *never* liked curry sauce. She hated the smell, disliked the colour, and positively despised the consistency.

And yet, what was the point in a deep-fried haggis supper if it wasn't slathered in the stuff? What was the point in *any* food, in fact, that didn't have an inch-thick gooey layer of the greenish-brown substance oozing all over the top?

Just fancy it, she texted. Then, in a follow-up message, added: *And five pickled onions*, then finished it with a kiss.

She had just returned the phone to her pocket when the driver's door was pulled open, and a wet and windswept DCI Filson flung herself into the seat.

"Jesus Christ!" Heather hissed, slamming the door behind her.

She shuddered—a full-body number that started at her toes and finished with a rattle of her teeth—then handed Sinead a plastic bag that was heavily beaded with rainwater.

"You get your sandwich?" Sinead asked, which won a mischievous sort of grin from Heather.

The smile faded after a moment, though, and the DCI shook her head. "Oh. What, did you actually think I was going for a sandwich? I texted Jack, told him to get me a red pudding." She poked at the bag. "That's for you."

"For me? What is it?"

"Look and see."

Cautiously, like it might contain a live venomous snake, Sinead peeled the top of the bag open. There, inside, was a long, narrow box. At first glance, she thought the picture on the front was a thermometer, and then the penny dropped.

"A pregnancy test?" she asked.

"Ninety-nine percent accurate, it says," Heather told her. "Results in one minute."

"Ah. Right." Sinead stared down into the bag for quite some time. "Thanks."

"You going to use it, then?" Heather asked.

Sinead looked across at the DCI. "What, here?"

Heather laughed. "Eh, no. Preferably not. At the station, I mean."

"Em..." Sinead quietly scrunched the top of the bag closed. "Maybe. I don't know yet. I might leave it until I get home. Or... tomorrow."

DCI Filson's smile remained fixed. Not a muscle moved. Not a line changed. "Aye. Right, yeah. Whatever you think," she said, and Sinead could sense something radiating off her. Disappointment. Or embarrassment, maybe.

"But, I really appreciate it," Sinead said. "It's just... it's all a bit..."

"Of course. Yeah. It's a huge thing. You do what works for you," Heather said, jerking her seatbelt across her chest. She fired up the car, and turned the wipers up to full. They swished violently across the glass, flinging the rain away. "Right. Enough of this bullshit. Work to be done."

Without another word, she floored the accelerator, and the tyres *screeched* as they sped out of the car park, and into the rattling rain.

———

Forty minutes later, the Incident Room positively reeked of cooking oil, fish, and vinegar, with a fairly heavy bottom note of chip shop curry sauce.

Sinead's had been awful. Inedible, almost. Yet, she'd gobbled up the lot with a level of enthusiasm that had drawn gawps of wonder from her colleagues.

"Bloody hell, has he been starving you, or something?" Logan asked, firing an accusing look in Tyler's direction.

"Eh, no. No," said Sinead, wiping a smear of sauce from her cheek with a paper napkin in what she hoped was a dainty fashion.

It was not.

"Just been a long day. Skipped lunch," Sinead explained.

She looked across the desk to where Hamza was sitting rigidly in his chair. He was eating slowly, chewing each morsel of food as many times as possible so as to keep his mouth full at all times. That way, he couldn't say anything that might get him into trouble.

"Right. Everyone done?" Ben asked, scrunching up his last few raggedy chips in their wrapper, before shoving it into the white carrier bag that the food had arrived in.

To his dismay, a corner of the crumpled paper punctured the bag, and everything he'd put in there fell right out through the arse of it.

"Well, that's no' exactly a bloody surprise, is it?" he muttered, gazing forlornly at the mess on the floor. "I mean, look at the bag. No wonder the bugger ripped. It's about as thick as an atom's eyelash."

"Worked alright on the way here, boss," Tyler pointed out, which earned him a scowl and a shake of the head from the DI.

"Aye, because the paper was *rounded* then, wasn't it?" Ben said, making a curved motion with his hands like he was tracing the outline of a ball. "It was wrapped around the food. As soon as you scrunch it up, the jaggy bits tear right through."

"Well, don't scrunch it up, then," Logan suggested. "Fold it flat."

"Fold it flat? Oh aye. Just hang on and I'll give it a wee iron, while I'm at it," Ben retorted. He tutted. "*Fold it flat.* I'm getting it ready for the bin, no' a night at the bloody *Ivy.*"

"Jesus, what's up with you?" Logan asked him. "Someone piss on your chips?"

"They'd bloody better not have!" Ben said, and he shot Tyler such a dirty look that the DC felt compelled to clarify.

"Eh, no. No, nobody pissed on your chips as far as I'm aware, boss."

Ben shook his head, and bent to pick up the scrunched up paper from the floor. "It's nothing," he said. "I'm fine."

He wasn't. Not really. He had called Moira a couple of times earlier in the day. He'd even left a voice message—a good one, too. Chatty, but not too much so. Friendly, but not desperate.

When he hadn't heard back, he'd almost sent a text, but had eventually decided against it. This was partly because he was worried it might make him seem a bit needy, and partly because he couldn't find his reading glasses, so he had no idea what he was typing.

Besides, Moira wasn't a fan of text messaging. In fact, she'd once described it to him as a 'harbinger of the Apocalypse.' Then again, she'd described quite a few things the same way, including internet pornography, twenty-four-hour news channels, and the career longevity of TV's Ant & Dec.

"Let's just crack on," Ben said. "What do we have?"

It took Sinead a few seconds to realise that everyone was looking at her. "Oh. Right. You want me to...?"

She glanced down at her notes, then at the Big Board. Neither one made immediate sense to her. Then again, most of her brain was currently occupied with other thoughts, and the details of the case were struggling for space.

"Actually..." Hamza swallowed, forcing down the food he had been storing in his cheeks like a chipmunk. "I spoke to the guy who found the body." He looked to Sinead, seeking her permission even as he threw her the lifeline. "Mind if I do the update?"

Sinead could've kissed him, but played it cool. "Eh, no, fire on."

"Cheers," Hamza said, wiping his hands on a napkin as he got to his feet and approached the board. "The new victim's name was Vikram Ganguly. Vik for short."

Heather startled him—and everyone else present—by

breaking into loud, joyous song. *"Ging gang goolie goolie goolie goolie watcha, ging gang goo, ging gang goo!"* She grinned around at the others. "Come on, none of you bastards ever in the Scouts? You not heard that song?"

"We've all heard the song," Logan said. "We just didn't think it particularly appropriate to sing it at the tops of our bloody voices, given the circumstances."

Heather's smile only widened. "Ging gang *goolie*? I'd say that's very appropriate, given the circumstances." She pointed to her crotch, made a whistling sound through her teeth, then sat back with her arms crossed, like she had proved her point.

Logan glanced at his watch, saw that it was already approaching ten o'clock, and sighed wearily. Christ. How had that happened?

"Right, Hamza, crack on."

"Eh, sure, sir, aye," Hamza said, with a hint of uncertainty. "So, um, Vikram is a bit of a local tech entrepreneur. Runs an online coaching business."

"Coaching what?" Logan asked.

"Him? Nothing. He's more the sort of facilitator," Hamza explained. "He set up the site, then recruited a bunch of people to do classes on a load of different things. Flower arranging, car maintenance, training your dog—the sort of stuff you can find on YouTube, if you look hard enough, but his is all in one place and more in-depth."

"And people pay for that, do they?" asked Ben. "Learning online?"

"Seem to, sir, aye," Hamza confirmed. "He's got an office in the city centre. Just expanded, and employing three full-time members of staff."

"Good for him!" Ben said, and he sounded genuinely pleased for Vikram before he remembered that all future expansions had been unceremoniously cut short.

"The neighbour, Ernie Peele, said he saw the victim entering his house just before noon," Hamza continued.

"And he was sure it was him?" asked Logan.

"Aye. They had a conversation. Definitely him," Hamza continued. "Ernie then returned to his house—he lives next door—before going round later with a couple of jumpers, shirts, and a tub of soup for the victim."

"What kind of soup?" Ben wondered.

Hamza checked his notes. "Leek and tattie. I, eh, I didn't ask," he said, feeling the need to explain. "He just volunteered the information. Twice."

"Nice," Ben said, then he gestured for the DS to continue.

Tyler had another question, though. "Why's he bringing him jumpers?"

"Just a present, as far as I can tell," Hamza said. "I got the impression he thought the victim needed his cast-offs."

"Seriously? Had he no' seen his motor?" Tyler wondered.

"Benevolent prejudice," Hamza said.

Tyler's frown made his lack of understanding clear. The, "Eh?" was just the icing on the cake.

"Benevolent prejudice," repeated the DS. "It's where you're racist but, like, in a positive way. Like, handing out food to black people because you think they're all poor. Or, I don't know, assuming Asians are all great at maths."

"Right. Gotcha," said Tyler, but he wasn't done yet. "So... is that better than real racism, though?"

"It is real racism," Hamza countered.

"No. Aye, I know. But, you know what I mean," Tyler said. "It's not as bad as normal racism, surely?"

"I mean, don't get me wrong, I'd rather get free soup than have the shit kicked out of me by a load of Nazis, aye," Hamza was forced to agree. "But it's still definitely racism." He gestured down at his notes. "Can I...?"

"Aye. Sorry. Fire on," Tyler said.

"Right. So, we've got time of death between noon and three-fifteen, when he found the body."

"Pathologist backed that up," Heather confirmed.

Something changed about Logan's face. A tightening, perhaps. "You spoke to Shona?"

"Yeah. We had a lovely long chat," DCI Filson told him, and something mischievous sparkled in her eyes as she turned her attention back to Hamza.

"Can't be the MacLeans, then," Ben announced. "They were here for most of that time, and at the gym for the rest of it. And Eva's on camera at the Eastgate."

"What do we know about the victim?" Heather asked. "Any connection to the first one?"

Hamza shrugged. "Well, there's the obvious," he said. "They were both the same colour."

"You think they're racist attacks?" asked Ben.

"I don't think we can rule it out, sir," Hamza replied. "Both Asian men. Inverness isn't exactly full of people who look like us, so statistically, that's a hell of a coincidence."

Ben couldn't argue with that. "Did they know each other, do we know?"

"Not from what we can tell," Hamza said. "Uniform's making some calls, but there are no personal connections jumping out so far. They might've crossed paths, but it's not looking like we're going to find anything more than that."

"Not friends?" Logan asked. "Two young Asian guys, similar age, both doing well for themselves..."

"Well, aye. But by that thinking, I'd be mates with them both, too, sir," Hamza pointed out.

"Since when were you doing well for yourself?" Tyler chipped in.

Hamza let out a single mirthless chuckle. "There is that, right enough." He looked quite deliberately at Logan. "But, no, sir. I don't think they were friends."

"Alright. Point taken," Logan said, holding up a hand in apology.

"I still think it's sexual," Heather declared. "I can't get past the method. There are a hundred easier ways to kill a guy. Hacking his bits to bits isn't just an attack, it's a message."

"A message sent to who?" Logan asked.

"Well, I'd imagine to the victims, boss," Tyler suggested. "I mean, that's going to come in loud and clear, isn't it? A big knife up the whatnots."

"Maybe to them," Heather said. "But maybe not. And maybe 'message' isn't even the right word. It might be more like..."

"A statement," Logan said.

Heather nodded. "Yeah. Yeah, something like that. I'd put money on the killer being someone who's been sexually assaulted. Or a close relative of someone who's been. Husband. Dad. Brother, maybe."

"Sexually assaulted by the victims?" Ben asked. "There's nothing in their pasts that ties them to anything like that, is there?"

"There usually isn't," Hamza said, which Ben had to concede on.

"It's not necessarily either of them," Heather said.

"How do you mean?" asked Tyler.

"Well, if you're taking revenge on your rapist, you stop when the job's done. You don't move on to someone else."

"Unless they were both in on it," Tyler proposed.

Logan stood up and regarded the Big Board. "We can't rule that out, but I'm not feeling it. We've got nothing to tie them together."

"So *far*," Ben added.

"Right. Aye. But assuming for a minute that they haven't been secretly bonding over their shared love of sexual assault, what are we left with?"

A silence fell as everyone considered the possible options.

"Might still be a racist thing," Hamza said. Then, before Heather could interrupt, he added, "And a sexual thing. The right wing's still got its whole obsession with 'Muslim grooming gangs' going on. Maybe one of them got carried away with themselves?"

"Were they Muslim?" Ben asked.

Hamza shrugged. "Does it matter? I don't think your average EDL knob-end is going to know the difference."

Logan shook his head. "I'm not feeling that, either. They're at that shite down south, but we'd have got wind of it starting up here."

"Unless this is it starting now," Hamza suggested, and his usual affable air had been replaced by something harder and colder.

"No, I'm still not buying it," Logan said. "I think Heather's right."

"That four-year Psychology degree finally paid off, then," DCI Filson remarked.

"Eh? You've got a Psychology degree?" asked Ben.

"No need to sound so bloody surprised," Heather told him, before Logan steered them back onto topic.

"The wounds—the method of attack—that was personal. That wasn't some vigilante fuckwit trying to earn brownie points with his wee basement-dwelling internet pals. That was someone driven by something that had happened to them. Someone with a personal grudge to bear."

Tyler, picking up on the shift in tone, offered up an alternative suggestion. "What if the killer was attacked by an Asian guy, but doesn't know who it was?" he said. "Like, maybe they're working their way through them, hoping to find the right one."

Logan looked back over his shoulder to Heather, who gave a shrug. "It's possible." She jumped down off the desk she'd been sitting on, and swiped at the back of her trousers like her backside might be dusty. "But I wouldn't be surprised if it's not even that specific. Maybe the victim—the rape victim, I mean, not the dead guys—maybe she's just lashing out at men who remind her of the attacker."

"We're jumping straight to 'she' are we?" Logan asked.

"Well, let's just assume for now. Psychology degree, remember?" Heather said. "She's lashing out at men who remind her of the guy who attacked her. Young Asian men. In positions of power, too, because that's what most sex attacks are about, after all. Power. She'd have felt helpless during the attack. Maybe seeing them—powerful, in charge of stuff, looking at least superficially like their attacker—maybe it triggered something."

Sinead, who had been sitting in silence for most of the conversation, sat up a little straighter in her chair. "So, she'd have to be someone who'd met them both. She meets them, they remind her of what happened..."

"It all comes rushing back," Heather concluded.

"And she... what? Loses it?" Ben asked.

Logan shook his head. "No. There was planning involved. This wasn't someone lashing out."

"You might want to tell that to the victims' bollocks, boss."

"OK. It wasn't *just* someone lashing out," Logan corrected. "They were organised. They got in and out of both crime scenes without being spotted. They left very little forensic evidence at the first scene, and I'm not holding my breath about the second. There was strategy involved, it wasn't just a spontaneous thing."

It was Ben who voiced what they were all thinking. "Meaning this probably won't be the last."

"No," Logan agreed. "Probably not." He looked around at the team. "So, we all ready for another late one?"

"Well, my calendar's empty," Heather said.

Hamza took his mobile from his pocket and gave it a little wave. "I'd better go give Amira a ring and let her know." He smiled weakly. "I'll take it outside, in case she blows your eardrums out."

"Good luck, son," Ben said.

"Anyone else need to make plans?" Logan asked.

Sinead got to her feet. "Eh, I should go and check in with my aunt. See if she's OK keeping Harris another night. I'm sure she'll be fine, but..."

"Aye. Of course. On you go," Logan said.

Sinead picked up the phone from her desk, looked at it for a moment, then set it back down again. She got to her feet, the carrier bag that held the pregnancy test tucked into the inside pocket of the jacket she'd hung across the back of her chair.

"Actually, I might go call from outside, too. Get a bit of fresh air while I'm at it."

"Whatever you think. Just be back in five minutes," Logan told her. "We've spent the day getting nowhere. I want progress made on this tonight."

CHAPTER THIRTY-SIX

SINEAD AND HAMZA stood at either end of the corridor, making their respective calls, one of which was going far more smoothly than the other.

Aunt Janet had been fine with Harris staying. Harris himself had sounded a little disappointed, but he understood. Besides, Janet let him stay up later, had faster internet, and gave him chocolate muffins for supper, so he knew which side his bread was buttered.

Hamza, on the other hand, had spent most of the call apologising. Kamila was four now, but 9 PM was still late for her to be up. She'd insisted on hanging on, though, convinced that her daddy was going to make it home in time to carry on their bedtime story.

No such luck.

Their calls ended around the same time. Hamza spent a few seconds standing with his eyes shut, giving the guilt some time to settle, then turned to find Sinead standing beside him, waiting for him to pull himself together.

"Oh. Shite. Sorry," he said. "Didn't know you were there."

"Everything OK?" Sinead asked.

"Uh, yeah. Just... I'd told Amira I'd be home by five. Cutting it a bit fine."

Sinead checked her watch, then winced. "Aye. You can say that again."

They stood around awkwardly for a few seconds, then both broke the silence at the same time.

"You didn't...?"

"I haven't..."

They both smiled, and much of the awkwardness evaporated.

"Thanks," Sinead said.

"No bother," Hamza replied. "You still haven't told him?"

Sinead shook her head.

"Why not?"

"Just... I don't know," Sinead said, sighing. "I mean, I literally don't know. I might not even be pregnant."

"And if you are?" Hamza pressed.

"Then... I don't know," she admitted. "I mean, we've discussed it as something we want to do down the line, but I just..." She ran a hand through her hair. It was still damp, and her hand came away wet. "I don't know how he'll react."

"It's Tyler," Hamza said. "*Annoyingly enthusiastically* is how he'll react, same way he reacts to everything."

Sinead came close to laughing at that. "Aye," she said. "Maybe."

"Trust me. He'll be bouncing off the ceiling," Hamza said. "In fact, do us all a favour and *don't* tell him, or we'll never hear the bloody end of it."

"Works for me!" Sinead said.

Hamza put a hand on her shoulder. "It's going to be fine, Sinead. Whatever happens. It's going to be alright. Alright?"

She nodded. Smiled. "Alright." Drawing in a deep breath, she reached into her jacket pocket and produced the pregnancy test, still wrapped in the bag. "I think I might..."

"Is that...?"

"Aye."

"Oh. Oh, OK!" Hamza said, eyes widening in something that might have been excitement, but could equally have been panic. "Now?"

"No time like the present," Sinead said.

"For what?" asked a voice from along the corridor.

Sinead froze. Hamza withdrew his hand from her shoulder with enough urgency to arouse suspicions on the other side of the country.

"What are you two up to?" Tyler asked, making his way towards them. There was nothing particularly accusing in his tone, mostly just his usual child-like curiosity.

"Nothing," Sinead said. "We were just coming back in."

"Oh. Right," Tyler said, stopping beside them.

They had both stepped apart now, and angled themselves so they were facing away from each other. If this was an attempt to look less conspicuous, it failed miserably.

"What's in the bag?" Tyler asked.

Sinead swallowed. "What bag?"

Tyler's frown was mostly amused. But only mostly. "That bag," he said, pointing to the plastic carrier clutched in Sinead's hand.

It wasn't quite as thin as the one from the chip shop had been, but it was wrapped tightly enough around the pregnancy test that it was possible to make out the writing. Tyler tilted his head, then his eyes went wide when he read the box through the bag.

"Whoa. Hang on! Is that a pregnancy test?" he gasped.

Sinead just stared back at him, mouth open, but no sound coming out. She jumped when Hamza snatched the bag from her hands.

"It's mine," the DS announced.

Tyler regarded his friend, blinking slowly. "It's yours?"

"Well, not mine personally, obviously," Hamza said. "It's, eh, it's for Amira. She asked me to pick one up, and I asked Sinead to get it for me."

Tyler bent over, placed his hands on his thighs, and let out a sigh of relief so powerful it moved his gel-hardened hair. "Phew! Thank God for that! Had me going for a minute there!"

"Um, aye," Hamza said, and the look that passed from him to Sinead went right over Tyler's head, both literally and metaphorically. The DS flashed Sinead a smile. "So, eh, thanks for doing that."

Sinead smiled. It was a flat, thin thing, yet somehow brimming with emotion. "No bother," she said. "Anytime."

"Right. Aye," Hamza said. He passed the bag from hand to hand, then nodded. "Well, I'll be..."

He turned the wrong way, took a step, then doubled back and headed for the Incident Room. At the door, he hesitated just long enough to meet Sinead's eye, then he pushed on inside.

"Bloody hell. He's a glutton for punishment, eh?" Tyler said. "He's got his hands full with Kamila, never mind another one."

"It might be good for them," Sinead ventured. "It could be... nice."

Tyler snorted. "Aye, we'll see if he's saying that when he's changing a shitty nappy at three in the morning!"

He set off in the direction that Hamza had gone, then called back when he realised his wife wasn't beside him. "You coming?"

"Aye. I'll be in in a minute," Sinead said.

She waited for him to head through the doors, then she shut her eyes, leaned her forehead against the wall, and wondered just what the hell she was going to do.

———

The next few hours plodded along, slowed by the tedious minutiae of a murder investigation. Statements from the door-to-door were collated. The preliminary forensics and Post Mortem reports were noted, read over, and saved.

The victims' lives were cross-referenced, looking for any sort of connection beyond the obvious ones. Nothing jumped out. They'd never worked together, met in person, or connected on social media.

The only tenuous link was that they'd both attended the same launch of a local arts festival a couple of years previously, but there had been a couple of hundred other people there, and there was nothing to indicate that Dev and Vikram had interacted in any way.

Vikram's family were still back in Bangladesh. He didn't appear to be in a serious relationship, though his phone had revealed that he'd been on a couple of dates in the last six months, neither of which had really gone anywhere.

Work seemed to be his big passion. Uniform had spoken with his employees, and they all seemed genuinely upset by the news. None of them had a bad word to say about their old boss —not uncommon when people spoke about the dead—but the general impression from the sergeant leading the questioning was that they'd have been equally as positive had he still been alive.

He gave extensively to charity. He was nice to his neighbours. He cared about the welfare of his employees, and treated them well.

And yet, despite all that, someone had brutally murdered him in his own home.

The pathology report more or less matched Heather's interpretation of events. He'd been attacked from behind while sitting down, the killer striking with his knife in an overhand downwards motion, then continuing when the victim was on the floor.

There were a couple of deep gouges further down both legs, suggesting that Vikram had kicked out at his attacker. A few slash marks on his hands and arms said he'd tried shielding himself from the blade, but to no effect.

It had been sudden, and it had been violent, and it had been brutal.

And it had been the second such attack in as many days. If they didn't hurry up and catch the bastard responsible, there was no saying where this would stop.

It was almost midnight when Logan called time. There was nothing more to be done tonight. No more avenues to pursue that couldn't wait until the morning.

"But I want us all back here first thing," he said. "And I want everyone chasing up leads, right off the bat. Anything new, or anything from before that we think is worth going over again, I want us on it. Alright?"

The rest of the team murmured their agreement, their jackets already half on.

"Sure thing, sir."

"No bother, boss."

"Right you are, Jack."

Logan dismissed them all, then allowed his head to sink into his hands. He still wasn't fully recovered from his bug—not even close—and the partial kicking from Mark MacLean hadn't helped matters, either.

He had been craving sleep for the past several hours, but had refused to let the team see that. You couldn't exactly inspire confidence while flaked out in your office chair, and he'd never ask them to pull a full day shift he wasn't prepared to do himself.

But, Christ, he was paying for it now.

"You look like shit," DCI Filson remarked.

He'd been dimly aware that Heather had still been in the room, but he hadn't cared. She'd seen him in far worse states.

Perhaps more so than anyone, in fact, she'd seen him at his lowest. Compared to that, he was now a picture of health and happiness.

"Cheers for that," Logan said, sitting upright. He blew out his cheeks, placed his hands on the desk, and then drew himself up into a standing position. Albeit a slightly wobbly one.

"I take it you don't fancy grabbing a drink?" Heather asked.

"You take it correctly," Logan said. "I need my bed."

A smirk began to spread across DCI Filson's face, but Logan quickly shut it down.

"Aye, no' like that," he told her.

"Spoilsport," Heather said. She looked him up and down, then shook her head. "I think I should drive us, though?"

Logan frowned. "Us?"

"Aye. I mean, all my stuff's still at yours, and I can't exactly go and get a hotel at this time of night..."

Logan groaned inwardly. Probably outwardly, too, though he was too tired to tell. Shona wasn't going to be happy about this. He wasn't exactly delighted about it himself, for that matter.

"Right. OK. But tomorrow, you go home," he told her. "Or, if you're sticking around, you find somewhere else to stay."

Heather smiled, but there was something wounded about it. "Course. Aye. Wouldn't want to cramp your style or anything. Far be it for me to get in the way of your married bliss."

"We're not married," Logan said, dragging his coat off the back of his chair.

Heather gave him another up-and-down look, and this time she let it linger for a while. "Aren't you?" she asked. "You could've fooled me."

———

Shona, as expected, had not been particularly enamoured by the thought of spending another night under the same roof as DCI Filson, but hadn't made any fuss about it. She'd even offered to make tea for all three of them, but both detectives had declined, and Logan had gone shambling up to bed, leaving Shona to dig out the spare blanket and pillows.

"Cheers," Heather said, squashing the pillows into shape and throwing them onto the couch.

Taggart, who had been lying on the rug in front of the TV, assumed the pillows were for his benefit, and quickly jumped up onto the couch, only to find himself unceremoniously dumped off it again by DCI Filson.

As the dog slunk off back to the rug, Heather gestured towards the stairs. "And don't worry about Jack. I think we just tired him out tonight." She shrugged. "Guess he's not as young as he used to be."

"Well, none of us are," Shona countered. "And don't *you* worry about him. He's got me to look after him now."

Heather ejected a little laugh. "For now," she said. "But, in my experience, Jack doesn't do 'domestic bliss' well."

Shona crossed her arms. "Yes. Well, things change."

"People don't. Not really," Heather replied. "Not deep down." She flashed another smile. It was a barbed, pointy thing, all teeth and malice. "Anyway, sweet dreams."

"Always do," Shona replied. Then, with a sniff and a raising of the head, she turned her back on the detective, and marched on up the stairs to bed.

CHAPTER THIRTY-SEVEN

THE SUN STREAMED in through the windows of Burnett Road station, and the Big Board shone in the light of a brand new day.

The storm had broken overnight, and the sky was an uneasy alliance of bright blues and pale greys. After such a prolonged period of rain—seventeen days, on and off, according to one of the women at the front desk—the sunny morning had brought renewed enthusiasm to the Incident Room, despite the early start.

Tyler had jumped straight on the phones, and was trying to follow up with the police in Bangladesh, who had been getting ready to go break the news to Vikram's family when he'd left last night.

The country was six hours ahead—or eighteen hours behind, maybe, he hadn't paid too much attention when he'd checked on Google. Either way, it would be early afternoon by now, so they should've spoken to the relatives by now.

He'd been worried about making the follow-up call, as to describe his grasp of Bengali as 'tenuous' would be a wild exaggeration. He hadn't even known that was what the language was called until he'd searched for 'How to say hello in Bangladeshi' and been corrected by the algorithm.

To his relief, everyone he had spoken to as he'd been passed around departments could speak excellent English, and his nerves had now given way to impatience as he was redirected through to yet another department.

Hamza, meanwhile, was investigating the HDMI device that had been taken from the *Refuge* security systems. Or, as Ben put it when Logan and Filson arrived, 'fiddling with his doohickey.'

Dave was back at his usual seat, busily checking in the forensic evidence from the scene the day before.

Most of the stuff being checked in was pretty mundane—Vikram's laptop, the clothes he'd been wearing—that sort of thing.

They did have a partial cast of a footprint taken from the grass behind the house, but it didn't tell them much. A trainer of some kind, size unknown.

There were a few interesting fibres that didn't match up with any clothing in the house, though they came with a bit of a proviso, as they *did* closely resemble fibres from the protective suits Palmer's team wore, and they hadn't been able to rule out contamination of the scene.

So, no smoking gun, but it was enough to keep Dave busy for a few hours.

Once Logan had removed his coat, he looked across to the Big Board, expecting to see DC Bell working away to update it. There was a small stack of paperwork on the desk nearest to it, and a pile of *Post-it Notes* waiting to be put to use, but the detective constable herself was nowhere to be found.

"Where's Sinead?" Logan asked, taking his seat.

"Toilet, boss," Tyler said, then he winced and spoke more quietly into the phone. "No. Sorry, that wasn't meant for you."

"Actually, I could do with going there myself," Heather

announced, pulling a perfect U-turn and heading back the way she'd just come.

The Incident Room doors opened as she approached, and DCI Filson came face to face with a pale, bleary-eyed Sinead.

"Jesus," Heather whispered. "You alright?"

Sinead nodded, gave her a look that positively screamed, 'I don't want to talk about it,' then hurried past her and picked up where she'd left off at the Big Board.

Heather let the doors swing closed, then took a seat next to Logan.

"Thought you were going to the toilet?" he asked her.

"False alarm," Heather said.

Sinead picked up the top sheet from her stack of printouts, skimmed it, then set it down in another pile. Managing the Big Board wasn't just about pinning up every scrap of information, it was about carefully selecting what went up and what didn't, so as to help form an accurate narrative of everything that had happened in the case.

Some things, like this particular printout, didn't make the cut, and would instead be filed away to be referenced as and when required.

It was only when she had set the page down that something told her to read it again.

She picked it up, leaned against the edge of the desk, and took more time over the list of financial transactions printed onto the page.

Something had jumped out at her. Something she hadn't consciously noticed, but that a nagging voice in her head was insisting she look at it more closely.

She was two-thirds of the way down the page when she stood up again.

"Um..." she said, and there was enough meaning in just that utterance to make everyone else look up from what they were doing.

Logan stood, too, sensing something. "What is it?" he asked. "What have we got?"

"Um, it's... I don't know, maybe nothing," Sinead said. "Just, these are financial records for Vikram Ganguly's company."

Heather opened her mouth to start singing again, but was silenced by a raised hand from Logan before she could get out the first note.

"And?" he asked.

"There's a payment here to *Shine & Sheen*. Made two weeks ago." Sinead shuffled through a few of the pages that followed on the pile. "It's monthly. He was paying them every month."

"*Shine & Sheen*?" Logan asked. It took him a moment to place the name. In his defence, he'd been burning up with a fever the one other time he'd heard it referenced. "Wait, the cleaning company?"

"The ones who found Dev Rani's body, sir, yes," Sinead said. "Looks like they were cleaning the second victim's office, too."

"Jesus Christ! How did we not know that?" Logan barked. He pointed to Hamza. "You were going to follow up with them, weren't you? Find out why they were there in the morning, and not the night before."

"Uh, yeah, sir," Hamza said. "I tried calling, but got no answer. Sort of fell by the wayside after that."

"Get back onto it," Logan ordered. "Why the change of schedule?"

"Will do, sir," Hamza said, returning the video capture 'doohickey' to the evidence bag.

"And you. Tyler. What are you doing right now?" Logan demanded.

"Eh, I'm on hold with Bangladesh, boss," Tyler said.

"So, in other words, you're doing fuck all," Logan said. "While you're waiting, get digging. Find out what you can about everyone working for that cleaning business. As deep a dive as you can."

"That's me on it now, boss," Tyler said, keeping the phone pinned between his ear and his shoulder as he rolled his chair over to his computer.

"Mind that Shona's wanting someone over this morning to go through the full PM results," Ben said, which drew a wince from Logan.

"Shite. Aye. She mentioned that this morning."

"I'll do it," Heather said.

"God. Do you ever stop trying to wind her up?" Logan sighed.

"I promise not to wind her up," Heather said, though her smirk said otherwise. She gestured around the room, which had suddenly come alive with purpose. "You stay here and keep on this. I'll take DC Bell."

"Sinead?" Logan asked. "I want her here."

"Aye, well, I want her with me," Heather countered. "You've got all this lot. Besides, she makes a good referee."

Sinead's face had turned a shade of green at the thought of looking over the body. "I'm not sure that's such a good idea..." she said, but Heather dismissed her protests with a jerk of a thumb and a shrill whistle through her teeth.

"Tough shit. With me," she instructed, making for the door.

"Don't be long," Logan said. "This could be big. I want to get on top of it."

Heather held the door open for Sinead, and shot a leering look back over her shoulder. "Aye, you always did like to get on top, right enough," she remarked.

And then, in the awkward silence that followed, she went strutting out into the corridor.

"Wee bit too much information there," Dave muttered, not taking his eyes off his screen.

"Boss! Boss!"

Tyler's phone fell from the crook of his neck and battered off the table. He didn't seem to notice, his eyes—wide and staring—fixed on something on his monitor.

"*Boss!*" he cried again.

"What is it, Tyler?" Logan barked. "Stop just saying, 'Boss!' and spit it out."

"It's her, boss."

Ben frowned. "It's *whose* boss?"

Tyler stared blankly at him for a moment, then shook his head. "No, it's her, comma, boss. I don't mean it's her boss, I mean it's her. It's Angela Sheen. From *Shine & Sheen*."

"What about her?" Logan demanded.

"She was assaulted, boss. Sexually assaulted."

Logan, who had only recently sat down, stood up again. "What? When?"

"Two years back. Just under," he said, scrolling up the screen. "Jumped coming off a job. Hospitalised."

"Jesus. Anyone done for it?"

"No, boss. CID looked into it, but nobody was ever identified."

"When was the last case update?" Ben asked.

"Eh..." Tyler clicked and scrolled, then straightened again. "Couple of months back. Sheen's lawyer got in touch asking for an update, but we had nothing new to give her."

"Nothing since then?" Logan asked. "What about before? How often did she chase it up?"

"Looks like about once every three to five weeks," Tyler said, his eyes darting across the screen. "And then she stops."

"Sick of waiting on the legal system to get up off its arse, maybe?" Ben guessed.

"Aye, well, she knows a thing or two about the legal system," Hamza said. "She's got a record."

Logan spun to face the DS. "Violent?"

"Theft," Hamza said. "Minor stuff. She's never done time."

"Aye, well, I suspect that's about to bloody change," Logan announced. "Get onto Uniform. Get on the phones. Punt her photo around to every bastard who'll look at it. I want her found, and I want her found *now*."

———

Heather waited until they had both clipped their seatbelts on before breaking the news. "Don't worry, I'm not going to make you come in."

Sinead turned and looked at her, her face a mask of surprise. "What?"

"You just looked like you could do with getting out of there," the DCI said, starting the engine.

"Oh!" Sinead said, and her whole body sagged with relief. "Oh, that's... Thank you. Thanks."

"Aye, well, that's the thing about a men's club." Heather pulled out of the car park, leaving the station behind. "Us non-men have got to stick together."

———

Angela Sheen had dropped off the face of the Earth. There was nobody at her home address, and while her van was parked on the street out front, none of the neighbours recalled seeing it move in a couple of days.

The back door to her terraced house on the northwest side of the city had been left unlocked, and a couple of more experienced Uniforms had invited themselves in for a nosy around. If anyone asked, they were simply securing the premises. No harm in that. In fact, it was positively civic-minded, and definitely didn't require the securing of a search warrant first.

The house had been devoid of Angela Sheen, or anyone else for that matter. A couple of the bedroom drawers and a wardrobe had been pulled open, and there was a notable lack of clothes that suggested she'd gathered up what she needed, and fucked off, sharpish.

From what they could piece together from the neighbours, she'd returned to the house shortly after her interview with Sinead—and soon after finding Dev's body—parked her van, and then had presumably gone inside the house. Nobody had actually seen her arriving, though, but one of them had noted seeing the van parked outside before noon, which she'd thought was unusual.

Friends and family had been tracked down and contacted, but they all claimed not to have heard from her. It had been months since her parents had spoken to her, they said. They lived in Fife, and she didn't get over often. Also, she owed them quite a lot of money, and they evidently had very different ideas as to what the repayment schedule ought to look like.

Still, they seemed concerned, and a couple of local plods were dispatched to ask them some questions, poke around in their relationship with their daughter, and generally make a nuisance of themselves.

Her friends had been identified through tags on Facebook, but most of them initially seemed confused when they'd been asked about her, like they couldn't quite place the name. Eventually, they recalled her from some night out or other—she was a friend of a friend of a friend who had tagged along—and none of them were any the wiser as to where she might be now.

"Looking very much like she's legged it, boss," Tyler said.

Logan couldn't really argue with that. He sat back in his chair, scratching the stubble on his chin, as the first few stabs of a headache threatened to ruin the rest of his day.

"We did manage to get hold of Josh Holder, the guy who works for her," Tyler said. "He's been trying to get hold of her, he says. He was supposed to be paid yesterday, and hasn't been. Didn't seem particularly impressed, boss."

"He works for her?" Logan asked. "So, he's the guy who was with her when they found the body?"

"That's him, boss," Tyler confirmed.

"He'll be one of the last to have seen her, then," Logan said. "Bring him in. Interview him. See what he knows."

"Will do, boss. Though, I think the answer will be 'not much,' going by what he said on the phone," Tyler said.

Logan threw up his shoulders in a weary shrug. "Fine. *Not much* is still better than *fuck all*, which is what we've got right now."

"Fair point, boss."

Logan turned to DS Khaled. "Anything from her bank or her phone company?"

"Nothing from the network, sir, no," Hamza replied. "Her phone must be off, and the last ping they have on her is in the area of her house, just about the time she returned there with the van."

"Bollocks. No help, then," Logan muttered. "And the bank?"

"Word just came in on that, actually. She took out seven hundred quid from the Bank of Scotland on the Longman around one o'clock on Thursday."

"That's just a few hours after she spoke to Sinead," Ben pointed out. "So, she's ditched the van, bundled together a load of clothes, took out a wad of cash, and cleared out."

"Sounds fishy to me, boss," Tyler said.

"Oh, well, thanks for that input, Sherlock," Logan said, glowering at the detective constable. "We'd never have picked up on that ourselves."

"Cheers, boss," Tyler said. He must've picked up on the sarcasm. He had to. And yet, his response seemed utterly sincere. "Anytime."

"The bank—they get her on CCTV?" Logan asked.

"Aye. Inside. They're going to send it over."

"Nothing outside?"

Hamza broke the news with a shake of his head. "Afraid not, sir."

"Great. And, I don't suppose anyone saw which way she went?"

Hamza pulled his mouth into something that was neither a smile nor a grimace. "No such luck. But, one member of staff reckons she might have got in a taxi." The revelation hadn't been given with any real enthusiasm, but what little it had contained almost immediately died away. "Although, she can't really be sure."

"And the chances of her remembering the name of the taxi company are...?"

"Zero, sir."

Logan grunted. No. Of course they didn't remember. They never did. It was never that easy.

"They did say that seven hundred quid was basically everything in the account," Hamza continued.

Christ. It went from bad to worse.

"So, wherever she is, she'll be paying cash," Logan muttered. "That's not going to make finding her any easier."

Ben picked up the phone from his desk. "I'll get onto Uniform. Make sure they're on the lookout for her."

Logan rubbed his temples with the middle finger and thumb of one hand. "She's got a two-day head start."

"Not if she killed Vikram Ganguly yesterday afternoon," Hamza pointed out. "That's a one-day head start at most."

Logan nodded. "Aye. Aye, good point," he conceded. "Either way, I doubt she'll still be knocking around Inverness now. We'll need to throw the net wider."

Dave, who had wheeled himself over to join the others, casually raised a hand. "I can get onto taxi companies, if you like? See if anyone can tell us anything." He shrugged. "Long shot, like, but we might get lucky."

"We might," Logan agreed.

We won't, he thought.

But it was worth a try. Right now, anything was worth a try.

"Bus and train companies, too," Logan suggested. "Get us the CCTV from the railway station, and start going through it. If she has left the area, then I at least want a direction to start looking."

"You think it's her, boss?" Tyler asked. "You think she did it?"

"I don't know, son," Logan admitted. "But we're no' going to find out by sitting here twiddling our thumbs. So, everyone know what they're doing?"

There was a consensus from the team that, yes, they did.

Logan's big brow furrowed as he glowered at the group around him. "Well, that's funny, because I see a lot of people sitting around with their fingers up their arses," he said. When nobody reacted, he let out a sigh. "That was your cue to move, by the way."

CHAPTER THIRTY-EIGHT

"HI HONEY, I'M HOME!"

Shona looked up from the *Pot Noodle* she was in the process of wolfing through, muttered something only marginally less unpleasant than the chicken and mushroom flavoured mush on the end of her fork, then set the pot down and got to her feet.

"Heather. Great. Of course it's you," she said with resigned acceptance.

"Ah-ah-ah! We're in work mode. It's DCI Filson," Heather corrected, and she took visible delight in doing so.

Shona dabbed at the corners of her mouth with a cotton swap, presumably having run out of anything else that might serve as a napkin.

"Not to me it's not," she said. "I don't work for you. I could call you anything I want."

"Like what?" Heather asked. It was a dare. A challenge.

"Like..." Shona's eyes darted around, searching for inspiration. She'd never been very good at being mean, and while Heather certainly brought it out in her, it still didn't come naturally. "Bum tits."

Heather all but flinched. Not at the harshness of it—

because the delivery was hesitant and uncertain, and it was hardly the most devastating of insults to begin with—but the unexpectedness of it.

"*Bum tits?*"

Shona stood firm. She straightened to her full height, which still made her three or four inches shorter than Heather, and nodded. "That's right. Bum tits. That's what I'm calling you. If you don't like it, you can feel free to leave."

Heather stepped closer, eyes narrowing. "Actually..." she began in a low growl, then her tone lightened. "I do quite like it."

She rubbed her hands together with gleeful exuberance. "Right. Where's this body, then?" she asked. "Sinead's going to wait in here while I check it out."

"Sinead?" Shona glanced over at the door on the off-chance that she'd missed someone else entering the room.

"Uh, yeah. She was behind me just..."

Both women set off on a march towards the door, practically shouldering each other out of the way in their race to get there first.

Heather had the advantages of being closer, and having longer arms, but as the DCI pulled the door open, Shona seized her chance to duck through, earning herself an important yet unspoken victory.

All thoughts of celebration stopped when she darted out into the corridor.

Sinead stood fifteen feet away, leaning against the wall with one hand, the other clutching at her stomach. Her legs looked fit for buckling. Her face was a grimace of pain, and of fear.

"Sinead?" Shona asked, and the word echoed in the empty corridor like the tolling of a funeral bell.

"It hurts," Sinead said. Part sob. Part whisper. "God... it hurts."

"Oh. Fuck," Heather muttered at Shona's back.

"Get help," Shona instructed. "Find a doctor."

"Where?"

"You're in a fecking hospital!" Shona spat, hurrying towards the struggling detective constable. "Use your imagination!"

———

"Take a seat, Mr Holder," Tyler said, ushering the cleaner into the interview room.

"Cheers, ta. You can, eh, you can call me Josh. It's fine."

"Nice one, cheers. I'm Tyler."

"Tyler," Josh said, like he was testing the name out. "Hello."

He pulled out one of the two chairs on the other side of the table. Being short and somewhat weedy-looking, this took both hands to achieve.

Once he'd manoeuvred the chair into an acceptable position, he lowered himself onto it and shuffled himself closer to the table.

"You sure you don't want tea or coffee?" Tyler asked.

"No. I'm fine, honest. Been buzzing off my tits on *Red Bull* all morning. Should probably lay off the caffeine. Or, you know, liquids in general."

Tyler chuckled, then took his seat. "Fair enough. You mind if we record this interview? Saves me having to write it all down."

"Fire on," Josh said. "Em, quick question, though. Who was the old guy we met on the way in?"

"Ben? I mean, Detective Inspector Forde?" Tyler asked. "He's just one of my many bosses. Why?"

"Just thought he looked familiar," Josh said. "Thought I knew him from somewhere."

"He's done some TV appeals and stuff," Tyler said. "Might be that."

"Might well be that," Josh said.

He waited patiently until Tyler had got all the formalities out of the way, then asked another question before the DC had a chance to start with his own. "They said this was about Ange. Has she turned up?"

"You know she's missing?" Tyler asked.

"Aye. She was supposed to pay me yesterday. And I was waiting to hear about shifts for this weekend, but nothing. She's not answering my texts, she's not getting back to me on Facebook. I even tried calling her. Nothing."

"She's never disappeared on you like that before?" Tyler asked.

"No. Not at all. I really didn't think she'd do something like that," Josh said. "I mean..."

He seemed to have second thoughts about what he was going to say, and shook his head, like that might erase those last two words.

Tyler, however, wasn't about to let them go.

"What were you going to say?" he pressed.

"No. Nothing," Josh insisted.

"If there's anything you can tell us that might help us find her, Josh..."

Across the table, the cleaner struggled to get the next few words out. "I just... She's never been anything but good to me. But, when I got the job—when I first started, I mean—I heard from a few people that she wasn't the most... reliable."

"How do you mean?" Tyler asked.

"Well, you know about the other companies, right? From before?"

Tyler shook his head. "Other companies? What other—"

A knock at the door stopped him, mid-sentence. It was opened with a sense of urgency, and Hamza appeared in the gap.

"DC Neish. I need a word."

"No worries. Just give me five minutes and I'll be out."

"I'm not asking, Tyler. It's an order."

For the first time since the door had opened, Tyler turned to look. There was something in Hamza's expression that made his stomach tighten. Something about his eyes. Something about the curve of his shoulders.

"What is it?" Tyler asked. "What's happened?"

"You need to come with me, mate," the DS told him, and the words were filled with cracks. "You need to come now."

————

"Here," Shona said. "Watch, it's hot."

DCI Filson studied the offered paper cup like it might be a beaker full of poison, then accepted it with a, "Cheers," and a nod of the head.

Shona didn't sit next to her, but instead took the next seat along. This, she thought, was quite close enough.

"What are they saying?" Heather asked.

Shona shrugged. "Not much," she said. "They're going to keep us posted."

She took a tentative sip of her scalding hot tea, concluded that it was currently impossible to drink, and so nursed the cup in her hands, instead.

"You get through to anyone?" she asked, leaning her head back so it rested on the waiting room wall behind them.

"Aye. Spoke to Ben," Heather replied. "They're going to blue light Tyler over."

"Jesus. Poor bastard," Shona muttered. "Does he even know?"

"That she's pregnant?" Heather shook her head. "No. I asked her this morning. Said she was building up to it."

"God. What a way for him to find out," Shona said. "Oh, and thanks, by the way. For helping."

"No, thank *you* for helping," Heather replied. "I don't know what I'd have done without you."

"No, *I* don't know what *I'd* have done without *you,*" Shona corrected.

To the untrained ear, it might sound like two people showing their gratitude for one another. Anyone paying closer attention, however, would see the contest they were locked in.

"No, but, I really appreciate you helping," Heather insisted. "Thank you."

"Thank *you,*" Shona retorted. "You were the one who helped me."

They sat in silence for a while after that, watching the constant flow of hospital foot traffic, but not actually seeing it. Not really.

Time passed like it was having to fight through treacle. Heather clocked her watch. Shona watched the clock.

"Can't believe that's only fifteen minutes she's been in," the DCI said, sounding mildly outraged by how little time had passed.

"It could be a while," Shona said. "You should go."

"Yeah," Heather said. Like Shona, she rested her head against the wall. "I'll hang on for a bit. If you need to get back, though..."

"I'm fine. My patients don't tend to be in any rush," Shona said, which drew a smile from Heather.

"No. No, suppose not." She tested her coffee. Far too hot.

A door opened along the corridor. They both looked, waited, then faced front again when a porter came through wheeling an old man on a bed.

Footsteps squeaked. The woman behind the ward's reception desk tapped away at her keyboard. Somewhere, a machine *bleeped*.

"You got kids?" Heather asked.

Shona blinked, taken aback by the question. "Um, no. No. You?"

"No," Heather said, without hesitation. She quickly turned the line of questioning back around. "Planning any?"

Shona hesitated, sensing a trap. "Uh, I don't know. I hadn't really... Planning's not really my strong point. Why do you ask?"

Heather frowned, like she wasn't quite sure of the answer to that one herself. "Just making small talk, I suppose," she said.

They both checked the time again. A couple of nurses and a smattering of patients walked by.

"He was a pretty shite dad, by all accounts," Heather ventured. "Jack, I mean. He'll tell you as much himself."

Shona closed her eyes, bracing for another argument.

"But I think he'd be different this time," Heather continued. "I think *he's* different." She shrugged. "Dunno. Must be all the fresh air, or something."

"Maybe he just needed to get away from you lot," Shona suggested. It felt cruel, so she softened it with a smile that Heather returned.

"Aye. Could also be that," she admitted. "I hate to say it—I *really* hate to say it—but I think it's been good for him. Coming up here. Meeting..." She started to gesture at Shona, then thought better of it and turned it into something vaguer and more all-encompassing. "...new people. I think it's made him more, I don't know. Rounded. So, I think he'd be better this time. As a dad. If that was... if that was something that was to happen."

"Yes. Well," was all Shona had to say on the matter.

"Just... do me a favour, will you?" Filson asked. She waited until she had Shona's full attention before continuing, sombre and straight-faced. "If it's a girl, name her after me."

Shona laughed at that. It was a sharp, sudden thing that

caught her off-guard, and almost spilled scalding hot tea all over her lap.

"You're a dick," she said.

Heather grinned. "It's a good Scottish name!" she insisted. "I mean, what's the Irish equivalent? *Four-Leafed Clover* Logan? Doesn't have quite the same ring to it."

"Shamrock Logan, sounds alright."

"Fuck off! It sounds demented," Heather said.

"Actually, hold on. Who's saying it'll be taking his last name?"

"What, seriously?" Heather snorted. "You'll be married before the year's out."

"Haha. Hold your horses there," Shona said. "We've never even spoken about marriage."

"You don't have to speak about it," Heather said. "The way you two look at each other?" She shuddered with revulsion. "It's practically oozing out of you both."

She sipped her coffee, which had now cooled just enough to be bearable.

"I've never seen him look at anyone like that before," she admitted. A moment passed. A silent mourning for a life that might have been. "Not anyone."

"I doubt that."

"Aye, well, I know him better than you do," Heather countered.

"Yeah. So you keep reminding me." Shona blew out her cheeks, building up to something. "You can stay another night. If you really must."

"It's fine. I'll get a hotel."

"OK. Fair enough."

"Unless you want me to stay?"

"No, I don't *want* you to stay," Shona replied. "I'm saying I don't mind if you stay."

"OK, I'll stay. Since you obviously want me to..."

Another door flew open, at the opposite end of the corridor this time. It was followed by the sound of running footsteps, and a frantic shout from a man more scared than he'd ever been in his life.

"Where is she?" Tyler cried. "Where's Sinead?"

———

"Sorry about that, Mr Holder," Hamza said, once he'd returned to the interview room and taken up Tyler's position. "I'm afraid DC Neish has had to go and attend to an urgent personal matter. I'm sure you understand."

"Yeah. Yeah, of course," Josh said. "You his boss?"

Hamza raised his eyebrows. "Sorry?"

"The way you came in and pulled him out," Josh said, nodding to the door. "You his boss?"

"I mean... technically, aye," Hamza said. "But we don't worry too much about that around here. We're pretty relaxed."

He clasped his hands in front of him, indicating that the small talk was over, and they were getting down to business.

"So, Josh, I had a quick check of the recording, and you'd mentioned something about Angela's other businesses," he said. "Could you tell me what you meant by that?"

"I don't really know too much," Josh admitted. "I just, I heard from people who'd worked with her before. They said she'd shafted them. Shut down the company and started up another one, sort of thing."

He began to count on his fingers.

"Before she was *Shine & Sheen*, she was *The Golden Sheen*, then *Sheen's Cleaning*, then *Sheen'll Clean It*, then *The Clean Masheen*. That's my favourite. She spelled it M-A-S-H-E-E-N." Josh grinned, like he really appreciated the pun, and when Hamza didn't seem as amused, he struggled to hide his disappointment. "I'm not sure that's the right order, but those were the names. You can probably look them up somewhere."

"Thanks. We will," Hamza said. "I spoke to the owners of the nightclub—"

"Didn't he own it?" Josh asked. "The dead guy. Whatever his name was."

"No. Well, partly," Hamza explained. "But he had investors. They reckoned that cleaning was usually done at night, after the club shut."

"That's right," Josh confirmed.

"So, how come that wasn't the case on the night of the attack?" Hamza pressed. "Why did you go in the next morning, instead?"

"Well, I mean..." Josh wriggled like he'd developed an uncomfortable itch. "You'd have to ask Ange."

"I don't know where she is, so I'm asking you," Hamza said.

"Aye, I know, but... I mean, it doesn't seem right that I should land her in trouble, or anything."

Hamza sat forward so suddenly Josh rocked his chair back onto two legs in his rush to get clear.

"Look, Josh, I don't have time to piss about here. We've got two men dead, potentially more to come, and we are all under a *lot* of stress today. Even more so than usual. So, how about we cut the shit, eh? Stop trying to protect your boss, and just tell me what you know."

Josh stared back at him in mute disbelief, still perched on those two back chair legs. He had the sort of look on his face that a member of the aristocracy might adopt should the hired help ever have the audacity to talk back.

"Are you allowed to speak to me like that?" he asked, once he'd finally found his voice. "It's not very professional."

Hamza sighed and forced a smile. "My apologies. Like I say, tough day," he said. "But the point stands. The longer we delay, the more chance there is of someone else getting hurt. If you know something, tell me. Please."

There was a slow *creak* as Josh returned the front two legs of the chair to the floor. He closed his eyes for a moment, took a deep breath, and then came out with it.

"Ange cancelled."

"How do you mean?"

"She texted me. About half an hour before she was due to pick me up. Said she was going to have to call off."

Hamza frowned. "Did she say why?"

"No. I wasn't all that bothered, because I was doing a livestream on Twitch. Did you check out my channel yet?"

Hamza had indeed taken a look, but only to confirm Josh's alibi. The thought of watching him run around shooting virtual soldiers for hours on end didn't appeal.

"I did, aye," Hamza confirmed.

"Aye?" Josh asked, his eyes almost doubling in size. "Nice one! Did you subscribe?"

Hamza was forced to admit that no, he had not.

"Oh. Right. Well, you should. There's a load of new content going up. I'm getting really into the *Horizon* series. Have you played that?"

"No, can't say I have. I haven't really got as much time for gaming as I'd like."

"No? Well, it doesn't matter if you're into the game. You can just watch for the banter. I do competitions and shout-outs. Stuff like that. You should definitely subscribe."

"I'll try and remember to do that," Hamza lied.

Josh's enthusiasm wilted before his eyes. "No, you won't," he said.

"No. I probably won't," Hamza admitted. "Like I say, I don't have a lot of time. Now, about that text message..."

"Right. Yeah. OK. Here. You can see yourself," Josh said. He produced his phone, tapped in the PIN, then found the text message. "See? Just says something had come up. Asked if I could do the early morning shift. Said she'd pay me extra." He flicked a look of disgust at the mobile. "So much for that, eh?"

"Do you mind if I take a picture of this text message?" Hamza asked.

"Help yourself. Or I can screenshot it and Bluetooth it to you, if you want?" Josh suggested.

"That'd be great," Hamza said. He took out his phone, accepted the connection request when it appeared, then raised a thumb to confirm the screenshot had been received. "Nice one, thanks," he said, returning the phone to his pocket. "What about next morning? Did she tell you why she had to rearrange?"

Josh narrowed his eyes, thinking back. "No. Not really. She apologised a lot, but I don't think she actually explained what had happened."

"And how did she seem? Was she acting... differently?"

"Not really, no," Josh said. "Although, I did think she seemed a bit rough. You know, like hungover, maybe? But she doesn't drink."

"Not at all?"

Josh leaned in a little, his voice lowering a fraction. "She had problems, I think. Alcohol-related. She's mentioned them before. Aye, not in any detail, or anything, but she's dropped some pretty big hints."

"You think she fell off the wagon?" Hamza asked. "You think that's why she called off the shift the night before?"

"I mean, I don't know," Josh said. "She might've just been sick. Or she could've just been tired. You do a lot of unsociable hours in this job."

"Tell me about it," Hamza said.

"Well, most businesses don't want you there when customers are..." Josh's voice trailed away when he realised his mistake. "Oh. You mean you. Yeah. Sorry."

"You don't know where Angela Sheen is now?" Hamza asked.

"No. Sorry. I wish I did." Josh chewed on his thumbnail until a moon-shaped sliver tore away. "Can I ask you something?"

Hamza nodded. "Of course."

"Do you think she did it? Ange? Do you think she's the killer?"

Hamza said nothing for a long time, like he was trying to think of the right way to phrase his answer. In the end, he didn't offer one.

"Do you?" he asked.

Josh didn't need to think about it. He immediately shook his head. "No. No way. Not Ange. She wouldn't do something like that."

"It's funny," Hamza said, sitting back in his chair. "That's exactly what you said to DC Neish about her disappearing and not paying your wages. I think maybe you have to accept that you didn't know her quite as well as you thought..."

CHAPTER THIRTY-NINE

THE ROOM TYLER was taken to was empty. This seemed to be as much of a surprise to the nurse as it was to him.

It wasn't just that Sinead was nowhere to be seen, the bed was missing, too. Someone had wheeled her away.

That couldn't be good.

"Where is she?" Tyler demanded. "Where did she go?"

"Sorry, I thought she was... I'm just back from my break," the nurse told him. "Wait here, and I'll go find out."

She darted out of the room, leaving him alone with a lot of questions and worry, and not a whole lot of anything else.

There was a drip stand next to where the bed should be. Monitoring equipment powered on, but connected to no one. The accoutrements of injury or disease.

Or worse.

He paced, watching the door, trying not to think about what might be happening to her, but failing miserably. Was she in pain? Was she scared? Was she crying out to him somewhere, wondering why he wasn't there with her? Why he wasn't there to hold her hand, and stroke her forehead, and tell her that everything was going to be OK?

He couldn't do this. He couldn't just wait. He should run out there, look for her, find her himself. He'd be quicker. He could do it. He knew he could.

With a spring, he launched himself out of the room, and collided with a large, sombre-looking black man in a white coat.

"Shit, sorry," Tyler said, once they'd both finished careening across the corridor.

Before he could set off on his search, the doctor risked stepping back into his path.

"Mr Neish?"

"What? Aye! Aye, that's me."

"You're Sinead's husband?"

"Aye. Where is she? What's happened?"

The doctor hesitated. "You don't know?"

"No. They just told me she'd been taken in. Stomach pains, or something. Is she alright? Can I see her?"

"She's fine. She's going to be fine," the doctor said.

Tyler let out a sound that he didn't think he'd ever made before. Maybe no one had. Tears welling, he sagged against the wall, all the adrenaline that had been coursing through his veins now deciding that its job was done.

But, perhaps, it had left him too soon.

The doctor stepped aside and gestured along the corridor, like Death ushering the recently deceased through the veil. "Mr Neish, there's something I think you should brace yourself for..."

———

Hamza returned to an Incident Room that was muted by worry and grief. The whole team had assembled there, with the exception of the two most junior detectives. Heather had come back, leaving Shona to pass on news from the hospital. She'd insisted that the agreement had been reached quickly, and with very little in the way of argument, though Logan had found that very hard to believe.

Even Detective Superintendent Mitchell was there. She was sitting in Hamza's seat, so only Tyler and Sinead's were vacant.

"Any word?" he asked, and the lack of response told him everything he needed to know. "Shite. Well, I've discharged Josh Holder. He doesn't know where Angela is."

"Right. Aye," Logan said.

"I should... I should write it up for the board," Hamza said. He looked over at the Big Board, all carefully arranged by Sinead's hand.

"She'll no' be happy when she comes back to find you've messed it up," Ben remarked, with a sort of forced joviality that didn't prove particularly infectious.

"Ha," Hamza said. "No. She won't be."

"*If* she comes back, she won't be happy to find you all sitting here like this, either," Mitchell pointed out, and the harshness of it got far more of a reaction than Ben's attempt had.

"She's coming back," Logan said.

Mitchell rose to her feet. "We don't know that. We hope it, of course—Lord knows, we hope it—but we don't know it. And that's our job, isn't it? Here, in this room, our job is to know things. And what we know right now is that there's a killer out there who has murdered two men. Two decent men.

"We owe Detective Constable Bell our sympathy and concern, of course we do. But we also owe those men something —our undivided attention. Our determination to bring their killer to justice. That's what we do. Us in this room, that's what we're here for. That's who we are."

"And that's what Sinead would want us doing," Ben agreed.

"Hallelujah!" cried Dave from his desk by the door. When everyone turned to look his way, he almost looked embarrassed. "Sorry, just felt right in the moment."

Heather raised the mug of coffee she'd been nursing in a toast. "Halle-fucking-lujah."

Logan gave a sigh. It was a deep and guttural thing, like the sound of the earth itself shifting. He stood up, so he was towering above the detective superintendent. She didn't blink, or flinch, or look in any way impressed.

He'd always liked that about her.

"Well, it's not quite how your predecessor would've phrased it, but that was some speech," he admitted. He tipped her a nod of his head. "So, aye. Halle-fucking-lujah. Let's all get back to work."

A knock at the door spoiled the drama of the moment a bit, and the poor uniformed constable who popped his head into the room was met by a litany of questioning stares.

"Uh, sorry to interrupt, um, ma'am, sirs. Got someone on the phone returning a call from DC Neish. Says she can't get him on the mobile number he left."

"Right. Just transfer it up to my desk," Ben said.

"Will do, sir," the constable said.

"Wait," Logan said, stopping the young officer from making his escape.

"Sir?"

"Who is it? Do you have a name?" the DCI asked.

The constable checked the scrap of paper he was holding. "Uh, yes, sir. It's an Angela," he said. "It's an Angela Sheen."

———

She'd looked scared when he'd been led into the darkened room. Scared, and more than a little shocked. He'd rushed to her side, and held her hand while the doctor lurked just inside the door, and a stout, grey-haired woman who smelled of fresh lavender ran a handheld scanner over Sinead's stomach.

"You alright? You OK?" Tyler whispered, suddenly feeling like he was in church.

She nodded, but said nothing, just squeezed his hand when he offered it, and stared in mute disbelief at the grainy black and white image on the screen at the side of the bed.

There was something there. He could see it. Something terrifying. Something *life-changing*.

"Oh God. Is it cancer?" he asked, his voice breaking.

The lavender-smelling woman stopped moving the scanner long enough to shoot him a look. It was a look that was both a question and an expression of sympathy. The sort of look usually reserved for the village idiot.

"No," Sinead told him. "No, it's not cancer."

Tyler let out a breath that had been trapped somewhere in his chest. He looked from Sinead to the screen and back again. "What is it, then?"

She bit her lip. Steeled herself.

"It's a baby."

Something in Tyler's brain appeared to misfire. He just stared at her for several seconds, saying nothing.

Sinead had just started to worry that she'd broken him when he kicked back into life.

"It's a what?"

She squeezed his hand. "It's a baby, Tyler."

She watched his eyes blur. Heard the tremble in his voice. And she knew then, that she had been worried for nothing. She knew then, that she should never have doubted.

"It's a baby?" he managed to say through his tightening throat. He turned to the screen, and when he looked back at her, his cheeks shone with tears. "We're having a baby?"

He pounced then, leaning across and hugging her, and earning himself a, "Watch it," from the lavender-scented nurse.

"Sorry, sorry!" Tyler said, withdrawing so quickly he catapulted himself onto his feet. He spun to face the doctor. "I wasn't sure that I could... I mean, after the operation, the doctors said it wouldn't be a problem, but I wasn't..." He went rigid for a moment, like his brain was doing another reboot, then he grabbed the doctor's hand and shook it vigorously. "It's a baby! We're having a baby!"

"Eh... not quite," Sinead said.

The doctor's sombre expression cracked into a smile. "Remember I said that you should brace yourself, Mr Neish?"

Tyler's face fell. Dread twisted its knife in his guts.

"What? What's wrong?" he asked, turning back to the bed.

It was the woman with the scanning wand who answered. She indicated the blob on the screen that Tyler had wrongly presumed to be a tumour. "Baby," she said, then she slid the scanner along Sinead's abdomen and pointed to the screen again. "Second baby."

"Twins?" Tyler said.

He was sitting down, he realised. When had that happened?

"It's... We're having twins?"

Sinead's smile was a toothy and terrified thing, full of worries both known and unknown.

Tyler didn't share any of them. Not now, at least. Not yet. The reality of it all could wait. For the moment, this was all that mattered. This. Here. Now.

"We're having twins!" he cried. "That's two! That's two babies!"

Sinead laughed, Tyler's joy proving too infectious to resist. "That is two babies," she confirmed. "We're having two babies!"

They hugged, and this time the lavender woman didn't have the heart to interrupt.

By the time Tyler pulled away, he had a big dollop of transparent gel on the front of his shirt. "Christ, that's cold," he remarked, pulling the fabric out so it wasn't in contact with his skin.

"Tell me about it," Sinead said. She put a hand on the side of his face and rubbed his cheek with her thumb. "So, you're OK about it?"

"OK?!" Tyler clutched her hand and held it, as another tear fell. "Sinead, it's the best thing that's ever happened to me."

Sinead smirked. "Oi! Second best."

"OK, aye," Tyler laughed. "Second best. But, at least this time I don't have to do a speech." A thought troubled him, and he glanced around at the medical professionals flanking them on either side. "I don't have to do a speech, do I?"

"Definitely not, Mr Neish," the doctor assured him. "All I want you to do is wait out in the corridor for a while, then we'll get Sinead back to the ward. There are some things we want to check out."

"Things? What things?" Tyler asked.

He was on his feet again. He hadn't noticed that happening, either.

"What is it?" he pleaded "What's wrong?"

"It's nothing to be concerned about," the doctor told him. "We just want to get to the bottom of Sinead's earlier discomfort. We're just going to run a couple of quick tests, then you'll be able to take her home."

"Home?" Tyler asked with a gasp of disbelief. "Should she be at home? She's pregnant with twins."

"Yes, of course she can be at home," replied the doctor. "Provided she takes it easy, she can go to work, she can exercise... With a few exceptions, she can go about her life as normal. But the midwives will give you more information on that."

Something about the word made Tyler giggle. "Midwives," he said, then he turned to his wife in the bed.

His family in the bed.

"It's really real, isn't it?" he said. "You're going to be a mum!"

Sinead smiled and nodded. "And you're going to be a dad."

Tyler's brain suffered another momentary malfunction. He stood in rigid silence, his limbs all locked, his face utterly frozen.

And then, like a starting pistol had been fired, he launched into life, pulled open the door, and ran out of the room.

Sinead winced as, "I'm going to be a dad!" echoed through the hospital corridors.

"Sorry," she said, looking from the doctor to the nurse. "He gets a bit over-excited."

"Really?" replied the doctor, as Tyler's whooping continued on the other side of the door. "You don't say…"

CHAPTER FORTY

ANGELA SHEEN SAT on a well-worn brown leather couch, tucked up at one end, like she was expecting a lot of company and wanted to be as far away from them as possible. She'd got to her feet when Logan and Filson had been shown into the room, and had shaken their hands without making eye contact.

"I'll be right outside if you need me, Ange," the man who had brought the detectives in assured her. Angela had asked him to leave the door open, before nestling herself back into the dunkle her weight had left on the seat.

Logan waited until the door was closed, then pointed to one of the room's three armchairs. "You mind?" he asked, and Angela replied with a shake of her head. He sat, while Heather remained standing by the door, saying nothing.

The room was remarkable for its lack of notable features. There was a small TV in one corner, with a row of DVDs lined up on a stand beneath it.

The walls had all been painted in matching magnolia, and the vertical blinds on the windows were competing to be an even less interesting shade, and somehow winning.

The carpet was grey. It was a little threadbare at the door, but otherwise, there was nothing much that could be said about it.

There was a camera up in the corner, fixed to the ceiling, casting its watchful eye across the room. Logan had welcomed it when the orderly had told him, and had requested that a copy of the recording be available for him when the detectives were ready to leave.

"You don't sound like him," Angela said. "The guy on the phone."

"That was my colleague, Detective Constable Neish," Logan explained. He introduced himself and DCI Filson. Angela didn't seem particularly impressed by either of them.

"Sorry I couldn't call him back. They take your phone for the first bit," she said. "I phoned back when I got his messages."

"I appreciate you doing that," Logan said. "We've been looking for you, Angela."

The woman on the couch drew her leg up beneath her. "Why would you be looking for me?"

"I think you know."

Angela met his eyes, but only for a moment. "Dev."

"Aye. Dev," Logan confirmed. "Do you have anything you'd like to tell us?"

"About what?" Angela asked. "About Dev?"

Logan nodded. Angela chewed her lip and looked to the window, and the small garden beyond it that was almost as uninteresting as the room.

"I don't think so," she said. "I think I told that woman everything. Detective something or other."

"DC Bell," Logan said. "And yes. You told her that you'd found Dev's body that morning."

"Me and Josh, yeah," Angela confirmed.

"And you're sticking to that, are you?" Logan asked. "There's nothing you'd like to add?"

"Why did you call off the night before, Angela?" Heather asked. Her tone was sterner than the other detective's. Harder.

"What?"

"You were supposed to be at the club the night before. The night Dev was killed," Logan said. "But you called off without any explanation. Why?"

Angela squirmed. Her hand gripped the arm of the couch, her fingers kneading the leather.

"I just... It wasn't anything. I just..."

"You just what?" Heather barked. "Spit it out."

"I just got caught up with some people," Angela replied. "That's all. I just got caught up."

"What people?" Logan pressed. "What do you mean by 'caught up'?"

"I just... I fell off, alright? I made a mistake. I saw some old friends, and I shouldn't have stayed out with them, I know I shouldn't, but I did. And I fell off. And it was stupid. After everything, it was so fucking stupid."

"Fell off?" Logan asked. "The wagon?"

He looked around them at the dull room, with its camera and orderly hovering somewhere outside the door. Inverness had a couple of rehab centres. This one was the cheapest.

"That's why you checked yourself in here?"

Angela's head shook. It was subtle, and could have been mistaken for a tremble. "No. I mean, yeah. I mean..." She took a deep breath. "After we found Dev... after I saw him like that, I felt... I don't know. I just had this urge."

She shook her head again, and there was no mistaking it this time.

"No. Not even that. This *need*."

"For a drink," Logan said.

It wasn't a question. He already knew the answer. He'd lived it himself.

"Yeah. Just to try and blot it out, or something. Numb it. I went home. I was going to do it. I was going to give in to it. And then, I don't know, something happened."

Heather crossed her arms, growing impatient. "Something like what?"

"Not... not a thing. Not an external thing," Angela said, trying to explain. She tapped the side of her head. "In here. Just for a minute. Just for a minute, I was strong. So, I bundled some stuff together, took out the cash I knew I'd need to pay for this place, and came here."

"First of all, well done," Logan said. "I know that can't have been easy."

Angela made eye contact then, and let it linger, perhaps seeing or sensing something in him that she recognised.

"Thanks."

"And you're saying that you've been here since then?" Logan asked.

"Yeah. Since the day before yesterday."

Logan didn't need to look to be aware of Heather sidling out of the room. She'd go and check that what Angela had told them was right. If it was, they were back to square one.

And yet, Logan found himself hoping that they were. He'd been where Angela was now. More than once. Different rooms, different couches, but otherwise identical.

An hour ago, he'd been planning to arrest her. Now, he found himself hoping he didn't have to, even if it left them with no other suspects.

"Your friends you were out with the night Dev died—they'd be able to confirm?"

Angela blew out her cheeks. "Probably, yeah. We were all pretty smashed. But, yeah. Yeah, I'd think so."

Logan took out his pad and asked for their names and addresses. She gave him what she could. It wasn't much, but it would be enough to provide her with an alibi for the first murder. And, if Heather came back with a confirmation, then her alibi for the second was pretty rock solid.

"Do you know a Vikram Ganguly?" he asked.

"Vik? Yeah. He's got the computer business. Programming, or something. We do his office a couple of times a week. Nice guy." Angela's face fell. "You don't think he did it, do you?"

"Um, no. No, we don't think he did it," Logan said. "I'm afraid he's dead."

"Dead? Vik? What? How? When?"

There was a sound from the door as Heather returned. Logan looked back over his shoulder and was met by a nod. Heather was visibly disappointed, not sharing Logan's affinity with the woman huddled on the drying-out couch.

"He was attacked. Yesterday," Logan explained. "At home."

"Jesus. Not like...?"

"Aye. Like Dev Rani," the detective confirmed.

"Oh, God. Oh, no, that's horrible. That's... that's horrible."

"We tried to find a connection between both victims, Angela, and you were the only one we could find."

Angela's eyes grew suddenly wider. "Me? How am I...? Oh. Because I clean for them both? Right."

She ran a hand through her hair. It was thick and shiny with grease, like it hadn't been washed in days.

"Poor Vik," she whispered. "I mean, poor Dev, too, obviously, it's horrible, but Vik was always so lovely. The whole time we've been cleaning for him, I've only seen him get annoyed once. And it was deserved, too."

"Deserved?" Logan asked.

Angela nodded. "The bollocking he gave us. Went through us like a dose of salts, he did." She shrugged. "It was Josh's fault, really, but it was an accident, and accidents happen. Anyway, the buck stops with the boss, doesn't it? So I took the blame."

"Blame for what?" Heather pressed.

"Josh had, I don't know, messed up the computers somehow.

Unplugged something or other. Said he was looking for some-where to plug the Hoover in," Angela said. "Knocked out their whole system—computers, cameras, the lot. Vik wasn't happy at all. Raging, he was. Though, give him his due, when he got it back up and running he phoned me to apologise. Not many would do that."

Logan had mostly tuned out upon hearing the word 'cam-eras.' He sat forward in the armchair until he was perching at the very front.

It wasn't Angela Sheen who was the connection between Dev Rani and Vikram Ganguly. It was *Shine & Sheen*, her cleaning company.

And there were two of them in that business.

"Josh Holder. What can you tell me about him?" he asked.

Heather was a step behind him, but catching up fast. She took her phone from her pocket, tapped the screen to bring up the dialer app, and quickly left the room.

"Josh? Eh, what do you want to know?" Angela asked. "He's a nice guy. Good fun. Gets on with the job, turns up when he says he will... Can't really ask for more in an employee, actually."

She lunged for her phone, which was balanced on the arm of the couch, panic lighting up her face.

"Shit! I still haven't paid him!"

"Leave that for now," Logan instructed, and the sharpness of his tone made her set the mobile down again. "How long have you known him?"

"About, six months," Angela said. There was a hesitancy to her response, like she could sense something dangerous waiting to lunge should she say the wrong thing.

"Where did you meet?" Logan asked.

The question made her visibly uncomfortable. She scratched at her arm, the nails leaving long white lines on her skin. "I'm, eh, I'm not supposed to say."

"Sorry?"

"We're not supposed to talk about it."

"What is it, Fight Club?" the DCI pressed.

Angela looked confused, failing to get the reference. "No. It's a... It's a church group. Or, no, it's a group in the church. That meets in a church, I mean. The Old High Church. By the river. You know it?"

Logan nodded to confirm that he did, though this wasn't exactly true. He could hazard a guess at which one she meant, though.

"It's not... We're not religious. Well, I'm sure some of us are, but that's not... That's not why we meet."

"Is it an alcoholics group?" Logan asked.

"What? No. No, nothing like that."

It hit him then. What it was. The only thing it could be. A group, huddled together in a place of sanctuary, sharing their secrets. Sharing their scars.

"Angela, I know this is difficult, but I need you to tell me the truth," Logan said. "The group—the group where you met Josh —it was for victims, wasn't it? It was for victims of sexual assault."

CHAPTER FORTY-ONE

BY THE TIME Logan and Filson made it back to the Incident Room, everything was in full swing. A couple of boys from CID had been brought in to help with the hunt while Sinead and Tyler were out of action. They and Hamza were all on the phones, while Ben spoke with a couple of uniformed sergeants over by his desk.

Hamza cut his call short when he saw the DCIs entering, and hurried over to intercept them.

"He's not at his house, and he's not answering his phone," the DS announced. He indicated the Uniforms talking to Ben. "In fact, these guys heard his mobile ringing out front. Found it in the bin. He must've ditched it on his way out."

"You looked through it?" Logan asked.

Hamza nodded. "Nothing of interest. It wasn't locked. There's almost nothing on it. I'd say it's probably a burner phone. We're contacting the networks, trying to see if he's got another one registered, but chances are it'll be a Pay As You Go, and not tied to his name."

"And we're sure it's him?" asked Ben. He'd dismissed the

Uniforms, and come over to join Hamza and Logan. "I thought he had an alibi?"

"He was on Twitch," Hamza said.

"Twitch?" Ben wrinkled his nose, correctly predicting he wasn't going to like the answer to his next question. "And what's that when it's at home?"

"It's a live-streaming video service," Hamza explained. "You watch people playing games."

"What, like... *Monopoly*?" Ben asked.

"Eh, no."

"I was going to say, it's bad enough having to play that bastarding thing, never mind watch someone else play it."

"It's for video games. Computer games," Hamza explained. "It shows the game on part of the screen, along with a live video of the person playing."

"What do you mean?" Ben demanded, sounding increasingly irate. "People sit and watch other people playing computer games?"

"Yes, sir."

"Why?"

"I, eh, I don't know, sir," Hamza had to admit. "For entertainment, I suppose."

Ben clicked his tongue against the back of his teeth. It was a sound that signalled his deep disapproval. "And that's where we've got to, is it? In the world? That's where we are? People watching other people playing computer games?" He shook his head, making his disapproval clear. "What's next, people watching other people having sex?!"

Heather leaned in closer to Logan. "Do you want to break it to him, or will I?" she whispered.

"Uh, anyway, it's possible to upload pre-recorded footage to Twitch, but usually there's something that indicates it isn't a live stream. Something that tells you it's a recording."

"But that wasn't on Holder's?" Logan asked.

"No, sir. That's why I thought it was live, and I didn't really think too much more about it. And that's my fault, because I should have thought about this."

He snatched an evidence bag from his desk and held it up. A small, rectangular piece of plastic with two HDMI ports sat nestled inside it.

Logan lowered his head and studied it. "And that is...?"

"It's like a video relay, but with an internal hard drive that gives it delay functionality," Hamza said.

"And in English...?" prompted Ben.

"Uh, think of it like a bucket, sir," Hamza explained. "Water pours in one side, and the bucket fills up. Then, when you want it to, the bucket releases out the other side. Except, it's video footage. Using one of these, Josh could record himself playing his game, set a delay, then appear to stream live at a scheduled time. Everyone watching thinks he's there in person, but he actually recorded it hours before."

"And that's what's on there?" Ben asked, pointing to the plastic device. "Him playing games?"

"No, sir. This one was taken from the nightclub. I hooked it up to my computer. There's just fifteen minutes of footage of Palmer's team on there, before it got disconnected."

"So we don't know he used one of these for his gaming shite?" Logan asked. "It's just a theory."

"Well, aye, sir, but I'm sure when we go over his computer, we'll have proof," Hamza said. "And I checked back to his other live streams. He answers questions from people. Comments on things viewers say in the chat. Constantly inviting them to subscribe to his channel. But, in this one, he doesn't. No interaction with anyone. He doesn't even acknowledge the messages. Because he wasn't seeing them."

"Because he wasn't there." Logan nodded. "Right. Good. No alibi for Dev Rani."

"Or the second victim," Hamza said. "Same thing again, streaming on Twitch. No interaction with anyone."

Logan came dangerously close to letting out a cheer. "Right. Now we're talking. No alibi."

"Nothing coming up on motive, though, Jack," Ben said. "Gone through his history. He never reported any sexual assault."

"That's no real surprise," Heather said. "We know most don't."

"Angela Sheen told us everything," Logan said. "Happened in Bristol while he was visiting relatives over Christmas. Two men. Both Asian. Attack was brutal, from what he told the group. They encouraged him to report it, but he was having none of it. Said he'd tried down the road, but some old school DI he spoke to more or less laughed him out of the place."

"Jesus Christ. No wonder he's angry. Poor bastard," Ben said. "And we're sure the victims weren't involved? It couldn't have been them who attacked him?"

"As sure as we can be, sir, yeah," Hamza told him.

"So, it's like we thought," Logan said. "Sexual assault victim sees men who remind him of his attacker, both in appearance and the power they hold over him—we know at least one of the victims lost the rag with him—and he acts out some sort of revenge fantasy."

"Basically, exactly what I said," Heather crowed.

"Aye, but you said it was a woman," Logan pointed out.

"OK, *almost* exactly what I said."

Logan heard a phone being hung up, and jabbed a finger at the CID man before he could pick up the handset again. "You. Forgot your name, sorry. I want everyone out looking for this bastard. If he's ditched his phone, he suspects we're closing in on him, so there's no saying what he might do next. Drag everyone in, and get them hunting him down."

"Should we clear that with Mitchell?" the other detective asked.

"Then she might say no. What she doesn't know can't hurt her. I'll take the bollocking, if it comes," Logan said, then he turned back to the others. "We confident enough to go to the press with this?"

"I reckon so, sir, yeah," Hamza said. "It was him who messed with the CCTV at the nightclub. It had to be."

"If it's him, it helps explain the lack of forensic evidence, too," Ben pointed out. "They've got all their protective cleaning gear, haven't they?"

"And Palmer found fibres," Hamza reminded them. "Similar paper suit to their own."

"Aye. Fuck it," Logan said, his volume rising as he addressed the room at large. "Get onto the media. Get his photo circulated, get his name out there. I want the whole bloody city looking for him. I want there to be nowhere safe for the bastard to go!"

He checked his watch. The day was already slipping away into early evening. It would be dark soon. Easier to hide. That didn't help his mood.

"And, for God's sake," he boomed. "Someone find out why we haven't heard from Tyler yet!"

———

"I'm going to be a dad, Ham," Tyler said. "No joke. Me. I'm going to be a dad!"

He was standing outside Raigmore Hospital, far enough away from the entrance that his excited pacing back and forth didn't trigger the sensors and fling the doors wide open.

It had been a nurse who had pointed out that he was causing this to happen, and sending 'a bloody gale' howling through the hospital corridors. She'd used some quite choice language, but he'd still been walking on air, so the hurled abuse had bounced right off him.

On the other end of the phone, Hamza didn't say anything for a few seconds. The silence became an awkward void that he then had to rush to fill.

"Aye? Oh, mate. Congratulations. That's amazing news!"

Tyler let out a cackled laugh. "You're a shite liar! You knew fine well. Sinead told me."

Down the line, Hamza sighed with relief. "Oh. Thank God. Sorry, I didn't want to keep it secret, but she made me."

"Nice to see where your bloody loyalties lie after all these years!" Tyler said, then he laughed again before Hamza had a chance to take it to heart. "No, I'm glad you didn't say anything. Would've been a terrible way to find out. No offence."

"None taken," Hamza said. "So... how is she?"

Tyler looked back over his shoulder at the hospital entrance looming behind him. "We're just waiting on some test results. I should get back inside, just in case. I just wanted to check in."

"Aye, good job you did. The boss was getting worried."

"Is that Tyler?" Logan gruffly demanded from somewhere in the background.

"Aye, sir," Hamza said, his voice becoming a little muffled as he pulled away from the phone.

"And? What's he saying?"

"He's going to be a dad."

There was a long silence. Tyler stopped pacing and pressed the phone to his ear, listening hard.

"Oh, for fuck's sake," Logan said. "God help us all."

"Cheers, boss!" Tyler called down the line.

"He says, 'Cheers, boss,'" Hamza said, relaying the message.

"Twins! Tell him it's twins!" Tyler said.

The word emerged from the mobile as a yelp of surprise. "*Twins? Seriously?*"

CITY OF SCARS 343

"Twins?" Logan echoed. "Jesus Christ. Well, in that case, I take it back. God help *him*."

"Right, I'd better get back," Tyler said. "Once I know more, I'll let you know."

"Aye, better get back to it here, too," Hamza said. "But congratulations again, mate. Um... I think."

They said their goodbyes, then Tyler hung up. Before he could return the phone to his pocket, the screen lit up, alerting him to a message received.

He thumbed the notification and saw a text from Sinead.

Doctor here now. Come quick.

"Shite!" Tyler hissed.

And he ran.

———

DI Forde checked his phone on the way back to the Incident Room, in case he'd missed any calls or texts. With everything that had been going on, it would be all too possible for him not to have heard the notification coming through.

There was nothing there waiting for him when he woke the mobile from standby, though. No messages of any kind.

It had been a good night, too. They'd had a laugh. Or he had, at least, and she'd certainly seemed to.

He'd tried calling her a couple of times. Sent a handful of messages, just checking in. Checking up. Other than a quick, 'Yes,' in response to a question on whether she got home safely, though, he'd had nothing back.

Was this what they called being ghosted? Well, if so, then he wasn't a fan.

He took his mug of tea, and a wee Jammy Dodger that he'd purloined from the canteen, then sat at his desk.

"Any updates on... anything?" he asked the room at large.

"Sinead's pregnant," Logan announced from his desk.

Ben blinked. "Christ, that came out of nowhere. I was only gone for ten minutes."

"It's twins," Hamza added.

Ben took a bite of his biscuit. The packet had been sitting open for a while, and it crumbled away between his teeth. "Bugger me," he muttered, staring blankly ahead like he was slipping into shock. "Who knew the lad had it in him?"

He took a gulp of tea and swiped the biscuit crumbs off his shirt.

"Anything on the case?" he asked. "Still no word on Mr Holder, I take it?"

"Nothing," said Logan. He nodded over to where DCI Filson was talking with the two detectives borrowed from CID. "Heather's going over everything with that pair, in case there's anything they've missed. Looks like he's gone to ground, though. Could be a long few days."

"Family and friends are being contacted, and we've put a press statement out," Hamza said. "You should have a copy in your inbox."

Ben gave his mouse a shoogle, waking the PC's screen. He polished off the rest of the biscuit while he waited for it to fully rouse itself, then searched the screen for several seconds until he remembered which icon opened his email.

Sure enough, there was a message from Hamza in bold at the top, indicating it hadn't yet been read. He was about to click on it when he noticed another unread email below it.

The name Moira Corson was there in the 'sender' column. The subject simply read, 'Fancy it?'

He opened that email first. There was no personal message in the body of the email—personal messages weren't really her strong point—but there was an attachment that, when opened, brought up an advert for the musical *Jersey Boys*, which was apparently running at Eden Court in a few weeks.

Ben closed down her email. Let her wait. Let her stew, the way she'd let him. Two could play at that game.

He moved the mouse pointer up to Hamza's email...

...then moved it back down again. With a double-click, he opened Moira's email, quickly typed, 'Oh, go on then,' and hit the button to send.

"How come you're looking so pleased with yourself?" asked Logan, peering at the DI over the top of his PC.

"Oh, nothing," Ben said, beaming from ear to ear. "I just appreciate a well-written press release." He sat back and laid his hands across his stomach, fingers interlocked. "I suppose all we can do now is wait, then."

Logan checked his watch. "Aye, well, you can do that at home," he said.

Hamza straightened, perking up. "Sir?"

"You heard," Logan said. He glanced around at Hamza, Ben, Dave, and the two CID officers. "You lot shoot off. Get an early night of it. But be back here early. And keep your phones on."

Hamza had started packing up after 'you lot shoot off,' and was already on his feet. "Absolutely, sir. No bother. Thanks."

"Aye, well, make sure your missus knows it was me who sent you home? Might make her hate me slightly less than she currently does."

Hamza grinned as he pulled on his jacket. "She doesn't hate you, sir," he said. "She just... strongly dislikes you."

The detective sergeant was long gone by the time the others finished packing up. Dave said his goodbyes, then rolled himself out the door, hot on the heels of the CID guys.

Ben hung back with his jacket on, his gaze moving slowly and deliberately between DCI Logan and his female counterpart, who sat on the edge of a desk with her legs crossed, and a foot trailing back and forth.

"Well, I'll, eh, I'll leave you two to..." He grasped for an ending to the sentence, then settled on, "...it."

The next look he shot Logan was a warning, then he zipped his jacket up to the neck, and headed on out into the corridor.

"Alone at last," Heather said, once the door had finished swinging closed. She reclined a little, supporting her weight on her arms. "Where do you want me?"

Logan laughed dryly. "Glasgow," he said.

The response curved Heather's mouth into a smirk. "Good answer," she said, hopping down off the desk. "I spoke to your *other half* earlier. We had a good long chat. Very enlightening."

Logan's face fell. "Christ. What did you say?"

"None of your business," Heather told him. "But... you've done alright. For an ugly bastard."

"Aye," Logan agreed. "Aye. I have."

Heather tapped a hand on her hip, looked around the room, then shrugged. "Right, fuck all point us staying here. Let's head back to your place."

Logan winced. "I'm not sure you coming back is such a great idea," he said. "Maybe we should find you a hotel."

"Ah, no need," DCI Filson replied, her grin splitting her face in two. "Me and your woman discussed it earlier, and she's *very* excited about the prospect of me spending another night..."

CHAPTER FORTY-TWO

KAMILA SPRINTED UP THE HALL, her dressing gown trailing behind her like a superhero's cape. Hamza dropped his bag in time to catch her, mid-leap, then spun around, tickling her until the giggles came squealing out of her.

"Stop! Stop!"

"Stop what?" Hamza asked, fingers wriggling in her tickly spots, making her crease and squirm in his arms. "What am I doing? Stop what?"

She exploded with laughter, then threw herself backwards, safe in the knowledge that he had her, and wouldn't let her fall. He bent, dangling her upside down so her hair brushed against the carpet, then swung her back up and over his shoulder in a fireman's lift.

Amira appeared from the kitchen, drying her hands on a towel. "Kamila, what have I told you about talking to strangers?"

"Good one," Hamza said, wagging a finger at his wife. "Funny."

Amira smiled. "I thought so."

She raised herself up enough to accept a kiss from her

husband, then took the opportunity to lay a playful slap on the bony bum that was perched on his shoulder like a parrot.

"Hey!" Kamila protested.

"Sorry, couldn't resist!" her mother laughed. She turned back to Hamza. "Dinner's on. Be about forty minutes. You been at any dead people today?"

"Not so far," Hamza said.

Amira looked him up and down. "Well, go shower, anyway. I want you clean." She leaned in closer and whispered, "For now."

"Oh. *Oh!*" Hamza said. "Right! Yes! Shower it is, then! But, I'd better let Kamila know I won't be long. Have you seen her?" He spun around, drawing more giggles from the girl on his shoulder. "Kammi? Where are you?"

"I'm here!"

He turned again. "Who said that?"

"Me!"

Another turn. Another outburst of laughter. "Me who?"

Amira stepped back to avoid her daughter's swinging legs, then pointed to her husband. "Forty minutes," she reminded him. "Don't be late!"

———

"So much for you getting a hotel, then," Shona said, holding the door open while Logan and Heather traipsed in.

Taggart barked excitedly at their feet, his whole back end moving from side to side like a fish powering itself upstream. Only a pat of acknowledgement from Logan got him to shut up, though the tail wagging only became even more frantic and excited.

"Didn't want to disappoint you," Heather said. She held up a plastic bag. "And we went to the chippy, if that softens the blow any?"

"Why didn't you say that to begin with?" Shona asked. "Finally, you're talking my language."

They all headed for the kitchen, the dog trotting along with his nose in the air, the thrill of seeing Logan now replaced by the anticipation of chips. Though, to be fair, the same could be said for Shona.

They decided to be posh, and grabbed plates and cutlery, rather than eating from the packaging as they all usually would have. It felt like a bit of a special occasion, though none of them, if asked, would be able to explain why.

Maybe it was the unofficial peace treaty. Maybe it was a celebration of Tyler and Sinead's news. Or, perhaps it was just the sense that the case was drawing to a close, and that this was, in many ways, a farewell meal.

"Fish for you, haggis supper for you," Heather said, dishing out the unwrapped Styrofoam trays. "Horse's cock for me."

Shona's gaze went to the jumbo smoked sausage Heather was in the process of sliding onto her plate, and nodded her approval.

"He was a big fella."

"You want a bit?" Heather asked.

"Would you mind? I'll swap you a bit of fish," Shona replied.

"No bother." DCI Filson picked up her cutlery. "Head or shaft?"

"Can we maybe no' refer to it as 'head or shaft'?" asked Logan, wriggling uncomfortably. He looked between the women, Shona on his left, Heather on his right. "And this is just fucking weird, by the way. Just so you know. You two being nice to one another."

"You think this is weird? Just wait until we start kissing," Heather said.

Across the table, Shona thumped violently at her chest after almost choking on a chip. Logan cracked open a can of *Irn Bru* and passed it to her so she could wash it down.

"Thanks for that," she wheezed, though it wasn't quite clear who she was aiming it at.

She took another swig from the can, cleared her throat a couple of times, then completed her transaction with Heather, swapping a piece of battered haddock for an inch and a half of smoked sausage sliced from the shaft end.

"So, what's the score with the case, then?" she asked, tucking into her fish.

Logan filled her in, with Heather chipping in here and there to add some additional colour and texture. It was only a matter of time now before they caught him, Logan said, though he didn't sound especially enthused by the prospect.

"What's the problem?" Shona asked, slipping half a chip to Taggart, who gobbled it hungrily under the table. "That's good, isn't it? That's sort of the whole point of everything. You catch the baddies."

"Aye. I know. But we had him," Logan said. "He was right there. Tyler spoke to him, then Hamza. He was in the bloody interview room. We had the bastard, and now..." He sighed and sat back. "He knows we're onto him. If we're lucky he'll go into hiding. Make it hard for us to find him."

Shona took a bite of the smoked sausage. "And if you're unlucky?"

It was Heather who answered that one. "He'll go after anyone else on his list. A lot of these fuckers, the way they see it, if you're going to go out, go out with a bang."

"God. That's not good," Shona said. "And do you know who he might go after?"

Logan shook his head. "We've notified all the cleaning company's other clients. Got Uniform keeping an eye. But none of them matches the profile—young Asian male, with a bit of power or authority."

"Right," Shona said.

Everyone at the table fell quiet. Even the sound of chewing abated.

"Sorry," Shona said, through a mouthful of sausage. "Who did you say interviewed him?"

———

The water blasted across his shoulders and cascaded down his back, hot enough to sting his skin and fill the bathroom with steam. He hummed to himself as he scrubbed, cheerfully anticipating the evening ahead.

A nice meal. Some quality time with Kamila, and a chance to finally finish that bedtime story.

And then, once she was asleep, he was on a promise—a rare thing these days, between his work schedule, and the demands of a young child in the house—and he wasn't going to pass up that opportunity.

He broke into song as he reached for the shampoo.

And, over the hissing of the shower and his own dulcet tones, he failed to hear the ringing of his phone.

CHAPTER FORTY-THREE

SINEAD PULLED ON HER JACKET, thanked the doctor, and strode out of the ward, trying very hard to ignore the massive grin Tyler was wearing on his face.

"Don't," she warned him. "Don't say a bloody word."

"Wind!" he said. Give him his dues, he was trying hard not to laugh. He just wasn't being particularly successful. "That's what you needed? A big fart?"

"At-at-at!" she snapped, raising a finger and holding it just inches from his face. "I said don't." She almost gave into a giggle, and slapped him on the arm like this was somehow his fault. "It's not bloody funny! I thought there was something wrong."

"There was," Tyler said. "I smelled it. That was like a whole new level of wrong."

She slapped his arm and told him to shut up again, then she took his offered hand and they walked out of the hospital and into the cool night air. The rain and the clouds had cleared, and a sky full of stars shone down on them.

"Twins," Tyler said again. "We're having twins. Well, you're having them, but I'll be in the next room cheering you on."

"The next room?" Sinead laughed. "My arse, you'll be in with me."

"What, during proceedings? With all the... gory bits, and the screaming?" Tyler asked. He wrinkled his nose and shook his head. "No. You don't want that."

"Yes, I do."

"OK, well, I don't want that," Tyler admitted.

Sinead smiled and tucked her arm around his. "Tough shit. You're coming in. I'll need something to grab onto. Like your neck."

"Aye, well, just make sure it's the neck you go for, and not anything else," he said, then his phone buzzed in his pocket before he could continue the conversation. "It's the boss," he said, tapping the icon to answer, and bringing the phone to his ear. "Boss?"

"Tyler. Where are you?" Logan asked. His voice sounded tinny, and the background noise suggested he was driving.

"Eh, just leaving the hospital, boss. Sinead's alright. She just needed—" An elbow in the ribs made him quickly change course. "A check-up. Everything OK?"

"I don't know," Logan said. "You got your car?"

"Eh, aye, boss. Why?"

"Get to Hamza's. No sirens," Logan ordered.

Sinead, who had been listening into the call, frowned. She saw the same look of concern creasing the lines on her husband's face.

"Hamza's? Why, boss, what's happened?"

"Hopefully nothing, son. Hopefully nothing," Logan told him.

There was the sound of a blasting horn in the background, and a muffled shout of, "Ah, fuck you!" from what sounded like DCI Filson.

"But get going. Now," Logan instructed. "And I'll explain on the way."

———

Hamza finished drying himself, stepped out of the en suite bathroom, and got himself dressed. Well, technically he got himself into a nice pair of fluffy *Elmer Fudd* pyjamas that he'd got in the *H&M* sale a few months ago, and had never got around to wearing.

When he'd bought them, he'd thought Kamila would love them, until it quickly became clear that she had absolutely no idea who *Elmer Fudd* was.

Now, if it had been *Peppa Pig*...

He pulled the drawstring of the pyjama bottoms tight, securing them around his waist. After a quick glance in the mirror, and a test of his breath by blowing into his hand and sniffing, he opened the bedroom door and stepped out into the hallway.

Amira stood there, by the door. A man was behind her. Large. Imposing.

"Oh, thank fuck for that," Logan said.

"That man said a bad word," Kamila observed, and Hamza saw his daughter half hidden by the kitchen door, spying on proceedings with one eye.

"Shite. Sorry. I mean..." Logan snapped his mouth shut, took a moment to compose himself, then tried again. "You alright, son?"

"Eh, fine, aye," Hamza said.

There was some commotion out on the front step, and Tyler popped his head into the house. "Nice jammies, mate."

"Eh... what's going on?" Hamza asked.

"We, eh..." Logan glanced at Amira, who glared back at him, a heavy wooden rolling pin clutched like a baton in one hand. His eyes darted past her to the wee girl in the kitchen doorway, before finally settling on the detective sergeant. "Maybe we can have a quick word in private?"

"You've got five minutes until dinner," Amira said. She waved the end of the rolling pin up at Logan. "Five. Minutes."

"Understood," Logan said, then he and Tyler followed Hamza through to the living room, and shut the door.

"What the—?" Hamza ejected, spotting movement in the darkness beyond the living room window. "Is that DCI Filson in my garden?"

"Aye. She's making sure the coast's clear," Logan explained.

"We think Josh Holder might be coming after you," Tyler said.

"Me? Why would he be coming after...?" Hamza's voice trailed away. He shrugged. "No, I suppose I can see it. Young successful Asian guys."

"Young Asian guys in a position of power," Tyler corrected. "That's not the same as successful."

"It's pretty much the same," Hamza argued.

"Well... is it, though?" Tyler asked, screwing up his face.

"You haven't seen or heard anything?" Logan asked.

"No. Not a thing," Hamza said. "It'd be a pretty ballsy move for him to come after me, wouldn't it? No pun intended."

"Aye. Aye, probably," Logan said. "We just... when we couldn't get hold of you on your mobile, we panicked."

Hamza looked genuinely touched. "Oh. Cheers, sir. Sorry, probably just didn't hear it in the shower."

"Right. Aye. Fair enough," Logan said. He looked to the window, and was met by a shrug and a shake of the head from DCI Filson. "Well, looks like the coast's clear. We'll get Uniform to keep an eye on things for tonight, just in case. Keep your doors shut. If you suspect anyone's milling about outside, then—"

"Don't worry, sir. I know the drill," Hamza assured him. "If I'm worried, I'll call in the cavalry."

"Good. Make sure you do," Logan said.

"Two minutes!" Amira called from next door, in a tone that made it clear this was not open to negotiation.

"Right. Well, I suppose that's our cue to piss off," Logan said. He caught Tyler's eye and jerked his head in the direction of the door. "But remember, if there's anything..."

Hamza nodded. "You'll be the first to know, sir."

He escorted them out, closed the door behind them, then locked it. After a moment, he slid the security chain into place, then turned and followed the smell of his dinner.

Outside, Logan and Tyler headed for their cars. They had abandoned them in the street outside the house, and left Sinead to deal with the build-up of traffic that was forming behind them.

"Bit of a relief that, eh, boss?" Tyler said.

"Aye. You can say that again," Logan agreed.

They each reached their cars and stopped at the driver's doors. Heather came jogging up from the garden to join Logan, while Sinead quit her traffic duties and headed for Tyler's passenger seat.

"Only thing is, though, if Holder's not here, boss, then where the hell is he?"

———

DI Ben Forde was staring blankly at the contents of his fridge when he heard the sound behind him.

It was sharp. Sudden. He jumped, gripping the fridge door with one hand, and clutching his chest with the other.

"Ooyah bastard!" he hissed, turning to where his phone was vibrating its way across the kitchen table. He pounced on it, hurriedly tapped to answer, and brought it to his ear. "Well?" he asked, skipping right over the niceties.

He listened to Logan on the other end of the line, and let out a big sigh of relief. "Oh, thank God," he whispered. "I've been climbing the bloody walls here. You're sure he's...? Aye. Good. And Uniform are going to keep watch?"

He sauntered over to the fridge and reached for the bottle of white wine that stood tucked inside the door, ready for action at a moment's notice.

"Make sure they bloody do," he said, tucking the phone between his ear and his shoulder. He took a glass from the cupboard, held it up to the light to check it was clean, then nodded his approval. "And get them to do a handover after one," he suggested, leaving the kitchen. "Don't want the buggers falling asleep on the..."

Out in the hallway, he stopped. The lights were off in the living room. He'd left them on. The telly, too. He was sure of it.

"Jack," he whispered. "Someone's here."

And the darkness came alive behind him.

CHAPTER FORTY-FOUR

BEN HISSED as the pain burned like fire through his flesh. He saw a flash of white, then a spray of red. Blood bloomed on his shirt, then tickled and trickled along his fingers.

His blood.

He was always surprised by the colour of it—a rich, almost purple-red, and not the vibrant hue most people expected.

He'd moved quickly at the sound of movement behind him. Despite his advancing years, and the lingering arse-ache from his recent night at the dancing, he could still shift when he needed to.

He'd almost made it. He'd almost dodged the blade that had come scything towards him through the dark.

Almost. But not quite.

The knife had caught him across the inside of the forearm. Deep. Bloody. But survivable.

The only escape route had been into the living room. He'd stumbled through the dark, blood dripping onto the carpet, half-blind in the darkness.

Footsteps came rushing up behind him now, *thump-thump-*

thump, like a drumbeat building to a frenzy. He felt the floor shake, saw the shape of a man reflected in the window.

He spun. Roared. Swung wildly with the wine bottle. He'd been aiming for the head, but found a raised hand, instead. A knife went clattering across the room, lost in the shadows.

He swung again, bringing the bottle back around in a wide *whumming* arc. Head height, or thereabouts.

There was a satisfying *thunk.*

Contact!

"Have it, ya bastard!" he bellowed, the impact jerking the bottle out of his grip and sending it flying across the room.

But the blow was a glancing one. The swing left him wide open, and before he could react, a foot connected with his ribcage.

A fresh new agony exploded. His breath left him, all in one puff. The kick's momentum sent him stumbling over a table, and deposited him sideways into his armchair.

The glass he'd been holding smashed in his hand. Shards embedded themselves in his palm and between his fingers, ripping the skin into ribbons.

He cried out at the pain and the shock of it, but his shortness of breath turned the sound into a strangled mewling.

His attacker was on the ground, half-swallowed by the shadows. Ben hoped that the blow from the bottle had hurt him more than he first thought, then he realised the other man wasn't injured. He was just searching for his knife.

"Wait, son. Wait," Ben wheezed, holding up his uninjured hand. Both the knife wound and the broken glass were on his left side, and that whole arm now felt like it was ablaze. "You don't have to do this. You don't *want* to do this."

"Don't fucking tell me what I want," came the hissed reply.

"Josh. It is, isn't it? You're Josh," Ben said. "I saw you. In the corridor. With Tyler. I saw you."

"Shut up," Josh spat back, still fumbling in the dark for his knife. "Stop talking, you old fuck."

Ben didn't stop talking. He daren't. He talked like his life depended on it.

"I know what happened to you, son. I know what you went through. And my heart breaks for you, Josh. It really does," he said. "But this won't help. This won't make it any better."

"Stop fucking talking!"

"I can't do that, son," replied Ben. His lungs were still cramping, and the words came in short, fitful bursts. "See, I know if I don't talk to you, you're going to kill me. And I don't want to die. Not today. Not like this."

There was a sudden movement as Josh found the knife. He jumped to his feet, and the light from the lamp post outside picked out the details of his face. His eyes seemed terrifyingly large in the orange glow. Inhumanly so, like something from a nightmare.

He'd been crying, Ben thought. His face was pale, his mouth hanging open like even he was shocked by this turn of events.

Ben hoped the hand holding the knife would be shaking. A trembling hand meant a shaky resolve. It meant there was a chance to negotiate.

A chance that this didn't end the way Ben feared it was going to.

But his grip was tight, the knife held firm and unwavering.

"I don't fucking care what you want," Josh told him. The knife hand was solid, but the voice wasn't. The words were broken. Just like him.

"OK, OK, but just... just tell me this, son," Ben pleaded. "Why? Why me? Why are you doing this?"

"Don't pretend you don't know."

"I don't, Josh. I don't know, son," Ben insisted. Pain flared up from his hand and met a second wave coming the other way.

He gritted his teeth. Pushed it down. Fought to ignore it. "Tell me. Talk to me."

There was a moment of silence. A pause, before the man with the knife was able to force the words out.

"I came to you. I came to you, and I told you what had happened. And you laughed. You fucking laughed at me!"

Ben shook his head. "No, son. No. You didn't. That wasn't me."

"*Don't lie to me!*" Josh roared, lumbering forward a few paces, forcing Ben to draw back against his chair.

"It wasn't, Josh. You know that. I'm sorry he didn't believe you. I'm so sorry, son, but you know it wasn't me. Like you know it wasn't them," Ben said. "Those men you killed. You know they didn't hurt you. You know it wasn't them."

Josh said nothing for a while. The only sound was his breathing. In. Out. Hissing as it passed through his clenched teeth.

"No, but they were the same," he croaked. "The two of them. They thought they were big men. Thought they could just do what they wanted, push people around. Treat them like shit." He ran a hand through his hair, the nails scraping at his scalp. "They would've done it. Sooner or later. To some-one. Someone had to stop them. Someone had to punish them."

"For something they hadn't done?"

"*But they would have!*" Josh roared. "I know they would. You can see it. You get to... to recognise it. The way they look at you. The things they're thinking about doing. You get to know." He shook his head. Snot and tears flashed in the light coming in from outside. "Nobody else could see. But I could. I saw. I knew they'd do it again. Because they were the same. They were the same."

He seemed to be shrinking, like he was being consumed from the inside by grief, or loathing, or some pungent blend of the two. The knife was wobbling now. Not a lot, but enough to give Ben hope. To give him a chance.

His left arm and hand were too badly hurt for him to use them, so he used his right hand to guide himself forward on the armchair. His legs shook beneath him as he started to stand. Fear squeezed all his insides together, so there was barely room for the words to get out.

"I can help you, son. I can listen. We can find those bastards, me and you, and we can make sure they're punished. We can make sure they pay. Properly."

Josh stood there, head pulled into his shoulders, a snivelling mess of a man. His eyes flitted down to Ben's offered hand.

There was a moment of hope.

A moment where things might have gone differently.

And then, his face bunched up in a sneer. The knife became steady in his hands.

"You shouldn't have laughed at me," he whispered. "I wish you hadn't laughed."

Ben saw the change in him. He saw it coming. He knew that there was no way he was talking his way out of this. No way he was getting through.

No way he was avoiding what was going to happen next.

He thought of Alice.

He thought of Moira, too.

And then, with a sound of thunder, the front door of Ben's house flew inwards, and the wrath of God came roaring in like a hurricane in a long, flowing overcoat.

"Holder! Stop right fucking there!" Logan barked, storming into the room.

Josh lunged, grabbing Ben with an arm around the throat and pressing the tip of his blade into the DI's kidney area until it drew a hiss of pain.

"Jack! Jack, wait!" Ben cried. "Just... just wait, alright?"

The room was already filling up. DCI Filson had entered at

Logan's back, with Tyler and Sinead both bundling in behind them.

Blue lights licked across the walls, and the crunching of tyres signalled the arrival of a squad of Uniforms.

"Just everyone hold their horses," Ben urged. "Josh here, he's just... he's upset. Understandably."

Tyler took a step forward, offering up a friendly smile. "Alright, Josh, mate?"

"*Back the fuck up!*" Holder bellowed, and Ben grimaced as the knife pricked deeper into his skin.

"Alright, alright," Tyler said, retreating with his hands held in front of him.

Logan was in no mood to appease the bastard, though. "Let him go, Holder. There's nowhere to go. You're well and truly fucked, son. Give it up."

Josh shook his head. He shook it so much it was like he was never going to stop. "You don't get to tell me what to do. You don't get to order me. I'm in charge here."

"You're in charge of fuck all, son," Logan barked back.

"Steady, Jack!" Ben warned. He half-turned his head until he was as close to making eye contact with the man behind him as he dared. "We get it, son. We do. What happened to you should never have happened. It's not fair."

Josh's reply was a scream in his face. "Don't fucking say that! You don't know what it's like! You don't understand!"

"I do."

Heather's reply was uncharacteristically soft, yet it rang out in the silence like a gunshot.

"I know," she said, risking a step forwards.

The others watched her. She deliberately avoided their gazes, like she felt cowed by them. Judged.

"I was... I was fourteen. Nearly fifteen. I was at a... like, a youth club. And, um..." She looked away, then down, then met his eye again with some reluctance. "They, um, they pulled me into the bushes. They were older. Twenties, maybe. I don't know. Two of them. Well, three, but one just... He just watched. Laughed."

She ran her tongue across her teeth. Cleared her throat. Steeled herself.

"I've never said anything. I didn't tell anyone. Not my mum or dad. Not my sister, or my friends. I didn't tell them what they did to me." Her voice became a whisper. Barely even that. "I couldn't. Because, if I told someone... If they knew what I'd done. What they'd... What they'd made me do... Then they wouldn't look at me the same way ever again. It'd never be the same. They'd look at me like I was broken. Like I was *soiled*."

Tears started to pool in her eyes, but she was having none of that, and forced them back until they fucked off again.

The other detectives stood around her, mutely watching and listening as she—finally—unburdened herself. Sinead's hand had gone to her mouth, already aware of where this story led, and of the damage that had been done.

"And if I said it. If I actually said out loud what they'd done, then it had all happened," Heather continued. "Then that would make it real. And so, I didn't. I told myself that I'd been up for it. That it was all consensual. Better to be a slut than a victim, I thought. If I was a slut, then I was in charge. I had the power. Me, not them."

Her voice broke then. She didn't cry, but a few feet away, Sinead shed a tear on her behalf.

"But that's not the truth. The truth is, I was a child, and those men raped me. And, if I could go back there now, I wouldn't just cut their cocks off, I'd feed them to them, bit by bit."

She took another step forward. Holder made no move with the knife.

"But I can't do that, Josh. I don't get to rewrite history like that. *We* don't. What happened to us, should never have happened. But it did. To both of us. And we'll carry those scars forever," Heather said. "But DI Forde isn't one of those men. Nobody here is. We're the people who do everything we can to stop those men."

She held out a hand. An olive branch. "You're in pain, Josh. You're in so much pain. Let me help you."

Josh inhaled sharply, filling his lungs. His arm tightened across Ben's throat.

"I'm sorry," he whispered. "I'm sorry!"

And then, with a *clunk*, the knife landed on the carpet at their feet.

CHAPTER FORTY-FIVE

"HOW'S THE INVALID?" asked Shona Maguire, stepping into the private room where Ben sat propped up in bed.

His arm was bandaged, while an assortment of wires and sutures held his fingers in more or less the positions he'd grown used to over the past sixty-odd years.

"Aye, well, I think my piano playing days are over," Ben said.

"I didn't know you played piano!" Shona said.

Logan, who stood at the end of the bed with DCI Filson at his side, shook his head. "He doesn't."

"Over before they've begun, I mean," Ben clarified.

"Ah!" Shona said. "Still, sad day for the musical community, I'd have thought."

"Very much so," Ben agreed.

Shona smiled, winked for reasons she didn't seem entirely clear about, then turned to Logan and Heather with a sort of calculated casualness that wasn't fooling anyone.

"Sooo," she began. "You got yer man, then?"

"We did, aye. Hamza's handling the report to the PF." He

turned to Ben, as an aside. "He says hello, by the way, and that he's glad it was you Holder went for, and not him."

"Oh, I bet he is, the bastard," Ben retorted.

Logan's attention returned to Shona. "He gave us a full confession. Told his solicitor he's pleading guilty. Not that he's really got a lot of choice on that front, given that he assaulted and threatened to kill a senior officer in a room full of detectives."

"Right. Right, aye. Great," Shona said. She shifted her gaze to Heather. "So... how about you? You heading off soon, then?"

"I am," Heather confirmed.

"Right. Because, you know, you could always stay for another night, if you—"

Heather shook her head. "Nah. Need to get back down the road."

"Thank Christ for that," Shona said. "Good riddance, I say."

Heather smiled. "I was saying to Jack, though, that I might come back and visit."

"That'd be grand," Shona replied. "We'd love to see you. Infrequently. Just give us a bit of warning and we'll find you a hotel."

"Nah. Rather just crash at yours," Heather told her.

Shona couldn't fight back her smile. She pointed between herself and the other woman. "Is this... is this where we kiss?"

Heather snorted, and jabbed a thumb in Logan's direction. "Aye. He bloody wishes."

Down in the bed, Ben's head had been moving from side to side like he was watching a fast-paced and—judging by his expression—quite confusing tennis match.

"Have I missed something?" he wondered, glancing up at Logan.

"Oh. God. Don't ask me," the DCI replied. He gestured to the door. "Want me to walk you out?"

"I think I can find my way," Heather told him. She pointed to Ben. "You. You're a rock star. Get on the mend, alright?"

"Is that an order?" Ben asked.

"Always," Heather told him. She turned, gave Logan a hug that was only fifty percent awkward, then went striding out of the room, pausing only to fire an air kiss in Shona's direction.

From out in the corridor there was a brief sound of scuffling, like Heather had come close to colliding with someone else.

"Sorry," she said.

The response she got was short, sharp, and not in the least bit forgiving.

"I should bloody think so, too."

The sound of sensible shoes on the polished hospital floor grew louder, then Moira Corson appeared in the doorway, her face fixed in a rictus of disgust.

"What's all this, then?" she demanded of the man in the bed. "Lounging about like a useless oaf."

"What the hell are you doing here?" Logan asked. He swung his gaze down to Ben. "What the hell's she doing here?"

He knew, of course. You didn't get to be a DCI in the polis without being able to put two and two together.

He knew. He just wished he didn't.

"No," he said, shaking his head. "No, no, no. I'm not having that. I won't allow it. I forbid it."

Shona tactfully slipped an arm around Logan's waist and steered him towards the door.

"That's not right," Logan muttered.

"We'll leave you to it," Shona said. She winked at Ben again, and this time they both knew exactly why.

"It's just not right," Logan muttered.

Then, he was led out into the corridor, and with a final glance back at Ben and Moira, Shona closed the door and left them in peace.

———

"You just going without saying goodbye, then?"

Heather tossed her bag into the back seat of her car, closed the door, then turned to find Sinead standing behind her in the hospital car park.

"Eh, aye. Just wanted to get off sharp. Long drive back down the road."

"Aye," Sinead agreed. "Aye, it is."

The silence that followed was an uncomfortable one, and it was Heather who raced to fill it.

"You're, eh, you're all OK, then?"

"Fine. Aye. Thanks."

"Did they find out what was wrong?"

Sinead groaned and blushed at the same time, but managed a half-smile. "Wind."

"Wind?!" Heather's face practically lit up.

"This big good-looking doctor had a feel about of my stomach," Sinead continued. "Totally farted on him."

Heather roared. That was the only way to describe it. She threw back her head and ejected a laugh that rolled right up to the heavens.

"Oh, God! Oh, God, that's amazing!" she wheezed.

"It was bloody mortifying, is what it was," Sinead muttered. "I genuinely thought Tyler was going to die, he was laughing that hard."

"I don't blame him," Heather said. She ran a hand down her face, controlling another hysterical outburst of her own. "But I'm glad you're OK. You gave us a scare for a—"

Sinead rushed in and threw her arms around the older woman, hugging her. Holding her.

It wasn't the sort of thing that DCI Filson generally tolerated, but she didn't resist. Not this time. Not today.

"I'm so sorry," Sinead whispered, and Heather, perhaps

through lack of experience with this sort of thing, just patted her robotically on the back.

"Thanks. But it's fine. I'm alright. It was a long time ago," the DCI said, finally pulling away. She opened the driver's door, put a foot inside the car, then stopped. "If you're ever looking for a transfer to the big leagues, you know where I am."

"Eh, thanks," Sinead said.

Heather glanced over to the front door of the hospital, where Tyler stood waiting for Sinead to return.

"But, you know, maybe get divorced first," she suggested. "I'm not putting up with that wee arsehole all the time."

Sinead laughed. "Somebody has to."

Then, she stepped clear, as DCI Filson got in her car, fired up the engine, and pulled out of the car park, headed south.

Tyler nodded after the car when his wife returned. "Everything alright?" he asked.

"Fine, yeah," Sinead confirmed.

"What was she saying?"

"She was offering me a job," Sinead replied.

"A job? What, in Glasgow?"

"Aye."

"You're not... You're not going to take it, are you?"

Sinead smiled. She slipped her hand into his, their fingers interlocking.

"What do you think?" she said.

And then, with Tyler by her side, they headed into the hospital.

All four of them.

CHAPTER FORTY-SIX

IT WAS several hours later when the phone rang. Logan was asleep, so he couldn't say exactly how many.

He peeled his eyes open as, beside him, Shona pulled the covers up over her head and groaned.

"It's alright. I've got it," he mumbled, his throat dry.

He slapped at the bedside table, fumbling for the phone. The screen was too bright, and his eyes were too blurry for him to see the name on the front, but he had a vague idea of where the button to answer it was.

"Hello?" he grunted, thumbing sleep from his eye. "Logan."

The voice on the other end was sharp. Abrupt. Angry.

But then, it always was.

"What? Slow down," Logan said. "What's happened?"

He listened to the voice on the other end of the line. Sleep—and the prospect of getting back there—fell away from him as he swung his legs out of bed.

"Right. OK. Aye. Jesus Christ," he said. "Aye. Just text me the address. And don't do anything stupid for fu—" He took the phone from his ear, stared at it, then put it back. "Hello? Hello, you...? Shite."

Logan threw the phone back on the bedside table. The *clunk* it made when it landed was the final straw, and Shona's head emerged from below the covers like a tortoise creeping out of its shell.

"What is it?" she asked. "What now?"

Logan sighed. He stood up, his full, towering frame blocking the moonlight coming in through the bedroom window.

"It's Hoon," he said, looking back over his shoulder. "He's in trouble."

NEXT IN SERIES

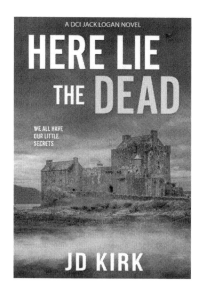

DCI Logan and his team return in HERE LIE THE DEAD, the 15th novel in the series.

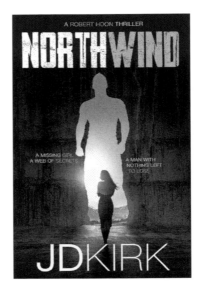

Northwind: A Robert Hoon Thriller

Discover a (slightly) softer side of Logan's old sparring partner, Bob Hoon, in the first in a series of new thrillers.

JOIN THE JD KIRK VIP CLUB

Want access to an exclusive image gallery showing locations from the books? Join the free JD Kirk VIP Club today, and as well as the photo gallery you'll get regular emails containing free short stories, members-only video content, and all the latest news about the world of DCI Jack Logan.

JDKirk.com/VIP

(Did we mention that it's free...?)

ABOUT THE AUTHOR

JD Kirk is the author of the million-selling DCI Jack Logan Scottish crime fiction series, set in the Highlands.

He also doesn't exist, and is in fact the pen name of award-winning former children's author and comic book writer, Barry Hutchison. Didn't see that coming, did you?

Both JD and Barry live in Fort William, where they share a house, wife, children, and two pets. You can find out more at JDKirk.com or at Facebook.com/jdkirkbooks.

Printed in Great Britain
by Amazon

80607016R00219